Political Justice

A Marc Kadella Legal Mystery

Dennis L. Carstens

Additional Marc Kadella Legal Mysteries

The Key to Justice

Desperate Justice

Media Justice

Certain Justice

Personal Justice

Delayed Justice

A Note from the Author

The following is a work of fiction. The names used are completely fictional and any comparison to real people, alive or dead is purely coincidental.

The inspiration for this book is very loosely derived from an 1890's scandal in France called the Dreyfus Affair. An innocent man, a French Army captain named Alfred Dreyfus was wrongfully framed and convicted of treason. He was alleged to have passed a list of secrets to the Germans.

An excellent account of this story can be found in the book, *An Officer and A Spy* by Robert Harris. If you have any interest in this event or history in general, I strongly recommend it. The style and writing are excellent.

Dennis Carstens

ONE

FOURTEEN YEARS AGO

"It's okay, really, I understand," Mickey O'Herlihy said into his office phone. "It's no big deal. I'll find someone else to go with. I'm not even sure how bad I want to go."

He listened for a moment then continued by saying, "Be careful and I'll talk to you later."

He replaced the phone in its cradle then picked up the two tickets lying on the pad covering the middle of his desk. Mickey swiveled around in his chair and looked out the window behind his matching walnut credenza. October in Minnesota can be a gift from the weather gods and this one was especially delightful. Mickey continued to stare out the window overlooking Snelling Avenue at the steady stream of traffic. He held up the two tickets and then returned his gaze to the political yard signs across the street.

"Does it ever end anymore?" he quietly asked himself.

Even though it was an odd-numbered year, the political season was not taking a break. St. Paul's city council and mayoral race were in full swing. The local populace was, once again, being bombarded with unsightly political signs, barely honest TV and radio ads and it was about to get exponentially worse. Next year was the quadrennial Presidential election. In fact, in Minnesota's neighbor to the south, Iowa, it had already been going on for months, a thought which brought Mickey back to the two tickets.

Michael 'Mickey' O'Herlihy was an institution in the Twin Cities. In his early seventies, he had been a very successful lawyer for almost fifty years, practicing in both St. Paul and Minneapolis. In the legal and political community of both cities, Mickey O'Herlihy was like Cher; only one name was necessary to identify him. If anyone in either the legal or political world used the names Mickey or The Mick, everyone understood it referred to only one person and no identifying explanation was necessary.

Mickey was also an Irishman's Irishman. At five feet nine inches, with his slight build, smiling blue eyes and Irish red hair, which had now gone mostly gray, Mickey could have played the part of a leprechaun. Underneath that Irish charm and affable exterior was the heart, mind and soul of a courtroom killer. Mickey received almost sexual gratification from turning a prosecution witness, especially a cop, into a confused

2

fool. Despite this, even cops and prosecutors liked and respected the man.

Mickey had also planted legal seeds all over the Cities. Like a very highly respected Super Bowl winning coach, Mickey had mentored many young lawyers over the years. He would bring one on for a couple of years, teach him or her the reality of the practice of law and trial work then turn them loose. They, in turn, had gone on to 'coach' other lawyers. The local legal talent that had branched out from Mickey's family tree had to be in the hundreds.

Mickey's office was located on Snelling and Kincaid Avenues, two blocks south of another institution of even longer standing than Mickey, O'Gara's pub on the corner of Snelling and Selby. Opened just a few years before Mickey came into the world, 1941, Mickey and his favorite watering-hole were growing old together.

Mickey owned what had been a six-unit apartment. It had been deeded to him by a client for his representation. A client who was currently doing a minimum of thirty years as a guest of the State of Minnesota. This particular client, a very shady businessman, had decided a divorce would be too costly. His wife's untimely demise would be quicker, more efficient and let him get on with his life and girlfriend. The idiot told the girlfriend, the girlfriend told the cops and Mickey got the apartment. It was a small, three-story that Mickey had converted. He turned the two units on the third floor into one large apartment for himself. He made the second floor into his law firm office and the first floor into rental space for two other small law firms whose monthly rent checks were a nice source of cash flow.

In back was a parking lot large enough for a dozen cars. Mickey had a one-car garage built on the lot for his Cadillac. While it was being constructed, an inspector from the city showed up. He shut down construction of Mickey's garage and started issuing citations because Mickey had not bothered with permits, inspections or any of the local bureaucratic nuisances normally required, not only for the garage being built but for all the renovations done inside the building. The Mick made one phone call to his good friend and one-time protégé, the current mayor of St. Paul, Kevin Stevens. Mickey then tore up the citations in front of the now apoplectic inspector. The next day that inspector was reassigned to building inspections on St. Paul's gang-infested East Side. Mickey's garage was completed without further ado.

Over the course of his career, Mickey had made millions. Not from his first love, criminal defense, but from personal injury cases. Unfortunately, four marriages had taken their toll on Mickey's money. The small apartment office was about all he had left. Mickey liked to joke that he had spent half his money on booze and women, the rest he just wasted.

Mickey O'Herlihy was a Twin Cities institution.

The young lawyer Mickey was currently mentoring was a man by the name of Marc Kadella. Marc had been recommended to Mickey by one of Mickey's former protégés about a year ago. Kadella had gone to work for an insurance defense firm right out of law school. The money was very good but after almost three years with them, he could barely remember what his children looked like and he had yet to meet a live client or see the inside of a courtroom. Kadella talked it over with his wife, Karen, who surprised him by being totally behind the move. Apparently, she was willing to take the pay cut to end her status as a single mom. Besides, between what Mickey paid him and what he made from his own cases, the pay cut was not as bad as it at first seemed. On top of that, Mickey O'Herlihy saw the potential of a first-class trial lawyer.

"Hey, Marc, what are you up to this evening?"

Kadella looked up from the brief he was writing for one of Mickey's cases and saw him standing in his office doorway. Another thing about Mickey was his affection for three-piece suits. Rumor had it that in fifty years no one had ever seen him wearing *anything* else. Standing in Marc's doorway, despite the slight paunch and mostly gray hair with fading red streaks, the old man looked as dapper as ever.

"I don't know," Marc replied. "Why?"

"I got two tickets to a fundraiser for this guy, Tom Carver, the presidential candidate. They're having a soirée at the St. Paul Hotel tonight."

"Soirée huh? I don't know, will they have beer and brats?" Marc asked with a laugh. "How did you get tickets? How much were they?"

"Twenty-five hundred bucks each and no, I didn't pay for them. I got them from a guy who couldn't make it."

"Because he's in jail?" Marc asked.

"No," Mickey laughed. "He probably should be but he's not. You want to go? I was supposed to take Loretta but she can't make it."

"Who's Loretta?" Marc asked.

"A, ah, friend," Mickey replied.

"Loretta? Why does that sound familiar?" Marc quietly, rhetorically asked. He snapped his fingers in recognition, pointed a finger at Mickey and said, "Isn't she Loretta Finch, a.k.a. Charmaine? You were going to take a hooker slash stripper to a political fundraiser?"

4

"Ssssh," Mickey said and held an index finger to his lips, not wanting his staff to hear.

"How appropriate," Marc laughed. "She'd fit right in."

"That's true," Mickey said with a big grin. "That's why I wanted to take her. Plus, she's a gorgeous woman."

"Yeah, she is," Mac agreed. "What is she anyway? Her ethnicity."

"I think she's about one-eighth black, one quarter American Indian, a little French, one-half white and one-half Vietnamese and just enough Latino to be a spitfire."

"What? She can't be…, never mind. Let me call Karen and see what's up at home. I'll let you know."

A few minutes before eight o'clock that evening, Mickey and Marc were in line at the St. Paul Hotel in downtown St. Paul. There were about twenty people ahead of them, mostly very well dressed couples. Looking over the crowd, Marc was glad he had a court hearing that morning and had worn his best suit for it and did not feel out of place now. Two serious looking men and one woman, all with an ear piece in one ear and a noticeable bulge under their suit coats, were checking tickets. They were also quickly waving a metal-detecting wand over each of the guests.

The line was entering the Promenade Ballroom. The room allowed for five hundred people and at twenty-five hundred bucks a ticket, a cool million and a quarter dollars would be raised tonight. The money was going toward the candidacy of the man the media was on the verge of proclaiming to be the next president, the current governor of Colorado, Thomas Jefferson Carver. As if his mother knew before he was born, she made sure he even had the name for the job.

Along with this very successful, charming and extremely photogenic governor was a wife and family cut from central casting. A one-time second runner-up in the Miss Illinois pageant, Darla Benton Carver was not your typical political wife.

The Carver's appeared to be the model of the new-age family and had been proclaimed so by Time magazine. Intelligent, educated—both graduates of prestigious law schools; him, Yale and her, Michigan. With great looks, charm, political appeal and an ideal pedigree, Tom, at 45, was a successful state attorney general and governor. Darla, age 40, a former assistant U.S. Attorney. And of course, they had the perfect, photogenic children: a daughter, Natalie age 16 and a son, Jefferson age 14. Little wonder the adoringly smitten media was proclaiming the race all but over a year before the election.

The couple had met twenty years ago. Tom was a paid staffer for a U.S. Senator running for re-election from Ohio. Darla was a staff lawyer with the local Ohio party. Someone they both knew had pointed Tom out to her as an up and coming political climber. After a couple of casual dates, Darla did her usual cunning calculations and decided he might just get her where she wanted to go and she would be the one to get him there. He had one serious flaw: he was a total, womanizing hound. This didn't bother Darla personally, he simply had to be carefully watched and his messes kept under control.

Mickey and Marc passed through the security screening and began mingling with the guests. In Marc's case, he followed Mickey around while sipping cheap, white wine. Mickey, it seemed, knew just about everyone and those he didn't know knew him and he pretended to know them. It took the two of them almost an hour to make their way to the buffet tables. Along the way, Mickey introduced Marc to the mayor, half the city council and at least a dozen state senators and representatives, all of whom Mickey seemed to know intimately.

"How do you remember all of them?" Marc asked at one point.

"Practice," Mickey replied. "You have to work at it, Marc. These people are mostly featherheads but it can't hurt to get to know them. Hello, your Honor," Mickey said to a female judge from Ramsey County who had walked up to them.

Mickey introduced her to Marc and the three of them amiably chatted for several minutes. The judge's husband joined them and a moment before they were going to move on, another woman stopped by.

"Excuse me, Mary," the woman, Patti Foster, a co-chair of the local party, said to the judge. "I must steal Mickey away. I'm sure he'd like to meet the next president."

"Absolutely, Patti," Mickey told her. "Marc, you want to meet the next president?"

"What's his name and is he coming tonight?" Marc irreverently asked knowing that would annoy the woman.

The judge, her husband and Mickey all laughed heartily at Marc's smartass comment. Patti Foster gave Marc a dirty look, took hold of Mickey's arm and dragged him off.

While Mickey went off to meet Tom Carver, Marc ambled a few feet to the bar. While standing in line to exchange his now warm, cheap wine for a fresh glass, he heard a female voice behind him.

"That was a pretty good shot you just took," the woman said.

Marc turned around to face the source of the comment. "I was just kidding," Marc said with a sly grin.

"It was pretty funny, all the same," she said. "Margaret Tennant," she said and held out her hand.

"Marc Kadella," Marc said as he shook her hand.

"If you're here with Mickey, you must be a lawyer. Are you his latest project?"

By this point, they had moved up to the bar together. Marc pointed at her glass and asked, "Would you like a refill?"

"Sure," she said. "What I'd really like is a vodka martini but I'm with my husband so I'll have to drive tonight."

"Oops," Marc said. "Yes, I'm with Mickey and I guess I'm his latest project or protégé or whatever," he smiled gladly changing the subject. "How about you?"

"I'm with Briggs, McKennan," she said referring to a well-known law firm in downtown Minneapolis.

The two of them continued to chat for another ten minutes or so. Her husband arrived and she introduced him to Marc. After another minute the husband announced they needed to mingle and led her away.

"She's a little young, even for you," Darla Carver snarled into her husband's ear while keeping a practiced smile on her face.

The worst kept secret of the "Carver for President Campaign" was Tom Carver's inability to keep his pants on. The inner-circle staff all knew it as did most of the media. Fortunately, Carver's charm had the media almost literally throwing themselves at his feet, wrapping their arms around his ankles and whimpering like love-struck puppies hoping Carver will scratch them behind their ears. In fact, Carver had already bedded three female members of his media entourage.

Carver ignored his wife's comment while he was introduced to another half a dozen donors. He smiled, shook hands, schmoozed them a bit then finally whispered in Darla's ear, "Try not to be such a cold, calculating bitch for one evening. Maybe find some well-hung, young stud to ride yourself. It would do you some good."

"Hello, Mr. Mayor," Darla said ignoring her husband. "It's good to see you again."

The two guests of honor maintained their position greeting their guests. At one point, Tom motioned for a man to come to him over. The man's name was Clay Dean. Dean was a very special aide to the Carvers who handled very personal and delicate assignments. The governor assigned him to see to it that the young volunteer Carver had eyed up and his bitch of a wife chastised him about would be waiting in his suite upstairs.

TWO

The head of Carver's security detail, a man in a dark, business suit with an earpiece in his left ear, stepped off the elevator on the twelfth floor of the St. Paul hotel. He turned left to walk down the hallway to his destination and saw a similarly attired, younger man standing in the hall.

"Morning, Al," Secret Service agent Steven Munson said to the agent guarding the Park Suite on the twelfth floor of the St. Paul Hotel. Munson was the agent in charge of Tom Carver's protection detail and the guard at the door, Al Tierney, worked for him.

"'Morning, Steve," Tierney replied. "All quiet. I haven't heard anything coming from inside yet."

"Is he alone?" Munson asked.

"I don't know. I didn't ask," Tierney replied.

"It's almost seven," Munson said referring to the time. "The Hellcat will be along pretty soon."

When Abraham Lincoln was president, his entire staff consisted of two young, male secretaries, John Nicolay and John Hay. The two of them worshipped Lincoln but despised his manic-depressive wife, Mary. Behind her back, The Hellcat was the name they used for her. Carver's protection detail used it to refer to Darla Carver, also behind her back.

"Should we check on him to make sure he's up and getting ready to go to Iowa?" Tierney asked.

"No way," Munson replied. "The last time I did that, The Hellcat threatened to castrate me. No, we'll wait here for her." Munson quickly put a hand to his right ear and said, "Copy that" into his mic.

"She's on the way," Munson told Tierney.

Barely five seconds later, the two men saw Darla Carver come around the far corner and head toward them. Hurrying alongside Darla was her shadow and number one, joined-at-the-hip aide, Sonja Hayden. Sonja was already on her phone checking news stories and sending text messages to favored reporters.

"Good morning, Mrs. Carver," the two agents said in unison.

Tierney had used the extra pass card to unlock and open the suite's door for the two women. Darla, without a word or even an acknowledgement of the men's presence, went through the door into her husband's room. Sonja offered the men a slight smile and a genuine good morning to them as she followed her boss. Before closing the door behind her, Sonja held out a hand and Tierney gave her the pass card.

As the two women walked past the suite's dining area, Darla muttered, "I wonder what we'll find this time."

8

When they reached the closed double doors of the bedroom, Darla stood aside. Sonja rapidly knocked three times then opened the door for Darla and stood back to let her in.

"Oh, for Christ's sake," a disgusted Darla said when she saw the mess.

Lying on the floor, his head on one pillow and half-covered by a sheet was the obviously naked Thomas Carver, still sound asleep. On the opposite side of the king size bed to Darla's left was the uncovered, naked young girl Carver had been lustfully looking over the previous evening, laying on her stomach.

"Wake the girl," Darla told Sonja. Darla then stepped up to her husband and firmly kicked the bottom of his right foot. He made a groaning sound and stirred while Darla looked over the mess that was the bedroom. On the dresser, she saw a vial that she knew was cocaine and several pills scattered about. Disgusted, she gave Tom's foot another kick.

"Get your ass up!" she almost yelled.

"What?" a groggy Tom Carver said as he blinked several times. His eyes focused on his angry wife and he sharply said, "Get the hell out of here."

"Mrs. Carver," an anxious Sonja interrupted. "We have a serious problem here. She is really cold. I'm not sure, but I think she's dead."

"Oh my God, no, tell me that's not true," Darla stammered as she hurried around the bed to check on the girl herself.

While his wife was checking for a pulse, the commotion and thought that his plaything might be dead, stirred Tom Carver and he staggered to his feet. He stood with the sheet wrapped around himself like a toga, his hair sticking up, and a befuddled look on his face watching the two women try to awaken the girl. After about a minute, succumbing to the futility, Darla gave up, stood and looked at her husband.

"What the hell did you do, you fool?" Darla said.

"I ah, I ah…it, ah, I don't know. It must have been the coke. She said she'd never tried it and I don't know, maybe it was too much. I don't know. I passed out and, I don't know…"

Darla took a deep breath, held out her hands' palms out and taking charge, calmly said, "Okay. Everybody stay calm. You," she continued pointing at Tom, "get in the shower. We're going down to Iowa like nothing happened."

She looked at Sonja and said, "Go get Clay, right now. Find him. He and I will take care of this."

"Okay," Sonja croaked as she turned to leave.

"Sonja! Calmly. Act like nothing's wrong and for God's sake, don't let any of the Secret Service people in here. Take a deep breath."

"Yes, ma'am," Sonja replied.

Darla turned back and saw Tom still frozen in place staring at the girl.

"Hey! Get your ass in gear."

"Yes, okay," Tom said as he turned and hurried into the bathroom.

Darla looked down at the girl. She had long, brown hair and was very attractive and very young.

"I'm sorry, sweetheart," Darla quietly said. "But I can't let this ruin my plans."

While Sonja went searching for Clay Dean, Darla began to check out the room. The first thing she did was to place the cocaine and pills in a small, empty plastic garbage bag she took from a wastebasket. She looked under the blankets on the floor and found a used condom by the bed. Darla took a Kleenex, picked it up and went into the bathroom. She flushed it down the toilet then went to the shower and opened the door.

"How many times did you screw this poor child?" she angrily asked her naked husband.

"Ah, just once, just one time," he replied his head still a little foggy.

"Let me tell you something, you moron. If Clay and I can get you out of this fiasco, this kind of bullshit is done! You will keep your dick in your pants and start behaving yourself. Do I make myself clear? You are not going to fuck this up for me. We make you President first, then me. That's the deal. You got it?"

Tom turned around to face her and sheepishly said, "Yes, I got it. I swear this is it. What are you going to do?"

"Clay and I have a contingency plan in place. The less you know, the better. You slept with me last night. You got it? Now get your ass in gear. I want you out of here and on the road to Iowa in ten minutes. I'll lay a suit out for you."

Darla closed the door as Tom shut off the shower. As she walked away, he heard her mutter "Dipshit" and he gave her the finger behind her back.

Darla laid out clothing for him and placed them on a chair. She then saw the girl's purse on the floor by the bed. Using Kleenex again so as not to leave fingerprints, Darla found the girls I.D. in her purse. Abby Connolly, age 19 with an address in Minnesota by the Wisconsin state line in Stillwater.

"Well, thank God she's not a minor," Darla whispered. She then made a mental note to make sure Clay got rid of the purse.

At that moment she heard the hallway door open.

10

In less than ten minutes Sonja was back in the bedroom with Clay Dean. Clay was a forty-year-old former Army Ranger/Special Forces soldier and Colorado state cop. While assigned to the protection of Governor Thomas Carver, Clayton Dean had a personal tragedy crash down on him.

He was the divorced father of a then eleven-year-old girl, the light of his life, Jordan. She had been diagnosed with leukemia and seeing an opportunity, Darla Carver had intervened.

Clay had shown himself to be exceptionally intelligent and resourceful. Darla believed he would make an excellent personal aide for her husband. Someone who could keep an eye on him, watch for the worst of it and clean up Tom's messes. All he needed was a gentle nudge to become as loyal as a Golden Lab. Darla had Tom take Clay aside and promise to move mountains for his daughter, which he did. The absolute best care was provided for Jordan at Sloan-Kettering and the Mayo Clinic. And the Carvers made sure Clay Dean never saw a bill for any of it. By the time Jordan was pronounced cured, Clay Dean was Thomas Carver's man for life.

The first thing Clay did, while Tom Carver got dressed, was to cover the poor girl's naked body with a sheet. He checked for a pulse and felt how cold she was and agreed she was dead.

"What room is that kid in?" Clay asked Sonja.

Even though he had not identified him by name, Sonja knew exactly who Clay meant. She opened up the folio she always carried with her and looked over a list of names and room numbers until she found it.

"820," she told him.

"Okay," Clay replied. "Mrs. Carver and I are going down to find him and talk to him. You stay here and get the governor out of here, in the car and on his way to Iowa as if nothing happened," he said to Sonja.

"All right," both women said.

"Let's go," he said to Darla.

In the hallway, Clay assured the agents—there were now five of them—that the governor would be ready to go in a few minutes. A moment later, Clay pushed the down button for the elevator and looked at the lighted numbers while they waited for the car.

"What do you think?" Darla quietly asked him.

"I think we planned for something like this and we'll make it work," Clay replied without looking at her.

There was something reassuring about Clay's strength and certainty for Darla. She also realized what a relief it was to have someone with her to take care of her husband's problems. Tom Carver could be a one-man wrecking crew. But he was an almost perfect candidate. He was going to be president and so was Darla Carver.

The two of them stepped off the elevator on the eighth floor and followed the wall sign to 820. Clay knocked a couple of times and a few seconds later, a young man opened the door. Shocked to see who it was he could barely stutter a coherent hello.

"Billy," Clay said with a smile, "mind if we come in? We need to talk to you about something."

"Yes, certainly. Good morning, Mrs. Carver. Please, take a seat," the young man said as he backed into his room.

"Good morning, Billy," Darla pleasantly replied. This startled the young campaign worker since he did not believe she even knew his name.

Darla and Clay took the two available chairs at a small table. Billy sat on the bed anxiously waiting for one of them to speak.

Billy Stover was a recent graduate of Colorado State with a degree in political science and a minor in communications. A family connection had placed him as a volunteer for Carver's campaign the day the committee was formed. Clay Dean had spotted him early on as a gullible kid who might come in handy for a situation such as the one they had on their hands this morning. Clay convinced Darla, who readily agreed, and Stover was put on as a full-time, paid staffer.

"Let me ask you something, if I may," Darla began. "Do you believe in my husband?"

"Of course," Billy quickly and earnestly replied.

"No, I mean, do you, in your heart, really believe and have no doubt that Thomas Carver not only could be elected resident, but for the good of America, the country we love, *should* be the next president?"

Stover leaned forward, folded his hands together as if in prayer and said, "Down to my soul, Mrs. Carver. He is a great man and will be a great president."

"What would you do to help make that happen?" Darla quietly asked.

"Anything in my power," Stover sincerely said.

"We have a problem, Billy," Clay interjected. "There's no good way to tell you this so, I'll just give you the straight, truthful version."

Clay leaned forward, his elbows on his knees; his hands folded reverently together and looked the young man directly in his eyes. Billy also leaned forward so the two of them were barely three feet apart.

"A young woman, apparently infatuated with the governor, somehow snuck into his room last night. She was obviously hoping to somehow seduce the governor, so we think. Anyway," he continued, "the governor did not stay in that room. In fact, we were only using it for meetings. As usual, he spent the night with Mrs. Carver in her room. This morning when they went to his room, they found this girl in the governor's bed." He paused and looked down at the floor and lightly sobbed before continuing. "Billy, it was terrible. The poor girl was dead. It looks like a drug overdose."

"Oh, my God!" Billy said. He straightened up, sat back and lightly bit down on a knuckle he had put in his mouth. "How horrible. But I don't understand. What can I do to help? Shouldn't we call the police?"

Before Clay could reply Darla lightly placed her left hand on Clay's shoulder and said, "Billy, you have to understand something. Even though the governor wasn't there all night and the girl was alone, well, you know what jackals the media people are. This campaign would be over. He would never become president."

"The same thing happened to Ted Kennedy only Governor Carver is absolutely innocent," Clay said.

"I remember learning about what happened to Senator Kennedy," Billy said. "What can I do? I'll do anything to help Governor Carver. He's a great man and whatever I can do to help him become president, I'll do. Anything," he repeated with emphasis.

That's what we were counting on, Darla thought while suppressing a smile.

Darla's phone rang. She looked at it, smiled slightly at Billy and said, "Clay will explain what must be done. I need to take this call."

The phone call was from her shadow, Sonja Hayden. While Clay told Billy what they wanted, Darla went into the bathroom to take the call.

Sonja quickly filled her in. Tom Carver was in the Escalade and on his way to Des Moines. He would arrive by noon for the luncheon and in plenty of time for the day's scheduled campaign events. Darla could catch up with him later.

"Okay, that's done. Now this will be the tricky part," Clay said to Darla, Sonja and Billy. They were all back in Tom's suite on twelve.

Clay had explained to the young staffer exactly what they needed to do. At first, Billy was unsure if he could do it for fear he would end up in jail. Darla assured him he would be provided with top-notch lawyers and if he did do some time, he would be well compensated and eventually pardoned by President Carver after the election.

"I'm worried about my mom," Billy told them. "She has cancer and…."

"She'll get the best care money can buy," Darla assured him.

That promise was all it took. Billy was in.

13

Clay had commandeered two empty serving carts he had found on another floor. They had pushed them together and carefully placed the naked dead girl on them on her stomach precisely as she had been on the bed. Sonja and Clay then covered her with a sheet.

"Sonja, you go get an elevator and hold it. Billy, you and I are going to wheel her down to your room and place her in your bed. Mrs. Carver, you go back to your room and wait for us," Clay said.

Ten minutes later now back in room 820 with the girl laid out on Billy's bed as she had been upstairs, a barely breathing Billy said to Clay, "I've never been so scared. How do you stay so calm?"

"Practice," Clay replied.

Clay took a step back and looked over the girl. Satisfied she was lying exactly as she had been found, he told Billy to get rid of the carts and the sheet from Tom's room.

"Take the carts down to another floor then come back here," Clay said.

"Are you going to call the police?"

"Yes, we need to do that," Clay replied. He placed a comforting hand on the young man's shoulder and said, "Just stick to your story. Don't make it any more complicated than that. I'll make sure they find the drugs and the bottle will have her prints on it. There's a good chance you won't even be charged with anything. It was an accident. Remember," he said solemnly looking directly into Billy's eyes, "you're doing a great service for your country."

Billy took a deep breath, puffed out his chest and said, "You're right, I am. I'll keep that in mind. Let's go."

14

THREE

A St. Paul patrolman, a black man in his late twenties, was first on the scene and was standing guard at the door of Billy's room. The cop's name was Eugene Coolidge and he was considered a rising star in the department. Everyone who knew him, beginning when he was a kid on St. Paul's streets, called him Max Cool. Coolidge calmly waited for the medical examiner and homicide detectives. Across the hallway leaning against the wall were Clay Dean and Billy Stover. Ten minutes after securing the scene, Max greeted the medical examiner, the first to arrive.

"Good morning, Doctor," Max said. "She's inside. You're the first one here."

"I got a call on my way into the office," the doctor said. His name was Anand Bhatt and his family was originally from India. Anand had disappointed his cardiologist father by becoming a pathologist which dad considered beneath his son. This, of course, pleased the Americanized Anand greatly. He also found pathology to be rewarding, interesting and important work. Annoying his strict, old-world father was just an enjoyable side-effect.

The doctor went into the room and began examining the body. Within another ten minutes, the crime scene unit and investigating detectives arrived. Max quietly told the two detectives what he had found when he arrived. Both men took a quick look in the room then came back out. While the two crime scene techs began to process the room, Max introduced the detectives to Clay and Billy. The detectives, Parker Mills, the older, more experienced one took Billy off to talk to him. The other detective, Nathan Hough, did the same with Clay Dean.

"Okay, Mr. Stover," Detective Mills politely said, "Can you tell me what happened?"

"Sure, um, yeah," Billy said. "We met, me and Abby, the girl in there, ah, met last night at the fundraiser for Governor Carver.

"She came with me to my room and we, well had sex. I used a condom," he added almost too quickly.

"Then, ah, she had a little jar of cocaine. I don't do drugs so, she did it, you know, by herself. We fell asleep and I, ah, overslept this morning and when I woke up I went right into the bathroom. I had to get going because I was running late. Anyway, when I came out I found her like this."

"Who is Clay Dean?" Mills asked.

"He is like, Governor Carver's main guy. His right-hand man. I called him and he came down to my room."

"Why didn't you call 911?"

"I was scared. I didn't know what to do. I called Mr. Dean because I was told if there was ever an emergency, I was supposed to call him. So I did. He came to my room and he called you guys."

At that moment, Dr. Bhatt came out of Billy's room into the hall. Mills told Billy to stick around and walked backed to the M.E. When he got there his partner was also there.

"Looks like she died, probably between one and three A.M. Probably an overdose."

"Has the body been moved?" Mills asked.

"I don't think so, no," Bhatt replied. "Why do you ask?"

"Because this girl is way too good looking to be screwing this idiot, Billy Stover," Mills answered.

"What's his story?" Mills asked his partner, referring to Clay Dean. Hough told Mills what he had learned from Dean which matched what Billy had told Mills.

"Let's get their phones. We'll have the techs check them. I want to know when Stover called this guy Dean and if they called anyone else."

Mills looked down at the much shorter M.E. and said, "Let me know as soon as you have a prelim C.O.D., Adnan."

"Will do, Parker. Probably later today."

By now, the word had spread—no doubt leaked to the media by hotel staff—that there was a problem related to the Carver campaign. The hallway on the eighth floor was becoming crowded with gawkers and a couple of local TV news crews.

More cops showed up, uniforms that were assigned to keep the crowd back. Max Coolidge was the first of the cops to go at the crowd and he was instantly hammered with questions from the TV people. "No comments" were all they received and after a few minutes four more uniforms arrived to help him.

Three separate teams of EMT's got off the elevator together squabbling vigorously with each other. Max had to step in between two of them to break up a potential fight. He questioned them and found out what they were really after was information they could sell to the national media. Max and another uniform pushed them all back onto the elevator and sent them down to the lobby.

While this was taking place, Detectives Smith and Hough were sneaking Clay Dean and Billy Stover down a freight elevator. They were headed back to the police department for a more thorough interrogation, not that it would do any good. Their story was set and would not change. The detectives also confiscated the two men's phones to verify the timeline of the calls.

16

Mills rapped lightly on the open office door to their boss, Lt. Linda Foster. She looked up from the paperwork she was working on as Mills and Hough walked in. Hough closed the door and stood while his partner took a seat in one of her chairs.

"The word's out," Foster said. "It's all over the news. We need to put something out and soon to dispel the rumors. I've gotten calls from the chief and the mayor himself."

"We just got a call from Anand Bhatt with a preliminary cause of death," Mills began. "Overdose of cocaine."

"Tell me about the victim," Foster said.

"Abigail Connolly," Hough began after opening his notebook. "Age 19. She was a student at Macalester College and a part-time volunteer for the Carver campaign. So far, that's all we have on her," Mills told her.

"I have been told her father is state Senator Don Connolly from Stillwater," Foster told the two men.

"Shit," Hough said. "Just what we need, more politics."

"You know him?" Foster asked Hough.

"No," Hough replied.

"Well, you're right though, he's not without clout. What about these two guys you brought in?" Foster asked.

"Clay Dean and William Stover," Mills answered her. "Dean is really close to Tom Carver. Top aide. Stover is a paid staffer that travels with the campaign. We found out Carver, the husband, left before this happened and Mrs. Carver left about an hour later. Dean says there's nothing unusual about that. He also says it's not unusual for him to hang back after the governor leaves in case of any last-minute problems."

"You buy this?" Foster asked.

"At this point, no reason not to," Mills answered. "It does seem a little off that the old man would leave and his wife and top aide didn't go with him. But," Mills shrugged, "I don't know what's normal for these people."

"Oh shit, here he comes," Foster quietly said looking through her office window into the squad room. A moment later, Hough opened the door so Chief Derrick Sommers and Foster's boss, Captain Eric Gettes, could come in.

"Good morning," Sommers said. Mills stood up and shook hands with the chief. Sommers took a chair and Mills brought him up to speed.

When Mills finished, Sommers asked Foster, "Do we arrest William Stover?"

"What do you guys think?" Foster asked Mills and Hough.

"We can," Mills said. "But we should run it by Marcus Dewitt first," he added referring to the Ramsey Count Attorney.

"I think we have a good case for manslaughter," Chief Sommers added.

"I'll call," Foster said and picked up her desk phone.

Two minutes later, having spoken to Dewitt himself, Foster hung up her phone.

"He agrees. He said the mayor wants a press conference ASAP to announce it," Foster said.

"I know," Sommers said. "It will be in an hour at the mayor's office. I want all of you there." He then added, after seeing the sour look on Parker Mills's face, "I know. I get it. Except, whether we like it or not, this is a major, national news story. We have a huge public relations problem and it is enormously political. We need to get out in front of this and make it look like we know what we're doing. You two," he continued referring to Mills and Hough, "arrest Stover and get him processed. Dewitt can take it to a grand jury if he wants to. What about the other guy, this Clay Dean?"

"We can kick him loose," Mills said. "We have nothing to hold him on. We had the techs check their phones and verify the calls and times they said they were made. If we want him back, I'm sure we can make that happen."

"Okay," the chief said as he stood to go. "I'll call Mayor Stevens and bring him up to date. I'll see all of you in an hour. Don't be late."

"Can I talk to Billy before I go?" Clay asked Mills and Hough. "You can be in the room."

"Sure, we'll give you a few minutes. But we haven't told him yet he's under arrest. We'll have to do that first."

The three of them walked down the hall to the interrogation room where Billy Stover was being held. When Mills informed him he was being arrested and read him his rights, Billy's face was white as a ghost.

"Mr. Dean wants to tell you something before we take you to be booked," Mills told him.

Mills was seated at the room's table next to Billy and Hough was standing along a wall to Billy's left. Dean was seated at the table opposite the young man.

"I just want to tell you a couple things. We're going to get you excellent legal representation. We know you didn't mean to hurt this girl and the Carver's appreciate your loyalty and the work you've done. It will take a day or two but you'll be okay until then. You're going to get through this okay?"

"Yeah, okay," Stover nervously croaked.

"Until then, just keep quiet and don't talk to anyone about your case," Dean added.

"I won't," Billy said.

"That includes anyone you meet in jail. Okay? Talk to no one. Can we get him in isolation away from other inmates?" Clay asked the detectives.

"We probably should," Mills said. "The last thing we need is for anything to happen to him in custody. We'll see to it."

"Thanks," Clay said.

He turned back to Billy and said, "Don't worry you'll be okay."

FOUR

The Carver campaign was making its fourteenth trip to Iowa and there was still more than three months to go before the caucuses. There are 99 counties in Iowa and so far, Tom Carver had personally visited more than 70 of them.

Every four years, the state of Iowa and its approximately three million people become the center of America's political universe. And every four years the politicians and the media invaded this Midwestern farm state like a ravenous horde of locusts. And every four years, by the time it's over, the citizens were thoroughly disgusted, disheveled and fed up with the whole thing. But four years later they would inflict this on themselves again.

The Carvers had a campaign rally scheduled for 7:00 P.M. at the Civic Center in Des Moines. Of course the story about the tragic death of Abby Connolly was all over the news. The media assigned to follow the Carvers were clamoring for information and a statement from Tom. By mid-afternoon, Darla had released a carefully drafted comment containing the usual pathos; "What a sad and tragic event. Our thoughts, hearts and prayers are with the family etc." The empty, meaningless, political rhetoric that always follows an event such as this.

Unsatisfied, one of the women reporters who had slept with the governor followed up on a rumor, a rumor that she had started. Her name was Tracy Windford and she cornered the Carvers' press spokesperson, Juliet Carne. Juliet was at the Civic Center helping the advance team get ready for the night's big rally. The indoor rally was for twenty-seven hundred big donors. The main event was afterward at Drake Stadium. There, they were expecting a full house of fifteen thousand.

"Hey, Juliet," Tracy whispered into Carne's ear from behind her. "Got a minute?"

Not knowing the reporter was behind her and concentrating on a seating chart, Carne jumped a foot when she heard the voice.

"Jesus Christ!" Carne yelled at Tracy. "You about gave me a goddamn heart attack."

These two women, both of whom having slept with the governor, and they both knew it, had no love for each other.

"Sorry," Tracy disingenuously said suppressing a smile.

"What now?" an obviously annoyed Carne asked.

"I'm tracking down a rumor…"

"That you probably started," Carne snarled.

"…that Abby Connolly's body was found in Governor Carver's bed. She had spent the night with…"

"That's bullshit, Tracy," Carne whispered and jabbed her between her breasts with a finger. "And I've about had it with you. You go anywhere with that lie and by the time we're done with you, you'll be doing weather reports for the Upper Peninsula of Michigan standing in snow up to your fake tits."

"Is that a denial?" Winford politely asked.

Carne calmed down, took a deep breath and said, "Yes, Tracy. There is absolutely no truth to it. Please don't damage Governor Carver with it."

"Relax, Juliet. If I can't get it confirmed, I won't say a word. But you're likely going to be asked about it. You might want to have him make a statement before tonight in front of the cameras."

"I'll talk to him," Carne said. "You're probably right."

"Okay, thanks," the reporter said. "Oh, by the way, they're real and they're spectacular," she laughed as she turned to walk away.

The four conspirators, Darla and Tom Carver, Sonja Hayden and Clay Dean, were holding a very private meeting in Tom's hotel suite. As usual, Darla carried the conversation and this time a chastened Tom Carver sat silently getting his instructions. Tom was about to do a brief press conference.

"Just stick to the talking points. Keep it short and simple. If the reporters start throwing questions at you, stick to the 'There's an ongoing investigation and we cannot comment on it'. Then add that they know as much as you do," Darla told Tom.

"And if one of them claims the girl was found in my room, I'll just deny it and say that's a rumor started by one of my opponents," Tom said.

"But act surprised. Don't be too quick to throw the rumor statement out there," Darla reminded him.

"I'm not an idiot, Darla…"

"That's debatable," Darla replied.

"I've done this before. I know how to handle it," Tom said becoming annoyed with his patronizing wife.

"Shit," Sonja quietly said while reading a text message she had just received.

"What?" Darla asked.

"It's from Juliet. A reporter, Tracy Winford with the Associated Press just ambushed her and asked her about a rumor she heard that the girl was found in the Governor's room," Sonja replied. "Juliet denied it and told Tracy it was bullshit and threatened to take away her access if she ran it."

"That bitch probably started the rumor herself," Tom said.

"They have nothing. Clay made sure the suite was cleaned. Even if the cops checked it, the place is too contaminated for them to find anything," Darla said.

"That's right, sir," Clay added speaking to Tom.

Darla looked at her watch then said, "We should go. We'll be just late enough to remind everyone that you're far more important than they are. We'll do a quick press conference then you speak to the donors at the Civic Center. We'll grab a bite to eat and then go to the rally at Drake. We just need to stay on the same page for the next 48 hours. This will blow over."

"Should I mention we are going to help Billy Stover with a lawyer?" Tom asked.

"Yes," Darla said after reflecting on the question for a moment. "That's a good idea. It will make us look compassionate. Tell them what a tragic accident it was, a young girl dying, blah, blah, blah. Look sad and sincere."

The next morning the two detectives who had caught the case were reviewing their notes and writing a preliminary report. It was almost 11:00 and their boss, Linda Foster was not in her office yet. At 11:00 she arrived and on her way to her office, she motioned for Parker Mills and Nathan Hough to join her.

"There are some holes in this story," Mills began after the three of them took their respective chairs.

"Like what?" Foster asked.

"We did a little digging," Hough replied. "This Clayton Dean guy told us the girl was found in Stover's room dead when Stover came out of the shower," he began.

Taking over, Mills continued by saying, "We found a couple people, wait staff employees of the hotel who had worked the fundraiser, who told us they saw her leaving the party around 10:00 or 10:30 with Clayton Dean."

"Who also made a point of telling us Governor Carver spent the night in his wife's suite with her," Hough interjected.

"So?" Foster asked.

"We didn't ask him. He volunteered it to make sure we knew," Mills said.

"And we found the maids who cleaned the twelfth floor, the floor where the Carvers had booked two suites," Hough said. "The two women, whose immigration status may be a little shaky, didn't want to talk to us. We leaned on them a bit and they admitted that Tom Carver's room had been slept in and the place was a mess."

"Did you guys check the rooms?" Foster asked.

"Yeah, both of them," Mills replied. "They were both scrubbed. The bedding was gone, sheets, blankets, pillow cases. The floors vacuumed. Even if we went back, both rooms are too contaminated to find anything."

"But," Hough continued, "one of the maids told us something odd. A sheet was missing from the governor's room."

"A sheet was missing? What the hell?" a puzzled Foster asked.

"If you wanted to move a body, what better way to do it," Mills said. "Wrap it up and…"

"Hold it," Foster interrupted him. "You're getting a little speculative here."

"Yeah, but you know how I hate loose ends," Mills said.

"Okay, let me fill you in. I just came from a meeting with Chief Sommers and Captain Gettes. A couple of high-end lawyers are in town and are representing this kid, William Stover. The political winds are blowing and I can tell you right now, if you think you're going after Tom Carver, you'd better have more than what you're telling me. Do you?" she asked looking back and forth at both men.

"No," Mills admitted. "But…"

"Do you think it's likely you'll get more?" she asked then held up a hand to cut off any comment. "I'll answer that myself. No, I don't think so."

"We should at least continue to investigate," Hough said. Mills remained silent. With many more years of experience, he had a pretty good idea what was coming next. He did not like it, but he was too close to his pension to make waves.

"Do you have a cause of death?" Foster asked.

"Yeah, we talked to Anand just before you came in," Hough said referring to Dr. Bhatt. "He's pretty certain accidental drug overdose. No sign of violence. She had consensual sex with someone who wore a condom."

"Okay, given that, I've been told in no uncertain terms that unless we have solid evidence of a homicide, which we don't, our investigation is over. Sorry guys. We have other cases and going after the next president without evidence of a homicide, with what are clearly an accident and a confession, is not good for anyone's career."

Both men looked at each other, shrugged, turned back to their boss and said, "Okay."

When they were walking away from Foster's office, Mills said, "I still don't buy it. Something's not right here."

"What do you want to do?" Hough asked.

"I don't know. I'm not sure there's anything we can do."

"Come in, gentlemen. Please, have a seat," Marcus DeWitt pleasantly said to the two New York lawyers who had requested this meeting even before arriving in St. Paul.

DeWitt was the elected Ramsey County Attorney. The two lawyers who requested this meeting were Nelson McGovern and Peter Simpson. Both men were from an expensive, politically connected firm with offices in most major cities, especially Washington D.C.

A fourth person was also in attendance. Her name was Gwen Bryant and she was the assistant county attorney assigned to Billy Stover's case. Bryant was already there when the two men arrived, seated alongside DeWitt's desk.

After introductions and handshakes, DeWitt asked the obvious question, "What can I do for you gentlemen?"

"As I told you on the phone this morning, we have been retained to represent William Stover. We wanted to have this meeting to find out where the case and investigation stood," McGovern said.

"He's being charged with first and second-degree manslaughter," Bryant told them.

"May I ask why?" McGovern asked.

"Because we believe he is guilty of first and second-degree manslaughter," Bryant replied as if speaking to a child.

"What I meant was that this seems like an unfortunate accident..."

"Which is why he is being charged with manslaughter and not murder," Bryant said. "He'll be arraigned tomorrow morning at around 9:00 in courtroom 1240."

"Are you licensed to practice in Minnesota?" DeWitt asked.

"No, I guess we'll need to get a local co-counsel. Could we put off the arraignment until tomorrow afternoon?" McGovern asked.

"Sure," Bryant replied. "No problem."

"Any suggestions who we might contact to get for co-counsel?" the other man, Peter Simpson asked.

"You could try Mickey O'Herlihy," DeWitt replied. He then found O'Herlihy's card in his old-style Rolodex and handed it to Simpson so the lawyer could write down the number.

"What about a plea?" McGovern asked.

"Sure, he can plead guilty tomorrow," Bryant pleasantly replied.

"What I meant was..."

"Maybe you should call Mickey first and go see your client. He's in segregation at the detention center," DeWitt suggested.

"Oh, yeah, that's probably the thing to do," McGovern agreed. "Well, thanks for your time. I guess we'll see you tomorrow."

"One last thing before you go," DeWitt said. "We have it on very good, reliable authority that the victim, Abby Connolly, never did drugs."

The New York lawyers were barely out the door when Gwen Bryant said to her boss, "These two have no idea what they're doing. Neither of them is a criminal defense lawyer."

"I know," DeWitt said with a big smile. "That's why I sent them to Mickey. Let him deal with these two. That will piss him off."

"They're here to get this thing swept under the rug as quickly as possible," Bryant said.

"Yeah," DeWitt agreed. "That's another reason I sent them to Mickey. Maybe this Stover kid will have one lawyer looking out for him."

FIVE

Marc's office door was open as usual so Mickey rapped once on the frame. Marc looked up as his mentor came in, closed the door and took a chair in front of Marc's desk.

"What's up?" Marc asked.

"Want an easy case? An easy five grand?" Mickey replied.

"There's no such thing," Marc said.

"This should be," Mickey said. "There are a couple of lawyers from New York in town to represent someone and they need local counsel. They called me but their client is being arraigned in St. Paul this afternoon and I'm going to Minneapolis. I have to be in federal court on that gambling ring case."

"Who's the client?" Marc asked as he reached across the desk to accept a piece of paper Mickey handed him.

"Kid's name is William Stover. Those are the lawyers," Mickey said referring to the names on the note he had given Marc. "Stover's the guy who was working for the Carvers. It was his room the dead girl was found in. They're going to charge him with man one and two."

"Do they even have a cause of death? How do they know...?"

"They're saying it was a drug overdose and Stover provided her with the drugs," Mickey said.

"The M.E. has the tox screening back already? It's only been, what, two days. What's going on Mickey?"

"The girl's dad is a state senator from Stillwater," Mickey told him. "There's political heat on this. The dad claims the girl never touched drugs before this, according to the New York guys."

"Ah, ha," Marc said rolling his eyes. "That's why you don't want it, the political heat."

"No," Mickey said shaking his head for emphasis. "I gotta be in Minneapolis this afternoon. I can't get another continuance. Look, Marc, it's almost eleven now. Give those guys a call. Let them buy you lunch then go to the arraignment. Get the check from them first."

"What if it goes to trial? I'm not doing that for five grand," Marc replied.

"Then get more money. I think they were sent here by the Carvers. Or the Carvers got one of their rich pals to pick up the tab for the fees. Either way, you'll get paid," Mickey said.

Marc looked directly into Mickey's eyes and said, "They're going to shove a plea down this kid's throat to sweep the whole thing under the rug and get it over and make it go away as quickly and quietly as possible, aren't they?"

"Maybe," Mickey replied. "I can't tell you that's not a possibility. Look, don't do anything you think might be unethical. You can always withdraw since he has other counsel. Don't let these New York guys blow smoke up your ass or push you around. You're a tough kid. You can handle these guys. Besides, I'll be around. There's a real chance that the Stover kid is guilty. He could've provided the drugs to her, they were too potent and it killed her."

"Yeah, that's true too," Marc agreed. "But I don't think I want to have lunch with these guys. New York lawyers? I don't think I want to sit there for an hour at lunch being treated like a rube from flyover country."

Mickey laughed at the image, then said, "I already told them I'd talk to you about it. Call them and meet them at the arraignment. Oh yeah, comb your hair and wash your face. There's sure to be media attending."

"Yes, Mom. I'll look my best."

At 12:55 Marc pushed through the door of courtroom 1240. As he walked up the center aisle to the gate he noted the dozen or so media people in attendance. Somewhat unusual, Stover's case had already been assigned to a judge who would oversee it through trial, if necessary. The judge assigned was Stanley Weaver, a sixty-two-year-old, twenty-year veteran judge with a solid reputation for fairness. He also was exceptional at handling highly publicized cases, which this one could be, with a very firm hand.

Dressed in a suit and tie and carrying a leather, satchel briefcase, Marc was obviously a lawyer. He passed through the gate and approached a middle-aged woman seated next to the bench. Her nameplate identified her as Maura Barkow, Judge Weaver's clerk.

Marc identified himself and she pleasantly told him the other lawyers were in the jury room conferring with Stover. Before Marc made a move to join them, the door opened and everyone filed into the courtroom, including a woman Marc new was an assistant county attorney, Gwen Bryant.

While a deputy escorted Stover to a table, Bryant shook hands with Marc. The New Yorkers, Nelson McGovern and Peter Simpson, also introduced themselves.

"I suppose we should bring you up to speed on what's going on," Bryant said. "Why don't we go back into the jury room? Your client can wait here for now."

"Okay," Marc agreed while thinking, *why don't I like the sounds of this?*

The four lawyers took chairs at the table and before they started, McGovern gave Marc a check from his firm's trust account and a retainer agreement to look over. Marc signed the retainer and pocketed the check while McGovern talked.

"You understand that Peter and myself will be main counsel for this case," he said smiling at Marc.

"Sure, I get that," Marc said while thinking, *except I'm the one that's licensed so, we'll see.*

"To cut to the chase, Marc," Bryant began, "we've already worked out a plea."

"You've what? Worked out a plea?" Marc said looking back and forth at McGovern and Simpson. "Have you been given any discovery? Police reports, autopsy results, witness statements…"

"Yes," McGovern said. "We have gone over all that with Mr. Stover."

Bryant slid a small stack of papers across the table to Marc. He picked them up and silently looked them over for a minute without reading them.

"As I said, Marc, we're lead counsel and…"

"No, you're not," Marc sharply replied. "In fact, you're here as a courtesy to whoever's paying you. I'm the one that's licensed and I want to talk to my client, alone, please. So, if you'll excuse me, I'll bring him in and satisfy myself that he knows what's going on here."

"Don't you want to hear the deal first?" Bryant asked.

"Sorry, sure," Marc sheepishly replied.

"He pleads to man two and we recommend twenty-four months, way below guideline. Also, he will be allowed to serve the time at a facility in Colorado, close to his home. We understand his mother is ill and we'll accommodate that as much as possible. He'll be on unsupervised probation for five years at the end of which the charge will drop to a misdemeanor. It's a good deal, Marc."

"Yeah, it is," Marc agreed. *Too good if he's guilty*, Marc thought.

For the next hour, Marc met with Billy Stover alone. He went over the police report and autopsy results with him, marveling at the swiftness of the lab results showing the level of cocaine in Abby Connolly's system.

Marc also explained there had been no time for the defense to conduct any independent tests, interview witnesses or prepare any type of defense.

At the end of the hour, Marc was satisfied that at least Stover understood what he was doing. Marc was not satisfied that he was doing the right thing. But if a client insists on pleading guilty, make sure he understands what he's doing and what his options are then get out of the way and let him do it.

When they took the plea in the courtroom, Marc thoroughly questioned Stover, for the record, that he had been advised by Marc not to do this.

Judge Weaver also spent several minutes satisfying himself that Stover knew what he was doing, was, in fact, guilty, not under the influence of any drugs or alcohol or coerced in any way. Finally satisfied, almost reluctantly Judge Weaver accepted the plea. He also agreed to the twenty-four months subject to concurrence by a court services review and report.

While Billy Stover was being led away, the media left to file their stories or film their reports. McGovern and Simpson scrambled to catch the next flight out and Marc took a seat in the jury box. While he waited for the courtroom to empty, Gwen Bryant joined him.

"What the hell was that, Gwen?" Marc asked.

"You know something, Marc? I'm not sure. Now that it's over, I can tell you this, word came down from up high to wrap this up as quickly and quietly as possible. So, I did. Why do I feel so shitty about it?"

"It does feel a little…I don't know, sleazy, doesn't it?" Marc replied.

"I hope your check cashes. You earned it. At least someone made an effort to look out for that kid. Those two…"

"Douchebags," Marc interjected.

"Yeah, douchebags," Gwen laughed, "sure as hell didn't. They couldn't get him in jail fast enough."

Marc looked at the empty courtroom and said, "Come on, I'll walk you out."

Two hours after Marc got back to the office Mickey arrived back from Minneapolis. Marc joined him in Mickey's office and told the older man what had transpired.

"Somebody's covering up something for someone," Mickey said.

"Maybe," Marc replied. "Stover stuck to his story though. He said he felt terrible about what happened and wanted to take his punishment and get it over."

"I'll do some checking around. Get me the paperwork and I'll see what I can find out."

"Why?" Marc asked. "It's over. What can we find that might get the plea withdrawn? Especially as adamant as William Stover was."

"Probably nothing. Even if we found something, the guy had three lawyers. The odds of withdrawing the plea are a little less than zero. Call it professional curiosity," Mickey replied.

Mickey was seated alone in his favorite back booth in O'Gara's. Finishing his supper, a shepherd's pie concoction, he then set the empty plate aside. He may have been sitting alone but all of the regulars, which was just about everyone in the place, made a point of stopping to say "hello". Audrey, the twenty-something doll who was waiting tables tonight, brought him his second Guinness and picked up his dirty dishes. Despite the fifty-year difference, Mickey still found ways to flirt with her. And, despite the fifty-year difference, Audrey was secretly flattered.

Five minutes later, two men wearing inexpensive suits with bulges on their hips from their guns entered the bar and quickly walked the length of the bar to where Mickey was waiting for them. Mickey took a sip of his beer while they slid into the booth across from him.

Parker Mills, St. Paul police detective, was a long-time acquaintance of Mickey's having testified many times while Mickey drilled him in court. Parker reached across the table and shook hands with the lawyer.

"Evening, Mickey," Parker said. "You remember my partner, Nathan Hough?"

"Of course, Detective," Mickey lied as he shook Hough's hand. "Thank you both for meeting me."

Audrey appeared and the now off-duty cops each ordered a glass of beer. Mickey told her to be sure to put it on his tab.

"Thanks for meeting me, Detectives," Mickey said again as he raised his glass to them. He took a swallow, set his glass on the cardboard coaster and continued. "I understand you were the investigating officers on the tragic death of that young girl at the St. Paul a couple days ago."

"Yeah, we were," Mills acknowledged.

Audrey set their drinks down and Mills waited for her to leave before continuing.

"Why? What's up?" Mills asked.

"What can you tell me about it?"

"You weren't involved, were you?" Hough politely asked.

"The young lawyer who is currently working for me was hired as local counsel for two lawyers from New York," Mickey explained. "A deal was made and the young man charged with her death took a plea at his arraignment. Very unusual."

Hough looked at Mills who set his empty glass down and said, "We heard that. I'll tell you what Mickey," Mills lowered his voice, leaned forward and continued. "There was something wrong from the get-go

30

about this. We're pretty sure that girl's body was moved. And we talked to the M.E. and he now believes that as well. The politicians threw a net over this thing and swept it under the rug."

"Who's the M.E.?" Mickey asked.

"Anand Bhatt," Hough replied.

"I know Anand," Mickey said. "There isn't a political bone in his body."

"I know," Mills agreed. "I'll tell you something else. We can't prove it but that Carver guy, the one running for president, his top aide, bodyguard or whatever he is, lied to us. He told us Carver slept with his wife in her room. But someone slept in Carver's room and the maids believe there were two of them."

"We found out that Carver is a total pussy-hound. Bangs everything with tits," Hough interjected.

"So you think she slept with Carver, died of an overdose in his bed and the campaign covered it up?"

"Could be. We went back to interview the maids that cleaned Carver's room," Mills said, "and both are gone. They quit and no one knows where they are. We can't find them."

"That's when the case was pulled from us," Hough added.

"And there's a sheet missing from Carver's bed. Exactly what you would use to move a body."

"What about DNA in his room?" Mickey asked.

"The place had been scrubbed," Hough said. "But that's another thing. There was hardly any DNA from the girl in Stover's room. They found some on the bed and nowhere else."

The three men chatted for another twenty minutes, enough time for another beer. Nothing else of significance came up and in the end, they all agreed there was not much they could do about it. Billy Stover's plea was done and to bring up anything about any possible involvement of Thomas Carver was career suicide, even for Mickey and certainly for the two detectives and Marc Kadella.

The next day Mickey told Marc what he had found out. The reality of it was the two detectives really had nothing solid. No real evidence and there was a confession and plea from Billy Stover. Case closed.

"Those two assholes from New York weren't real lawyers looking out for their client," Marc said with clear disgust. "They were bagmen for the Carver's."

"No doubt," Mickey agreed.

SIX

ONE YEAR LATER

The election was now four days in the past and Marc Kadella was barely out of his funk, what he called his post-election blues. Even though the result was predicted by everyone, knowing what he knew about Tom and Darla Carver, Marc was hoping for a last minute turn around.

The one-term incumbent the Carvers defeated—they made it clear that Tom and Darla were a package deal—was a good and decent man. Curtis Baker was an elderly, old-school politician. Over a forty-year career, Baker had held numerous government posts, including legislative and cabinet-level. The Carvers came across as young, new-era, modern, forward thinking and the country decided it was time for a fresh face change and a new era to begin.

Carver's political opponents had dragged out several women with whom Tom had some brief flings and a couple of long-term affairs. There were also stories and people claiming the Carvers had used their political position to line their pockets. None of this seemed to matter or stick to them.

The Bimbo Problem, or so it was labeled, went nowhere. The attitude seemed to be if Darla didn't care why should we? This was a private, marital matter. With each new revelation, it took Darla three days to calm down. Not because her husband had been unfaithful—she knew all about that—but because of the damage these women might do to Darla's political ambitions. As for the ethically questionable investments from which they had enhanced their wealth, nothing was ever definitively proven. Plus, knowing Darla Carver, the people involved had every reason to keep quiet and cover up any possible wrongdoing.

Election Day exit polling showed that the margin of victory was primarily due to women. Apparently, the tall, charming, handsome Tom Carver had smitten enough women, especially younger, single women, to push him across the finish line.

"So, are you done pouting? Is it safe to talk to you yet?" one of Mickey's staff, a middle-aged woman named Alice, asked Marc on the morning of post-election day five.

Marc was arriving at the office a few minutes late and everyone but Mickey was already at their desks. Mickey's office had three offices for lawyers along the north wall with a nice sized conference room. Mickey's office itself took up the entire front of the building overlooking Snelling Avenue. The common area where the staff was situated was a large, open space in the middle with the windows to the south. Just inside the back entryway door to the right was a lunch/coffee room. Alice and another legal assistant, Marge, and Mickey's paralegal, Kevin Stuart, were standing at the coffee machine when Marc walked in.

"Yeah, I'm all right," Marc said with a slightly embarrassed smile. "Sorry I haven't been very cheerful the last few days." Marc held out a cup and Marge filled it for him.

"What do you have against Tom Carver?" Marge asked.

"I found out some things a while back. They're not who you think they are," Marc said.

"What, they're ambitious politicians? So what? They all are," Alice replied.

"And Tom's a hunk. No wonder women go after him," Marge chimed in.

"And you're okay with that?" Marc asked.

"Not my problem. It's her husband, not mine," Marge said.

Marc looked at Kevin, the paralegal, who shrugged his shoulders and said, "I'm with you. I voted for Baker. The Carvers seem a little too slick, too sleazy for me."

"A voice of reason in the wilderness of adolescence," Marc said as the two men fist bumped.

"Where's Mickey?" Marc asked.

"Haven't heard from him yet," Alice replied. Mickey strolling in at odd hours was hardly unusual and certainly no cause for alarm.

A short while later Marc was seated at his desk, his feet on an open desk drawer, scanning through the morning paper. He was in the Metro section when a small headline and short article caught his attention. Out of curiosity he quickly read it with increasing shock. When he finished, not completely believing what he had just read, he read it again.

It was a brief story from the AP about a young man found dead in a prison cell in Colorado. What put it in the Metro section of the St. Paul paper was its connection to Minnesota. A little over a year ago the man had pleaded guilty to manslaughter while in St. Paul. At the time, he was a staffer with the Carver campaign who admitted to having provided the drugs that caused a local woman's overdose death.

William Stover had been discovered hanging in his cell two days ago. The Colorado authorities were ruling it to be a suicide. A spokesperson for the Carver's issued a brief statement expressing their shock and anger that the Colorado prison people responsible for the safety and security of their inmates could have allowed this young man to take his own life.

Marc did a quick calculation of Billy's time served and realized he would be paroled in less than three months. Stover had already completed the bulk of his sentence. It was then Marc wondered if this occurring two days after the election was merely a coincidence.

"Sonofabitch," Marc quietly whispered to himself. "Could they have..." he started to say but was stopped by a voice from his doorway.

"Marc! We just got a call," Alice said with obvious anxiety. "Mickey's had a heart attack. He's at Regions."

Before Alice finished, Marc had tossed the paper aside and was putting on his suit coat. He grabbed his overcoat and sprinted toward the parking lot door. Before he got there, Kevin Stuart caught him and asked if he could go with him. The two men were in Marc's ten-year-old Buick and on Snelling headed toward the freeway in under a minute.

Despite Mickey O'Herlihy's less-than-stellar record of adherence to Catholicism, his funeral was held in the Cathedral of St. Paul. Locally known simply as The Cathedral, it is the third largest church in America and the fourth tallest.

Situated on Cathedral Hill, the copper-domed building had one of the most distinctive views in Minnesota. It overlooks downtown St. Paul, the Mississippi River and the state Capitol barely a mile away. In 2009, the beautiful church was designated as a National Shrine of the Apostle Paul by the United States Conference of Catholic Bishops and the Vatican.

The head of the archdiocese, Archbishop Connor MacBreen, personally conducted the service. Aside from being a fellow Irish Catholic, the good archbishop was a poker-pal of Mickey's. About once a month or so, a very secret poker game would be organized; a friendly game for a few politically connected friends—bipartisan of course. Mickey would somehow procure enough Cuban cigars for everyone and the archbishop's favorite single-malt. Mickey was always welcome even if he lightened everyone's wallets a bit.

The Cathedral seats approximately 3,000 and every seat was filled. If a bomb had gone off, a good section of the Twin Cities bar would have been eliminated. Of course, any number of irreverent jokes would have followed.

The previous day there had been a day long visitation for the man at a funeral home a block from his office. Many of the people attending the funeral and several hundred more, including Marc's wife, Karen, and their children, had paid their respects during the day. To move the funeral along, the archbishop limited the eulogies to just two people. The mayors of both St. Paul and Minneapolis would do the honors, much to Marc's relief.

Unknown to Marc, Mickey was an army veteran having served just before Vietnam escalated into a nightmare. It was Mickey's wish and privilege earned to be buried with his peers at Ft. Snelling. Most of the people attending the service skipped the procession to the cemetery. Even so, there were at least a thousand people graveside or as close as they could get. The November weather cooperated, a live bugler played out taps and a twenty-one-gun salute brought Mickey to his final resting place.

Marc turned away from the flag-draped casket sheltered by the canopy and began making his way through the crowd. He could not help thinking how much he was going to miss Mickey, which brought more tears to his already red eyes. The crowd was moving slowly and with the amount of traffic in the narrow cemetery streets, Marc was in no particular hurry. It was going to be a while before traffic cleared. He had barely progressed twenty feet when he felt a gentle hand on his shoulder and a familiar voice from behind.

"Hey, Marc, you got a minute?"

Marc turned around and looked at two of the three children of Mickey O'Herlihy. Mickey's two sons, Brian and David, both grown men in their forties, much older than Marc, were standing there.

Working with their dad, Marc had met both of them and their younger sister, Sheila, many times. All three were as affable as their dad and Marc got along quite well with them.

"Sure, Brian," Marc said to the older of the two. "David," he nodded at the other. "What's up?"

David took Marc gently by an elbow and the three of them stepped away from the crowd.

"Listen," Brian began, "we might as well tell you, we've decided to sell dad's building. Sorry, but…"

"It's okay," Marc said. "I figured you would. Do you have a buyer?"

"No, not yet. We really haven't done anything yet," David said.

"We have no interest in it and well…" Brian said.

"Brian, it's okay. Really. I can find office space," Marc assured them.

"What about the staff?" David asked.

"They're already looking for jobs. They'll have no trouble finding one. Don't worry," Marc said.

"We hate to kick anyone out on the street," Brian said. "It will be at minimum two or three months."

"If you want to find financing, we would give you first crack at it, if you want it," Brian replied.

Marc thought for a moment then said, "I don't see it. My practice is coming along and with my cases and the ones your dad had open, I'll be busy for quite a while. But I don't think I could afford that."

"One of the firms on the first floor is interested. They're looking into it," David said. "They said they're going to move upstairs. But they'll give you time, they told us that."

A short, well-dressed, attractive woman with dark hair and large sunglasses joined the three men.

"Hey, Connie," Brian said as he gave the woman a warm hug. "Thanks for coming."

"Are you kidding? Your old man? I wouldn't have missed it. The Mick had a great life," she replied.

"Marc," Brian said, "I'd like you to meet an old friend of my dad's, Connie Mickelson."

"Nice to meet you," Marc said as they shook hands.

"Are you Mickey's latest project?" she asked.

"Yeah, you could say that," Marc replied.

"Listen, is it true?" she asked looking at Marc. "Did he have a heart attack in the sack with one of his hooker clients?"

Horrified that she would ask such a thing in front of Mickey's sons, Marc's eyes grew wide and he completely froze. Not knowing how to respond he stayed this way for two or three very long seconds. Then Brian and David both started laughing at the question and Marc's obvious discomfort.

"It's okay," Brian said. "We knew our dad pretty well."

"Besides, we both know it's true," David added.

"It is?" Connie asked. "Good for him." She turned to Marc and said, "These guys both know that their dad and me, well, we had a thing for a while."

Finally breathing again, Marc looked around and said, "Okay, yes, it's true."

"Hey, Connie," Brian said, "Marc's looking for office space. Do you have any?"

"You selling your dad's place?" she asked.

"Yeah," Brian replied. "You interested?"

Connie thought it over for a moment then said, "No, I don't think so. I don't have time to take care of a place in St. Paul."

She looked at Marc and said, "I have a building on Lake and Charles in Minneapolis. Uptown. I have an office sharing space with me and a couple other lawyers. If you're interested, I do have an office available. You must be a litigator if you're working with Mickey."

"Yeah, I am," Marc replied. "And I'd be interested."

"There are two guys with me, Chris Grafton who does corporate work for small businesses. He needs a litigator and I can throw work at you, too. The other guy is an old fart who was a friend of my dad. He does mostly probate stuff. Between you and me, I wish he'd retire or die."

"How much you want for rent?" Marc asked.

"I don't know. It's been empty for two years," Connie said. She reached in her purse then handed Marc a business card. "Give me a call then come see me. We'll see about rent based on what you can afford. Don't worry about it."

"I'll do that," Marc said holding up the card.

"Come here, you two. Give us a hug. I gotta go," Connie said to Brian and David. "Marc," she continued, "nice to meet you. Give me a call."

"I will. Probably next week."

"All rise," the sheriff's deputy, acting as courtroom bailiff, ordered.

Marc stood up at the defense table while his surly, orange jumpsuit-clad, uncooperative client remained slumped in his chair.

Judge Ross Peterson of the Hennepin County District Court in downtown Minneapolis took the bench. He gave Marc and his disrespectful client a dirty look then told Marc and the prosecutor, Rhea Watson, and the few court onlookers to be seated.

"My condolences on the death of your associate, Mr. O'Herlihy," Peterson started off by saying.

Marc knew that Peterson's comment was disingenuous, at best. In fact, Peterson probably celebrated when he heard the news. Peterson disliked defense lawyers—except insurance defense lawyers—in general and Mickey in particular. Knowing this, Mickey, over the years, had never missed an opportunity to tweak Peterson's bias.

"I understand you want to withdraw as counsel for the defendant. Is that correct Mr. Kadella?"

"Yes, your Honor. Mr. O'Herlihy was assigned his case. I was merely assisting and do not feel qualified to..."

"Are you a licensed attorney, Mr. Kadella?" Peterson asked.

"Well, of course, your Honor."

"For how long?"

"Not quite four years, your Honor," Marc replied.

"What's your position on this, Ms. Watson?" Peterson asked the prosecutor.

"We're opposed, your Honor. Any further delay would cause severe hardship to the victim's family, your Honor," Rhea Watson replied.

"And she doesn't want to have to deal with a more experienced defense lawyer, your Honor," Marc blurted out.

"Speak when you're spoken to in my courtroom, Mr. Kadella," Peterson admonished him.

"What about you, Mr. Traynor?" Peterson said to the sulking man sitting next to Marc. "What do you have to say? Want a different lawyer?"

Traynor sat up then looked around the courtroom as if noticing it for the first time. He looked up and down at Marc who was still standing, then turned his head to the judge.

"He'll do. What do I care? It's all a joke anyway," Howie Traynor said.

Howard Traynor was accused of murdering the aunt of one of the wealthiest, most powerful women in America. It had happened while Traynor, a professional burglar, and another man burglarized the woman's home. There was ample evidence of his guilt. The only question would be what degree of murder had he committed?

"I'm glad you find this amusing," Peterson dryly said. "Motion to withdraw, denied, Mr. Kadella. It's all yours."

SEVEN

Marc Kadella parked his rented Chevy in a slot in the prison's visitor's area parking lot. He had flown into Denver the previous morning, rented a car and driven to Colorado Springs. Having spoken to Billy Stover's parents several times over the phone, they were waiting for him although not anxious to see him. It had been over two months since their son was found hanging in his cell and they were not happy to reopen wounds that had barely begun to heal and never would completely.

Following their directions, Marc had easily found their middle-class, suburban-style home. Dan and Estelle Stover were Midwestern pleasant and polite despite their obvious grief. Marc spent an hour with them reviewing the investigation reports of Billy's death they had already sent to him. At the end of the hour, Marc sensed the couple had had enough and had nothing more to offer. He politely made his exit from the obviously relieved parents. Dan walked him to his car and told Marc unless he found something solid, they did not want to be bothered again. It was a sentiment Marc clearly understood.

Marc drove South out of Colorado Springs on I-25 to Pueblo. There he picked up U.S. 50 and took it Northwest to Canon City. Canon City is noted for having nine state and four federal prisons and bills itself as the "Corrections Capital of the World". This was a claim Marc found to be more than a little odd and a bit unsettling.

Marc found the Best Western where he had his reservation. He checked in, obtained directions to the appropriate facility he wanted and arrived for his appointment with a half-hour to spare.

After being passed through the prison's security, Marc found himself waiting patiently in the reception area of the warden's office. He paged through a three-week-old Time magazine while waiting. Ten minutes after sitting down, a phone buzzed on the desk of the oldest administrative assistant. Marc set the magazine down and heard the matronly woman cryptically respond to the caller.

"The warden will see you now, Mr. Kadella," the woman politely said when she hung up the phone.

The other administrative assistant, her desk closer to the large, double doors of the inner office, rose and opened the door for him. He quietly thanked her as he walked past.

Entering the nicely appointed office, Marc saw the warden, James Carlyle, seated directly ahead, sitting behind an exceptionally nice and obviously expensive, large walnut desk. To Marc's right were two corrections officers seated on a couch. Marc nodded slightly to the men on the couch, walked the ten or twelve feet to the desk and stuck out his hand.

"Marc Kadella, Warden Carlyle. Thanks for taking the time to see me," Marc said introducing himself.

James Carlyle may have only been a big fish in a small pond but he was a very big fish in that pond. He preferred to be called by his title and this out-of-state lawyer would get no special treatment. He shook Marc's hand as the two officers stood up. Carlyle introduced them as Captain Howard Munson and Sergeant Albert Bass. Marc took one look at Bass and had to fight the urge to flee. Bass was a good six foot five and a solid two fifty. The look on the man's face could, at best, be described as serious.

"Have a seat, Marc," Carlyle said.

When all four of the men were in their respective places, Carlyle said to Marc, "Since you're here about William Stover, I asked Captain Munson and Sergeant Bass to join us. They are much more familiar with this tragedy than I am."

"No problem, Warden," Marc replied. "As I said over the phone this is probably a fool's errand anyway."

Without being too noticeable, Marc took a quick look around the warden's office. One of the photos on the man's vanity wall was a picture of Carlyle and the soon-to-be inaugurated President-elect Thomas Carver. The photo was several years old and must have been from when Carlyle was Colorado's governor. Marc was about to make a comment about it, thought better of it and decided to ignore it. The room was significantly nicer and better decorated than what might be expected for a prison warden.

"And, as I said, when we spoke this trip was mostly for me to meet Billy Stover's parents and offer my condolences," Marc continued.

"A lawyer with human feelings," Captain Munson chimed in from the couch.

"Will wonders never cease," Sergeant Bass added.

The two corrections officers heartily laughed at their combined wit and even fist bumped each other.

Marc turned to look at them, slightly smiled and said, "It's rare, but it does happen."

He turned back to Warden Carlyle and continued, "I figured as long as I came this far, I thought I'd stop here and see if you knew anything different than the reports had. I didn't know Billy well but he seemed like a really good kid. When I saw the story in the St. Paul paper, I was a bit shocked."

"The investigation was done by the state attorney general's people and was very thorough. He ripped up one of his sheets from his bed and hung himself on the bars with it. Terrible thing. Fortunately, it rarely happens," Carlyle said. He was leaning back in his executive chair, his hands laced together on the vest covering his ample belly. Carlyle looked and acted as if he did not have a care in the world and a lawyer looking over his shoulder was little more than a nuisance to be brushed aside.

"So you were satisfied no other inmates were involved, nothing like that?" Marc asked.

"Hey, no other inmates were involved. I can guarantee it," Captain Munson almost yelled as he jerked forward on the couch toward Marc. "Get that out of your head, lawyer. We're good at our jobs."

This sudden and inflamed outburst caused Marc to think, *methinks thou dost protest too much.*

"No other inmates were involved," Warden Carlyle quietly concurred. "Prison affects people differently, as you can imagine," he continued. "I'm sure you've seen the psychologists report on Stover. He was having problems. It's not unusual."

"But not so bad that he should be on a suicide watch?"

"Not according to the prison shrink," Munson said, more calmly this time. "He never informed us there might be a problem or we would have kept a close eye on him."

Marc turned a little more to his right to look at the other guard, Sergeant Bass.

"Did you know Stover, Sergeant Bass?" Marc politely asked.

"Yeah, and he gave me no reason to believe he was suicidal," the guard answered him. But he said it as if he was reading it off of a card. Obviously, Bass had been briefed to keep his mouth shut and offer nothing.

By this point Marc was certain he would get nothing more from these three; certainly nothing useful. He made a little more small talk, looked at his watch and decided to go. He shook hands all around and Carlyle walked him to the door.

"Is it always this nice here in January?" Marc asked as Carlyle opened the exit door for him.

"Weather can change quite a bit here in Colorado. It can turn on you and bite you on the ass anytime," Carlyle replied.

"Interesting. Well, thanks again, Warden," Marc said as he headed out into the reception area.

A guard was waiting for him and silently escorted him out of the building. While Marc was walking across the parking lot toward his rental car, he thought, *these guys don't realize it but they are all really bad liars.*

"What do you think?" Munson asked Warden Carlyle as soon as Marc was gone.

"I checked this guy out," Carlyle said. "We have nothing to worry about. You two get back to your duties. I have a phone call to make. Bass, make sure you keep an eye on him until he's gone."

"Yes, sir," Bass replied.

The two corrections officers left, and using a cell phone even his wife did not know about, Carlyle placed a call. Before the first ring ended, a familiar, curt-sounding voice answered.

"Mr. Dean," Carlyle respectfully said to Tom Carver's man, Clay Dean.

"Did you meet with him?" Dean asked after Carlyle identified himself.

"Yes, and it went fine. He was fishing and got nothing. The official reports are finished and quite definite. We're covered."

"Does anyone else know anything about my bosses' interest in this matter and who they are?" Dean asked.

"Absolutely not," Carlyle replied. "I'm the only one and you can rest assured I will keep it that way."

"Thank you, Warden. I'll pass it along," Dean abruptly replied.

"Thank you and pass on my congratulations…" Carlyle began to sputter. It was too late. Dean had already hung up.

Without making Marc aware of it, the officer escorting Marc out of the prison was under orders to delay him. This was to give Al Bass time to change out of his uniform and get to his own vehicle, a new Ford pickup truck courtesy of a grateful Carver campaign slush fund. Bass was going to keep an eye on the nosy lawyer.

On the drive back into Canon City to the motel, Marc spotted the bright red pickup after going barely two miles. Without seeing him, Marc knew who was following him. It had taken a little too long to exit the prison. Obviously, this was to give Sergeant Moron a chance to follow him. Marc thought about giving him a run around then decided not to. Why let them know he knew they were hiding something? Instead, he drove directly to the motel and acted as if nothing was out of the ordinary. What Marc had not noticed was the small SUV in front of him.

Al Bass followed Marc right into the motel's parking lot. He parked his truck and watched while Marc went inside. Bass stayed on post for another hour using his cell phone to make periodic calls to Munson to check in. He stayed for a total of two hours then Munson made the decision that Marc was not going anywhere and Bass could call it a night. Unknown to Bass, while he was watching Marc, another man was watching him until Bass left.

Just before 6:30 P.M., Marc was escorted to a small table in the motel's dining room. The place was about half-full including the bar area. He ordered his meal and quietly sat contemplating his predicament. He knew the three men at the prison were lying. This, of course, likely meant Billy Stover had been murdered. At least maybe. He may still have committed suicide but the motive was unclear. Regardless, Marc was at the end. Stover's parents were not going to help and without a case or client, what could he do?

"You were right," Marc quietly said to himself sipping his beer. "This was a fool's errand."

His meal arrived and having not eaten since breakfast, Marc was famished and dug right in. Halfway through the meal, a man suddenly appeared and without a word took the chair opposite him at his table.

Holding the steak knife firmly in his right hand, Marc said, "Please, have a seat."

Ignoring the sarcasm, the man, who looked to be in his mid-twenties, athletic with a small scar above his left eye said, "Did you know you were followed when you left the prison?"

"The guy in the red pickup," Marc said.

"Al Bass," the man said.

"And you are?"

"I work at the prison. I don't have any proof about what happened but I knew Billy Stover. I'm a guard where his cell was. And Billy Stover was not suicidal. And he was not even seeing the prison shrink. Billy was doing fine. He got along with the other cons and was looking forward to getting out. Billy would not have killed himself."

"Why should I believe you?" Marc asked still conspicuously holding the knife.

The man sat quietly, hesitating for several seconds thinking about his answer. He had thought about this moment and was not sure he could trust the lawyer. It was now decision time.

"Because me and Billy were in love. I loved Billy Stover and we were planning a life together. We were both in the closet but when he got out we were going to move. California probably and come out and be together. Billy told me he had never been so happy."

"Jesus," Marc said quietly. "I'm really sorry for your loss."

"Thanks," the man replied as he wiped his eyes with a napkin.

"I'll tell you something else. Billy had nothing to do with that girl's death in Minnesota. He had never been with a girl and never did drugs. I just wanted you to know this. Can you do something?"

Marc thought about the question then answered, "I don't know. Did he tell you the truth about what happened in Minnesota? How that girl died?"

"I have to go," he suddenly said. "I've probably said too much."

He pushed his chair back and started to step away from the table. Marc grabbed his left wrist and pulled him back.

"Who did it? What caused the death of Abby Connolly?" Marc demanded.

The man stopped, looked down at Marc and with a sad defeated look quietly replied, "What the hell, you'll never touch them anyway." He leaned down and whispered in Marc's ear, "Darla Carver handled the cover up. Billy believes it was Tom who gave her the drugs.

"Darla and some guy named Clay Dean talked Billy into taking the hit for the Carvers. He helped them wrap her up in a sheet in Tom's suite then move her to his room. The rest you probably know."

A stunned Marc Kadella did not notice but an instant later, the man was gone. And Marc did not even know his name.

The next day, Marc returned the rental at the Denver airport and caught his flight back to Minnesota. During the one and a half-hour plane ride, he again mentally reviewed everything he knew. The problem he kept coming up with was not what he knew but what he could prove. Plus, there was not a prosecutor, state or federal in America that would touch what he had.

By the time the plane touched down, Marc was practically inconsolable. He knew the truth about two homicides and there was nothing he could do about it. And to make matters significantly worse, the people responsible were about to take over the most powerful office on the planet.

Three days after his meeting with Marc Kadella in his office at the prison, Warden James Carlyle was found in the front seat of his new Lexus. The police report, because there was no evidence to the contrary, was written up as a one-car accident. Carlyle had gone off the road and down an almost two hundred foot drop. His blood alcohol level was 0.11 which made him legally drunk. Those who knew him would have sworn, if given a chance, that 0.11 for Jim Carlyle was probably a little lower than most days.

44

EIGHT

INAUGURATION

Darla Carver ran her hands over her hips to smooth out her dress as she walked through the massive hotel room. The word "room" hardly gave justice to where Darla and the President-elect were staying. They had arranged for the Trump Townhouse in the Post Office Hotel on Pennsylvania Avenue. The view included the most famous address in the world; 1600 Pennsylvania. Darla loved to look at the old mansion and envision them setting up housekeeping—not that she had ever personally done any housekeeping—for the next sixteen years. On her list of things to accomplish was the repeal of the Twenty-Second Amendment. A dream perhaps, but if they could get it done, who knows how long their stay would be? Perhaps permanently.

On her way through the Trump Townhouse, Darla marveled at the place. Over six thousand square feet of hedonistic opulence that only someone as narcissistic as Donald Trump could create. Among its many amenities were two huge bedrooms, a private workout area, a private study for Tom's meetings and a dining room for twenty.

Again Darla ran her hands over her hips, proud and happy of the fact she had lost fifteen pounds since the election. She reached Tom's bedroom door, lightly knocked and went in. The President-elect was standing in front of a bureau mirror perfecting the knot of his tie. He turned to greet her as she approached him.

"I'm going to skip the meetings today with the congressional people," Darla told him as she reached up to fix the knot for him. "You're better at that than me and I have other things to work on for the inauguration."

"Okay, no problem," Tom said.

Darla looked up at her husband and with genuine affection said, "We really made it, didn't we? We're really here."

"Yeah, we are," Tom said smiling at her. "And we couldn't have done it without each other."

"And now, we're going to make history and change the world," Darla said.

"And get filthy rich in the process," Tom added with a big grin as Darla clapped her hands together and laughed.

Sonja Hayden found Darla in front a window overlooking Pennsylvania Avenue. Darla was silently staring at the famous mansion that was the center of the most powerful office on the planet. Sonja stood next to her and silently waited for Darla to notice her.

"We made it, Sonja. I never doubted that we would but there it is. Believing it and the reality of it are two very different things. It's amazing."

"Yes, ma'am," Sonja said, her reflection in the window's glass showing a large smile.

In contrast to Sonja's grin, Darla's expression was one of grim satisfaction. Sonja, for all of her slavish devotion, had never been able to get inside Darla's head. She'd never been able to figure out what drove the woman and why she never seemed to take any real joy in any of the Carvers' achievements. Here they were, at the pinnacle of power, the most beloved, respected and, at the same time, reviled couple on the planet and Darla was, seemingly, not enjoying it.

"Mrs. Carver," Sonja quietly said, "You've earned the right to enjoy this. No one has ever worked harder or deserved it more…"

"In my way, I am enjoying it," Darla replied slightly smiling at her aide. "And I can't thank you enough. Your future is secure, Sonja. Stick with me, kid, and we'll enjoy the ride."

"Always, Mrs. Carver," Sonja said.

"Did you find out how many inaugural balls were thrown for Baker?" Darla asked referring to their predecessor.

"Yes, ma'am. Sixteen and they, the President and the First Lady, attended six of them," Sonja replied. "We have eighteen, including the big one at the MGM National. I have you scheduled to attend eight," Sonja added as she handed Darla a single sheet of paper listing the events.

"Good. Just so we do more than the Bakers," Darla said looking over the list. "Well, let's get to work. There are still a thousand details to go over."

"Everything is going smoothly. You don't need to worry about every little detail. Plus, Jefferson and Natalie are waiting to see you," Sonja said referring to her children.

"Oh, that's right," Darla sighed. "I forgot about them. Let's go. I'll deal with them first and yes I do have to worry about every little detail. I want this to go perfectly."

They found the two teenage children, Jefferson and Natalie, waiting in a small room off the dining area. They were watching a cable news show of a panel discussion of their parents. The panel members, all media journalists, were glowing in their opinions for the next four years.

"Hello, you two," Darla said as she entered the room.

"Hello, Mother," Natalie replied barely looking at her and without getting up to greet her.

"Hi, Mom," Jefferson said as he embraced her.

Natalie pointed at the TV and said, "They really like you. They think Dad is going to make a great president."

"Don't you?" Darla asked as she took a seat on a couch facing her daughter. Jefferson returned to his seat while Sonja sat next to Darla.

"Yeah, I guess," Natalie shrugged.

"Please turn the TV off," Darla said.

Natalie picked up the remote and hit the power button while Darla continued.

"Do you both understand what you need to do during the inauguration?"

"Yeah, smile like idiots and stay out of trouble," Natalie quickly replied. "We got it. It's not like we don't have any experience being used as political props," she added.

"Do it for your father, please."

Natalie, at sixteen, was a fairly normal teenage girl. This, of course, meant she and her mother butted heads virtually every time they were in a room together. Fortunately, Natalie was still Daddy's girl and would dutifully play her part for Tom.

Jefferson, barely thirteen, was still young enough to be desperately seeking his mother's love and affection. This made him eager to please and would present no problem for Darla. Once the inauguration was over, Darla would hustle them back to Colorado and their exclusive boarding schools.

To be sure both of her offspring understood their parts, the four of them, surrogate mother Sonja included, thoroughly went over what was expected. Since they were still too young to be out all evening at inaugural balls, Darla made sure they would be back in the White House as early as possible.

"That reminds me," Darla said to Sonja after they left the two kids. "Are the Bakers about moved out? I don't want to have to wait all day for that fat-ass cow to vacate the premises."

"Yes, ma'am. I'm told they are on schedule. Your movers will start moving in while we are at the swearing-in ceremony," Sonja replied.

"Good. It was bad enough I had to spend an entire afternoon with her while she showed me around the place. The sooner they're out of town, the better."

"They have been extremely gracious and helpful during the transition," Sonja reminded her.

"We're letting them use the plane to go back to Texas, aren't we? They *should* be gracious."

"Yes, ma'am," Sonja said.

The two women heard voices coming from the living room. When they got there, they found Stevenson Wingate, Chairman of the Inaugural Committee, with another man. The two of them were obviously uneasy with each other and Wingate was quite red in the face.

"Good morning, Mrs. Carver," Wingate said to Darla as they shook hands. "This is Arthur Oberly, the hotel's general manager," Wingate added introducing the second man.

"Mr. Oberly," Darla politely said as she shook the man's hand. "What can I do for you?"

"It's an honor and a privilege to meet you, Mrs. Carver," Oberly said. As he let go of Darla's hand he shifted his eyes to Wingate.

"It's, ah, about the bill," Wingate practically muttered.

"I don't understand," Darla said. "What bill?"

"The hotel bill, ma'am," Oberly said. "We need to know who to send it to. It's over seven hundred thousand dollars. The townhouse alone is over twenty-two thousand per night and it's been three weeks and with the other rooms and suites, plus meals…"

"You mean that cheap sonofabitch, Trump, is gonna make us pay for this? Are you serious?" Darla practically screamed.

Knowing her boss was about ready to explode, Sonja quickly stepped in between her and the hotel manager.

"We have no orders to the contrary," Oberly calmly replied.

"We'll look into this, Mr. Oberly," Sonja said to the man.

While Darla stomped around the living room, her eyes on fire, her face beet red, Sonja took Oberly by the arm. She led him to the door and when she got there, took the invoice he was holding.

"Let me look into this. One way or another, we'll get this paid," she said.

"Thank you," Oberly said. Unspoken was the fact that Donald Trump himself had called and told Oberly to do this. Trump had known the Carvers for years and was waiting for Oberly to call him back with Darla's reaction. Trump had warned him and as Oberly rode the elevator down, he could barely contain his laughter.

Sonja returned to the living room to find Darla jabbing an index finger into Wingate's chest.

"You got it? Find the goddamn money and take care of this. The last thing we need is for news to leak out we skipped out on the bill. And I know Donald Trump. He'll have the media all over this."

"Yes, ma'am," Wingate stammered. "I'll get it taken care of."

"I, Thomas Jefferson Carver…" With his right hand raised and his left placed gently on the Bible, Tom Carver was sworn in as President of the United States by Chief Justice Irene Morgan. When the oath of office was fully administered, the enormity of what he was undertaking fully hit him. For one to two seconds, unnoticed by anyone else, he experienced a brief, dizzy spell. Tom inhaled deeply, leaned down, kissed the Bible and shook Chief Justice Morgan's hand.

Late that evening, just before midnight, Tom and Darla made their final appearance. They made a grand entrance at the MGM National Harbor as the eighty-piece orchestra played the traditional "Hail to the Chief" while several thousand party-goers enthusiastically applauded.

The next day, mildly hungover, President Carver held his first cabinet meeting. Although there were still several nominees being reviewed by the Senate, all of them were in attendance.

Already having laid out his agenda for the first one hundred days, there were no big surprises. The real purpose of the meeting was to give everyone a chance to meet each other. All of the men and women present were known to each other but not all of them had ever met. Plus, Darla insisted on making a photo op out of the occasion. Let the American people know the Carver Administration was going to hit the ground running.

When the pool photographer and reporter were finished and gone, Tom thanked them all and ended the get-together.

"Let's all work hard toward a prosperous four years for the American people," he said. "And a peaceful four years."

Despite being forewarned by his predecessor of the coming danger of radical Islamic terrorists, Carver and his top advisors had shrugged off President Baker's concerns. Sore loser, they believed. Besides, Carver's charm would turn the world around.

NINE

The red New Delhi TATA Motors mail truck with the three yellow stripes that resemble the Nike swoosh logo on its side pulled up to the guardhouse. The driver, a man very familiar to the three Marine guards, smiled and waved to them through the windshield. The senior of the three men, Corporal Max Klinger approached the driver while the other two Marines began their inspection. Max was not really Klinger's name. David was. Ever since basic training, thanks to the smartass drill instructor he had, he was known as Max in honor of the transvestite character on the TV show M*A*S*H.

The driver had the window down by the time Klinger got to the door and as usual, greeted the guard with a huge, obsequious grin.

"Hey, Fahd," Klinger said using the man's Hindu name. "What do you have today?"

"One small bag," the driver said in his heavily accented English.

Klinger heard one of the other guards close the truck's back door. That Marine came around from the back and told Klinger everything looked good. The third guard was back inside the guardhouse and already opening the electronic gate. Having checked Fahd's deliveries too many times, the routine of checking his truck had become far too routine. The three young men had become a little too bored and a little too careless. Besides, Fahd Chopra, whose real name, his Muslim name, was Kaleel Mirza, was well known, friendly and obviously harmless.

"Thank you, Corporal Max," Fahd said as he drove the small truck into the U.S. Embassy compound in New Delhi.

When Fahd got past the gate, instead of turning to his right to go to the door to drop off the mail, he pushed the accelerator to the floor and drove straight ahead. While the bewildered Marines watched, Fahd drove down an incline and crashed through the door of the Embassy's underground parking lot.

"Jesus Christ," Klinger yelled. "Come on," he said to his two friends. The three of them took off at a sprint to chase after the truck.

Fahd, with sweat pouring down his face, his eyes wide open and unblinking, continued into the garage. As he did this, he muttered over and over, "Allahu Akhbar". When he reached the middle of the parking area, he pushed the button on the detonator. By this time, the Marine guards chasing him had reached the smashed and shattered door. The explosion blew all three of them backward instantly killing them. Max Klinger's head was found amid the wreckage of the guardhouse. The other two young men were so mangled DNA testing would be needed to verify their identity.

Covered by bags of mail and easily discoverable by a thorough inspection of the truck was two hundred kilos of ammonium nitrate fertilizer and nitromethane. Coming from under the Embassy, the explosion blew up the first two of the building's floors and almost collapsed the structure completely. By the time the tally was complete, one hundred and eight people, mostly native Indians, were killed and an equal number injured. More than forty of the survivors lost at least one limb and several lost two or more.

Fahd Chopra had falsified his way into a job with the India Mail Service. Kaleel Mirza, his birth name, was a radicalized Muslim. Hatred for the West, especially the U.S. and Britain, had been hammered into his head from birth. At age twenty, his vaporized remains, so he believed, had reconstituted themselves and were now in Paradise in the company of the awaiting 72 virgins.

While Fahd Chopra f.k.a. Kaleel Mirza was delivering his nightmare to the American Embassy in India, a young couple, obviously very much in love, was sitting on a bench holding hands, seemingly oblivious to the crowd. It was mid-morning in Paris on what looked to be a beautiful June day. The bench they were on was under the Eiffel Tower. The man was wearing a T-shirt which proudly proclaimed him to be a tourist from Spain and a fan of FC Barcelona. The French guard, a soldier barely ten feet away, paid the couple very little attention because of the T-shirt.

That same French soldier was dressed in combat camouflage fatigues, highly polished boots and a black beret while alertly watching the crowd around and under the huge structure. The security guard, one of at least twenty strolling the grounds of this best-known symbol of France, was carrying a fully automatic rifle.

The young woman sitting on the bench looked at two men standing in one of the lines waiting for the elevator to go up to the observation platform. One of them looked over his shoulder at two other men in another line, then back at the woman. He barely nodded his head at her. She turned the corners of her mouth up in an imperceptible smile and then whispered in the ear of her lover.

Her boyfriend stood up and casually strolled over to the soldier. In very bad French, the bench sitter started to ask a question. The guard, not comprehending, gave the young man a puzzled look. In an instant, the supposedly Spanish tourist pulled an eighteen shot Beretta from his back waistband. Before the poor soldier could comprehend the act, the pistol was an inch from his forehead. A quick shot and the soldier collapsed.

The crowd of several hundred people heard the shot, saw the soldier drop and had no time to respond. The four men in the two elevator lines each pulled an identical handgun and started shooting. The young woman jumped up from the bench and joined in as her 'lover' took the soldier's assault rifle and began spraying the crowd with bullets.

Bedlam broke out as the tourists began to scream, run and fall. Other soldiers stationed in the area, more than twenty, came sprinting to the scene. In less than ten minutes it was over.

The six terrorists were all dead. Each had been riddled with bullets by the French soldiers. When all of those who had been critically wounded and could not be saved were added to the total, fifty-four innocent people, including thirteen children, had died. Another thirty-two had been wounded including several who would lose limbs and one who would spend the rest of her life in a wheelchair.

Within minutes of the attack at the Eiffel Tower, three other Islamic terrorist attacks were taking place. One, an attack in Berlin at the Brandenburg Gate, a major tourist attraction, was exactly like the one in Paris. Six people, couples, armed with semi-automatic handguns had opened fire on the crowd. The tally was not quite as high as Paris. Before the German Police killed all six attackers—one committed suicide—eighteen people were dead. Eleven more were wounded, several severely including a three-year-old girl from Sweden who would never walk again.

The fourth attack was by a man and a woman in Istanbul, Turkey. They arrived at an open-air market in a small Fiat. There were two armed policemen within twenty feet of them who, cameras would show, paid no attention to them. The couple removed semi-automatic assault rifles from the Fiat's backseat and casually began shooting. The first to die were the two inattentive policemen. When it was over, the terrorists were both dead along with twenty-four shoppers and the two cops.

The fifth and final one was by far the worst. A small truck with four men in the back drove into a crowd in Antwerp, Belgium. The driver killed a dozen people as he ran them over. He came to a stop by crashing the truck through the doors of a shopping center. The four men in back, along with the driver, exited the vehicle and began running through the mall spraying machine gun fire at the people. This went on for over an hour as the men hunted down shoppers, mostly women and children, before the police could get to the terrorists, kill them all and stop the massacre.

The final total from Antwerp would be almost two hundred dead and another one hundred wounded. Almost all of the victims were women and children.

All five attacks, including the embassy bombing in India, had occurred within minutes of each other. They were obviously well planned and coordinated.

Tom Carver hurriedly passed through the security door of the White House Situation Room. With him was his National Security Advisor, Leland Arkwright, a former Harvard professor who was supposedly an expert in international relations.

Waiting for them were several staff members of Arkwright's national security team. Among them was his chief deputy, Nancy Oswald. Oswald had been a favorite student of Arkwright's mostly because she was a very attractive woman with whom Arkwright, a married man, had been engaged in a twenty plus year affair.

"Where is everyone?" Carver demanded to know, referring to the other senior members of his national security committee.

"On the way," Oswald replied. "All of the principals have been contacted and they will all be here shortly."

The room's door opened and a serious looking black man walked in.

"Mr. President," Vice President Julian Morton said as the two men shook hands.

"I'm glad you're here, Julian," Carver replied while the two men took their seats, Carver at the head of the long table, the Vice President to his right.

"Should we wait for…" Arkwright started to say.

"No," Carver emphatically replied. "We can fill them in as they get here."

He looked at Oswald and said, "Tell me what we know."

Oswald stood at a lectern and using satellite photos and her notes, quickly filled in Carver on the attack in New Delhi.

"So, we don't know a whole hell of a lot at this point," Carver said when she finished. "Has anyone claimed responsibility?"

"Not yet, sir," Oswald answered.

As she said this, three more people, two men and a woman, came in. One of the men was in uniform. He was Air Force General Parker Ellerbie, head of the Joint Chiefs. The woman, who had been driven to the White House with Ellerbie, was Secretary of Defense, Christina Kyle. The third person was CIA Director Malcolm Brewster. Brewster was a politician and because of his fund-raising expertise, had been rewarded with the top job at CIA, a position for which he was totally unqualified. Like most politicians, the man could not keep a secret if his life depended on it. In fact, Brewster had been Darla Carver's choice to head the CIA. The news of this meeting would be leaked by the end of the day. The short, bald, extremely unattractive DCI was sleeping with a beautiful network reporter who was using him to enhance her career. The three newcomers all grimly greeted Carver and the veep, then took seats at the table.

"Mr. President, we have more news," Brewster said. "There are reports of attacks in Berlin, Antwerp and Paris and an unconfirmed attack in Istanbul."

"What kind of attacks?" Carver's National Security Advisor, Arkwright, asked before Carver could.

"Right now, the news is a little sketchy. It appears our embassy was the only bombing," Brewster replied. "From what we are hearing, the others were all done against shoppers and tourists by individuals using firearms."

"Any word on casualties?" Carver asked.

"Nothing definite yet, Mr. President. But the death toll will be high."

TEN

The remaining members of Carver's national security team arrived within a few minutes of each other. The Secretary of State, Alan Danver, Attorney General Godfrey Colm, Director of National Intelligence, General Ralph Thomas and Carver's Chief of Staff, Noah Flake. Not surprisingly, General Thomas took a seat next to his long-time friend and fellow four-star General Ellerbie. The others, with the exception of the politician Noah Flake, were all former members of academia. None of whom had any practical, real world experience dealing with anything more contentious than a committee squabble.

As the day wore on, news came in little by little although initial reports of casualties were sketchy. First estimates had the numbers either far too low or significantly higher than the truth. Throughout the day Carver took and made calls from and to other world leaders. All of them were in the same basic situation Carver was; waiting with a room full of advisors for news from first responders and waiting for a claim of responsibility.

Lunch was sent for and while they waited for it to arrive, Carver asked everyone to take a seat. On one side, to his left, were the academics for State, Defense, Justice and his NSA, Arkwright. On the opposite side, to his right, were the veep, the generals and his Chief of Staff. Toward the end of the table, almost by himself, was Brewster, the CIA Director.

"When we find out who did this, and we will," Carver began looking down the table at Brewster, who nodded in return, "how should we respond?"

Arkwright, the NSA, was the first to reply and calmly, with a very careful, measured response. "We don't want to go off like a bunch of cowboys with guns blazing." This statement was made by Arkwright while looking at the two generals. Both of them looked across the table at the Harvard professor with an impassionate, almost uninterested expression.

Secretary of State Danver jumped in with his emphatic approval of Arkwright's statement. Joining in with her fellow professors was the Secretary of Defense Kyle.

"General Thomas?" Carver asked looking at his Director of National Intelligence.

"Mr. President, I think we need to find out who did this before we can make any kind of recommendation. Is this ISIS? Is it Al Qaeda? Some other group we either know about or don't know? We just don't have enough information, yet," Thomas replied.

"The last thing we want to do is get involved in another Mideast War and send in a hundred thousand troops..." Arkwright started to protest.

"Professor," General Ellerbie interrupted him using his academic title as if talking to a child. Arkwright believed it was out of respect. Ellerbie meant it as a reminder of where he was; not in a classroom. "Why do you always jump to that conclusion? Make that announcement before you even know what we are up against? No one's talking about sending any troops in anywhere."

This started a minor squabble across the table, mostly from the civilians. Unnoticed by everyone but Carver, Brewster turned his head to answer his phone. He spoke very briefly with the caller, hung up and looked at his boss.

"Mr. President, we're getting a video feed we need to watch," Brewster said which quieted those at the table.

A second later, an image of a man wearing a black, Muslim turban, his face completely covered with a black cloth except for his dark eyes was speaking in Arabic and there was a simultaneous translation into English.

The man spoke for twenty minutes and claimed full responsibility for all five attacks. Most of his diatribe was the usual palaver about how the West was evil and Allah was sending his group to convert the world to the one true religion, Islam. They were avenging the war the West was waging on Islam and they were going to destroy the West and its evil, wicked ways.

He identified himself as a member of a group calling itself Dayira of Islam, the Circle of Islam. "Circle" because it would circle the globe and bring all to Allah's will or kill the infidels who refused to convert. He went on to claim the group was far more committed to jihad than ISIS or Al Qaeda but were brothers and sisters of these groups who would ultimately achieve the same goal.

"All right, everyone," Carver said after the performance had ended. "We now have some information. Not much, admittedly, but more than we had. First thing we need is to find out who these people are and where they are. Have your lunch then get on the phones and let's find out what we can about these people. Julian?" he said looking at the Vice President.

"I've already thought of at least a dozen people to call," the veep replied. Julian Morton was the chairman of the Senate Foreign Relations Committee before becoming Vice President. His knowledge and connections would be invaluable.

"I'm going out to release a statement to the public. Get on it and I'll be back," Carver said. He started to rise and everyone at the table started to stand also. "Keep your seats. Noah," he continued looking at his chief of staff. Noah Flake was already on his feet to leave with his boss. Without another word, the two men left the room.

"That's not much of a statement for Juliet to make to the press," Darla Carver said, referring to Carver's press secretary, Juliet Carne.

When President Carver and Flake left the situation room, they went immediately to Flake's office. They were using his office to avoid the usual interruptions Carver dealt with from staff members who came to him with problems for his attention. Darla, without her shadow Sonja Hayden, joined them. All morning long, while the news of the attacks came in, both Tom Carver and Noah Flake were mentally processing how they could take political advantage of the situation. Darla was way ahead of them.

"It will have to do," the President replied. "It's all we have, for now."

"It's about time we had a serious crisis to handle," Darla said. "One and a half years into the first term. I was beginning to wonder when this would happen."

"There have been attacks by Islamic radicals," Tom reminded her.

"Muslims killing other Muslims. Who gives a damn? We needed a genuine attack. I was beginning to think these guys had crawled back into their holes," Darla said.

"Never let a good crisis go to waste," Noah Flake reminded them.

"With the midterm election coming up, this could be perfect for us," Darla continued. "A chance to act tough..."

"But not too tough," Flake interjected. "It's been so long since 9/11 that a majority of people, according to our polls, believe Bush overreacted."

"Good point," Darla said. "This should be exactly what we need to hold the House and Senate. With only an eighteen seat majority in the House, we could lose it if we aren't careful and use this to our advantage. The Senate should be okay. Our enemies have more seats up for re-election than we do. In fact," Darla continued, "Noah and I have been working on a list to go after when we go up for our re-election. I've already got Spencer working on it," she added referring to Spencer Collins, their campaign manager.

Spencer Collins was the architect, along with Darla Carver, of every election Tom Carver had won. The day after the inauguration, Collins and his highly paid team began the re-election campaign. In the year and a half since the inauguration, they had secretly accumulated over one hundred fifty million dollars for the re-election campaign. This was the seed money they were using to target voting patterns down to the precinct level for the next election. Darla, the true take-no-prisoners politician in the Carver household, was leaving nothing to chance.

"And?" Tom asked her.

"Spencer is coordinating with the national party headquarters to go after vulnerable opponents," Darla reminded him.

"Yes, Darla," Tom answered annoyed at her condescension. "I'm aware of that."

"What we need to do," Flake quickly interjected to head off the domestic spat he knew was about to erupt, "is figure out a response to the attacks that will strengthen us and weaken our opponents."

"Enemies," Darla said.

"Something forceful but not over the top," Tom said to Flake.

"Exactly," Flake replied.

"Tom," Darla said after calming down, "you do what you do best. Go run the government and be the commander-in-chief. Leave the politics to me."

By late afternoon, despite a good deal of acrimony, stress and frazzled nerves, the people around the President were starting to get results. A fractured and incomplete picture of who and what the Circle of Islam was.

"It looks to be a splinter group that broke off from ISIS," General Thomas, the DNI said. "No one seems to know much about them at this point."

"Sir, we have some information, some people in the Mideast who we've heard from," Malcolm Brewster interjected. "These sources believe it was founded by at least a couple of very extremist Imams. You're going to love this, Mr. President," he continued. "The word is they believe ISIS is not radical enough. That the leadership of ISIS is too lenient toward non-believers."

"ISIS is too lenient, too liberal, too forward thinking," Carver said in exasperation.

"How did they pull this off without giving off even an inkling of what they were up to?" Carver asked looking around the table. "We didn't hear anything at the NSA? They picked up nothing?"

"No, Mr. President. Not a peep," DNI Thomas answered him. "And that's extremely worrisome."

"Why?" Flake asked.

"Because, and we can only speculate," Brewster said, "they're operating off the grid. Entirely underground."

"What does that mean, Malcolm?" Carver asked.

"It means they don't use modern communication methods. No radios, no cell phones, internet or anything we can trace."

"They use messengers like the Mafia. They use people to carry messages and smuggle arms and probably bombs. It is much slower but makes them very difficult to find," General Thomas said.

"We've believed," Arkwright added, "that ISIS and other groups have infiltrated the refugees flooding into Europe. It's not that difficult…"

"Their borders are even more porous than ours," Thomas said.

"This attack was only a matter of time," Arkwright added.

"Why our embassy in India? Why there and not another target?" Carver asked.

"We don't know," Brewster answered. "It may have been as simple as it was a more easily accessible target. The preliminary reports are the suicide bomber was delivering normal mail. He might not have been as closely inspected as he should have been if the guards knew him."

"That speculation does not leave this room. Those young Marines gave their lives and we will not have them blamed for this," Carver said emphatically.

"Thank you, Mr. President," General Ellerbie said.

"Find these people so we can hit them back," Carver ordered.

"What do we release to the public?" Arkwright asked. "The video we saw is on the internet."

"I'll take care of that," Carver said. "As far as the rest of you are concerned, what was said in this room, stays in this room. Thank you all."

ELEVEN

The two men in the big Suburban were heading north on Cedar Avenue going past Eagan, Minnesota. They crossed the big bridge over the Minnesota River barely half a mile from their destination. Now in their thirties, the two of them had been best friends since kindergarten. They had been born three days apart in the same hospital and grew up together less than a block away from each other in Apple Valley, a suburb south of the Twin Cities. They went through school together including two years at Normandale Community College. They even went through Army Airborne training together and served overseas with each other.

Today they were on a mission that neither of them was enthused about. The man at the wheel was married to his pal's sister. She had a birthday coming up and they were on their way to get her a special present.

"I hate this place," the passenger, Corey Taylon, muttered again as the driver exited onto Killebrew Drive.

They were going to Macy's at the Mall of America. The Mall was located on the grounds of the old Met Stadium in Bloomington. Way back when, the street had been named for one of the Twins' greatest and most popular players and it still carried his name.

"I know, that's at least the seventh or eighth time you've mentioned it," the driver, Nick Pederson, replied. "No sane person would want to come here. We will be in and out in ten minutes. You'll see."

"What's the name of the stuff she wants?" Corey asked.

"I don't know. It's some French perfume shit I can't pronounce. I wrote it down. Macy's has it. We'll be in and out in no time," Nick said.

"And why do I need to be here?" Corey asked.

"Because she's your sister and I shouldn't have to suffer going to this place by myself."

"Oh, okay. I'm glad you have a sensible reason," Corey sarcastically replied.

"Stop your whining."

Nick drove the big SUV into the West garage up to the second floor in the southwest corner of the Mall. As he maneuvered into a narrow parking space, Corey's head turned as he looked at a van several spaces away.

"Hey, you carrying?" Corey quietly asked.

"Always. Why? Aren't you?"

"Sure but I don't think they allow guns inside the place," Corey said as he continued to watch the three men exiting the van.

"That's why they make shirts that you don't tuck in," Nick said as he set the transmission to park.

"Check this out," Corey said to his friend.

Nick turned to his right to see what Corey was referring to. As he did, two of the black men were removing bags from the van while the third was obviously keeping guard.

"Somalis," Nick quietly said.

"Yeah. What the hell are they up to?" Corey whispered.

While they watched, the three men bent down and unzipped the black, nylon bags they had.

"Something's wrong with this picture," Nick said. "Let's get inside and find security."

"You go," Corey said. "I'll keep an eye on these guys and we'll use our phones to stay in touch."

"Watch yourself," Nick, the ex-airborne Ranger, said to his friend, another ex-airborne Ranger.

"Always, bro," Corey replied.

While Corey waited in the SUV, Nick hurried across the second-floor skyway into Macy's. Being midday on a Saturday the store was fairly busy. As Nick hurried through Macy's to find a security guard, he took a quick look and mentally calculated at least two hundred people in the immediate area. If what he thought was about to happen did happen, this could be a bloodbath.

Nick reached the inner part of the huge mall and stopped. He checked his watch and noted he had left his truck barely a minute ago. Nick looked to his left and saw what he was searching for come around a corner walking toward him, an alert man in a guard's blue uniform with a gun on his belt. Nick sprinted the forty feet to the man who watched him coming with his hand on his gun.

"We may have a problem," Nick said to the man.

As the two of them walked back into Macy's retracing Nick's route, he explained to the guard what he and Corey had witnessed.

"It could be nothing, but it could be a disaster," Nick said.

"Okay," the guard, whose name was Phil Hanlon said, "Sir, you need to get out of here and let me handle this."

Using the radio mic attached to his shoulder, he quickly called for backup. While he was doing that, Nick's phone rang. It was Corey with word that the three young men were on the move.

"Sir…" Hanlon started to say again.

"My friend and I are both Airborne. We did four tours in Iraq and Afghanistan. You're gonna need some help and we're it," Nick said.

He then told Hanlon the three men were heading their way carrying their bags.

"Are you armed?"

"Yes," Nick replied then lifted his shirt enough to show the man his weapon.

"Okay. I'm a Marine and a sergeant with Minneapolis SWAT. You follow my lead. Remember, this could be three guys shopping," Hanlon told him.

"I hope so, but I don't think so," Nick replied.

By this time the two of them were almost through Macy's and the three men they were looking for were entering the store. The shoppers, somehow sensing trouble, began to quickly move away from the scene. As Nick and Hanlon got closer, Nick saw Corey bringing up the rear. He motioned slightly with his head for Corey to move off to Hanlon's right and stay slightly behind the targets. Nick moved away from Hanlon by sliding off to the left where a young woman was still standing behind a cosmetics counter.

The clerk was apparently oblivious to what was happening so Nick smiled at the young girl then showed her his semiautomatic handgun which was now in his hand. The girl stood frozen with a terrified look on her face staring back at Nick.

"It's okay," Nick whispered. "I'm with security. Please lie down on the floor and stay there."

"Excuse me, gentlemen," Hanlon said holding up a hand to the three young men. "I'll have to take a look in those bags."

"Why?" the closest one to him asked. The other two were a couple of feet behind him. All three had the same style black, nylon bag slung over a shoulder. Each bag the size of a large gym bag and obviously filled with something fairly heavy.

"Because anyone entering the Mall carrying a bag, by law, agrees to allow us to search them," Hanlon said. He had no idea if this was true. Being a cop lying to suspects was simply part of being a cop. You worry about the consequences later.

"You are a racist…" one of the other two said in a Somali accent.

The first one, the leader, held up a hand to stop the other from saying anything else. He smiled slightly to Hanlon and began to unzip the bag he carried.

"Of course, Security Guard Hanlon," he said reading Hanlon's nametag. "We will gladly cooperate."

When he finished opening the bag he quickly reached in and came out holding a handgun. He pointed it at Hanlon, fired one shot and missed. Anticipating this move, Hanlon went down and to his right the instant he saw the gun.

62

The shooting lasted barely five seconds. Nick and Corey were both less than fifteen feet away. They saw the gun and their training took over. When it was done, there were three radicalized, terrorist wannabees from the local Somali community lying in a pool of their own blood. Not a single shopper received as much as a scratch.

Nick helped the young girl up from behind the counter who ran as fast as she could. Nick and Corey, guns still drawn, joined Sergeant Hanlon and the three of them looked at the dead men on the floor.

"I sure hope you guys have permits for those guns," Hanlon said.

"Now's a fine time to ask," Nick replied.

"We do," Corey answered him. He then introduced himself to Hanlon. "Speaking of guns," Corey continued, "You'll probably need these."

"Put them on the counter right here," Hanlon said. "The place is gonna be crawling with cops in a few minutes. You guys will have to stick around for a while."

Thirty seconds later, the three men were joined by a dozen Mall security people. Taking charge, Hanlon sent them all back to various entrances and had them shut down the big building completely. No one in or out until the police cleared the place and gave the okay. It was a task that would take several hours.

It would be almost 10:00 P.M. before Nick Pederson and Corey Taylon would be allowed to leave but a grateful Macy's manager made sure Nick had a five-ounce bottle of the perfume with the unpronounceable French name when he did leave. It was a good thing, too. They were both national heroes but Nick's wife, Corey's sister Meghan, ripped them both apart for sticking their necks into something like this.

And, of course, the media and the FBI would descend on the Somali community in Minneapolis. Over the next several days, every Somali who had ever met any of the three dead men would be interviewed by both the media and the Feebs. All of these people, especially the Imams who ran the Mosque where the three dead, would-be terrorists worshipped, expressed astonishment that this happened. Not a single person in this small, close-knit community had the slightest inkling of their radicalization. Other young Somali men who knew them well now claimed they had hardly ever spoken to them and knew nothing of their radicalization.

The FBI conducted a complete and thorough search of the homes where the dead terrorists had lived. Their laptops were confiscated and in them were searches of various jihadist websites but no other evidence of who had recruited them was found. After several days, when the dust had settled, an older sister of one of the men took a bus to the police department in downtown Minneapolis. She brought with her a poorly written pamphlet that she translated for them proving to be a recruiting document for the Circle of Islam. Despite their best efforts at keeping this out of the public, its discovery was leaked and made public the next day.

The two men and two women who had come to Minnesota to recruit in the Somali community for the Circle of Islam quietly left the Cities. They had been in the Somali community recruiting for several months and had sent seven young men and women to Yemen. Yet again, no one in the Somali community would admit to knowing anything about them or the missing young men.

TWELVE

President Carver and Chief-of-Staff Noah Flake walked side-by-side through the White House toward the Oval Office. The two most powerful men on the planet were going to a briefing and were running a few minutes late. Tom Carver certainly had his share of flaws but punctuality was not one of them. And despite his politicians' polished, public persona, everyone in the Carver Administration learned early on that his temper had a short fuse that was quickly lit if you were late for a meeting with him. Since he demanded promptness from others he expected it from himself as well.

Flake held the door open for his boss then followed him into the most famous room in the world. As they did so the members of Carver's National Security Council that were seated stood to greet him.

"Please forgive my tardiness," Carver sincerely requested. "Everyone, please find a chair. Then we'll hear what Director Wiggins has to say," Carver said as he shook hands with FBI Director Peter Wiggins.

Carver took the President's customary chair to the right of the fireplace. The couch to his left and right were both full and there were several others seated in chairs. Director Wiggins was on the couch to Carver's left, the closest seat in the room to the President.

"Apparently, according to our local office personnel in Minneapolis, the media stories about yesterday's thwarted attack are essentially true.

"Two men, special forces veterans, spotted three suspicious looking men in a parking garage. One of the two vets stayed with the Somalis…"

"Are we sure they're Somalis?" Leland Arkwright, Carver's National Security Advisor, asked.

"Yes," Wiggins replied looking at Arkwright. "All three have been identified as members of the local Somali community in Minneapolis. Our agents and the Minneapolis PD will go through there with a fine tooth comb and find out everything about them."

"Why do you ask, Leland?" Carver asked.

"It would have been better if they had been White Supremacists or some other such far right nut group," Arkwright answered. "Don't you agree, Alan?" Arkwright asked Secretary of State Alan Danver.

"Oh, yes, absolutely," Danver agreed.

"I see," Carver blandly said while making a mental note, again, that Arkwright and Danver had to go after the election. Carver was sick to death of P.C. driven academics. "Go on, Director."

"A search was done of the terrorist's homes which turned up very little. The Minneapolis PD did obtain a document which we believe is a recruiting pamphlet from the Circle of Islam."

"So, there it is," Carver said. "Little pinpricks by these people for the past two years, always small but quite deadly coming from under the radar and now they are here in America."

Carver's last statement, the one proclaiming terrorists in America, elicited an understated storm of discussion and squabbling. One side of the argument not wanting to hastily jump to that conclusion, the other taking the stance that they had no choice.

The squabbling went on for three or four minutes until finally, Director Wiggins, the most nonpolitical person in the room, stood up.

"They are here!" he vehemently declared. "The President is absolutely correct. To deny that will get Americans killed. Face reality everyone!"

"Director," Carver quietly said.

Wiggins looked at Carver who mouthed the words "please sit down" at him.

"Sorry, Mr. President," Wiggins said as he took his seat.

"No, that was great. I liked it," Carver told him. "And," he continued addressing everyone else, "he's right. It's time we got serious about this group. We got really lucky yesterday. Let's not kid ourselves that this attack was thwarted through some brilliant level of diligence on our part. It was thwarted because two well-trained, armed, brave young men happened to be there."

"The governor of Minnesota has asked their attorney general to bring charges against those two guys," Godfrey Colm, the U.S. Attorney General, said.

"For what?" a half a dozen voices asked in unison.

"Apparently this shopping mall where it happened is a gun-free zone. They were not allowed to be in there armed," Colm replied.

"How stupid is this guy?" CIA Director Malcolm Brewster asked referring to the Minnesota governor.

"Why is this stupid?" Defense Secretary Christina Kyle asked. "Do we want cowboys running around shopping centers with guns?"

"Christina, come on," Brewster said.

"These were hardly cowboys running around with guns, Christina. They're national heroes today," Carver said while thinking, *another one to be rid of.*

"All right everyone, this is what I want. We have to find out who the hell these people are. I want a thorough report and briefing in thirty days. It's been two years since the New Delhi embassy bombing and we still don't have any information on this group. Let's find them!"

66

"This is a godsend for us," Darla Carver said with barely disguised glee. Later after Tom's meeting with his national security team, she was on a couch in the Oval Office. Present were the President, Noah Flake, Sonja Hayden and their re-election campaign manager, Spencer Collins. Technically this meeting was probably a violation of federal campaign laws. A political election meeting such as this is barred from being held on federal property. Since the Carvers had taken on the attitude that the White House was their permanent residence, a violation of federal law within it was a laughably minor matter.

"The only way it could've been better is if there had been thirty or forty people killed before these fanatics were gunned down," she continued.

"Darla, for God's sake!" Tom said.

"Oh, hell. I didn't say I wanted it. I just meant politically with the election in barely three mouths, the country would have rallied behind us," Darla replied waving a hand at the President as if chasing off an annoying insect.

"Or, they might have blamed me for it," Tom said.

"True," Darla agreed. "It turned out okay. Here's what we'll do. We're working on contacting these three guys, the ones who shot the terrorists, and..."

"That reminds me," Tom interrupted. "We need to send a back door message to Minnesota's governor. He's looking to bring charges against the two civilians, the Army vets who helped stop the attack."

"For what?" Darla asked.

"The mall where it happened is a gun-free zone and..."

"How big an idiot is this guy, what's-his-name?" Darla asked in astonishment.

"Mark Clayton," Noah Flake answered her. "Pretty good size idiot," he continued. "He did one term in the Senate and was annually voted the least effective Senator in the place."

"How did he get elected?"

"Mega-bucks rich," Flake said. "Heir to an oil pipeline company and has spent tens of millions of his own money on multiple political campaigns. Don't worry, Mr. President, I'm already on it."

"Okay," Tom said.

"Next week, we'll shoot for Monday afternoon early enough for the evening news cycle, to have these three guys flown here for a ceremony," Darla continued. "We'll have them bring their families. Maybe have them in D.C. for several days."

"We'll pick up the tab for everything," Flake said.

"If we have to, we can find the money from the campaign," Collins mentioned.

"Is that legal?" Tom asked.

Collins shrugged his shoulders sipped his coffee and said, "Who cares? We'll find a way to cover it. No problem."

"You need to hand out medals," Darla said. "Sonja?"

"We suggest the Presidential Citizens Medal for the civilians," Sonja Hayden said. She was sitting behind Darla and had been waiting for her cue. "The Public Safety Officer Medal of Valor for the other man, the mall guard..."

"He's also a Minneapolis cop. He was off-duty working security," Darla said.

"It's considered the cops' equivalent of the Medal of Honor," Sonja added.

"That thirty or forty dead would have helped us get some legislation through transferring more war powers to the executive branch," Darla said wistfully.

"The polls will tighten up after our opponent's convention," Collins said.

"We can use this to emphasize that you as Commander-in-Chief have kept us safe..."

"And our honorable opponent," Darla chimed in with obvious sarcasm, "has consistently voted against increasing the military budget for twenty-four years."

Senator Byron Meldrum was the opposition party's nominee. Their convention would be held in two weeks. Tom Carver's nomination would take place two weeks after that. This would give both sides an opportunity to prepare for the real campaign to begin after Labor Day. Approximately ten days after Carver's nomination.

Polls showed Tom Carver with a twelve to fourteen-point lead. His re-election was all but assured. Byron Meldrum's nomination was the result of few quality candidates running for his party's nomination. Meldrum received it almost by default. He was not so much a nominee as a sacrificial lamb. Darla Carver had yet to begin to go after him. Her excellent researchers, especially a well-known muckraker with a New York tabloid, had provided her with plenty of ammunition. Most of it was fairly petty, even childish and silly events, that Darla's viciousness would make look like this mostly decent man was as bad as a child molester. She even had that. Clay Dean had found a sealed juvenile court file over forty years old that showed Meldrum having had sex with a fourteen-year-old girl. Of course, at the time, Meldrum was only fifteen himself, but that fact would be conveniently overlooked when the dirt was released to the right media hacks.

68

Between spouses, children, parents and Corey Taylon's girlfriend, there were seventeen people, including the three medal recipients from Minnesota. They were all respectfully waiting in the East Room of the White House shaking a lot of hands of a lot of politicians, Congress members, generals and cabinet members. Also included were three children belonging to Sergeant Phil Hanlon and two belonging to Nick and Meghan Pederson. The kids, much to their parents' relief, were shockingly well behaved.

Fifteen minutes after they had arrived and five minutes before he was due, the President was announced. He walked in, ignored the politicians and went right to the three heroes and their families. Having been briefed on who was in attendance, Carver showed off an amazing skill. In barely five minutes before arriving he had memorized everyone's name, including the children. Remarkable even for a politician.

Corey Taylon's girlfriend, Jennifer Leighton, was a male eye catcher, to say the least. The instant Darla met her she made a mental note to keep an eye on her husband. The man's self-control at moments like this could sometimes be a problem. Darla need not have worried. Jennifer Leighton was totally in love with Corey, and as an intelligent adult, knew the kind of man Tom Carver was and she was no fan. Despite this, before the photo-op was over, Corey was getting a little hot at the attention Carver gave her. And Darla had to get Tom away from her twice.

The moment the party left the building, Jennifer whispered to Corey that she was anxious to get back to the hotel.

"Why, what's wrong?" Corey asked.

"I need to take a shower. That man makes my skin crawl."

As they were walking back to the First Lady's offices, Sonja whispered to Darla so the Secret Service agents would not hear her.

"We have another problem."

"What?" Darla asked.

Sonja held up a slip of paper so only Darla could see it. On it was printed one word: "Bimbo".

"Sonofabitch," Darla whispered barely loud enough for Sonja to hear it. "How bad?" Darla asked.

"Pretty bad," Sonja answered.

"Get Clay," Darla said.

"Already waiting for us," Sonja replied.

THIRTEEN

Darla, with Sonja Hayden almost attached to her hip, arrived on the second floor of the Executive Residence. The two of them, followed by two Secret Service agents, went directly to a private sitting room attached to the President's bedroom. Upon entering, Darla went immediately to a small, dry bar to her left. She poured a healthy dose of Drambuie into a Waterford crystal snifter.

"A little early, isn't it?" Clay Dean asked.

Clay was already in the room waiting for the two women. He was seated on the suede loveseat in front of a window, patiently waiting. His hands were folded loosely in his lap with his legs crossed, looking at Darla with a disapproving expression. Clay Dean was probably the only person on the planet who could speak to Darla like that, admonishing her for drinking alcohol this early in the day. Darla Carver was hot for the man and Clay knew it. She had never overtly acted on her feelings toward him. In a strange way, this ultra-aggressive female was hoping Clay would come after her and sweep her off her feet. It seems even powerful women can have romantic fantasies.

As for Clay, the thought of being involved with Darla sent a chill down his spine. He would rather put his hand into a rattlesnake pit up to his elbow. He secretly had grown to despise her, especially for the way she treated her husband and everyone around her. Knowing she was his for the taking allowed him a little more latitude, but not much more, while dealing with her.

"For what I have to hear about my hot pants husband, no, it isn't too early for a little fortification," Darla replied, then took a healthy swallow.

Darla took a chair that matched the loveseat Clay was on. He was to her left with a small table between them. Darla set the brandy snifter on the table, turned to the now seated Sonja and gestured for her to begin.

"Um, well, ah…" Sonja began with a stammer.

"Get on with it," Darla demanded.

"We've been contacted by a woman who…"

"What's her name?" Darla asked.

"Lynne Hartley," Clay answered her.

"Lynn Hartley? That name sounds familiar," Darla said looking at Clay.

"She works for a lobbyist for big Pharma. Secretary or something," Sonja said. "And, um, well…."

"What?" Darla asked.

"She did the same thing in Denver when we were there," Clay interjected.

At this point, seeing Sonja's discomfort, Clay took over.

"What Sonja's trying to avoid telling you is that the President and this woman knew each other in Colorado. In fact, she claims they've had an off and on affair for almost ten years. It broke up her marriage.

"Now, she's claiming the President is trying to break it off again and she says she has had enough. She has film."

"Goddamn that idiot," Darla snarled. "Have you seen it? Have you seen her home movie?"

"Yes, ma'am, I have. So has Sonja. We figured we had better check it out before we came to you with it," Clay said. "In fact, it's a little too explicit."

"What does that mean?" Darla asked.

"I think she had help. I think someone else did the filming, probably through a one-way mirror. There are close-ups, wide shots, and different angles."

"Jesus Christ!" Darla yelled loud enough for the agents in the hall to hear her. She stood, picked up her drink and began pacing about the room. As she did so, she drained and refilled the glass she held, all the while Sonja watched with trepidation. This went on for almost five minutes. Finally, Darla looked at Clay.

"What does she want?"

"Money and a lot of it," he replied. "Five million. I'm sure she has to share it with someone," Clay replied.

Darla sat down again in the same chair and asked Clay, "Do you have the tape or DVD or whatever it's on?"

"I have a DVD," he said.

"Let's have it," Darla said holding out her hand.

Clay removed the plastic case with the disk in it from his inside coat pocket. He handed it to Darla who turned to Sonja.

"Have you seen it?" Darla asked her.

"Well, ah, yes, part of it. It's disgusting," Sonja said.

"Why, what's wrong? Haven't you ever seen a little porn before?" Darla asked rolling the plastic case over and over in her hand.

"Well, ah, no one I ever knew…"

"Forget it," Darla said to Sonja more calmly. "When does she want the money?" Darla asked Clay.

"Before the convention or she puts it on the internet. She says she's tired of the President using her like a whore then telling her to get lost," Clay said.

"She *is* a whore," Darla snarled. "All right," she continued, "do nothing until I get back to you. Let me think about this."

"Should I see if I can find out if she filmed this alone?" Clay asked.

71

Darla thought about this for a moment then said, "Very discreetly. We don't want to spook her into doing something rash."

Late that evening, Darla sent a message via the Secret Service, whom she treated like servants and not the professionals they are, to her husband. She often communicated with the President like this, by hand-delivered messages. This normally signaled something ominous.

The President was in his private office at the time. He was watching a panel discussion on Fox News. The talking heads, a pair on both sides of the political spectrum, were agreeing his re-election was all but assured. And they all agreed, even the people from the opposition, that he deserved it.

Carver was on the couch with Noah Flake, each man nursing a scotch and soda, when they heard a soft knock on the door. Darla's Secret Service messenger entered and stepped over to the President with the note in his hand.

Flake was closer to the man so he took the note and gave it to the President. Carver looked at it, sighed, shook his head, and then looked up at the agent who was starting to backpedal.

"I apologize, Rob," Carver said to the man. "She shouldn't be using you guys like this. I'll talk to her, again."

"Yes, sir, Mr. President," the agent said then left the room.

"What does Her Majesty want this time?" Flake asked. Noah Flake and Tom Carver were friends for over twenty years. He knew Darla quite well and was well aware of their relationship. A model marriage it was not.

"Who knows?" Carver answered. When he read the note again he said, "I've been summoned to a meeting. She's requesting my presence at nine o'clock."

"Lynne Hartley?" Flake asked

"Maybe," Carver said. "I know she's pissed. But she has to understand there is a campaign about to kick off."

"You want me to..."

"No, Noah. Stay out of it. I'll handle it. If the media gets wind of you snooping around her...."

"They'll assume it's from you," Flake said.

"Exactly." Carver stood up and took his friend's glass, went to the bar, and fixed them each another drink. "If I have to deal with Darla tonight, I'll need another drink."

Darla heard her husband's soft knock on the door and watched him enter before she could respond. She was waiting for him in the same side room attached to his bedroom where she met with Sonja and Clay earlier that day. The TV was on but the screen was blank.

"Hi," Tom said as pleasantly as he could. He walked to her, bent down and kissed her cheek. "What's up?"

Without a word, Darla stood up, went to the TV, picked up the remote and started the DVD player. Immediately the screen filled up with the image of a naked Tom Carver on his back being ridden by an equally naked Lynne Hartley. She paused it at a particularly salacious point.

"Shut this off," Tom demanded.

"Oh, no," Darla replied. "Let's get to the good part. There's a lot more. It gets better."

"All right. You made your point, Darla. Now shut it off!" he yelled.

Darla pointed the remote at the screen and hit the power button stopping the show. Steaming, her eyes were narrowed into infuriated slits on her face. She glared at him for several seconds, the indifferent look on his face causing her anger to go white hot.

"How could you be so fucking stupid?" she screamed.

In the hallway were three Secret Service agents, two men and a woman. Every member of the protection detail had been through these episodes before, some several times. One of the men was standing in front of the door fighting off the smile that was coming. The woman, the supervisor of the other two, looked at each of them and gently wagged an admonishing finger.

"Hey," Tom shrugged then smugly said, "She's a great piece of ass. What can I tell you?"

This answer was the last thing Darla Carver wanted to hear. The TV remote was still in her hand and without a word, she threw it at him as hard as she could. It hit him in the forehead just above his right eye. The force was such that the plastic remote broke into several pieces.

"Oww!" Tom yelled on his way to the floor. He landed with a heavy and very loud thud.

All three agents, guns drawn and pointed directly at Darla were in the room in less than two seconds. Their training having taken over, they were resorting to the absolute first rule of the Service: protect the president.

"Don't shoot her!" Carver yelled at them. He was sprawled on the floor, his right hand covering the wound, blood seeping through his fingers.

Darla stood in place, the fury still obvious in her eyes. As the agents took over to get an emergency medical team going, Darla stepped forward and kicked her husband strategically between his legs.

"The President fell and hit his head on something," Darla said as she stared down at her husband. He was holding both his head and his crotch as he moaned in pain while writhing around on the floor.

With a satisfied look on her face, she said, "Maybe now you'll start thinking about what you're doing." She turned to leave, snapped at the agents in the doorway, "Get out of my way," and then stomped off.

There is a medical team, including a physician, on-call for the president twenty-four hours a day. The wound on his forehead looked worse than it was; head wounds always bleed profusely. The doctor closed it up with four stitches. Being the President, nothing was left to chance. Despite the doctor administering a concussion protocol which came up negative, Carver was airlifted to Bethesda Hospital for a more thorough exam. It was determined his pride was far more hurt than anything else.

The next day a press release was issued. The President slipped getting out of the shower and hit his head on a vanity in the bathroom. The truth took less than a day to leak out but the Washington press generally liked Tom Carver and no one reported it.

It would be a week before Tom and Darla Carver spoke to each other again. During that time, Clay Dean, among others, acted as a go-between for them. There was still the matter of what to do with the President's paramour, Lynne Hartley.

Four days after the President's 'accident', a Friday during rush hour, Clay sat waiting on a bench in Union Station. On the floor between his legs was a cheap, pseudo-leather briefcase containing half a million dollars in twenty dollar bills, weighing roughly 55 lbs.

Clay could see a clock from where he was sitting and it read 4:50, twenty minutes after the agreed upon time. He decided 10 more minutes then he would leave. Three minutes later a man in a bad disguise sat down next to him. The two of them sat silently for almost a full minute while the intruder tried to casually look around.

"This isn't a spy movie," Clay finally said. "No one's paying any attention to us."

"You're Clay Dean?" the man said.

"Yeah, genius," Clay said. "I have a half mil in the briefcase. That's all you're gonna get. You tell Lynne she should be ashamed of herself. She's an adult and she knew what she was getting into. We better not hear another word about this. Do I make myself clear?"

"That sounds like a threat," the man said trying to sound tough and confident.

"It is, dummy," Clay said. "And if you're recording this, I suggest you destroy it or someday I'll shove it up your ass. Understood?"

"I'm not recording it," the man said.

"Good," Clay said. He lifted the briefcase, set it on the bench between them, and then stood up.

Clay looked at the man who also stood up and was trying to pick up the briefcase.

"Heavy," the man said.

"Get lost and don't call us again," Clay said, then turned and walked off.

The next day, Saturday afternoon, Clay was in the President's private office with the President and Noah Flake. He had photos of the man he encountered the day before and a drawing of him. The drawing was done by removing the hat, glasses, beard and nose putty the man had used as a disguise. It took Tom Carver less than two seconds to recognize the man from the drawing.

"It's her husband," he said. "Or more accurately, her ex-husband, Ryan Hartley."

"The guy is using porn movies starring his ex-wife for blackmail?" Flake asked.

"I'm not surprised," Carver said. "He knew about us for a long time. She said she didn't care. In fact, he liked the idea that the President was attracted to his wife."

"She's a beautiful woman, what did she see in him?" Flake asked.

"I don't know," Carver shrugged.

"Well, we know who we're dealing with, sir," Clay said. He then thought, *Darla will want this taken care of as soon as the election is over.*

The re-election of Tom and Darla Carver was just short of a Reaganesque landslide. They carried forty-four states and increased their majority in both the House and the Senate. Not by much, but enough to get most of their second term agenda passed.

Just before Christmas the bodies of Ryan Hartley and his ex-wife, Lynne, were removed from the rubble of a house fire in Boulder, Colorado. The cause of death was ruled to be asphyxiation caused by smoke inhalation during the fire. The medical examiner could not and did not rule out homicide. However, the Fire Marshall ruled the cause of the fire to be accidental. But all ten fingers on the male victim were severely broken, as if he had been tortured.

When queried by Darla Carver, Clay Dean claimed he believed that Ryan and Lynne Harley had given up all of the DVD copies. Of course, he had to admit he could not be positive. Over the next few months, while Darla waited for a copy to turn up being mailed to a reporter, she could only hope for the best. After several months and none appearing, Darla was satisfied the Hartley problem was behind them.

FOURTEEN

ONE YEAR LATER

Saad Aswad drove his rickety delivery truck toward the Amman Souk in downtown Amman, Jordan. This particular open-air marketplace was very popular with tourists and Saad appeared to be making his normal delivery.

Twice each week for the past year, Saad had driven into the city with a load of produce and melons. His boss was a man Saad hated because he was as bad as the Jews. All he cared about was making money. He was not devout and worst of all, because Saad was Syrian and not Jordanian, the man treated Saad like a dog.

Saad was a twenty-year-old Syrian refugee who had lived in Za'atri since being brought here by his parents four years ago. The camp was like all refugee camps throughout history; a place of squalor, poverty and despair. His father had left them two years ago to go back to Syria to fight the hated Assad. Barely a month later the family had received word that he had been killed by a Russian bomb. It was then Saad began to find his true path in life.

"Saad" meant good luck or good fortune in Arabic. Every time he thought of this he either laughed at the irony or anger welled up from inside. His life had been anything but lucky or fortunate, especially since the Civil War began in Syria. And life in the camp had been a nightmare.

His hatred, as brought out by the Imam, had grown fierce and burned within him. Today he would join his beloved, martyred father in Paradise and join the ranks of the Circle of Islam martyrs for Islam.

Saad had always routinely passed through the checkpoints leading into the city and to the souk. Under his right leg was the switch he could use at any time. If the soldiers at any of the checkpoints had tried to detain him, he would have used the device and blown them all to pieces. Fortunately, he had cleared the last of them and was entering the souk and his destination with immortality.

As Saad reached his goal, instead of turning to deliver his goods as he normally would he jammed the accelerator to the floor. Before the soldiers could react, he screamed, "Allahu Akbar!" and pressed the switch to ignite the bomb.

Unfortunately for Saad, one of the melons had developed a leak and the juice had dribbled onto the main detonator wires shorting them out. Instead, only a small amount of the explosives hidden under his load ignited. And it was the explosives behind the truck's passenger seat. Instead of a huge blast throwing thousands of small, metal pellets through the market, the explosion caused only one casualty. That was Saad himself.

The explosion blew out most of the truck's small front end and threw Saad out of the driver's side door. He landed almost twenty feet away from the burning vehicle. Within seconds, loyal Jordanian soldiers surrounded him. The men quickly determined that Saad, though unconscious, battered and probably seriously injured, was still very much alive.

"Nineteen more attacks just this year that this Circle of Islam has taken credit for," President Carver said with obvious exasperation. "And we're no closer to finding them than we were in the beginning."

The President was in the Situation Room with his second term National Security Council team. Gone were the academics from the first term. Some had proven useful to help bring the country together after an acrimonious campaign. During the first four years, radical Islam had increased and the academics all believed if everyone in the West would slap a COEXIST bumper sticker on their car, all would be well. If we just showed radical terrorists what swell, well-meaning huggers we are, they would see the error of their ways and drop their desire to kill all of us. By the time of the second inauguration, Tom Carver was truly sick of them.

"All of these attacks are barely pinpricks, Mr. President," his new Secretary of State, Travis Gregory, reminded him.

"True, Travis," Carver agreed. "But collectively they are having an effect."

"Our intel tells us that radicalization across the spectrum among Muslims is on the rise," one of the first-term holdovers, Direct of National Intelligence, Ralph Thomas said.

At that moment another member of the original team entered the secure room. The Director of the CIA, Malcolm Brewster arrived profusely apologizing for his tardiness. Brewster was another one Tom Carver would have liked to jettison. The best that could be said for the man was that he was competent. What saved him was he was Darla's man through and through. If she told him to jump into a burning building he would do so holding a gallon of gasoline.

"I am extremely sorry, Mr. President," Brewster said before taking his seat. "But I do have some good news."

Carver replied, "Great, let's hear it."

"The suicide bombing attempt in Amman, Jordan last week, the one that caused no casualties," Brewster said, then paused and looked over the people at the table.

"Go on," Carver said.

"The driver survived. The Jordanians grabbed him and now we have him."

"It was reported he died," the new National Security Advisor, Lieutenant General David Deaver, former Director of the Defense Intelligence Agency said.

"That came from our guy on the ground in Jordan. He got to the Jordanians and they agreed to put it out that he was dead. But he survived. We have him. A Muslim interrogator got it out of the young man that he is a Syrian refugee and a member of the Circle of Islam," Brewster told the group. "And no, they assured me, they did not torture him. In fact, the interrogator convinced him that it was the hand of Allah that saved him, that Allah delivered him to us to help us. The man's name is Saad, which means good luck. The interrogator used that to convince him it was good luck and the will of Allah to survive and be delivered to us. The man's singing like a canary."

"Where is he?" the President asked.

"I guess he's pretty beat up. The bomb was mostly a dud but it did manage to blow him out of the truck," Brewster said. "I have a plane on the way with a full medical team to get him. The Jordanians are fully cooperating."

"One good ally in the Arab world," Deaver said.

"We already have the names of at least one Circle of Islam radical Imam and a couple of guys that are recruiting in the refugee camps. We'll have them picked up by morning," Brewster said.

"Great news, Malcolm," President Carver told him. "Well done. And tell your people, well done."

"Thank you, Mr. President," Brewster replied. "The best part is we just might have a crack to open up and find out who this Circle of Islam bunch is."

The Jordanian Security Forces conducted a raid that same night on the Za'atri refugee camp. With the information Saad had given them and the intelligence they already had, they knew exactly where to find the Imam who had turned Saad into a radical. With the help of an informant who had been recruited by them, they also nabbed the two Circle of Islam recruiters working with the radical Imam. The raids took place at exactly 3:00 A.M. All three men were literally dragged out of bed and taken to a secret, secure location.

For the next month, while Saad rested comfortably in a secure American hospital in Virginia, Imam Ahmad Halim, an Egyptian and the two recruiters were held incognito in a Jordanian secured facility. The two recruiters, code-named Barney and Frank, had limited knowledge of anyone else outside of the terrorist cell in which they were involved except for one thing. Barney had a brother in a different cell working as a bomb and munitions man in Oman. Within twenty-four hours of obtaining this news, the Omanian authorities had the brother in custody. Another thread in the cloak of secrecy covering the Circle of Islam had been pulled.

In the meantime, Saad was enjoying the first comfortable bed and set of clean sheets he had ever experienced in his short twenty-year life. He also found out how convenient a flush toilet was, hot showers and plentiful food. His interrogators were also hinting that they were going to get his mother, younger brother and two sisters out of their living hell. And unlike what the Imams had pounded into his head, he was finding that America was not a hell-hole that hated Muslims. While in reality he had limited knowledge of the Circle of Islam, he was a fountain of information about who they were, what they were about and how they recruited.

Over the course of the next six months, a dozen members of the Circle of Islam vanished. All of them, including the first Imam captured, were being held in a top-secret location. The CIA was given operational control of this facility and little by little a picture of this most hate-filled, radical enemy of the Western World was taking shape.

Of course, so many missing people did not go unnoticed by the top hierarchy of the organization. Because of their disdain for modern communication, which also kept them safe, discourse among them was slow. But not so slow as to hinder them significantly. They had many trusted members who could travel anywhere in the world, several with diplomatic passports and cover. They were the messengers and the ones with knowledge about who and where the upper-level leaders were. They were also the number one targets of Western intelligence.

FIFTEEN

Marine four-star General Harley 'Mad Max' Maxwell was seated in the back of his Army limo. The driver, Bruce Kerrigan, was a Marine Sergeant Major who had saved Mad Max's life twice during Desert Storm. The general, now Chairman of the Joint Chiefs, had known Kerrigan since Maxwell was a shavetail second lieutenant and Kerrigan a light corporal. Maxwell had brought Kerrigan along for almost thirty-five years as his personal guy. Or, Maxwell wondered, did Kerrigan bring him along? Despite their personal relationship, in all those years, not once did Kerrigan ever call the general by anything but his rank.

"ETA, Sergeant?" Maxwell asked from the backseat.

"Traffic is fairly light, sir," Kerrigan replied. "Ten to fifteen minutes."

Maxwell was on this way to a meeting with the President, the CIA Director and the DCI's boss and Maxwell's good friend, Ralph Thomas, Director of Nation Intelligence and a former four star. Maxwell stared out the heavily tinted window at the grimy, late-winter streets of D.C. and failed to even notice them. Already the politicians were sending out feelers to see who would succeed Tom Carver. Before summer was over they would descend on the state of his birth, Iowa, like a swarm of locusts. God how he hated these people.

Since the failed suicide bombing of the Amman Souk and the intelligence obtained afterwards, there had been more than thirty attacks by Circle of Islam followers including eight in Europe. Now, several months later, the intelligence community was stalled. The leads they had derived from the Syrians and those captured as a result, had dried up. None of these people, because they were all restricted to small cells, could help them obtain information about the leadership of the Circle of Islam, about who was in charge.

How it operated was simple. They were organized into small, self-sufficient cells. Messengers were used to relay orders throughout the group and each cell had almost no knowledge of other cells. Except for recruiting, they stayed off of the internet, didn't use phones or other modern communication systems and were proving difficult to track.

An hour ago, General Maxwell had received a call from his friend, the DNI General Thomas. A meeting was being set up with a select few people at the White House. General Maxwell's presence was requested and there was some good news to be had.

Maxwell entered the White House Situation room to be mildly surprised by the small number of attendees. Already seated and waiting for the President were the DNI, General Ralph Thomas, the President's National Security Advisor, David Deaver, himself a retired Air Force three-star and at the end of the table near the lectern was CIA director Malcolm Brewster.

Maxwell shook hands with each of the men and took a chair on the table's left side next to Deaver. As he did this, Deaver picked up a secure phone, dialed a two-digit number and told the President all were in attendance. Five minutes later, President Carver came in with the Vice President Julian Morton and Carver's Chief-of-Staff, Noah Flake, right behind him.

After greetings, while the veep and Noah Flake took their seats Carver began.

"We finally have some very interesting intelligence, or so we believe. As you all know, it has been almost a year since we grabbed some members of the Circle of Islam group. Unfortunately, we've run into a wall. We got what we could out of the people we have, enough to get a partial picture of this viciously, fanatical bunch. But we have not been able to get much further. Until now," Carver concluded. "Director Brewster has a report to make."

"Thank you, Mr. President," Brewster said as he stepped to the lectern and began.

"As you know, the attacks by the Circle of Islam have increased in frequency and viciousness. In just the past month, there have been eleven suicide attacks, mostly in the Muslim world but four in Europe. The death toll is getting worse with each attack. It seems as if they are killing people, including fellow Muslims, just for the sake of killing.

"Two weeks ago," Brewster continued, "we were approached by Saudi Arabia's intelligence people."

With the mention of Al Mukhaborat, the Saudi's General Intelligence Directorate, there was a noticeable stirring among the men at the table.

Brewster held up his left hand and said, "I understand. They're not necessarily the most trustworthy of sources, but let me finish. On the whole, they have been quite helpful trying to track down the heads of the Circle of Islam. They claim they have lost seven agents who infiltrated the organization, were discovered, tortured and brutally executed."

A picture of a young, good-looking Middle Eastern man in an obviously expense three-piece suit appeared on the screen.

"This man is Khalid Ibn Al Saad, a member of the Saudi royal family and the Saudi's Deputy Ambassador to the United Nations. His father is a very wealthy oil sheikh and something like sixteenth in line to be king. He has a long way to go to become king, but I say this to let you know these people are high up in the Saudi pecking order.

"The Saudis have been suspicious of this guy for over a year. The old man is a devout Wahhabi and the Saudis believe that junior here," he said referring to the man on the screen, "has been radicalized."

"How did they come to that conclusion?" the President's NSA, General Deaver asked.

"Good question," Brewster said. "He's thirty-one years old, has a wife and three kids in the kingdom. He has been at the UN for almost six years. During the first four years he was there, he was quite the patron of the MHA, the Manhattan Hookers Association. He liked to party which is hardly unusual. The Saudis don't much care, most of the Muslims at the UN drop their façade of devotion to Islam when the wheels of their luxury jets touch down at Teterboro.

"A couple of years ago, young Khalid stopped his wicked, Western ways. He started attending services at a mosque in Brooklyn run by this man," Brewster said changing the picture on the screen. "Imam Mustafa Raheem. We, meaning the U.S. and the FBI, have had our eye on Raheem for several years. We are convinced he's no friend of the West, especially America.

"About a year ago the Saudi intelligence people started monitoring Khalid. He has a private jet, a diplomatic passport and the money to go anywhere, anytime. He has made a lot of trips, ostensibly on behalf of his UN duties, but he's not fooling the Saudis. They haven't been able to find out who he meets but he spends a lot of time in what are believed to be radical mosques."

"He's a courier for the Circle of Islam?" DNI Thomas asked.

"The Saudis think so," Brewster said answering his immediate superior. "And one more thing," Brewster said again changing the picture on the screen. Photos of two Mid-Eastern men, dark hair and beards, wearing pilot's uniforms appeared. "These two are Khalid's permanent pilot and co-pilot. They are on call twenty-four seven for him. About a year ago, right after the Saudis started tailing him, these two went to work for him. The Saudis believe they are both radicalized and were assigned to him by the Circle of Islam."

"How convinced are we of this?" President Carver asked.

"I have been in discussions, as you know, Mr. President," Brewster continued, "personally with the Saudis since they came to us with this, which by itself is very rare. My people, who started out being pretty skeptical about it, are now about ninety percent convinced. And I apologize for not informing anyone sooner."

"That was my idea," Carver told the people at the table. "That's why there are only you people here today. We're going to keep a lid on this. I don't want to read about it in the Times."

"Now what?" DNI Thomas asked Brewster.

"Khalid will be landing in Teterboro this afternoon. He will be met by a limo, as usual, but driven to a safe house in New Jersey. He'll be told by Saudi officials that his diplomatic passport has been revoked by the Saudi government. We will then interrogate him for information and try to flip him. The Saudis will tell him if he does not cooperate, his entire family, father, mother, brothers, sisters, aunts, uncles, and cousins, you name it will be arrested as co-conspirators within twenty-four hours. Including his wife and children. The entire bunch will eventually confess to treason and be executed," Brewster flatly told them.

"My God," Vice President Morton said. "Do we want to be a party to this?"

"Relax, Julian," Carver said. "The Saudis are bluffing." He knew that was a lie but it was time Julian Morton was brought into the real world of fighting terrorism.

"Any questions?" Carver asked the people at the table. When no one made a move to ask anything, Carver said. "Okay, Malcolm. Tell your people good work. I want another meeting of just this group in two days. You'll have an update for us then."

"Absolutely, Mr. President," Brewster replied.

"Wait a minute," General Maxwell said. "The Saudis are going to just hand this guy over to us? What do they want in return?"

"Yeah, I was wondering the same thing," DNI Thomas said.

"Better relations," Carver said

"And access to the intel," Brewster added.

"I was skeptical also," Carver said. "Let's take it one step at a time and see what comes of it. They could be wrong, too. This guy could be innocent. We'll see."

"Where is the Secretary of State?" the veep asked.

"Not here" Carver bluntly replied.

"Why not?"

"Because the State Department leaks like a bucket with a five-inch hole in the bottom. Too many career know-it-alls there who think they know what's best for this country," the President candidly told the veep.

With that, Carver stood, as did everyone else and said, "I'll see all of you back here Thursday, same time."

"This could be heaven sent," Darla Carver said. She was pacing around the room, silently scheming about how to use the information her husband had given her to enhance herself politically.

She was in the West Sitting Hall in the second floor living quarters. The room was adjacent to the President's bedroom and was often used for private discussions. With her were the President, Sonja Hayden and Noah Flake.

"Darla, this is one-time you are going to put national security ahead of political ambition," Carver sternly told his wife. The President was seated on an antique, upholstered Queen Anne watching his wife. On a matching sofa sat Noah Flake within arm's reach of his boss and Sonja on the opposite end.

"Of course," Darla sincerely said patting her husband on the shoulder as she paced past him. She took a chair next to Sonja opposite the President and continued.

"It's just that people are getting tired of these attacks. Our polling shows terrorism is the number two issue in the country right now. The TV talking heads blather on about nothing else, especially on FOX. But the other networks are doing more stories about it, too. Your numbers are weak on terrorism. If I am to succeed you, we have about one more year to do something about this."

"I'm aware of all of this, Darla," Tom replied. "There's still time."

Khalid Ibn Al Saad came down the stairs of his Gulfstream and walked the twenty or so feet to the waiting limo. The driver, a man he did not recognize, was respectfully holding the door for him.

"Where is Asad?" Khalid asked the man, referring to his normal driver.

"Ill, your excellency, my apologies for any inconvenience," the driver replied.

Without another word, Khalid entered into the back seat. A copy of the Daily News, as usual, was on the seat waiting for him. And as usual, he quickly opened the paper to ignore the drive back. Except that this time, instead of going toward Manhattan, the car was heading southwest farther into New Jersey. Fifteen minutes into the drive, Khalid finally noticed.

"Where are you taking me?" he screamed at the driver. "Do you know who I am? You are in serious trouble!"

Two days after the original meeting during which they were first informed about the Saudi courier, the same people were back in the White House Situation Room. DCI Brewster had a very satisfactory update for the small group.

"Khalid is singing like a canary," Brewster informed them. "He was very quickly convinced it would be in his best interest to cooperate."

"Was he tortured?" Vice President Morton asked?

"No, Mr. Vice President, he was not. No one laid a hand on him. We didn't have to. The local head of the Saudi security detail, the man assigned to their UN delegation, was in the room. Khalid knows him. The man explained Khalid's and his family's situation and..."

"I don't like this one bit," the veep said disgustedly tossing the pen he was holding onto the tablet of paper on the table in front of him.

"Julian," Carver said, "this isn't a mischievous Cub Scout. He is a treasonous fanatic and is responsible, or at least partially culpable, for hundreds of murders. Our hands are clean."

The veep sighed and said, "Yes, I suppose you're right. Sorry, Director, please proceed."

"This is going to be a long process. He does not know many names but he does see a number of these Imams. He believes there are thirteen or fourteen of them scattered around the Mideast. Khalid also claims he, himself, was beginning to have doubts about his commitment."

"Probably missing the good life with the girls in Manhattan," Noah Flake said eliciting chuckles from the other men.

"That's probably more accurate than we think. Anyway," Brewster continued, "he's willing to cooperate. He's going to get us names, places and pictures of these guys, these Imams running the Circle of Islam."

"Why don't we grab the ones he knows now?" Carver asked.

"Because even torture won't make them talk. Plus, the rest of them would go underground. No, the best thing we can do is find out who they are then drone them with hellfire suppositories," Brewster said.

"Cut off the head. Right now they look like winners. We need to send the message that sooner or later we will get you if you persist in messing with us," General Maxwell grimly said.

"Where is he now?" Carver asked.

"He's at the UN, back at his duties. The Saudi UN Ambassador knows what's up but he and their security chief are the only ones. Even the Saudi Ambassador here in Washington doesn't know about this," Brewster replied. "We've got a team in place and Saudi cooperation. I feel pretty good about this, Mr. President. We're going to get these guys."

"Okay," Carver said. "Any questions?"

This opened the discussion up and for another half-hour, questions were tossed out and answers and opinions kicked around the table. Finally, satisfied for now, the meeting wound down.

"One last thing," Brewster said. "We've code-named Khalid, Rosebud."

"Like in Citizen Kane?" asked General Thomas.

"The same," Brewster replied smiling.

SIXTEEN

Through the spring and summer, Khalid/Rosebud was proving to be a fountain of information. He personally had provided his CIA and Saudi handlers with the names and locations of ten ultra-radical Imams. He also came up with the identity of another courier, a Pakistani general who was the deputy commander of the Pakistan intelligence agency, the notorious ISI. His name was Major General Ali-Mohammed Dehwar. Unfortunately, the Pakistani authorities would not be as cooperative as the Saudis.

The CIA put their own surveillance net around the man and came up with the names of four more Imams. Two in Pakistan and two Afghanistan. All four were well known to the CIA and U.S. military intelligence, the Defense Intelligence Agency. They were originally hardcore members of the Taliban who had grown disillusioned with them. They had split from the Taliban because the leadership seemed too willing to negotiate with the Americans. The Taliban and Al Qaeda were too soft for them.

The name of the fourteenth hate-mongering Islamic cleric had been obtained a few days ago. Rosebud had gone over the full list and believed that these constituted the full leadership of the Circle of Islam.

The DCI, Malcolm Brewster, was the first to arrive at the White House. The meeting was scheduled for 9:00 A.M. and it was barely 8:30.

Brewster had surprised everyone, especially the President, with the job he had done at CIA. Originally a political appointee forced on Tom Carver by Darla, lately, Brewster had done a very respectable job and had earned the President's gratitude. It helped that his East Coast political connections—he was a former governor of and senator from New Jersey—were a significant asset. And his place at CIA had been used to gather dirt on political opponents. It was stunningly illegal, but Darla did not let minor details like that deter her. Unknown even to her husband, Darla also had three well-placed 'friends' at the IRS.

By ten minutes before nine, all of the members of this small, select group had gathered around the Situation Room conference table. It was the Friday before Labor Day. D.C. was unbearably hot and humid and all of those present were in a hurry to get out of town for the long weekend.

"Okay, what do you have for us, Malcolm?" the President asked his CIA Director.

Brewster moved to the lectern and began his slide show.

"We have obtained a total of fourteen Islamic clerics who we believe constitute the leadership of the Circle of Islam," Brewster said.

86

"It wasn't easy but we have photos of all fourteen and at least some biographical data on them."

"It was my idea," President Carver interrupted Brewster and addressed the group, "to have this meeting and show you this. There are only three copies of the photos and information you are about to see. I have one, Vice President Morton has one and Director Brewster has one. Don't be offended by this. I trust all of you absolutely. For now, the fewer copies, the better. Please, proceed, Director."

"Yes, sir," Brewster replied.

For the next two hours, Brewster conducted his slide show going over the photos, bios and locations of each of the fourteen. Of course, the group had numerous questions and much discussion occurred while he did this. After finishing with the fourteenth man, the group went silent for almost twenty seconds.

"Now what?" General Maxwell broke the silence by asking while looking at the President.

"That's the question, isn't it, Max?" President Carver replied.

"From what Director Brewster has described concerning the security these guys have around themselves, going after these guys with Special Forces is extremely problematic. Putting a force together large enough to do it would be difficult, to say the least," Maxwell said. "Security alone would be a huge problem and we cannot guarantee the results we want with small groups of our guys."

"I know, Max," Carver said. "We're looking at drones. We're going to have to use drones to target these guys."

"We're going to need assets on the ground," the DNI, Ralph Thomas said. "It's going to take some time. And the best way is to do it all at once which is not probable."

"Yes, I know," Carver said.

"Mr. President, let me play Devil's Advocate here," Vice President Morton chimed in. "If word gets out that we are deliberately targeting Islamic clerics who have not been convicted of anything, who we only suspect of being at the head of this radical group, the Islamic world is going to light up. More radical groups will spring up and recruiting will use this…"

"Julian, I, for one, am sick to death of worrying about crazy Muslims recruiting based on what we do. If we do nothing, we appear weak and they use that to recruit. If we do go after these people, the far left gets hyperventilated claiming this just adds fuel to the fire. The people preach hatred because that's what they use to keep their followers under their thumbs.

"We need to fight back. These fanatics kill more Muslims than they do anyone else. And they are dedicated to coming after us. Hundreds of years ago the Christians used fear to control their followers. Now, the Muslims use hate. Very powerful emotions. They need something or someone to hate. They use us and the Jews to blame all of their problems on so their own people won't get tired of their bullshit and come after them. Hate. It's all they have.

"They hate the Jews most of all and not just those in Israel. They don't give a shit about Israel but they sure care about killing all of the Jews. If they could, they'd finish the job Hitler and the Nazi's started. Well, not on my watch, Julian. And if you want to sit in this chair, you better figure that out.

"It's about a year to the next party conventions. I want to help our nominee win to secure my legacy. By the time I leave office, I want this Circle of Islam bunch destroyed.

"Malcolm, let's get some assets on the ground. We're going after these murderous assholes," Carver said.

"Yes, sir. We're already working on it," Brewster replied.

"Are you sure it's absolutely necessary for me to be there?" Noah Flake asked his boss.

Flake and the President were on the Truman balcony looking out over the south lawn of the White House. It was a few minutes past 3:00 P.M. on the same day as their meeting that morning about the Circle of Islam clerics. Flake was referring to a meeting that was not on the President's official schedule as to what it was really about. The official schedule merely referenced a meeting in the second floor West Sitting Hall.

"Yes, if I have to be there for this than by God you're going to be there, too," Carver replied smiling at his friend.

Noah Flake was not only the President's Chief-of-Staff and an exemplary one, he himself was Carver's best friend. Perhaps the only true friend the man actually had. Certainly in this town. Lonely is the head that wears the crown, indeed.

Carver was smoking one of the two or three cigars he allowed himself each day. He loved a good cigar with a scotch and soda. It also had the side benefit of annoying Darla, a thought that always brought a smile to the President.

"Who is going to carry the conversation?" Flake asked.

Carver took a large puff of cigar then wickedly smiled at his friend and said, "I think you should do that, you have the least to live for."

"That's not funny, your Highness," a title Flake used when the two men were alone which always caused the President to laugh. "Why don't I just fall on my sword for you, now?"

"What, are you afraid of her?" Carver said, teasing the man.

"Yes!" Flake said. "You tell her."

Carver sighed, sipped his scotch then said, "I will. It has to be done. The party people are right. She'll understand."

"You're probably right," Flake agreed. "But just in case, I'm gonna sit on the other side of the room, away from you. I don't want to be listed as collateral damage."

Carver laughed again, then they heard a woman's voice behind them from the open door.

"Everyone is here, Mr. President," the female Secret Service agent said. "Including Mrs. Carver."

"Thank you, Sherry. We'll be right there," Carver replied.

The President watched the shapely agent through the door's glass windows as she walked away then quietly said, "Yeah, that would be okay."

"No, no, no," Flake said. "Do not start screwing Secret Service agents."

"Relax, I was just thinking out loud."

The two men entered the West Sitting Hall to find Darla, with Sonja at her side, on a sofa, chatting amiably with three people. They were Senate Majority Whip Colton Piper, Senator Sally Newport and Party Chair Paul Janzen.

The three of them had been driven to the White House together. The two Senators were senior members of both the Senate and the Party. In addition, Sally Newport was a friend of Darla Carver's going back over twenty years.

On the mostly silent ride from the capitol, it was Sally who had broken the silence by saying, "Why do I feel like we're going to a funeral?"

"Because it may be," Paul Janzen replied. "It could end up being ours."

"Who's going to tell her?" Senator Piper asked.

There was a full minute of awkward silence among them. Each waiting for one of the others to volunteer.

"Maybe the President will tell her," Senator Newport said, hopefully.

"Stop it," Janzen said. "She's an adult, we're adults. We can deal with her and she'll understand. I'll tell her. It's probably my place anyway as head of the Party apparatus."

"Okay," the two Senators replied in unison.

"You're probably right. It's just that I know Darla has been working her entire life to get a shot at becoming the first woman president," Sally Newport added.

"And she still can and probably will be," Janzen said.

When the President and Noah Flake entered the room, everyone except Darla stood to greet him. Carver went to the three politicians and warmly greeted them. He then took a chair next to Darla and Flake, true to his word, sat in the chair nearest to the door.

"Darla," the President said, beginning the conversation.

"Why do I feel like this is an intervention of some kind," Darla said smiling at everyone. "Let me save you the discomfort, Tom," she continued patting her husband on the hand. "You're here to tell me it's not my turn. That you don't believe the country will let me succeed my husband. Is that about it?"

"Yes, Mrs. Carver," Paul Janzen replied. "Our internal polling shows that you winning a third term, a third Carver term, is unlikely."

"I see," Darla said, still smiling. "And if I politely say, 'fuck you, I'll run anyway' then what?"

"Darla," Salle Newport jumped in, "your turn will come. Don't do this."

"All right, I'm listening," Darla said with a disappointed sigh.

"We think it's time, that the country is ready for the first black president," Senator Piper said. "We think it's best to get behind the Vice President. It will be good for the country and good for the Party."

"If he wins and gets eight years, my chances of a third straight president from the same Party will be almost zero," Darla said.

"The country is shifting to us, Darla," the President replied. "Julian Morton will be a great president and he will solidify the African-American vote."

"Julian Morton is a limp-dick weenie," Darla said clearly annoyed. "Why should I do this?"

"Mrs. Carver," Janzen said. "After the election, you establish residency in Connecticut. Wendell Brighton's Senate seat will be available in the off-year election. We will hand it to you on a platter."

"Brighton is retiring?" Darla asked. "I didn't know that."

"He doesn't either," the President said. "He'll be persuaded that it is time for him to spend more time with his family."

"And less time with his hooker girlfriend," Sally Newport added.

"Six years in the Senate would look good on your résumé," Newport said.

"If Julian wins a second term, we could probably get you a significant cabinet position, say, Secretary of State or Defense for two or three years, also," Janzen said.

"That's an idea," Darla agreed.

"We have an opportunity to make a historic run," Sally said. "We could elect the first black president and follow that with the first woman president. Besides, I'd love to have you in the Senate with me."

Darla looked at her friend, reached across her husband and took Sally's hand. They held the pose for a few seconds, smiling at each other. Darla released her friend's hand. Looked around the room and put on the best face she could.

"Okay, I'm a good soldier. I'll wait my turn," she said while thinking, *No way am I going to wait eight years and hope to succeed a man who should be carrying my bags.*

SEVENTEEN

Chairman of the Pentagon's Joint Chiefs of Staff, General Mad Max Maxwell was in the back of his Army-provided limo. Once again he was being driven to the White House for a meeting about the Circle of Islam. These bi-weekly, sometimes more often, updates on the CIA's attempts to infiltrate the Circle of Islam were almost becoming a nuisance. A little progress would be nice.

Memorial Day was less than two weeks away. The Washington weather was near perfect this spring. The cherry blossoms outside the general's window around the city were as gorgeous as they had ever been. Maxwell barely noticed as the car turned through the gate and onto the White House grounds. As they made the final approach to the building, Maxwell could not prevent a silent scowl because of this morning's progress report meeting. He hoped they had something to say that was worth the bother of taking him away from his full schedule.

The progress, if it could even be called that, was snail's pace slow. This particular branch of Islamic fanaticism was cautious in the extreme. First, a new recruit had to be nominated by a current member. Then he had to prove he was willing to commit suicide for the cause. Since so many current members were killing themselves in a suicide attack, this limited the number being nominated for inclusion.

Step two involved weeks of constant surveillance and training. Then, finally, when the higher-ups were satisfied the recruit was not communicating with anyone, the final test. You were forced to 'make your bones', as the Mafia would say, by committing a murder. And it could be anyone, including a family member who was considered insufficiently devout.

What the CIA was finding out was there was there was no shortage of volunteers. It was estimated that for every candidate selected, as many as three or four were turned down. The Circle of Islam was beginning to get the reputation among the Muslim world as the place to be. The holiest of holies for fighting jihad, striking a blow for Islam and a ticket straight to Paradise.

"Thank you, Sergeant," Maxwell said to his driver and also to the Marine saluting as he held the car door open for the General. He was at the back entrance to the West Wing. Maxwell checked his watch and saw he was ten minutes early. As he walked towards the door he thought of one good thing: the Vice President, whom Maxwell considered to be a weak appeaser, was too busy campaigning and would not be in attendance.

92

"Good morning, everyone," the President said as he entered the room. "Please, keep your seats."

Following behind the President was CIA Director Brewster and Noah Flake. Apparently, Brewster had met with Carver before the two of them joined the small group. In addition to Maxwell and the usual attendees, DNI Ralph Thomas and Carver's National Security Advisor, David Deaver, was the Attorney General, Rachel Compton.

Compton was a fifty-eight-year-old former federal judge and before that, a U.S. Attorney in Michigan. She had earned the reputation of being tough and no friend of people caught leaving America to fight for jihad in the Middle East. On the surface, she looked like everyone's favorite grandma or aunt. Cross her and she could crucify you. President Carver had grown fond of her and valued her advice.

Conspicuously absent, still, were the Secretaries of State and Defense. The State Department leaked like a sieve. Too many self-absorbed intellectuals who knew what was best for America and could not keep their mouths shut. The Defense was run by what the President called his biggest mistake, Secretary of Defense Lou Barker. Barker was a powerful politician in the party and if Darla was going to be president someday, she was going to need the former governor and senator from Ohio. In the meantime, Tom Carver would have as little to do with the man as possible. Since Barker rarely made an appearance at the Pentagon anyway, avoiding him was not overly difficult.

"Director Brewster has some good news for us, finally," Carver told the group after taking his seat at the head of the table. Brewster stood behind the lectern next to the viewing screen and addressed the assemblage.

"As you know, it has been very difficult to get close to these people. I won't go through it all again now, but we have finally planted people in two of the groups and are getting close to several others."

A photograph of a heavily bearded, turban wearing man of obvious Middle Eastern heritage appeared on the screen next to Brewster. By the look on the man's face, he appeared about as pleasant and happy as a man suffering from golf ball size hemorrhoids. Deep-set, dark eyes and very black, bushy eyebrows added to the image of a man harboring a good deal of hate.

"Sheikh Abdullah bin Safar, a Saudi, is currently residing in Yemen. We are informed that he has ordered and orchestrated at least twenty suicide attacks that have resulted in more than three hundred dead. This includes the attack at the Israeli security wall that killed four Israeli soldiers and nineteen Palestinians waiting to enter Israel to go to their jobs. And he was the one who released the acceptance of responsibility message in which he claimed he would gladly kill a thousand Palestinians for each Israeli—he, of course, said 'dirty Jews'—he could kill."

"That is our first target," the President said.

"When?" DNI Thomas asked.

"As soon as we can get a drone over him and a clear shot," Carver replied.

"Today is Tuesday," Brewster said. "We're gonna try to get him by the end of the week."

"How good is our on the ground intel?" Maxwell asked.

"Communication is a problem," Brewster admitted. "He has to be extremely cautious. If he's caught, his death will not be pleasant. Right now, this Sheikh is in Mukalla, a port on the Gulf of Aden. That helps us. We can launch from a carrier group and be over him in a couple hours. We just need to know where he'll be. We could get over Mukalla now, but these guys are very cautious. They switch cars and buildings and are hard to tail."

"Why don't we get him in his mosque on Friday?" Noah Flake asked.

"Lot of collateral damage," Carver said.

"Not if we shoot before the call to prayers," Flake said. "Besides, anyone in this guy's mosque is likely next week or next month's suicide bomber."

"Rachel?" Carver asked looking at the Attorney General.

"Noah has a point about this guy's parishioners or whatever they're called. If the media finds out we deliberately targeted a mosque there would be hell to pay. They would howl war crime under the Geneva Convention for deliberately targeting a place of worship. Articles 25 and 27 would be violated, especially Article 27. We can certainly argue it was a target of military necessity, which is allowed."

"The Geneva Convention never anticipated the barbarians that are radical jihadis. I'd like to see them accuse us of war crimes while they put POW's in cages and set them on fire," DNI Thomas said.

"We'll worry about that later," the President said. "In the meantime, let's go get this guy."

Later that afternoon, while the President was in the Oval Office at his desk, his direct line buzzed. He answered it and heard his wife ask if she could drop in for a few minutes this afternoon.

"Sure, come down now. I'm going over some documents for signing, but we can talk."

Five minutes later one of the President's personal secretaries knocked on the door then opened it for Darla. Darla walked in even uncharacteristically thanking the secretary and pleasantly greeted her husband. He came out from behind his famous desk. Tom took Darla's hand, kissed her on the cheek and led her to a couch in front of the fireplace. He sat down on the couch opposite her and waited for her to begin.

"I'm getting a little curious about these very discreet meetings you're having with what looks to be a select group of your national security people. We're not supposed to have secrets, Tom. Are you going to tell me what's up?"

"I knew you'd catch that. I'm surprised it wasn't sooner," he replied.

"It was sooner," Darla said. "I've known for months. It's about this Circle of Islam bunch, isn't it?"

"Yeah, it is."

"And that's why certain people are not invited, State and Defense, isn't it?"

"Right again," Tom said chuckling at his wife's ability to catch these things.

"Can you tell me about it?"

The President shrugged then said, "Sure, you'll find out soon enough, anyway."

The President quickly gave her a Cliff's Notes summary of where he was with the search for the heads of the Circle of Islam.

"So, you're not angry I didn't bring you in on this sooner?"

"No, not at all," Darla replied. "You know I trust your judgment on these things. And don't worry, I'll keep my mouth shut."

"It's a nest of fanatics who have killed at least a thousand innocent Muslims. If the Islamic world can't see that, then we have a bigger problem than any of us realize."

"Good point," Darla said. "How many other names do we have of these guys?"

"We have a list of fourteen in total. Only myself, Brewster and Vice President Morton have a copy."

"Which brings me to another subject," Darla said. "Have you decided if you are going to campaign for Morton?"

"Now that he has the nomination all but sewn up, yes, I will, after the convention."

"What about the convention? Are you going?"

Tom hesitated before answering. He had been leaning forward with his elbows on his knees while conversing with Darla. He sat back, crossed his right leg over his left and his left arm across the back of the couch.

"What do you think?" he asked.

"The convention should be for Morton. It should be his moment. If you go, it will steal the spotlight from him. On the other hand, the man is so weak I'm not sure how much we should do for him. I mean, how closely do we want to be associated with a man who is likely to do a mediocre job, at best?"

"Good question," Tom agreed. "Looks like Timmons is going to be his opponent," Tom continued. He was referring to Governor Gary Timmons of Missouri.

"Now there's a featherhead weakling," Darla said almost snarling with contempt.

There was a knock on the same door Darla had come through. The same secretary opened it and reminded the President of his next appointment. The first couple stood and Darla said, "By the way, I've decided to accept that Senate seat from Connecticut. We'll have to establish residence when we leave."

"Okay," Tom said. "It's close to New York. Actually, this will work out better. I've got some ideas to make a lot of money. You being in the Senate won't hurt any of that."

EIGHTEEN

CREECH AIR FORCE BASE, LAS VEGAS, NV

Captain Mariana Reyes poured herself a cup of coffee in the operation center lunchroom. Reyes was the shift supervisor for the mid-watch coming on duty in thirty minutes at 2300 hours, local time. She would also be the one to pull the trigger if any shots were to be taken. Included on her team were four other Air Force personnel; a first lieutenant, Jack Prescott, and three enlisted people, two men and a woman.

One of the men was eighteen-year veteran, Master Sergeant Ken Doyle who was Reyes' senior advisor and the person she relied on most of all. Rock solid and thoroughly professional, he was Reyes' leaning post whenever she need one, which was becoming less and less frequent.

"Hey, Ken," Reyes said. She was leaning against the countertop in the break room sipping her coffee when Doyle walked in.

"Evening, Captain," Doyle replied. "Did you know Colonel O'Connor is with us tonight?"

"No," Reyes casually replied. O'Connor was the commanding officer of the UAV Operation Group at Creech AFB outside Las Vegas. His presence meant there was a serious operation on for tonight. With the time difference between Nevada and the Mideast, most of the shooting was done during evening-watch from 1500 hours until 2300.

"What's up?" Reyes asked. Normally having your boss looking over your shoulder during your watch was not a welcome event. Reyes liked and respected O'Connor. He had been on hand during several of her team's shifts and rarely interfered. What his attendance really signified was the target must be high level. As commanding officer, O'Connor was ultimately responsible and liked to be on hand when something of a significantly high value went down.

"He didn't say," Doyle replied while filling his cup from the thirty cup coffee maker. "When I asked, he said he would brief us when we are all here."

At exactly 2300 hours, Reyes' team was at their stations and ready to go. Colonel O'Connor had given them a brief rundown of the target, which amounted to little more than the fact the guy was a verified, certifiable asshole who needed to be turned into smoke.

2300 hours in Nevada is 11:00 P.M Nevada time and 10:00 A.M. in Yemen. For the first two hours of their shift, Reyes and her team did little but watch the large screen in front of them while the Predator on station over Mukalla, Yemen cruised overhead beaming back video. At 22,000 feet the clarity of the cameras was amazing. As good as if it was just above rooftops.

The bird itself required a team of two to pilot it. One to handle the joystick controls to maneuver the bird and one to manipulate the sensors and cameras. With enough time in the cockpit, so to speak, the pilots, Reyes and Senior Airman Dejuan Taylor, a black man who had escaped the Bronx via the Air Force, could practically do it in their sleep.

For the first two hours of their shift, the Air Force crew mostly watched the video feed on the large monitor on the wall. With the camera on the drone set to a wide angle, they had a clear view of the entire city of Mukalla. It was midmorning in Yemen, a cloudless sky with no wind or weather to deal with or account for if and when they took the shot.

A few minutes before noon local time, a signal via satellite came through. It contained GPS coordinates transmitted by someone on the ground, an 'asset' who would 'paint' the target with a laser. The missile, when launched would lock on to the laser and explode one second after going through the target's roof.

With the signal and coordinates coming in, the drone's cameras were positioned by Senior Airman Taylor to focus on that exact spot. While he did this, Captain Reyes toggled the aircraft a little closer to the target to get the best angle for the missile's flight and its fastest delivery time. At 22,000 feet it would take approximately ten seconds to strike once it was fired.

While they waited, despite their professionalism and calm demeanor, everyone in the room tensed up noticeably, including Colonel O'Connor. Less than ten minutes after receiving the GPS signal, they saw a group of ten to fifteen people exit a building on the left side of the dusty street they were watching. As soon as this happened, every other pedestrian began to walk away noticeably faster.

"Are they afraid of this guy or do they know what's coming?" Reyes quietly asked no one in particular.

At that moment, as the entourage surrounding the sheikh moved across the street, a voice came over the crew's headsets and the room's intercom.

"The target has been positively identified as the man in the middle of the group in the street," the male, disembodied voice said to them. "Our asset," the voice continued, "is the man in the red hat coming onto the roof of the building the group just exited from."

"Roger that," O'Connor replied.

"Wait until they are inside the building they are walking toward. We will receive a signal that the target is painted and you will execute the mission when we so inform you," the voice said.

"Roger that," O'Connor said again.

They again watched the group of jihadis, most of them carrying what were clearly Kalashnikov automatic assault rifles, the weapon of choice for the dedicated terrorist of all denominations. The group reached the building and one of the men held the door for the sheikh. While this took place, a crowd of unarmed men, conspicuously no women, began to gather at a door on the opposite side of the building. It was Reyes who noticed it first and knew what it meant.

"Colonel, this is a mosque. Those people are being called to prayer," she said.

"Hold your position, Captain," O'Connor said. "Maintain the mission."

"The target is being painted, you are ordered to fire," the voice said.

"There are civilians present," O'Connor replied.

"Affirmative. We are aware. Fire your missile," the voice responded.

"Has this been ordered from…?" O'Connor started to ask.

"The highest level," the voice said obviously growing irritated with the hesitation. "You have your orders. Carry them out, now."

"Roger that," O'Connor said. "Captain, fire the missile."

Reyes sat still, unmoving, not speaking for several seconds. When she did this, knowing what O'Connor would say next, Sgt. Doyle quickly took

up a position to her right.

"Captain," O'Connor said in a louder, more authoritative voice, "take the shot or I will relieve you."

Doyle leaned down and whispered in her ear, "Mariana, take the shot."

"Missile away," Reyes confirmed.

The targeting site of the drone's camera remained fixed on the roof of the mosque. Each person on the team silently counted down the ten seconds everyone in that building still had to live. Just before the missile hit, for the briefest of instants, the Hellfire came into view. It went through the roof and the floor of the mosque into a basement warehouse in less than a second.

The explosion that followed shocked everyone watching, the people at the CIA in Langley where the voice was and especially those, including President Carver, in the White House Situation room. What they saw was a fireball and mushroom cloud that resembled a miniature atomic bomb. Before it began to recede, the boiling cloud would reach a height of almost a mile high. The fireball and subsequent shock wave knocked down every building surrounding the mosque and would cause serious damage to all others up to a quarter of a mile away. It would take several days to know and the exact figure would never be certain, but it was reasonably estimated that at least five hundred people died from the blast. Being a mostly poor, residential area, dozens of houses collapsed killing hundreds of people including many children.

Speaking for the entire crew whose eyes were locked on the image being transmitted, Senior Airman Taylor put their thoughts very succinctly. "Holy shit! What the hell was that?"

"A Hellfire does not pack enough explosives to cause that," MSgt Doyle replied. "They were using the mosque to store munitions. Probably a shitload of C-4 or Semtex. Something along those lines."

"Well, Sarge," Taylor quietly said, "I guess we got the sonofabitch."

At the end of their shift, all members of the team were requested—ordered—into the colonel's office for a chat. When they were all seated, O'Connor began.

"Are you all right, Mariana?" he asked Reyes.

"Yes, sir," she replied. "We didn't do that. They did. But I'm still a little sick about it."

"Good, me too," O'Connor replied.

He looked at the faces of the team seated around the office and said, "I'm not gonna give you the usual bullshit about war and casualties. You've all heard it before. I just wanted to get you together and see how everyone is doing. If you have any feelings you want to express, any guilt or anything at all you want to get off your chest, now's the time. As always, what happens in Vegas stays in Vegas. What happens in this facility, stays in this facility."

No one spoke for over thirty seconds then Captain Reyes, knowing her team and believing she spoke for all of them said, "It's hard sometimes. No one signed on for this but it's the enemy's fault for using a church to store explosives. If we do our job," she shrugged, "people die. We're here to defend our country and our way of life. These assholes want to take that from us. If they stop, we'll stop."

"Well said, Captain. If there is nothing else, you're dismissed. You did a good job tonight. Try to get some sleep."

There was one final note from the attack before the political and moral outrage hit. The onsite asset, the Muslim man who signaled for the strike and held a laser guidance device on the target, went down in the rubble of the building he was on. He was a Saudi army officer, Major Awad Maloof. He had worked undercover for four months to get close to the sheikh. Amazingly, he was found in the rubble by rescuers the day after the attack. Seriously injured with a broken leg, arm and several ribs, he spent three weeks in a hospital due to internal bleeding and injuries.

However, upon his release, he was given a hero's welcome by the Circle of Islam for having survived the attack. His 'street creds' had been enhanced. Fortunately, the laser he used was never found.

NINETEEN

"Good morning," the President's press secretary said to the assembled media. Justin Havens had become press secretary during Carver's second term. Prior to that, he had been a reporter for a cable news network. Because he had been one of "them", the White House press corps did not routinely savage him. In fact, Havens was a friend of many of them and had a decent sense of humor which helped with his credibility.

He started off making a brief statement concerning the President's schedule for the day. Justin barely finished when the hands went up. Knowing what the hot topic of the day was going to be and having decided whom to call upon ahead of time, Justin pointed at a reasonably unbiased reporter from the AP.

"It is being reported that the huge explosion of another mosque, the one that occurred yesterday, was not an accident but the result of a drone strike by the U.S. Air Force," the woman said. "Would you care to comment?"

The event the AP reporter was referring to was the fourth missile strike against a leader of the Circle of Islam. The first one, the day before the Memorial Day weekend, had resulted in the huge explosion in Mukalla, Yemen. What little government there was in Yemen conducted an investigation. They determined that an unidentified terrorist group was using the mosque to store explosives, possibly as much as two tons of plastique. Because of the explosion and subsequent fire damage and the incompetence of the investigators, the cause was undetermined. It was concluded to be an accident and the investigation was closed.

Yesterday, the same thing happened to a mosque in the Sudan. This was the fourth drone attack against Circle of Islam leadership. Numbers two and three occurred in June. Number two took out a nasty Jihadi Imam who had used children as young as eight years old to act as suicide bombers. He was blown to pieces in the middle of the night along with one of his favorite mistresses, the wife of a follower he had had murdered. Or so it was rumored.

Number three went up while in the back seat of a car on a road in Syria. A homing device had been attached to the car by a traitor to the cause to track him. Three of his bodyguards died with him.

Yesterday's strike hit a building in an isolated compound approximately fifty miles from Mogadishu, Somalia. There was a total of five buildings of various kinds in the compound. On the ground, intel had located the place as a training ground for fighters and a warehouse for weapons and explosives. The missile hit the warehouse and when the smoke and dust settled, there was a crater eighty meters wide and twenty meters deep. None of the buildings were still standing and there were no survivors to be seen from the sky.

"First of all," Havens began. "We believe it was not a mosque. It was a compound outside of Mogadishu that reports we have made clear was a training camp for radical Islamic terrorists."

"How do you know that?" a man's voice leapt out of the crowd.

"I can't get into that, Sandy," Havens replied.

In the President's work office, Carver, Noah Flake and Carver's National Security Advisor, David Deaver, were seated in front of a TV. Normally, Tom Carver did not like to keep his press secretary in the dark. The air campaign that was being waged against the Circle of Islam was an exception. Everyone involved agreed the less Justin Havens knew, the better. At least this way, he was not personally lying to the press and by extension, the American people. The fallout from targeting Muslim clerics required it. Sometimes, even in Washington, secrets had to be kept.

The briefing moved on to more mundane topics and with relief the President used the remote to turn off the TV.

"He's good at his job," Deaver said.

"Yes, he is," Carver replied. "I hate keeping him in the dark but it's necessary. Someday I'll apologize to him."

"There was enough hell raised over the deaths of numbers two and three," Flake reminded him. "We were lucky we got our Muslim friends to get the story out about what scumbags they really were."

"Governor Timmons is going to be officially nominated in two weeks," Flake continued. "Then it will be our turn."

"Are you attending the convention, Mr. President?" Deaver asked.

"No," Flake said.

"Yes," the President replied.

"I thought you had decided not to go," Flake said. "Why the change?"

"Julian asked me if I would introduce him for his acceptance speech," Carver answered him. "He caught me off guard and I couldn't think of a good reason to say no."

"Lucky you," Flake said with a large smile. "St. Louis in late August. Enjoy."

"If I'm going, you're going," Carver said.

"Come on," Flake protested. "You don't need me there."

"Relax, Darla's not coming. She's still pissed. She thinks this should be her turn."

Three days later, in the early evening hours after dinner, Darla and her sidekick, Sonja Hayden, were in the White House residential quarters. The two of them were enjoying an adult beverage while watching a campaign rally for Governor Timmons on Fox News.

"I marvel at this man," Darla said making an ironic comment.

"How so?" Sonja asked.

"He's about as interesting, exciting and capable as a monk. How the hell he ever became a governor let alone the nominee of a major political party is beyond me," Darla explained.

"Have you ever met him?"

"Once, many years ago when Tom was the Attorney General in Colorado. We met him at a convention in Chicago for state attorneys general. He was so unimpressive I didn't remember him at all. Tom reminded me a few months ago."

"The President has an amazing memory for people, faces and names," Sonja remarked.

They continued watching the rally, neither saying anything for almost fifteen minutes. Darla finished her drink and handed the glass to Sonja for a refill.

"It's disgusting," Darla said. "I could have crushed this featherweight. Morton will win but we're in danger of losing the Senate because of him."

Darla was looking at her aide when she said this. It was this precise moment that the light went on in her head. She jerked her head around and continued to watch Timmons for another thirty seconds while Sonja refreshed their drinks.

"Yes," Darla whispered to herself. "This will work."

She quickly stood up and while slipping her feet into her shoes said, "Never mind that. We have something more important to do. Come with me."

The two of them went into Darla's bedroom where she quickly found a ring of keys in her dresser. They hurried through the halls and down the stairs of the old mansion until they reached the Oval Office.

"I need to find something," Darla snapped at the agent guarding the door. He stepped aside and the two women went in.

Less than a minute later, after using her key to unlock a secret drawer in the famous desk, Darla held up a single sheet of paper. She scanned down the list of names on it and said, "This is it."

Darla sat down in the President's chair and picked up a notepad of paper with the White House logo on it. She tore off the top sheet, found a pen and quickly copied the names from the list. While she did this, Sonja nervously kept an eye on the doors.

When she finished, Darla put the original typed list back in the drawer, locked it and the two of them left.

Instead of leaving through the door they entered, the two women went out through the secretary's area. On the way, Darla stopped at a copy machine, neatly tore off the White House logo from the sheet of paper and made a single copy of the list. She already had in mind exactly what to do with it. When they were back upstairs, Darla wrote another note on plain stationary, folded it with the handwritten list and placed both in a plain, white, letter size envelope. She wrote a man's name on it then licked and sealed it.

"The convention is next week," Darla said to Sonja as she handed her the envelope, "Get this to him," she continued referring to the name she had written on it. "Tell him to use it Monday, the first day of the convention."

"Yes ma'am," Sonja replied. Having been with Darla as long as she had, Sonja knew exactly what she was up to. Being almost an extension of Darla and the puppy-loyal, toady she was, Sonja did not ask a single question.

TWENTY

Carla Suarez, as usual, beat her boss into the office on Monday morning. This was the first day of the St. Louis convention to nominate Julian Morton for the party's Presidential candidacy. Carla, who was the White House Deputy Chief-of-Staff and whose boss was Noah Flake, was looking forward to a slow news week in the White House. The attention of the media should be on the convention and election.

Carla filled her coffee then went into her office to tackle her first task of the day. It was her job to go through the half dozen newspapers on her desk and pick out stories her boss and the President would want to see. On the top of the stack, lying face down, was the New York Times. Standing at the corner of her desk casually sipping her coffee, Carla picked up the paper and flipped it over to see the front page, top of the fold headline. What she saw and read across the entire front page was like a slap in the face. In large font, bold letters, it read:

ADMINISTRATION TARGETING ISLAMIC CLERICS

Carla took a deep breath, sat down in her executive chair and read the story. When she finished, she quickly went through the other papers to see if any of them had the story. Before she finished, Noah Flake stormed into her office. There was fire in his eyes and knowing he must have heard about it on the news, Carla handed him the Times.

Flake dropped his briefcase and sat in one of the chairs at Carla's desk. He started reading the story and almost immediately stopped. In the very first paragraph, the reporter claimed he had a list of Muslim clerics that was a hit list of Imams who were to be, in his words, hunted down and summarily executed.

When he finished, Flake sat quietly for several seconds staring down at the newspaper on his lap. It was Carla who broke the silence.

"Is there such a list? Are we targeting…"

Flake held up a hand to silence her and said, "Don't ask and you don't say anything to anyone, especially the media. I've probably got a dozen messages on my office phone already and my cell has been buzzing since I got up. That's why I hurried in. I heard this on the morning news, too."

Flake looked at his watch and noted the time as being 6:15 A.M. "I have to get upstairs. Do any of the others have this?" Flake asked referring to the other papers.

"No," Carla replied.

"Okay," Flake said. He stood up and still holding the Times said, "No comment to anyone, including staff, about this."

Seeing his briefcase still on the floor. Carla told him she would put it on his desk. Without answering her, Flake hurried from her office.

Flake sipped his coffee from the White House china while he waited for the explosion. Flake and the President were in the private sitting room next to the President's bedroom. Carver put the paper on the table next to where he sat and calmly swallowed half of the coffee in his cup.

"How the hell did this happen?" he asked his Chief-of-Staff not really expecting an answer.

"There were only three copies," Flake replied. "Yours, the Vice President's and Director Brewster."

"Has to be Brewster," Carver said as he stood up and began pacing about the room still dressed in his pajamas and bathrobe.

"He would be most likely," Flake agreed. "But why? Why would he do this?"

Carver stopped, looked down at the still seated Flake and stood silently thinking for almost a full minute. Obviously, something had occurred to him and when he did not say what it was, Flake asked him.

"Nothing," Carver abruptly answered him. "Nothing," he said again repeating the obvious lie.

"Okay, here's what we do," Carver said, "we hunker down, no comment this and…."

He was interrupted by a knock on the door. Both men turned toward it as Carla Suarez slowly opened it and stuck her head in.

"Excuse me, Mr. President," she said. "I thought you would want to see this. Turn on CNN."

"Come in, Carla, and close the door please," the President said while Flake turned the TV on and found CNN. Of course, the main story was the list of Muslim clerics being targeted as claimed by the New York Times. The story had just taken a turn for the worse.

"WikiLeaks has released what they claim is the list reported by the Times. They also claim there are a total of fourteen names on the list and four of them have already been killed by U.S. drone attacks," the male announcer solemnly reported.

"Thank you, Carla. Please leave us alone for a few minutes," Carver politely told her.

"Yes, sir," she replied. As she opened the door to leave she said to Flake, "I'll be in my office if you need anything."

The two men continued to watch for another ten or twelve minutes until the President had enough and told Flake to shut it off.

"We better get ahead of this," Flake said. "We need to leak it to our media people that these are not benign religious people. They're fanatic, murderous radicals who use children to blow up other Muslims. We can tell them we got the information…"

"No," Carver said cutting him off. "Let's sit on it for a few days and see what the reaction is first."

"You think that's a good idea?"

"I don't know but let's not run around leaking classified information, yet," Carver said.

"The rest of the people on that list are gonna go underground now. We'll be lucky if we find any of them and a lot of people are going to die because of this," Flake said.

"I know," Carver sighed. "WikiLeaks. What a dumbass name. It always makes me think of little boys out playing and waiting too long to go in the house to pee. So they have to run into the bushes and WikiLeaks."

Flake laughed and said, "We should use that at the next press briefing." Turning serious he said, "You better have a meeting with Justin before he meets with the press today."

"Set it up," Carver said. "I'll be down in half an hour. I'll want him, you and Cassandra in my office first thing."

Cassandra was Cassandra Bligh, the communications director. It would be her job to coordinate the messaging from the White House and to make sure that everyone was on the same page.

By the time the President was finished shaving and showering, Al Jazeera was reporting the news of the list and the names on it. Somehow they were able to broadcast pictures of those already dead. By the end of the day, the Muslim world was hysterical. At least two dozen embassies across the region slammed their doors closed and the Marines loaded their weapons. Fortunately, only bottles and rocks were thrown at the buildings. Very little damage was done and there were no American casualties.

There were, however, reports of at least fifty fellow Muslims killed in the rioting. Most of them were killed by their carried away co-religionists who had a difficult time controlling themselves.

There were also a couple dozen calls by the usual suspects for U.N. action. Third world dictators, tyrants and assorted despots never missed an opportunity to blame the West in general and America in particular for their country's problems and bad mouth America in the UN.

"Could you give us a few minutes, please, Sonja?" President Carver asked his wife's talking appendage. He was in the First Lady's office in the East Wing and needed to talk to her alone.

108

"Certainly, Mr. President," Sonja answered him. She gathered up her leather folio and phone then silently left.

"What do you want, Tom?" Darla asked not bothering to hide her annoyance at the interruption.

"Have you been watching the news?" the President asked as he sat down opposite the desk.

"Of course. How are you going to handle it? I think you should…"

"Did you have anything to do with this?" Tom abruptly asked cutting her off.

"Anything to do with what?" she replied. She tried to sound innocent and pulled it off except for the quick blinking of her eyes and a barely noticeable flicker in them as she briefly looked away from him.

"With leaking this information to the Times' reporter," Tom said.

"Of course not! How dare you…"

"Cut the bullshit, Darla. Don't give me the indignation. Did you leak this story to the New York Times?"

Darla leaned forward, glared at her husband for two or three seconds then said, "No! Absolutely not. Why would I?"

"Because I know you. You don't want to follow Julian Morton. You might be thinking it would be easier for you to run in four years and beat Timmons."

"Julian Morton will destroy the party, Tom," Darla replied. "He's weak and should have stayed in the Senate where he was just one of a hundred and couldn't do the damage he'll do as President and you know it. But I had nothing to do with this leak.

"Tom," she continued more softly, "you need to investigate, quietly, anyone who night possibly have access to the list. It could be a good job for Clay. He knows how to do something like that discreetly."

The President watched his wife for a few seconds while she stared right back at him. Finally satisfied, he looked at his watch and stood.

"I have a meeting. I'll see you later. Are you coming to St. Louis on Thursday?"

"Are you flying back on Thursday night after the festivities?" she asked.

"Yes. You should be there," he replied.

"Okay," she said and stood herself. She came around the desk, put her hands on the President's cheeks, pulled his face down and kissed him.

"You're right," she said. "Party unity. Besides, I'm beginning to like the idea of being in the Senate. It will be good experience."

After he left Darla's office, while walking back to the West Wing, the President replayed the little drama that had just taken place. No matter how sincere she acted, he knew she was lying.

Sonja saw the President leave Darla's office. She quickly went in to find out what had happened. When she got back to her boss, Darla was staring out a window deep in thought. Sonja took a seat and silently waited for her to speak.

"Where is Clay?" Darla asked.

"He's in St. Louis. He's involved with security for the convention and the President's visit," Sonja replied.

"Good. Get a hold of him and tell him I'm going to want to see him when we all get back."

"We're going to St. Louis?"

"Yes," Darla said as she sat down at her desk.

TWENTY-ONE

President Carver sat with his back to the window while the CNN staffer put the finishing touches on his makeup. Darla was seated on a couch patiently waiting for the woman to finish with her husband so the interview could begin.

They were in the Presidential Suite of the Four Seasons Hotel in downtown St. Louis. The window behind the President offered a spectacular view of heartland America. The Gateway Arch, the Mississippi River and the fields of Illinois should have reminded the Carvers of where the real America was.

Tom Carver joined his wife on the couch while the woman who applied the makeup closed the curtain. After a technician finished a light and sound check, the interview was ready to begin.

Because of the revelation on Monday that the government was targeting Islamic clerics, every media source in America had been yammering for a Presidential interview. The White House press secretary had a very tough week staying on message with denials and spinning the story the political people had come up with. The entire episode was being blamed on the Russians. They were the ones who had made up and then leaked the so-called "Hit List" in an attempt to embarrass President Carver and influence the election.

This interview with CNN had been agreed to because the reporter, John Forsyth, was well known for pitching softballs to anyone in power and politically motivated celebrities. The White House communications staff, the ones who had set it up, made it clear that the interview was to be about the convention and election only. Besides, the attention span of the American media and people being what it is, the "Hit List" story was already dying down. Even the Muslim world was beginning to settle back to normal.

It was now Thursday afternoon, four days after the list was revealed. The convention news, despite the fact that there really was no news coming from it, was back on the front pages.

Hovering in the room behind the lights and camera were Cassandra Bligh, White House Communications Director, Justin Havens, the President's press secretary and the omnipresent Sonja Hayden.

Sonja was completely distracted and paid virtually no attention to the interview. She knew her boss could chew up John Forsyth and spit him out if necessary. She also knew that would not be necessary. Most of the questions were almost childishly silly and Darla's face would be sore from the fake smile she wore throughout the interview. Tom and Darla Carver were professionals at handling the media.

What occupied Sonja's thoughts was a conversation, in reality, a bushwhacking, that happened to her in the elevator on her way up to this suite on the 19th floor. While standing in the background not watching the interview, it replayed over and over in her mind.

Sonja stepped onto the empty elevator car, pushed the button for nineteen, and stepped to the back wall while the doors started to close. An instant before the doors came together, a hand grasped hold of one of them causing them to part again. A man she immediately recognized came aboard and looked down at her with an unnerving smile. The doors started to close again when an elderly couple came rushing toward them. The man jammed his thumb on the 'Close Door' button, held up his other hand to the man and woman and said, "Sorry, full," to them.

"Hello, Sonja. I've been looking for a chance to talk to you," Melvin Bullard, the New York Times reporter said to her.

Bullard was a large man. Well over six feet tall and pushing three hundred pounds. He was also a very homely, if not downright ugly man with a large nose veined from alcohol abuse and dull teeth stained by cigarettes. Sonja often thought it was a shame that such a hideous creature was endowed with a great, full head of still dark hair.

"What do you want, Melvin?" Sonja asked.

"I want you to pass on something to your boss. You see, I expect to get exclusive information from you two from now on."

"Don't count on it," Sonja said.

"Oh, I *am* counting on it. I don't know if you read what was in the envelope you gave me, but what Mrs. Carver passed along, well, she requested that I destroy it. A foolish mistake. I haven't destroyed it and I'm not going to. You see it's in her handwriting and I'll bet her fingerprints and DNA are all over it."

With that, he took another step toward Sonja and with a serious look quietly said, "So don't give me any shit about you not cooperating. In fact," he continued, "I have kind of thing for Darla Carver. An attractive woman with a lot of power is a turn on, I have a nice hot tub at my house. The three of us should get together for a little threesome. My treat."

At that moment the elevator car arrived on nineteen. As the doors started to open, Sonja, her stomach convulsing, stepped around the reporter.

"I'm looking forward to it," Bullard said to her back as she hurried through the opening to get away from him.

While the President and First Lady were being interviewed in St. Louis, Omar Hussain, an American-born Muslim of Syrian heritage, was driving a van through the Lincoln Tunnel in New York. He was going to Midtown Manhattan from his home in New Jersey.

Four days ago, Monday afternoon, Omar was walking out of the Union Station subway when his conversion to radical Islam became complete. At nineteen, like most teenagers and young men, he was undergoing a crisis of identity. His parents and siblings were mostly Muslim in name only. This, of course, was also Omar's attitude for most of his life. Then two years ago he was befriended by Ali, a man several years his senior. It was Ali and Imam Nader who had opened his eyes to the wickedness of America and its determination to eradicate Islam.

On Monday Omar had exited the subway station, one of the busiest in the city, and while bothering no one, was accosted by four young men. They swore at him, called him the vilest names and joked about the murders of Imams by the Americans. Omar had glared at the four imbeciles which caused two of them to spit on him.

Despite the fact that at least a dozen passersby berated these infantile morons, Omar made up his mind at that moment. He admitted to himself his hatred for America and determined that he would strike a blow at the Great Satan.

This morning while the friends of Ali prepared the explosive in the van, Omar made his peace with Allah. He also made a suicide video to be released by the Circle of Islam after the event. Omar was so certain of the righteousness of his cause he was impatient to begin. Plus, being a virgin himself, the thought of the seventy-two virgins awaiting him filled him with a warm glow.

Omar drove south to 14th Street and turned left to go east to his destination.

The interview was completed and ready for editing, the CNN crew was wrapping up and putting away their equipment. John Forsyth, practically drooling over the President and First Lady was obsequiously thanking them.

Simultaneously, Sonja's phone went off and Noah Flake burst into the room. Upon seeing the TV crew still there, Flake stopped dead in his tracks. President Carver saw the look on Flake's face and knew that something was up and it was not good news.

"Oh my God!" Sonja practically yelled into her phone. "Are you sure?"

Flake heard Sonja's exclamations and correctly assumed she was receiving the same news he had. He looked at her, held an index finger to his lips and shook his head at the same time. Forsyth, although a very pretty, well-groomed man and not the brightest bulb, was able to pick up that something serious had happened.

"I'm sorry, I have to ask you to clear the room," Flake loudly announced. He went back to the door, held it open and began demanding that everyone but Sonja, Darla and the President get out. He even told the TV crew to leave any equipment they had to but to exit right away and come back for it later.

When they were gone, the President said, "They're going to want to know why you threw them out."

Flake, walking to the TV, replied, "They'll know in a minute anyway."

He turned on the television and the four of them took chairs to watch the news. With a mixture of horror, anger and revulsion, they sat silently watching in while the cameras brought them the scene in New York.

The suicide bomber had driven an older, gray van into the middle of Union Square Station. It was rush hour and there were hundreds of people rushing about. In addition, it was a beautiful late summer day and the area was more crowded than normal. According to surviving witnesses, an Arabic looking man stopped the van in mid-traffic and blew it up. First responders believe that the bomb was not just an explosive device. There were clear signs that the device had been covered with hundreds of metal objects. Things such as ball bearings, screws, nuts and bolts had been attached to turn the bomb into an enormous Claymore mine. Of course, this also significantly increased the carnage and casualty list.

"Get that, will you please, Sonja?" the President quietly asked referring to a knock on the door.

Sonja opened the door and found the Julian Morton standing there amid a small crowd of Secret Service agents. Sonja stepped aside to let him pass into the President's suite.

"Any word on casualties?" Morton asked as he took a seat.

"The TV people are guessing but saying at least fifty dead and a couple hundred injured," Tom Carver replied.

The President's personal phone rang for about the tenth time only this time he did not ignore it. His National Security Advisor, David Deaver had been calling since the news hit the air. He talked quietly with Deaver who had no more information than the President. The conversation lasted less than two minutes.

"What about tonight?" Morton asked referring to his nomination acceptance.

"Noah," Carver said, "set up a press briefing for an hour from now. Get a statement ready for me. Wait, make that thirty minutes. We need to assure the nation.

"Julian, we obviously can't act as if nothing happened but we'll go forward."

"I'll amend my speech to include a statement about hunting these people down and bringing them to justice," Morton replied.

A much-subdued convention completed the formality of nominating Julian Morton to succeed Thomas Carver. By the middle of the following week, the terrible toll of the attack by Omar Hussain would be one hundred twelve dead, including four children under age ten. In addition, there was another two hundred twenty-seven injured of which nineteen had lost an arm, a leg, one of each or both.

Twenty-four hours after the attack, Omar's suicide video, blaming America for all of the evil in the world, was released. Omar's statement, having been written for him, included a five-minute rant about the hatred Americans had toward Muslims. He also accused the American government of the cowardly, vicious murders of peace loving Muslim Imams with missile strikes.

This last part was given an inordinate amount of air time by the U.S. media. Al Jazeera replayed the entire statement with an Arabic translation more than thirty times. Of course, the news of the attack sent the Muslim world into a frenzy of celebration that cost the lives of at least twenty Muslims enjoying the festivities.

A small army of FBI agents descended on Omar's former life. Within a few days all of Omar's co-conspirators, including Imam Rasheed, were identified. Unfortunately, every one of them was gone. It would be two years before they were all located and quietly brought to a well-deserved final justice.

TWENTY-TWO

In the southeast corner of the White House living quarters is the Queen's Bedroom. This bedroom is called the Queen's Bedroom because it is specifically reserved for Queen Elizabeth II of the United Kingdom. When the Carvers moved in, Darla latched onto it as her own bedroom. Since sharing a bedroom with her husband was out of the question, what better place for her than a bedroom reserved for a real queen? Of course, when the real Queen Elizabeth II found out about this, she made it clear there would be no trips scheduled to the White House while the Carvers were in residence.

Attached to the Queen's Bedroom was the Queen's Sitting Room. Darla had this room redecorated and new locks installed to assure her privacy to use it away from the prying eyes and gossiping lips of the White House staff. Not trusting anyone, especially her husband, Darla had Clay Dean sweep it for bugs—listening devices—at least once a week. Being more loyal to the President than he was to Darla, Clay told the President this who had a hearty laugh over his wife's paranoia. It was in this room that Darla and Clay, along with Sonja Hayden, held a very special, private meeting in early October, less than five weeks before the election.

"What progress have you made with the reporter?" Darla asked Clay. She was referring to Melvin Bullard.

"He is still being protected twenty-four-seven by armed guards provided by the Times," Clay answered. "After the attack before Labor Day during the convention, he received so many death threats..."

"Yes, yes, I know all that" Darla interrupted him, annoyance in her voice.

"But from what I hear, things are quieting down and the Times is getting tired of the expense," Clay said.

"Goddammit!" Darla exploded. "The sonofabitch is blackmailing me, Clay."

"I understand," Clay calmly replied. "Maybe this weekend. Be a little patient, Darla. I can't get to him for a private chat while he's being protected like this."

"I know, I know," Darla replied more calmly. "It's just, well, it needs to be done soon. It can't wait until after the election."

"I understand," Clay calmly said again.

"Are you all set with the other thing?" Darla asked Clay.

"Yes, I've told you that before," Clay answered her. "All I need is a chance to talk to the reporter."

116

"What if Bullard comes forward? What if he changes his mind? The last time he contacted me," Sonja said, "he was getting impatient. He said he wanted…"

"I don't give a damn what he wants," Darla interrupted her, "He's blackmailing the President's wife. It needs to be stopped. Besides, he would go to prison."

"If he survived long enough," Clay added.

"So, we're ready for our October surprise?" Darla asked Clay.

"Yes," Clay said. "All set. As soon as I can have a little chat with the fat man."

Clay Dean was a loyal "soldier" for the Carvers. Ever since Tom had gone out of this way to help his daughter beat cancer, Clay was Tom Carver's man, body and soul.

Because Darla was married to his master, Clay would do anything for her, too. In fact, he had, up to and including murder. And he had done so without batting an eye or giving it a second thought. He so thoroughly believed in the Carvers that for Clay, the ends really did justify the means.

The problem with this latest assignment was not the deed itself. In fact, Clay could not help but admire Darla for coming up with it. A very intelligent and clever man himself, Clay was even a bit awed by Darla's ingenuity. Even if there were a couple of loose ends to clean up, the most serious complication with this project was keeping the number of people involved down to a minimum. So far there were only three Confederates he had used and two of them would have to go. They were collateral damage to be disposed of, for the greater good.

Clay Dean, seated alone in a nondescript Chevy he had rented with a fake ID, watched the front of the apartment building. He was parked on Third, a few blocks from Central Park. It was nine o'clock Saturday evening and New York was covered with a light rain that made Clay think he was in a 40's film noir movie.

He had been on station for over an hour. While he watched he smiled whenever the doorman took an occasional nip from a flask he kept in his uniform pocket. While he patiently waited, he could not help wonder how a prostitute could afford an apartment on the Upper East Side of Manhattan. She must be exceptionally good at her trade which begged the question, how could a New York Times reporter afford her?

At precisely 9:30, the hooker, making excellent use of her time, hustled Clay's quarry to the building exit. Melvin Bullard stood under the building's canopy and lit a small cigar. He turned the collar of his overcoat up and smoked while waiting for a cab to come along. While he continued to watch the man, Clay could not help thinking, *if I was a woman there isn't enough money in the world to get me to do this hideous clown.*

Right on schedule, the cab that Clay had signaled when Bullard came out of the building, arrived. The driver pulled it over to the curb. The doorman opened the door for Bullard as he tossed the cigar onto the wet street. He got in back and the cab pulled away with Clay following in his rental. He was able to stay well behind the cab because he knew what its destination was. It also gave him the opportunity to be sure no one else was following the reporter.

Clay looked at his watch then back at the fat man in the chair. They were in the basement of a rented home in Union City, New Jersey. Clay was sitting on an uncomfortable, metal folding chair. On each side of him was a powerful spotlight on a five-foot metal tripod pointed directly at Melvin Bullard. He had been gassed into unconsciousness in the back of the cab. The cab was on its way back to Manhattan to be left on a street by itself, unlocked, motor running with the keys in it.

Bullard started making grunting and groaning noises as the effect of the gas wore off. In another minute or two he would be back and Clay could get the information from him. Bullard was strapped to a chair with metal arms. Attached to the chair's arms was an ordinary set of jumper cables. These were connected to the home's electrical power system. Clay sincerely doubted the use of the cables would be necessary but why not be prepared?

Bullard shook his head a couple of times, tried and failed to move his arms, then squinted at the lights while looking at the silhouette of Clay.

"Who," he started to say, then stopped to clear his throat. "Who are you?"

"I need some information," Clay replied.

"About what?" Bullard asked trying to shield his eyes from the lights. "Do you know who I am? You're in a lot of trouble, asshole."

"Of course I know who you are, moron. Now, shut up until I tell you to speak."

"Go to hell! Let me go right now!"

Clay loudly exhaled, bent down and picked up a device off the floor. It was an electric current inducer. Turn the dial and electricity would flow at an increasing rate. Clay turned it to the lowest setting and Bullard yelped and tried to jump out of the chair.

"It gets worse from here," Clay said.

"You bastard. Are you going to torture me?"

"Only if you make me. Now, shut up and listen. Where is the list of Muslim names you were given? The ones to be killed by the drone attacks?"

"I can't tell you that. Besides, what good would it do you? It's already been published."

Clay turned the dial again, this time a little farther.

"Ahhh! Sonofabitch. Why…"

Clay gave him another jolt, he screamed a little louder and began sweating profusely.

"The room is soundproof. No one will hear you."

"Okay, okay," Bullard muttered. "Please stop. I'll tell you."

"Remember, if you lie to me, it will only make things worse."

At 3:00 A.M. Clay and another man, a lean, muscular, rough-looking former Special Forces compatriot of Clay's entered Bullard's two-bedroom Manhattan apartment. Clay found it amusing that Bullard could not afford a place with a doorman but his hooker friend could.

Having been provided with the alarm code and exact layout, Clay knew exactly where to go. While his friend stood guard, Clay went into the bedroom Bullard used as an office. Wearing surgical gloves, he found the items he wanted taped under the desk's middle drawer inside a manila envelope, exactly where Bullard said they would be. Clay then removed a single sheet of stationary from his inside coat pocket, placed it in the manila envelope and taped it back on the underside of the drawer. The two men were back in Clay's rental and on their way in less than three minutes.

That same Sunday morning, two shabbily dressed men were seated on a pier near the Holland Tunnel. It was barely 10:00 A.M. and the two men were already drunk from the cheap wine they shared. They were also fishing in the Hudson River, or at least giving the appearance of fishing.

"What's that, Henry?" one of the men asked his inebriated friend.

"What's what?" Henry replied.

"There, dumbass," the man said pointing at an object in the river. "That thing floatin' right over there."

Henry set the bag-covered wine bottle down, peered at the spot his friend was pointing toward and waited for his eyes to focus.

"Holy shit," Henry said. "I think that's a body."

Special Agent Sam Arnold was in his fifteenth year with the FBI. He had been transferred to the Manhattan office two years ago and he came to hate New York with a passion. In fact, he was seriously thinking

119

about getting out. Today, a Sunday afternoon, he and his partner, Gayle Lockett, had been called by their boss and told to get to the apartment of a New York Times reporter.

Both Sam and Gayle knew Melvin Bullard and neither shed a tear when they heard his fat-ass was dragged out of the Hudson. Of course, since it was one of their own, every reporter in America was howling about the apparent murder. The Republic was in dire peril because one asshole journalist had been thrown in a river. Sam had laughed.

When they arrived at Bullard's apartment there was already a crime scene team there going over the place. Sam's orders were to get in there and find the list Bullard had been given with the names of radical clerics on it.

The two agents went over every scrap of paper in the place. When they finished that, starting in the bedroom/office, they went to work on tearing the place apart. Sam went after the desk and within five minutes found the envelope taped to the underside of the middle drawer.

Wearing gloves, he carefully removed the single sheet of paper. It was folded into thirds and he unfolded it while Gayle looked over his shoulder.

"Gotcha," Gayle quietly said.

When Clay arrived back at the house where he was holding Bullard, he gave his two co-conspirators their instructions. Neither of them had any knowledge about what Bullard had told Clay, nor did they have any interest in it or what Clay had found. They were well paid, which they knew came with orders to keep their mouths shut.

Clay drove to the Newark airport, returned the rental and caught an early flight to Washington.

Back at his apartment, he put surgical gloves on again to handle the items found at Bullard's. Darla had only requested that he find the list. She had said nothing about the envelope or the note she had written to Bullard. Having been told by Sonja that the note and the envelope were destroyed led Clay to believe Darla did not know they still existed.

Clay had all three items laid out on a kitchen counter. Having seen Darla's handwriting hundreds of times over the years he clearly recognized that she had written the list, the note and Bullard's name on the envelope. Clay stared at the three items trying to decide what to do. "How much do you really trust Darla Carver?" Clay quietly asked himself.

He retrieved a Ziploc plastic bag from a cupboard and placed the envelope and note in it. Later, he would get a copy of the list and keep it as well. What to do with the original was the decision he needed to make.

TWENTY-THREE

Clay Dean was a familiar face to the President's secretarial staff. It was not unusual for them to see him around the office and with the President himself. No one seemed to know exactly what he did or what his job title was. Formally he was listed on the payroll as an advisor to the President. This, of course, was ambiguous enough to cover a multitude of sins.

The Monday afternoon following the death of Melvin Bullard, Clay showed up outside the Oval Office. He went straight to the woman nearest the back door leading to the office, smiled his best smile, gave her a note stapled closed and asked her to slip it to the President. The note was a request for a private, after-hours meeting with just the two of them.

The secretary, Marlys, went in right away while Clay waited for a response. She was back in less than a minute with his answer. He would have time for Clay at 6:00 P.M.

At 5:45 Clay took a seat along the wall opposite Marlys' desk. Exactly fifteen minutes later, the President opened the Oval Office door and gestured for Clay to join him.

Carver closed the door behind Clay, patted him affectionately on the shoulder and said, "What's up? You look awfully serious. What's on your mind?"

The two men sat down on separate couches facing each other. Carver patiently waited for his man to begin.

"Mr. President, I'm not sure you're aware of something and it's time you were told," Clay began.

He reached into the inside pocket of his suit coat and removed a clear, plastic, Ziploc bag. Inside was a single sheet of notepaper with handwriting on it.

"This is the list of Muslim Imams that the reporter was given," he said as he handed it to the President. "I know it is genuine because I retrieved it from him early Sunday morning."

The President held up the bag and looked at the note. When he saw the handwriting he immediately recognized it and the color drained from his face. He stared at it for a minute then looked at Clay.

"Do you recognize the handwriting?" the President asked him.

"Yes, sir."

"Have you told anyone?"

"Of course not, sir," Clay said sounding almost offended.

"Sorry," Carver softly said. "I should have known you wouldn't."

The President lowered his chin and held the bag in his right hand between his knees while looking at it.

"Jesus Christ, Darla. What the hell have you done?" he quietly asked himself. He looked up at Clay again and said. "There's more, isn't there?"

"Yes, sir," Clay replied.

"Okay. Let's have it. I want all of it, everything you know. And don't worry about Darla retaliating."

It took almost a half-hour for Clay to go through everything up to and including the murder of Melvin Bullard. What should have been a shock to the President, the murder of a prominent reporter for the Times, barely caused him to blink.

When he finished, an extremely angry Tom Carver went to his desk and buzzed the secretaries.

"Find my wife. I don't care where she is. Tell her she is to meet me upstairs in the sitting room next to my bedroom."

He looked at Clay and said, "Is that everything?"

"Everything I know, Mr. President," Clay replied.

"Okay, let's go."

The instant Darla entered the room and saw Clay and the look on her husband's face, she knew what this was about. Instead of being concerned, she decided to go on offense and take charge.

"Clay," she began, "will you excuse us, please?"

"He stays," the President said.

"No, he doesn't," Darla replied. She walked across the room to the small stand of liquor and mixed herself a sharp vodka tonic.

"Go ahead, Clay," the President quietly said. "Wait for me down the hall," he continued clearly defeated by Darla's presence.

Darla turned back to her husband and waited for Clay to leave. She took a healthy swallow of her drink, looked at Tom and sharply asked, "What?"

In response, the President silently held up the bag with the list in it.

"He got it back. Good. I've been calling him for two days wondering if he did," Darla said. She stepped over to Tom and took the bag from his hand. She looked at the list.

"That was pretty stupid of me to put it in my handwriting. I thought that fat asshole from the Times would be cooperative."

"Darla," Tom said looking directly at his wife, "are you out of your goddamn mind? You've committed treason, for chrissakes."

"Oh, stop it," Darla said. She put her glass on a table, opened the bag and removed the list. "You're being hysterical. We, you and I, cannot commit treason. We, collectively, are the Presidency. Remember?"

122

"Why?" Tom asked.

"Sit down, Tom," Darla said.

She took the list and tore it into a dozen pieces and tossed it into a wastebasket by the bar. She sat down in a chair next to her husband and calmly, as if speaking to a child, explained.

"If we let Julian Morton get elected, there is no way I will succeed him. He's weak, lazy, inept and will do a terrible job and you know it. If he's elected it will be at least eight years after him before our party nominates a candidate that can win."

"You don't know that," the President said but he sounded uncertain when he said it.

"And if he were to miraculously win two terms, it will be sixteen years, maybe more, before I could run and win. By then, it will be too late. No, it is four years from now. We get that fool Timmons elected then I run in four years and kick his worthless ass."

"But why…"

"We needed a scandal. Did Clay tell you who our patsy is?"

"Yes, and I'm appalled," Tom said.

"Oh, bullshit you are. In fact, I know you well enough to know if you had thought of it you would think it's a brilliant idea."

"The country is going to explode," Tom said.

"I'm counting on it," Darla laughed. "And Julian Morton is going to have it tied to his political tail."

"What about my legacy?"

"You are going to get the credit for finding out what happened. Don't worry. It's all falling into place. You'll see," Darla said. She stood up preparing to leave then said, "Have the guys sneak in your latest little girlfriend. Have a good time. Remember," she continued smiling down at her thoroughly whipped husband, "leave the politics to me."

While Clay was having his meeting in the Oval Office with the President, another meeting was taking place. It was in the conference room of the FBI Director, Peter Wiggins. Six members of the FBI, including Wiggins' number two, Sharon Parson and the team who were handling the investigation, attended it.

Wiggins was seated at the head of the conference room table silently reading a report. It was the third time the director read through it and the others in the room were trying to remain patient.

"Are you sure about this?" Wiggins said when he finished. He placed the document in front of himself, removed his reading glasses and spoke to the deputy director.

"Yes," Parson replied. "Those are his fingerprints all over the list. We've tested them several times."

"Jesus Christ," Wiggins quietly said shaking his head. "You realize what this is?"

"It's a political nuclear bomb," Parson answered him. "Peter, we can't sit on this. Election or no election, we have to do…"

"I know, Sheila," Wiggins said holding up a hand to stop her. "Okay," he continued as he looked at everyone seated around the table. "We have to be one hundred percent perfect on this. No screw-ups. Every 'i' dotted and 't' crossed perfectly. This is going to be an explosion of historic proportions and if we screw up anything, this agency will be in for holy hell.

"Janice, do you have everything lined up?" he asked the Special Agent in Charge, Janice Coffey. It was Janice who was lead agent of this investigation team.

"Yes, Director, We've been over it with a fine tooth comb and everything is in order. Arrest warrant, search warrants, supporting affidavits and reports, all are in order," Coffey replied.

Despite her calm, assured exterior, Janice Coffey wished someone, anyone else was sitting where she was. If anyone messed up even one little thing, it would be her ass lopped off.

"The subject is under surveillance and I just got a text that he is home," she said.

"We have a net over him," Sheila Parson added.

"When do you plan on making the arrest?" Wiggins asked.

"When he leaves for work in the morning," Coffey replied. "We'll execute both the search warrants at his home and office."

"For God's sake," Wiggins implored, "be gentle at the office. Restrict yourself to his work area only."

"Yes, sir," Coffey said.

While one of the uniformed Secret Service guards checked her lunch container, Hyun Kang showed her ID card to the other one. This was a daily ritual the South Korean woman went through each day as she arrived for work. Hyun was a member of the White House cleaning staff. She was on the day shift which started at 6:00 A.M. Hyun was assigned to the upstairs residence and spent each day cleaning the second floor quarters.

Hyun was in her twelfth year of employment and was generally quite happy with her job. Most of the people in the White House were polite and courteous, especially the President himself. It was not unusual for Hyun to see either or both of the First Couple. Fortunately, the rude, spoiled children had moved out leaving only Darla Carver to deal with. Most days, the First Lady acted as if Hyun was invisible.

By 3:00 P.M., as usual, she was finished with her duties and her shift. While preparing to leave she was able to sneak the small, white plastic garbage bag into her empty lunch container. While cleaning the President's Sitting Room, she emptied the wastebasket and replaced the garbage bag. She had noticed several scraps of torn paper in it and would give these to her nephew. He was collecting these things for his personal interest in White House history, or so he told her. Hyun never really understood why he wanted trash from the White House. But he was her favorite nephew and to please him she occasionally brought him things he might like.

That evening, wearing blue surgical gloves, Hyun's nephew, Jae Pak, carefully placed the scraps of torn paper on a table. It took him about three minutes to reassemble them but when he did, he believed he might have something of value for the friend who would pay him for this.

TWENTY-FOUR

Samir Kamel was an American success story worthy of Hollywood. Samir—Sammy to all who knew him—was a thirty-one-year-old graduate of West Point and an Army major. He was also an immigrant and naturalized citizen having been born in Egypt. His father and mother, Jahid and Dendera Kamel, had moved to America when Sammy was still a toddler. Four siblings, two boys and two girls, came along within a few years. When Sammy was five, the family moved to Minnesota and significantly prospered. Jahid was a shrewd and intelligent businessman.

By the time they moved to Minnesota, the parents and Sammy had become American citizens. Growing up, Sammy, a very good-looking boy with his mother's thick, black hair and dark eyes, had little trouble attracting girls. He was also a fair athlete who grew to love American baseball, somewhat to Jahid's displeasure, a die-hard soccer fan who still followed a couple of Egyptian teams.

With excellent grades and his successful father's political connections, Sammy was accepted to the US Military Academy at West Point. He graduated in the top one-third of his class and opted to become an infantry officer.

Sammy saw combat in Afghanistan and Iraq. Because he was taught Arabic at home, he was eventually transferred to Military Intelligence. Several commendations followed and two years ago he applied for and was accepted to be a member of Vice President Morton's National Security Advisor's staff.

On an Army major's salary, living in expensive Washington on his own was next to impossible. Even across the river in Alexandria required that he have a roommate. Despite his family's wealth, Sammy always insisted on getting by on his own. Fortunately, he was able to find a colleague to room with him. Captain Oliver Edgar Townsend III, an offspring of a Massachusetts Brahmin Family with roots going back to pre-Revolution days.

Oliver's family was also very well off and unlike Sammy, Oliver had no qualms about living off of his family's trust fund. It allowed him to drive his own car, a year-old Mercedes C-class, into the city, have a very nice, expensive apartment and charge Sammy only one-third for his share of the rent. Since the two of them worked together on the Veep's NSA staff, Sammy was not above accepting rides into work. Recently, though, Sammy had started detecting a touch of anti-Muslim prejudice in his roommate. Being a casual Muslim, at best, the little remarks he picked up from Oliver did not really bother him. But there was something in the back of his mind that was sending tiny warning signals to him.

This morning Oliver had left early claiming he had a report to prepare by 8:00 A.M. This meant Sammy would have to ride the Metro to work. For some reason, he actually felt a little relief at not having to listen to his obnoxious roommate making snide comments about all of the little people. Especially the "little-colored people" as he called them.

Sammy checked himself in the mirror in the hallway, as he always did, one last time before heading out. He was a proud soldier and took pride in his appearance and bearing. He placed his officer's hat on, checked it to be sure he had it just right, then went into the living room. When he got there, he was startled by a knock on his door. Before he had a chance to take even one step toward it, the door blew open and the next thing Sammy knew he was on the floor with his hands cuffed behind his back. For the next hour, he laid on his living room floor like this while a team of FBI agents tore the apartment apart. Several times Sammy tried to ask a question only to have one of them scream in his ear to shut up.

While Sammy's apartment was being ransacked under color of a valid search warrant, Special Agent in Charge Janice Coffey was meeting with the Julian Morton's Chief-of-Staff. Coffey had coordinated her entry into the Veep's offices in the Old Executive Office Building next door to the White House with the entry team at Sammy's apartment. Having called ahead to inform the Chief-of-Staff, Leo Enzler, they were coming, Coffey anticipated no problems. While she talked to Enzler and showed him the warrant, the two agents she had brought along stood guard at Sammy's cubicle.

"This is outrageous," Enzler almost bellowed. "The FBI is serving a search warrant on the office of the Vice President! A man who will be the next President of the United States. Are you crazy? Before you do anything, I'm calling our chief counsel."

"Sir, you are free to call whomever you choose," Coffey politely replied. They were in Enzler's office and Coffey was glad she had closed the door. "But we're going to search Major Kamel's workstation. We'll be careful and respectful but…"

"Get the hell out of my office," Enzler practically screamed, "and kiss your career goodbye!"

"Yes, sir," Coffey politely said then quickly exited closing the door behind her.

It took less than thirty minutes for the three FBI agents to confiscate and box up everything from Sammy's workstation. His immediate supervisor almost turned purple she was so angry while they did it. Coffey showed her the search warrant and explained that the agents all had the necessary security clearances. Coffey assured her that any classified material would be completely safeguarded. Coffey sincerely hoped that was true.

While this was taking place, everyone on the Veep's security council staff gathered to watch. There were several loud protests, ignored by Coffey and her agents. Silently watching with a grim, disapproving look on his face to match his co-workers was Captain Oliver Townsend. The look on his face showed grave concern over this intrusion. He even joined in and made a couple of derisive comments about the FBI. Inside he could not have been happier.

It was the desire of the FBI to keep the arrest of Major Samir Kamel quiet for as long as possible. The handwritten list found in the apartment of Melvin Bullard had been checked for fingerprints. There were six clear prints and several too smudged to read. Of the six, every one of them belonged to Major Kamel. Because Sammy was an officer with a security clearance, his prints were in the FBI database. There were none that could be from Bullard. The techs chalked this up to the man having enough sense to use gloves while handling it.

They also dusted the envelope the list was in from the underside of Bullard's desk and found no prints of anyone. This fact was also attributed to Bullard wearing gloves.

The fingerprint evidence was courtesy of a blank sheet of paper taken by Captain Townsend after he saw Sammy handle it. It was also enough for an arrest warrant and search warrants for his home, car and workplace. The list of names written on the sheet of paper was courtesy of Clay Dean and an excellent forger. The FBI was trying to keep the arrest quiet until they could come up with more evidence. What they especially wanted was a handwriting analysis to compare Sammy's writing to the envelope. Again courtesy of a note pilfered from Sammy's desk by Oliver Townsend, the writing would be a match. Washington being Washington, the news of Sammy's arrest was kept secret for almost four hours.

President Carver heard about it the same way and at the same time as everyone else. In midafternoon, Noah Flake came into his work office and turned on the television. It was tuned to CNN, jokingly known as the Carver News Network. They watched together while Flake went from channel to channel. Every one of them was almost breathlessly reporting the same story. An arrest of an aide of Vice President Morton had been made. The list of targeted Muslim clerics had been discovered at the apartment of Melvin Bullard. It was a handwritten list and there were several fingerprints on it that were identified as being from an Army officer, Major Samir Kamel. Three of the news shows even had a picture of Sammy to display.

While he watched, the President's anger and curiosity both spiked upward. When he had finally seen enough, he told Flake to shut off the TV.

"If this is true," Flake said, "Julian Morton is finished. Timmons will hang this right around his neck. How can he be trusted with the presidency when this happens right under his nose? I can see the campaign ads now."

"You're probably right," Carver quietly answered him.

"What's wrong?" Flake asked.

Still seated at this desk, Carver looked at his friend and sadly shook his head. "This whole thing sickens me. If this man is a Muslim..."

"Oh shit, I hadn't thought of that," Flake said. "There could be an explosion, a literal as well as a political one."

"Precisely," Carver said. "Well, there's not much we can do about it. Go tell Cassandra and Justin to put out a statement. We cannot comment on an ongoing investigation. You know the drill."

"Yes, sir. We'll take care of it," Flake replied.

Flake had barely closed the door when Carver made a call on a private cell phone he used. Clay Dean answered it before the first ring finished.

"Where are you?" Carver asked.

"Across the street at the Vice President's office," Clay replied.

"Come over here right away. Now," Carver said. "We need to talk."

Jae Pak was in the office of the family's grocery store watching the news on the small flat screen. The announcer was claiming that the original list leaked to the murdered reporter had been found in the reporter's apartment. Jae had checked online and the list of names revealed by WikiLeaks, purchased from Bullard, matched the list he had from the White House. While he watched, something did not seem quite right to him. Perhaps he was simply worried that his list would not be as valuable as he thought.

He checked the clock on the wall and saw it was time to go. Jae had a meeting with the Russian in fifteen minutes. The man had never admitted it but Jae believed he was a member of the staff at the Russian Embassy. Why else would he pay Jae hundreds of dollars for whatever trash his aunt could smuggle out of the White House?

TWENTY-FIVE

Viktor Ivanov's official title with the Russian Embassy was that of an assistant trade representative. In reality, he was a high-ranking member of the SVR, the Russian Foreign Intelligence Service. His official rank would be the equivalent of an army major general. Normally someone with this rank would not be assigned to an embassy. The United States, being what it is, required it. Plus, Ivanov spoke fluent English.

Ivanov was a dedicated Russian patriot. He had also been, when he was obviously much younger, a dedicated party man of the communist regime. He started out as a very young officer in the office of a rising KGB star, Vladimir Putin. When the crash came, Viktor Ivanov was able to ride out the storm and stay out of prison.

Viktor finished his afternoon tea, stubbed out the American cigarette he favored and straightened the paper pile on his desk. Because of his position, Viktor's office was the second most opulent in the embassy. Only the ambassador had a larger, better-appointed room than Viktor.

He looked at the clock and frowned. Viktor had another dull, boring diplomatic party to attend. This time at the Swedish Embassy in a few hours. He quietly laughed to himself at the news of the day. The Americans had made an arrest of an obscure army officer, a man with a Muslim sounding name. Fools that they were, it would take several years to give this traitor a "fair trial". *What a waste,* Viktor thought. In Russia, he would get his fair trial in a matter of months, then a shallow grave.

"Enter," Viktor answered the knock on his door.

A moment later, his number one assistant, a bright and capable young man came in and closed the door.

"Yes, Mikhail, what is it?" Viktor politely asked.

"Sir, I have something you must see," Mikhail Sokolov replied. He had a plastic case in his right hand and held it out for his boss as he approached the desk. He placed it on the blotter in front of Viktor.

"Please, sit," Viktor said. "What am I looking at?"

"It is the pieces placed together of a list of Muslim names," Mikhail began.

"I see that," Viktor shrugged. "So what?"

"These are the names of the Muslim clerics the Americans have been killing with drone strikes. As you can see, sir," he continued, "several of them have check marks next to their names. We have confirmed that these are the ones they have killed, so far."

"So, these are names of the Imams that are making the Muslims go crazy. So what? They are on the internet, are they not?"

130

"Yes, sir. But this list came from the White House. And we have determined who wrote them down."

"Who?" Viktor asked, now genuinely curious.

"It is the handwriting of the First Lady, Darla Carver," Mikhail said.

"That is interesting," Ivanov said his interest elevated. "How do we know this?"

"We have a writing sample, her fingerprints and DNA on file. We obtained them when she visited the Embassy," Mikhail replied. "Sir, we also identified a number of good fingerprints on it, several belonging to her. Plus, we have identified two other fingerprints. They are those of the reporter, Melvin Bullard. We believe this is the real list, the one that was leaked to this Bullard. It is likely it was retrieved, brought back to the White House, and then Melvin Bullard was murdered."

Ivanov bolted upright in his chair and jerked backwards so hard his assistant thought he might tip over. The two men sat silently while Ivanov stared at the plastic case as if it might jump up and bite him. He thought it over for a minute then looked at Mikhail.

"Are you absolutely certain about this?"

"Yes, sir," Mikhail nodded and said. "We have the reporter's fingerprints also. It is standard procedure to add anyone's prints to our database…"

"Yes, yes, I know that," Viktor impatiently said.

"We ran the tests three times by three different technicians. Every time they came back with a ninety-eight or ninety-nine percent match."

"Who else knows about this?"

"The three technicians. I ordered them to tell no one, sir," Mikhail said.

"Are they still in the building?"

"Yes, sir."

"Get them up here. I must talk to them."

A few minutes later Mikhail opened the door and three nervous embassy employees came in.

Viktor came out from behind his desk, smiled at the three men and gestured at a leather couch. "Please, sit down."

The three quickly followed the suggestion.

"I'm not trying to threaten you. I tell you this bluntly so you understand how serious this is," Viktor started out. He picked up the plastic case with the list in it and held it up for them to see.

"Mikhail tells me you three know what this is and who wrote it. First, let me commend you for your good work. Now," he continued, "this is a very dangerous item. I must warn you that if any of you ever speaks to anyone about this, all three of you, and any family you have with you, will be on the next plane back to Moscow. You will be tried for espionage and if you are lucky, only sentenced to a long prison term. Do you understand me?"

All three, too nervous to speak, nodded in unison.

"Good, I tell you this as a friend and for your own good. To protect you. Now you may go and, once again, well done."

The next day, Viktor Ivanov and Mikhail Sokolov, along with a diplomatic pouch held tightly by Mikhail, were in the first class section of an Aeroflot flight to Moscow. Viktor would bring his assistant and the plastic case to a private meeting with his long-time mentor, Vladimir Putin.

The next morning in Minneapolis, Marc Kadella trudged up the back stairs of the Reardon Building. He was on his way back to his office after a pretrial conference downtown. He stopped halfway up the set of creaky, wooden stairs in the old brick building and once again replayed this morning's case, marveling at how idiotic people can sometimes be.

His client, Derek Frazer, was the twenty-one-year-old son of a business client of Chris Grafton's. Chris was one of the lawyers who had an office in the same suite as Marc. Connie Mickelson owned the building, was their landlord and she also had an office with them.

On Derek's twenty-first birthday he had decided to really make a night of it. To celebrate his arrival at the legal drinking age, Derek and friends had started out at a Happy Hour of a well-known sports bar. By 9:30 P.M. Derek had consumed enough shots to get his blood alcohol content up to a staggering 0.27, more than three times the legal limit.

Instead of taking his car keys and putting him in a cab, his pals, probably as drunk as he was, let him drive off to visit an ex-girlfriend. Derek got about a mile away when, on a side street near his destination, he began to bounce off parked cars like a pinball. He finally came to a halt when he crashed into the back end of one of the cars parked in front of a Lutheran church.

Derek managed to get his door open and fall out of the car and onto the street. A small crowd was exiting the church at that moment and they quickly gathered around Derek. A couple of the men, including the owner of the car he rear-ended, helped him to his feet. Instead of being angry and wanting to lynch him for the damage he did to their cars, the people were quite sympathetic and helpful. These were members of Alcoholics Anonymous and had just finished a meeting when young Derek came crashing along. Of course, they were not so sympathetic as to not call the police.

Back in the judge's chambers at the pretrial, the judge, prosecutor and even Marc could not help getting a good laugh out of the irony of the encounter. Derek's severely angry father was picking up the tab for the attorney fees. Marc made the best deal he could, meaning he kept the jail time down to a minimum. After court both Derek and dad thanked Marc for his help and dad assured Marc that his idiot kid was going to repay every dime of the damage he did.

Marc entered the suite of offices and on his way to his private office picked up the A section of the morning paper. Not being a big fan of TV news, Marc had yet to hear about the arrest the day before. He quickly scanned the headlines then the subheading that identified Samir Kamel as a local from Minnesota.

"Oh my, God," Marc said while staring at the paper. "They arrested Sammy!"

He dropped his briefcase at his feet and stood still while he silently read the story. When he said this about Sammy, Connie Michelson came over and stood next to him.

"You know this guy?" she asked.

"Yeah," Marc quietly replied while he continued to read. When he finished he casually held the paper and looked at Connie. He was silent for several seconds while Connie and the staff waited for him to speak.

"I don't believe this for an instant," Marc finally said. "This guy wouldn't... No, no, not a chance."

"Who is he and how do you know him?" Connie asked.

Marc wrinkled his face then said, "Of course, it's been a while, at least ten or twelve years but..."

"But what?" Connie almost yelled.

Marc looked at her as if just now realizing where he was and said, "Samir Kamel. I represented him back when I was with Mickey," Marc said. "Everyone called him Sammy. Great kid. I think he was eighteen at the time. Straight A's in school, never been in trouble. He was at a party that got busted. You know, kids and beer. No big deal. But Sammy had been accepted to West Point. He couldn't have this on his record. So, I got them to divert it subject to dismissal if he had no further problems. I think the old man paid a hundred bucks in court costs.

"But this," Marc said holding up the paper, "this is not the kid I knew. He was the guy you'd want your daughter to bring home."

"Maybe he got radicalized," Connie said.

"I guess," Marc said. "Could be, it's just hard to believe."

133

TWENTY-SIX

Layne Doyle stood with his back to the bathroom mirror. In his left hand was a small, handheld mirror that he held up to get a good look at his ponytail. Lucy Darnell, one of Layne's most devoted acolytes, stood in the doorway watching with the normal adoring look on her face.

Layne Doyle was a sixty-eight-year-old graduate of the 1967 Class of Berkeley with a degree in radical politics. He also held a J.D. from Harvard, Class of '70. Unlike most of his fellow Sixties radicals, Doyle had not caved into the temptation of normal society. Of course, Doyle had never married or taken much responsibility for the seven children he had sired either. Layne Doyle floated far above such petty bourgeois concerns. His calling was to continue the fight against The Establishment, to bring it down and return power to the people. At least that was the image he sold.

In fact, Layne Doyle was a millionaire many times over but not from the practice of law. For Doyle, the law was merely a means to an end and the end was the promotion of Layne Doyle.

His wealth was earned the old-fashioned way; book sales and speaking fees. Over the years Doyle had learned the fine art of injecting himself into causes, and the more inflammatory, the better. His current cause and maybe the best one ever was Samir 'Sammy' Kamel.

"How does it look?" Doyle asked his latest bed warmer, Lucy.

"Perfect," she said smiling while holding up his shabby, tweed sport coat, the one with the fraying elbows. Doyle slipped into the coat then surveyed himself in the mirror. A two-day growth of salt and pepper beard, a twenty-year-old, dingy-brown flannel tie loosened at the collar, a wrinkled blue shirt and worn jeans gave him the exact appearance he wanted. The pro bono warrior for truth and justice was about to have his fourth press conference regarding Sammy Kamel.

"What are you watching?" Tom Carver asked Noah Flake. The President was having a leisurely day and he had wandered into Flake's office. Noah was at his desk, leaning back in his big, leather executive chair, with his feet on the desk watching TV.

The calendar read December ninth and the two men were finding out what being a lame duck President truly meant. After eight years of constant stress, they were both enjoying it immensely.

"The lawyer for Major Kamel is on again," Flake answered his boss.

"He gets more air time these days than I do," the President said as he took a chair to watch. "Is this live?"

"Yeah, it is," Flake answered.

"What's he foaming at the mouth about now?" Carver asked.

"The usual," Flake replied. "The military industrial complex is destroying an innocent man. Samir Kamel is an innocent stooge of the establishment politicians. He can't wait to bring it to trial so he can have twelve honest citizens stick it to the man. Blah, blah, blah. Why do I get the feeling this guy's as phony as a three-dollar bill?"

"Because he is. This reminds me, the Pentagon and the DOJ are fighting over jurisdiction of this case," Carver said.

"I heard," Flake replied. He dropped his feet from his desktop, picked up the TV remote, turned off the set and looked at the President. "So what? What are we supposed to do?" Flake asked.

"I think we should stick it to this asshole," Carver said pointing at the darkened TV, "and give the case to the military."

"Why?"

"This guy is doing everything he can to inflame the situation. It's just now starting to die down. You remember what it was like. Before the election, the country was on fire. Half the people wanted to lynch this guy and the other half wanted to set him free," Carver replied. "Even the DOJ is starting to think it might be better for the military to take it. They can seal off a base from protestors and picking a jury won't be a problem. Plus the judge would issue a gag order with some real teeth in it and shut this guy up."

"What does Rachel have to say about it?" Flake asked referring to the Attorney General.

"I haven't talked to her about it. I thought you could. You know, just let her know which way I'm leaning."

"Is that proper?" Flake asked.

"No, but we have barely six weeks to go. Besides, she doesn't have to listen to me," Carver said. "Who cares if it leaks out that we put in our opinion?"

"Good point."

"Besides, giving it to the military will take it out of the hands of President-elect Timmons and his people. And it will negate this lawyer's attempts to influence the jury pool. Isn't he already confined to quarters at Ft. Myers?" The President asked, referring to the Army post across the Potomac in Arlington.

"Yes, he is," Flake replied. "About the only people allowed to see him are family and lawyers.

"I'll give the attorney general a call and let her know what you're thinking. I'm guessing she may want to let the Army take it, too. Less expense for the DOJ."

"And if they can't convict him, it's on them," Carver interjected.

Just before Christmas, it was announced that the case against Samir Kamel was being given to the Pentagon. As an officer in the U.S. Army, they had jurisdictional rights to the case as did the civil authorities. The U.S. Attorney General decided justice would best be served by allowing Kamel's employer to handle the case.

By this time the nation was almost evenly divided along political lines over Sammy. Thanks to the media attention given to the gang of Sixties radical lawyers—Layne Doyle had brought in three of his pals, two men and one woman—many people, almost half the country if polls were to be believed, saw Sammy as a patsy.

In fact, Sammy had not even been arrested or formally charged, yet.

Under The Uniform Code of Military Justice, Article 32, no charges can be made until there has been a thorough investigation. Because of the indecision regarding who would have jurisdiction, the Army had not assigned an investigator. Due to the holiday season, one was not assigned until after the New Year. This gave Layne Doyle and his cronies opportunity to howl for a couple more weeks about the gross injustice being heaped upon his client. Since Sammy had not been arrested or charged, but merely put on restricted duty, the military's attitude was let them rant and rave all they wanted.

A four-person team from the CID—Criminal Investigation Division—was assigned on January second. Their job was to get the evidence already obtained by the FBI, re-interview witnesses, which was done in a few days, and recommend charges.

It was decided that there would be only one charge, a single count of treason. The Judge Advocate General's office assigned a prosecution team and the case of The United States vs. Major Samir Kamel began.

Sammy's defense lawyers, The Gray Haired Ponytail Team, so dubbed by the media, all arrived at the gate to Ft. Myers. On one side of the entry to the post, on their left, were the protestors supporting Sammy. On the right-hand side of the entryway were those that were in favor of a quick lynching. On both sides, filming it all, were at least a dozen camera crews filming the crowds and the fifteen to twenty MP's keeping the peace.

Layne Doyle himself was behind the wheel of the 1972 rust-bucket Volkswagen van they arrived in. He stopped short of the gate and all four lawyers in tattered old clothes got out for an impromptu press conference leaving the van sitting in front of the gate causing traffic to go around it. The Army master sergeant in charge waited twenty minutes before, politely for the cameras, asking Doyle to move it. Doyle made a nasty comment for the media about fascists then agreed to move along.

The team was present for Sammy's arraignment as was his father. Much like a civilian court, Sammy appeared before a JAG appointed judge, an Army Colonel. He waived reading of the charges, his rights were read to him and he entered a plea of not guilty.

Of course, the media in attendance acted as if this was significant news. All day, TV talking heads replayed the story as if they had received new information about the Kennedy assassination. There was also a number of them hinting at shock because Sammy dared to plead not guilty.

Sammy had been assigned a small house to be used as his quarters. MP's were assigned to it as around-the-clock guards. After the hearing, Sammy was taken back to the house by MP's. The lawyers followed Sammy's dad back to the house for a conference. Most of the discussion centered around the media coverage, the press conference at the gate and courthouse and how well the lawyers had performed for the camera. When this topic was exhausted, Doyle told the others he needed to talk to Sammy and his father, Jahid, alone.

"I haven't brought this up before," Doyle said when the others were outside, "But since I'm not being paid, I need something from you."

The three of them were in the small living room. Sammy and Jahid were seated on the twenty-year-old government provided sofa and Doyle in a chair across from them with a rickety coffee table in between.

"As you know, I do all of my work pro bono. But we do have expenses to cover, not just for your trial, but for everything we do…"

"I can pay you," Jahid interrupted him to say.

"That won't be necessary," Doyle replied with his best, most charming smile. "But what I would like is for you to sign this," he said to Sammy. He pulled a two-page document from his satchel briefcase and laid it on the table.

"It gives me book rights, movie rights, things like that. This is how we fund our free legal clinic to help the poor to protect their rights against what the government is doing to people like you."

Layne Doyle was in Sammy's living room because he had gotten to Jahid before any other lawyer. It was Jahid he had charmed and convinced to let him have Sammy's case. Of course, the DVD Doyle had with him that gave Jahid twenty minutes of Doyle's brilliant career helped do the trick. Sammy, trusting his father's instincts, had gone along with him.

"I see no problem," Jahid said when Sammy looked to him for guidance.

137

Sammy merely shrugged and signed where indicated.

While replacing the document in the briefcase, Doyle continued.

"As we've already discussed, someone has framed you for this and it is going to take some time to find out who. Our investigation team is already working on it but you are going to have to be patient. At least you aren't in jail. It could be worse. But again, we cannot be hurried into court. Remember, time is our ally."

When he got outside, his team members were gathered together by the van. The three of them were passing around their second marijuana cigarette waiting for Doyle.

"Did you get it?" The woman, Aubrey Hollandia, asked as Doyle took a hit from the joint.

"Oh, yeah," Doyle said holding in the smoke.

Hollandia was dressed in wooden clogs and a baggy dress straight from a second-hand store. Doyle passed the smoke to her and she said, "Good. Let's go so I can get out of these rags and into some decent clothes."

TWENTY-SEVEN

TWO YEARS LATER

Assured that Maddy Rivers was going to be all right after being attacked in her apartment, Marc Kadella, with his good friend Tony Carvelli, exited the hospital.

When they reached the sidewalk, Tony said, "That's something, isn't it? All along they had the right guy and didn't know it."

"I feel like an idiot," Marc answered.

"Why? How would you know? Besides, you did your job. I feel bad for Jake though. Threw it all away because he thought he was protecting his brother and look at that now."

"What do you mean?" Marc asked.

"You haven't heard? Daniel Waschke was found in his car in the garage yesterday with the engine running. His wife found him when she came home. Rumor has it he wrote a note to Jake. It says he's innocent. The only thing bothering him was his wife was having an affair," Tony related to an obviously stunned Marc who was staring back at him, his eyes and mouth wide open.

"Well, counselor, it's almost 7:00 A.M. and I've been up most of the night. See you later."

"Wait a minute," Marc said. "How'd you find out about Maddy?"

"Cop friend called me from the hospital. He knew I knew her. I'm gonna take off. See you later," Carvelli said as he turned and walked off down the street.

Marc, still a bit shocked by the events of the past twenty-four hours, strolled over to a small retaining wall that circled the hospital's entryway. He sat down on it watching the light, early morning downtown traffic cruising past him on the wet street. He sat there contemplating those events with a sense of wonder and relief. After about fifteen minutes he heard a voice from beside him say, "Hey sailor, looking for a good time?"

He turned his head toward the voice, smiled at the sight of Margaret Tennant and as his heart picked up a couple beats, said, "God, is it nice to see you."

"How is she?" Margaret asked as she sat down next to him and slipped an arm through his.

"She'll be fine," Marc answered. "With the scars she'll have, no more posing for Playboy anytime soon, but I don't think that's a problem," he said smiling at her as he lightly brushed his fingers across her cheek.

"How about you? How are you doing?" she asked.

139

"Me?" he asked, "I'm okay," he shrugged. "No. No, that's not really true," he continued as he turned away from her to look straight ahead. "I feel a little shitty, truth be told."

"Well, little wonder. The guy you believed was innocent..." she began to say.

"No, that's not the problem. In fact, that doesn't bother me at all," he interrupted her. "You know what's bothering me?"

"What?"

"I'm beginning to believe every rotten thing you've ever heard about lawyers is absolutely true."

"Why?" she asked, laughing softly.

"This morning, on the way down here, after Tony called and told me what happened and I knew that Maddy would be all right, well, all I could think of was: after Carl went out that window, there isn't a snowballs-chance-in-hell that Joe Fornich is going to pay me now."

"Come on," Margaret said as she stood and pulled on Marc's arm. "We'll go down the street to this little restaurant and I'll buy you breakfast."

"Best offer I've had today," Marc said.

"Are you going into the office today?"

"Yeah," Marc replied. "I have a pile of stuff sitting on my desk that I've been neglecting. I better get at it."

When they finished breakfast, Marc and Margaret parted company. The judge had a full calendar and left to walk down Seventh toward the government center and Marc turned back toward the hospital to his car. It was already time to go into the office but first, it was home to shower and change clothes. The biggest trial of his career was over and it was back to the mundane, everyday details of the practice of law. Such as trying to make a living at it.

Marc had barely been in the shower three seconds when he heard the landline phone in his bedroom ring. He ignored it, finished showering and while getting dressed checked the caller ID. It was someone from the office, likely Carolyn Lucas, one of the secretaries and Marc's office mom.

"What's up?" Marc asked. He called back and Carolyn answered the phone.

"First of all, we're all worried to death here," Carolyn said. "How's Maddy?"

"She's gonna be fine. She lost some blood and is a bit beat up. She'll be in the hospital for a day or two, but she'll be fine. Carl didn't make out so well."

140

"Tough shit," Carolyn said. "The reason I called, you have a couple people waiting for you. They called at eight o'clock when I got here and made an appointment for ten. They're already here waiting."

"Okay, thanks. What's it about?"

"You had better come in and talk to them yourself," Carolyn replied.

"Okay, I'll be there in maybe fifteen minutes."

When Marc arrived, everyone in the office quickly surrounded him to find out about Maddy Rivers.

Madeline Rivers was an ex-cop with the Chicago Police Department in her early thirties. In her three-inch heeled suede half-boots she liked to wear, she was over six feet tall. She had a full head of thick dark hair with auburn highlights that fell down over her shoulders, a model gorgeous face and a body worthy of Playboy. In fact, foolishly posing for that magazine was what led her to quit the Chicago P.D.

Maddy, as she was called by her friends, had moved to Minneapolis after quitting the Chicago cops following her Playboy pose. At the same time, she went through an ugly breakup when she found out the doctor she had fallen for was married. After arriving in Minnesota she got a private investigator's license. Maddy was befriended by Tony Carvelli, a private investigator and former Minneapolis detective and she was now doing quite well for herself.

Maddy had worked for Marc on a serial killer case he had finished the day before. She had served as his investigator and had come up with crucial evidence that helped acquit Marc's client. Unfortunately, that client was, in fact, guilty and later that night he had attacked Maddy in her apartment. He likely regretted trying it while he plummeted eight stories down to land on a car. Despite having been knifed by the man, Maddie threw him through her living room window. The police found her passed out on her living room floor and got her to the hospital. Marc was called by their mutual friend, Tony Carvelli.

"So the long and short of it is, she'll be fine with a couple day's rest," Marc announced.

Much to their relief—Maddy had become like one of the office members—the little crowd broke up to go back to work. As they did, Carolyn silently looked at Marc and pointed behind him at the conference room/office law library. Marc turned and through the window he saw two men, one standing at the exterior window with his back to him looking outside and the other seated at the conference room table. The one sitting was dressed in an Army officer's dress blues. On his shoulders were gold-bordered epaulets with the silver eagle of a full colonel.

Marc opened the conference room door and went in. As he did, the well-dressed man staring out the window turned to look at him.

"Mr. Kamel," Marc said instantly recognizing him. Of course, due to his son's situation, Jahid Kamel had been on TV many times the past two years.

"Hello, Marc," the slightly built Egyptian said with a warm smile.

At the same time, the uniformed soldier stood up and extended his hand.

"Earl Dorn," the man said.

Marc shook the man's hand and silently, almost rudely, stared at the man's face. Colonel Earl Dorn was the spitting image of the actor Tommy Lee Jones.

Marc released the man's hand and finally said, "I'm sorry. I didn't mean to stare, but..."

"It's okay," the Colonel smiled. "I'm used to it. In fact, call me 'Tommy', everybody else does."

Back to reality Marc walked around the table to Jahid Kamel and placed his left hand on the man's shoulder while they shook hands.

"How's Sammy holding up?" Marc asked.

"Okay," the older man said with a slight accent. "He's doing better than me."

"Please," Marc said, "have a seat. Let's talk."

Jahid sat down next to Tommy Dorn while Marc went back around the table to a chair opposite the two men.

Marc looked at the Colonel's uniform and recognized the gold crossed feathered pen and sword superimposed on a laurel wreath.

"By the insignia on your collar, Colonel," Marc began, "can I assume you're JAG Corps and one of Sammy's lawyers?"

"I am," the Colonel replied nodding, "and that's why we're here."

Marc looked at Jahid and said, "Mr. Kamel, why don't you tell me why you're here? What can I do for you?"

"It's his lawyers, Marc..."

"The Gray Haired Ponytail Team?" Marc asked. "Yeah I follow the news," he smiled.

"Yes," Jahid said nodding for emphasis. "They do nothing except hold press conferences and talk loudly about how bad America is and how they are here to fight for justice and make the government..."

"I've heard them enough myself," Marc said. He looked at Colonel Dorn and continued, "What you have here are 'cause lawyers'," Marc said making air quotation marks with his hands around the word cause. "Do they seem more concerned with their cause than their client?"

142

"Absolutely," Dorn replied. "In fact, that's where I came in. I was assigned by the judge handling Sammy's case about four months ago. I was appalled at how little they had done."

"And?" Marc said once again looking at Jahid.

"And we're looking for a litigator," Dorn answered for Jahid. "You see, I'm not, or at least, I haven't been for many years. I don't know how familiar you are with the military Marc, but I've been passed over for my star twice and…"

"That means you're on your way out," Marc quietly said.

"Exactly," Dorn said. "I've got almost thirty years in, eight months to go and I'll be expected to retire."

"Sorry," Marc said.

"Oh, don't be," Dorn said with a wry smile. "There are worse things than a thirty-year pension on a full colonel's grade."

"True. Trying to make a living in private practice being one of them," Marc replied causing both men to smile.

"Sammy asked us to come and see you. He wants you, Marc," Jahid said. "We followed your trial in the news and on the internet. He knows you, trusts you, and I will pay."

"I don't know, Jahid," Marc said. "To come in at this late date and try to pick up the pieces, plus, I know nothing about the rules and procedures of military courts martial."

"Trial rules aren't much different than a civilian trial," Dorn said. "Rules of evidence things like that. The biggest difference, about the only real difference, is the jury. You don't get people off the voting rolls. You get military personnel."

"Where's the case, timewise?" Marc asked.

"Well, there's the problem," Dorn replied. "All these guys have done is drag their feet and get one continuance after another. I've spent the last four months filing motions for discovery and to suppress evidence."

"Any luck?" Marc asked.

"I think we have all of the discovery. Actually, there isn't that much evidence. I've lost every fight to suppress any of it. No witness list, yet. But I have a pretty good list of who they'll call based on the evidence but the Gray Haired Ponytail Team has been too busy giving 'stick it to the man' speeches to do any witness interviews."

"Don't you have an investigator?"

"There were a couple assigned by CID. Warrant officers and good investigators. I know both of them and Layne Doyle fired them. He said he wouldn't use military lackeys who would rat out the defense to the, and I quote, 'fascist Nazis framing an innocent man'. You can guess what these two investigators told him."

"What about a trial date?" Marc asked.

"Well, that's another problem. We had a scheduling conference a couple days ago. One of the Ponytail Team showed up. The judge set a trial date and told him no more continuances. Mr. Ponytail went off on the judge and told him he was denying his client all of his rights, blah, blah, blah. The usual blather. He then spent a night in the stockade for contempt. Doyle is really raising hell in the media. The whole thing's a circus."

"It is my fault," Jahid Kamel said. "Hiring them was my idea. This Doyle person, asshole, he convinced me."

Marc sighed and looked at both men knowing he was being drawn in. He had just completed a high profile, media-frenzy case and this one would be worse. Still, he remembered the Kamel family, what good people they are and could feel himself caving in.

"Trial date?" Marc asked.

"Two months," Dorn replied.

"Two months! Are you serious? I can't possibly..."

"There isn't as much evidence as you might think," Dorn said cutting off Marc's protest. "I'll admit what there is, is pretty damning. But what we really need is a good team of investigators to do some digging."

"Please, Marc," Jahid said looking at him with the eyes of a worried parent. "Just come to Washington. Talk to Samir. Look at the case. We are desperate and he trusts you."

Without responding, Marc took out his phone, found the number he wanted and made a call. It took almost ten rings before a groggy voice answered.

"Hello," Tony Carvelli growled.

"Hey, what are you doing?" Marc cheerfully asked him.

"Thinking about how much I'm going to enjoy torturing you before I slowly put you to death. I'm sleeping, goddamnit."

"Why? Never mind. We're going to Washington," Marc said, "not the state, the capital. Anyway, get up and I'll call back with the details."

"Why are we going to Washington?"

"A case. The United States vs. Samir Kamel. It's been in the papers."

"Seriously?" Carvelli asked now wide-awake.

"Yeah, I told you I knew him. His dad and his Army lawyer are here with me. We're just gonna check it out. I haven't agreed to anything."

"Bullshit," Carvelli said. "A case like this is mother's milk to you shysters. You couldn't resist it if your life depended on it."

144

Not wanting to say anything in front of Colonel Dorn and Mr. Kamel, Marc cryptically replied. "Probably. Get your ass out of bed. We've got a plane to catch."

TWENTY-EIGHT

"So, what do you think?" Sally Newport, Indiana's senior senator asked Darla Carver.

The two women were office shopping in the Russell Senate Office Building. It is the oldest of the Senate Office Buildings having been built in 1903. Beautifully ornamented in the Beaux-Arts style, the office they were in was currently occupied by 88-year-old Louisiana Senator Cameron Totz who had announced his retirement and was, for all practical purposes, already gone.

"It's gorgeous," Darla replied. "I thought offices were allocated by seniority. I haven't even been elected yet. The election is still three months away."

"Oh, shit," Newport said waving away Darla's concerns with a flip of the wrist. "The election's a formality and trust me, all we have to do to get what we want is whisper the words 'gender discrimination' and they'll run for cover. A bigger pack of eunuchs you will not find than politicians. In fact, it would be nice if there were a few men around this place. The thought of any kind of discrimination claim will have them in election mode panic. Trust me, we can have this decorated for you before the election."

"Okay," Darla said. "I'll take it. Let's get some lunch."

Twenty minutes later a government limousine pulled up to the curb in front of Gregory's, a trendy, and very expensive, Georgetown restaurant. One of the doormen was ready before the big Lincoln completely stopped. Within a minute the two politically powerful women were seated at a very private table with a view of the garden behind the building.

"Since I no longer have a government expense account," Darla said after the sommelier departed, "looks like this lunch is on your expense account."

"No problem," Newport replied. She held up her glass filled with a two-hundred-dollar per bottle red wine. Darla did the same and they clicked their glasses together.

"How are things between you and Tom?" Newport asked.

"Couldn't be better," Darla replied. "We see each other about once a month, usually at a political function, or fund-raiser. I'll say this for him, the man's bringing in the money. He's getting four hundred grand plus lavish expenses for a speech."

"How's your fundraising going?"

"Good. We have over fifty million already banked," Darla said. "And I have another book coming out in a week."

"I've heard. It's big news. Did you really get a twelve-million-dollar advance?"

"Fourteen," Darla said as she set her glass on the table.

"Will the publisher make that up?" Newport asked.

"Not even close," Darla laughed. "So what? The advance is nonrefundable and they get a nice write-off."

"After the election, Tom's speaking fees will go up," Newport said.

"A lot," Darla replied. "We'll need the money. Since I won't be getting that much, I'll be too busy, he'll need to make it up."

"You need to start a charity, a 501(c) that you can use for living expenses, travel expenses, things like that."

"Tom's doing it. It will be up and running by the time I take office. We already have commitments for over two hundred million. It's a sweet deal. We use the donations as expenses to do work for the charity and we don't have to declare it since it is not a salary. They are expenses incurred on behalf of the charity. Private planes, five star hotels, lavish fundraising meals to gather political support all laid on the charity. And the donations are tax deductible. Plus, we put our staff and friends on the payroll. The taxpayers pay for all of it," Darla said.

The two women smiled at the idea, clicked their glasses together again just as the waiter was arriving.

They ordered seventy-five-dollar shrimp, chicken caesar salads and another bottle of wine.

"Seventy-five bucks for a salad seems a little excessive, doesn't it?" Darla asked.

"Who cares? It's on the generosity of the American taxpayers. Who deserves it more than their faithful public servants?" Newport replied with a wink and a smile.

"I hear the trial of this Samir Kamel for treason may actually get underway soon," Darla said. "What's it been, two years?"

"I'm hearing some things through the grapevine that his lawyers aren't ready. In fact, all they've done so far is rant and rave about the government and how corrupt America is. It looks like they want to put the government on trial claiming this Muslim traitor was framed," Newport said.

"Do they have anything?" Darla coyly asked.

"Who knows? I doubt it. All these 60s assholes do is piss and moan about the government. They're all trying to relive the glory days of their youth when they were protesting the war. Hell, half of these dipshits weren't even there. Or if they were, they were social misfits hanging around the fringes hoping they might get a date and maybe lose their virginity before they turned thirty."

This last statement elicited hearty laughter from both women. It did not hurt the mood that the wine was starting to take effect.

"Probably true," Darla said.

"Besides, from what the press is reporting, this Muslim is in deep trouble," Newport continued. "So, when do we start planning your election to the White House? It's never too soon," Newport asked.

"Between you and me, Tom's already working on it. Timmons is such a weak, worthless man I'll be surprised if he gets nominated again," Darla replied. "After Tom zapped a few fanatic Muslim Imams with drone strikes, the others dove for cover. But with Timmons attitude, this Circle of Islam bunch is starting to come back."

"I know. I have a friend on the Senate Intelligence Committee. The massacre in Baghdad near our embassy a couple weeks ago was them. Or at least CIA says it was. So does the Pentagon. Timmons won't fight back unless he's absolutely sure there will be no civilian casualties. That reminds me, we haven't talked about committee appointments for you, yet."

"Sally, I haven't been elected yet. Are you trying to jinx me?" Darla asked.

"Have you seen the polling? Don't get caught in bed with a German Shepard and you'll win," Sally replied while pouring each of them more wine from the new bottle.

"That's disgusting," Darla laughed.

"Committee appointments?" Newport asked. "I was thinking Armed Services and Foreign Affairs."

"Isn't that up to the majority leader?" Darla asked.

"Trust me, that won't be a problem. Besides, the party national committee, or so I hear, is already lining everything up for the next president, Darla Carver."

"Ssshhh, you're not supposed to know that. They're supposed to be neutral, remember," Darla said.

"Oh hell, were they neutral when they shoved that black asshole, Julian Morton, down our throats?"

"Sally," Darla said, "keep your voice down. Somebody could consider that statement to be racist"

"Yeah, yeah, okay. Still, I'm putting in my bid now for a cabinet appointment."

"What do you want?" Darla asked. Sally's support would be crucial in the Midwest. Darla knew it and had no problem promising her a cabinet position for it.

"State would be nice. Or Defense," Newport replied.

"I'll get you something good, don't worry."

"I'm not," Newport replied.

An hour and another expensive bottle of Napa Valley Cabernet Sauvignon later, the two women finished their lunch. While Newport signed for their lunch she muttered, "Seven hundred fifty bucks for lunch, these people should be ashamed of themselves for charging such prices. Thank God I don't have to pay it."

"We could have eaten at McDonald's" Darla said.

"And rub up against the unwashed crowds in those places? No thanks."

TWENTY-NINE

With Tommy Lee Dorn at the wheel of the Army issued Ford, the car stopped at the entrance to Ft. Myer. Jahid Kamel was in the front passenger seat while Marc Kadella and Tony Carvelli rode along in back.

They had checked into a Days Inn near the post. The drive to enter Ft. Myer took them along Arlington National Cemetery. Never having seen the most sacred place in America, both Marc and Tony watch it roll by with a mixture of sadness and awe. The headstones of more than four hundred thousand seemed almost endless at Robert E. Lee's former plantation. By the time they reached the entrance to Ft. Myer, both men, even the hard-case ex-cop, were teary-eyed.

"Where are the protestors?" Marc asked as they were being passed through the entrance.

"They're not around much, right now," Dorn replied. "Don't worry, when we get closer to the trial date they'll be back."

It took him almost fifteen minutes to get to the little house where Sammy was confined. By the time they got there, both Marc and Tony were totally confused as to where they were.

Dorn returned the MP's salute, the one stationed in front of the house, as they made their way to the front door. Sammy must have been watching out the front window. When they reached the door, he was standing there waiting for them.

Sammy and Jahid embraced, then Sammy turned to Marc. While shaking hands he said, "Mr. Kadella, you haven't changed a bit."

Marc laughed, then said, "That's a really nice lie, Sammy."

Marc introduced Carvelli and the four of them followed Sammy into the tiny living room. Sammy and Jahid sat on the couch. Dorn and Marc took the remaining two chairs across from them. Carvelli retrieved a chair from the dining room table adjacent to the living room.

"Did Colonel Dorn tell you about my case?" Sammy asked Marc.

"Look, Sammy, I haven't agreed to anything," Marc said ignoring the question. "I agreed to come here and meet with you. That's all."

"Mr. Kadella..." Sammy started to say.

"Marc," Marc interrupted him. "Please call me Marc. You're not in high school anymore."

Sammy smiled and leaned forward, his elbows on his knees. He looked Marc directly in the eyes and said, "I am innocent. I had nothing to do with any of this. I am not even a very religious Muslim let alone the radicalized fanatic the people in the media are making me out to be."

He turned his head to Dorn and asked, "Did you tell him about the case? About the evidence?"

"No, Samir. I wanted him to meet you first."

150

Sammy turned to Carvelli and asked. "Are you a lawyer?"

"No, I'm an investigator."

"He works for me," Marc interjected. "As such, he's covered by attorney-client privilege. Your father is not."

"He already knows everything," Sammy said. "Besides, I'm not going to say anything that can be used against me anyway."

"You don't know that," Marc told him. "You could say something that may sound innocent enough that the prosecution could twist into something to use against you."

Marc looked at Jahid and politely said, "If we get into anything of substance, I will ask you to leave. Please don't be offended."

Jahid looked at his watch and said, "It has been a long day. I think I will go upstairs and lie down for a while. Wake me when you are done."

"Thank you," Marc said.

For the next hour, while Carvelli sat silently listening, the other three men went over the entire case. When they finished, Marc sat back in his chair thinking it over.

"Will you help me?" Sammy asked Marc.

Marc looked at Dorn and asked, "Will the Army help with fees and costs?"

"My dad will…" Sammy started to say. He was stopped when Marc held up a hand to him.

"I have a budget for some of it," Dorn replied.

"How much?" Marc asked. Before Dorn could answer Marc looked at Sammy and said, "We might as well try to get the government to pay some of it."

"Twenty-thousand dollars," Dorn replied.

"Twenty? That's it?"

"That's it. We can apply for more as we go along, but good luck. We would have to justify every penny," Dorn said.

Marc looked at Carvelli and asked, "What do you think?"

"I'm going to need help. We're gonna have a lot of witnesses to track down, especially people who can testify as to his character. Does this mean we're in?"

Marc looked at Sammy and asked, "Are you sure you want to change lawyers at this point? Barely two months before trial?"

"I don't have a lawyer, except Tommy Dorn, here," Sammy said. Using Dorn's nickname, a superior officer, caused Marc the Air Force veteran to arch his eyebrows.

"Tommy?" Marc asked.

"Colonel Dorn," Sammy said with a big grin.

Marc let out a noticeable expulsion of breath rolled his eyes to the ceiling as if looking for some divine guidance, looked at Sammy and said, "Okay, we're in."

"Yes!" Sammy exclaimed. He jumped up, reached across the table and shook Marc's hand. Carvelli stood up and Sammy took his hand as well.

"I'm gonna need Maddy," Tony said.

"I know," Marc said. He looked at Sammy and said, "Trust me, you'll like her."

"Who is she?" Dorn asked.

"Another investigator," Marc replied. "Trust me, she can get things others can't." Marc looked at his watch and said, "Look, it's getting late. I'm tired and hungry. We'll be back in the morning and get started."

"What about a preliminary hearing?" Marc asked Dorn. "When do we get that so we can hear from their witnesses?"

"It was done a long time ago, almost two years," Dorn replied. "It's called an Article 32 hearing. It is done at the time of charging. After the CID investigators gathered up everything from the FBI, they put it together and recommended charges. There was a hearing very similar to a civilian court's probable cause hearing. They put the evidence before a JAG judge and called enough witnesses to testify as to the authenticity of it. Afterwards Sammy was charged with one count of treason. His previous lawyers sent one of them to sit in and Sammy thinks he was high on something. He didn't ask a single question or objection."

"Weren't you there?" Carvelli asked.

"No, I was only assigned a few months ago," Dorn replied.

It was the next morning and the four of them, Marc, Carvelli, Dorn and Sammy were meeting again. Jahid had agreed to stay at the motel for the day. The four men were seated around the small oak dining table, the only decent piece of furniture in Sammy's quarters.

Tony Carvelli was looking over a report from the search done at Sammy's apartment. He put the report down and looked at Sammy.

"Tell me about your roommate, this Captain Oliver what's-his-name?" Carvelli asked Sammy.

"Townsend," Sammy said. "What do you want to know?"

By now, Marc and Tommy Lee were listening in. Dorn was about to say something when Marc held up a hand to stop him.

"What's he like? Was he a friend? Someone you could trust? Likeable? Asshole? What?" Carvelli replied.

"At first I thought he was okay. Kind of an entitled rich kid, but he was okay. We got along fine. He seemed to be pretty sharp, good at his job," Sammy said.

"At first? Then what?" Carvelli asked.

"I think he's a bit anti-Muslim. Actually, more like a bit of a bigot. Kind of had an idea that he was better than most people because he was a rich, Boston white-guy. Why?"

"What are you thinking?" Marc asked Tony.

"This list of the names of these radical assholes," Tony said holding up the copy they had been given. "The FBI says they found Sammy's fingerprints on the original."

"We'll get it and have it tested," Marc said.

"Sure and I'll bet you a C-note it comes back as being Sammy's prints. It's the FBI, Marc. They don't make up shit like that," Tony continued. "If they are your prints and you did not write this list, then how did your prints get on the original?"

"I don't know," Sammy said.

"Someone must have given somebody a blank sheet of paper who knew your prints were on it. Who?" Carvelli continued.

"Could've been any number of people," Marc said.

"True," Tony agreed. "But," he continued looking back at Sammy, "who is the best candidate?"

Sammy looked at Carvelli as he nodded his head in agreement and quietly said, "Oliver Townsend."

"And who could have come up with a good sample of your handwriting for someone to get that list forged?" Carvelli asked. "If you didn't write it then someone forged it. Is this your handwriting?"

"Yeah," Sammy quietly replied. "Sure looks like it."

"The reporter for the New York Times was murdered," Tommy Dorn reminded them. "Who did that?"

"Oliver Townsend's life is in serious jeopardy," Carvelli said.

"Maybe," Marc said. "Maybe not. How will it look if he gets whacked while Sammy is under guard?"

"Could have an accident," Dorn interjected.

"So, what do we do?" Sammy asked. "Wait for Oliver to get killed to prove our theory?"

"I could interview him," Carvelli said. "When I do it I could not so subtly warn him."

"I know Oliver," Sammy said. "He won't talk to you. He'll tell you to get lost before you say anything."

The room went silent for a minute then Carvelli sat up straight, looked around the table with a smile and smug look.

"What?" Marc asked.

"I know a way," Carvelli said.

By the look on his face, Marc realized what he was getting at.

153

"Yeah, I think you're right. We need to get Maddy here. Captain Oliver Townsend will be sitting up barking like a seal before she's done with him."

"Exactly," Tony chuckled.

Marc checked his watch then calculated the time difference in Minnesota. He picked up his phone, found the number and dialed it.

"Hi, hope I didn't wake you," Marc said when Maddy answered it. "How are you doing?"

"Much better. I'm waiting for the doctor to check me out. I'm getting discharged. I was about to call you. I need a ride home," she said.

"Oh, oh," Marc quietly replied. "Um, well, ah...."

"Where are you?"

"Northern Virginia," Marc said.

"Is Tony with you?"

Marc held his phone up and pointed it at Carvelli.

"Good morning, sweetheart," Tony said.

Marc put the phone back to his ear and explained what they were doing.

"You're taking the case against this guy? The one charged with treason? Are you nuts? Do you want to end your career?" Maddy asked.

"He's innocent and we're going to need your help," Marc replied.

"Is she getting out of the hospital?" Tony asked Marc who nodded his head in reply.

"Does she need a ride?" Tony asked him and Marc nodded again,

Carvelli picked up his phone and made a call while Marc and Maddy conversed. A minute later he put the phone back down and looked at Marc.

"Tell her there'll be an MPD squad car waiting for her in front of the hospital. They will wait for her."

Marc relayed this news to Maddy.

"I'm getting a police escort?" she laughed.

"Tony knows every cop in Minneapolis and most of the ones in St. Paul," Marc said. "And most of them owe him a favor. Tell you what, I'll be home tomorrow. I have some things on my desk to attend to then I'll fly back. We'll come back together. We only have two months to prepare. Are you in?"

"Of course. Call me when you get back. Say 'hello' to the paisan," Maddy said referring to Tony.

THIRTY

Marc, Tony Carvelli, and Maddy Rivers found the car and driver waiting in front of Reagan National. The driver, an Army three-striper, literally tripped on the curb trying to help Maddy with her small suitcase. His name was Larry Esterhazy and he informed Marc he had been assigned to him as his driver.

Maddy and Marc got in the backseat while Tony spoke to the driver.

"Just so you know, she carries a gun," Carvelli told the smitten young man.

"Now that's really hot!" he replied causing Tony to laugh and shake his head as he got in the front passenger seat.

While Marc and Tony were gone, Jahid Kamel had rented a very nice, four-bedroom house for them. It was a couple miles from Ft. Myer in Virginia and would provide both living quarters and a workplace for them for the duration.

Instead of going to the rented house in Arlington, Esterhazy drove them directly to Sammy's quarters at Ft. Myer.

"Do you know where the house is where we'll be staying?" Marc asked the driver while Maddy and Carvelli walked up the narrow sidewalk to the front of the little house.

"Yes, sir," he answered.

"Would you mind taking our luggage there? And can you wait there for us? We have more clothes being sent there by FedEx. They're supposed to be delivered this afternoon."

"No problem," the sergeant replied.

"Let me have your phone number. I'll call you when we're done. Oh, and," Marc continued in a whisper, "she carries a gun."

Esterhazy broke into a large grin and whispered back, "Yes, sir. The other gentleman warned me." He leaned in a little closer and asked, "I can look, can't I?"

"Good morning, Sergeant, we're back," Marc politely said to the man guarding Sammy's front door.

"Yes, sir," the man said as he reached to open the door for them. "And if I may say so, sir, I'm glad to see you, again. That other guy, the gray-haired guy with the ponytail, well sir, he treats us all like we're servants. Acts like he's so much better than we are."

"I'm an enlisted vet, sergeant," Marc said.

"Ah, that explains it. You're a human."

"And these two are ex-cops," Marc said wagging a thumb at Tony and Maddy.

"Excellent," the sergeant replied.

They went inside to find Colonel Dorn on his phone and Sammy waiting for them. Marc introduced Maddy and they went into the dining room where Dorn was listening with a concerned look on his face. The four of them took a seat at the table and silently waited for Dorn.

"Thanks, Dave. Keep me informed when you find out anything else," Dorn said then ended the call.

He looked across the table at Marc and said, "You're gonna love this. That was a CID investigator I know. He was at Sammy's apartment. The one he shared with Captain Townsend. Oliver Townsend was found sitting in his car in his garage. He's dead. It looks like an accident."

"Isn't that the guy you wanted me to get information from?" Maddy asked.

"Are you serious?" Marc asked Dorn ignoring Maddy's question. "Sorry, of course you are. Dumb question." He looked to his left at Maddy and said, "Yes, he was."

"Was he a drinker?" Dorn asked an obviously stunned Sammy.

"Um, yeah, ah, yes," Sammy muttered. "He liked to party a bit. Why?"

"What did he drink?" Dorn asked.

"Um, ah, vodka. Vodka martinis. Thought it made him cool, like James Bond. Why? What happened?"

"They're not sure, yet. It looks like he made it home then passed out in the car in the garage with the engine running. There was an empty vodka bottle on the passenger seat. There will be an autopsy and investigation. It's a civilian case but when the cops found his military ID, they called the CID. My guy will let us know what happened as soon as he finds out."

"How did he know to call you?" Carvelli asked.

"He was one of the investigators originally assigned to work for the defense. One of the guys Doyle fired. He remembered Sammy had a roommate and he thought it was Townsend. He called to check with me."

"Holy shit," Marc whispered. His head went up and he silently began looking around at the walls and ceiling. He then held a finger to his lips and looked at each of the people at the table.

Marc found a blank sheet of paper from the pile on the table. He quickly scribbled something on it and handed it to Dorn. Dorn read it, looked at Marc, shrugged his shoulders and shook his head.

"Can you go outside?" Marc asked Sammy.

"Yes, if there's a guard with me," he answered.

"Let's go," Marc said and got up.

When they got out front on the front steps Marc told the MP what they were up to. The man told him to go ahead and followed them onto the small lawn. He then kept a reasonable distance so that they could talk.

"I asked the colonel about the house being checked for bugs and I don't mean by Orkin," Marc told the other three.

"It hasn't been checked," Dorn said. "At least not to my knowledge."

"You think...?" Maddy started to ask.

"Maybe," Marc said. "We were talking about questioning this guy a couple days ago and this morning he turns up dead."

"Quite a coincidence," Carvelli said.

"You know of anyone in the area to call?" Marc asked Dorn.

"Well, I've never done it but I could probably find someone," Dorn replied.

"I'll do it," Carvelli said. "I'll check with a guy I know in Minnesota. I'll see if he can recommend someone good and not owned by the government. In fact, give me ten minutes."

Carvelli took out his phone, checked its directory and found the number he wanted. Before he could dial it, a new, shiny black Lincoln Continental screeched to a stop in front of Sammy's quarters. The driver had barely come to a stop when Layne Doyle and another member of the Gray Haired Ponytail Team were stomping across the yard toward them.

"You gotta lot of goddamn nerve soldier-boy," a steaming mad Doyle said to Tommy Lee Dorn while pointing a finger at him.

"Gee, Mr. Lawyer-for-the-people," Dorn said. "Where's the beat-up VW van or is that only used when cameras are around."

"Never mind that, asshole," Doyle snarled. He turned to look at Marc, Tony and Maddy and said, "Who the hell are you? What the hell is this shit Sammy? I bust my ass for two...."

"You haven't done dick for two years," Sammy said. He stepped up to Doyle to look him directly in the eyes. "All you've done is stall."

"That's the best tactic," Doyle said. "The longer we drag it out the better."

"Better for who?" Sammy asked, his eyes narrowed to tiny slits of anger. "Better for you and this dickless wonder," Sammy said flipping a hand at the other lawyer who stood watching.

"Which one of you is the lawyer?" Doyle said turning back and taking a couple of steps toward Marc, Tony and Maddy.

"That would be me," Marc calmly replied.

"Do you realize who I am? I'll have you disbarred for this you little shit. You don't know who you're messing with."

157

"Damn," Marc said. "Now I won't sleep tonight."

"You're fired, Doyle," Sammy said. "You and your little gang. Take your 'cause' and shove it up your ass. I need a lawyer to represent me, not your radical bullshit anti-government cause. Now beat it."

Doyle turned back to Sammy, took a deep breath and more calmly said, "Sammy, listen, we know what we're doing. Who's this nobody? He'll get you thirty years. We know how to put pressure on the government. They'll make a good deal. You'll see."

"I think it's time for you to leave," said Maddy.

Doyle turned to Maddy who was now barely three feet from him.

"Wow," he said with a sarcastic smile as he took a step toward her. "Bring it on, girlie."

"Oh shit," Carvelli muttered.

Marc started to yell, "Maddy, no!"

Before he got the words out, Layne Doyle was laying on the ground holding his midsection trying to breathe while Maddy stood over him staring down at the prostrate lawyer.

"What did you see, Sergeant?" Dorn asked the MP. The guard had been inching closer to the scene in the event there might be trouble. When the exchange between Maddy and Doyle occurred, he saw it as a chance to play hero for her. Instead, he was stopped cold by the swiftness of her attack.

"Sir, the sergeant saw the lawyer with the big mouth trip over his feet and fall on his ass, sir," the MP replied wearing a large grin.

"That's what I saw, too," Dorn said. "You should be more careful, Mr. Doyle. Now get your ass off of this post before I have you arrested and charged with trespass on a federal facility."

While Doyle's friend was kneeling over him, Sammy went to him, leaned down and said, "I am rescinding my permission to give you the right to use my story for any books, movies or anything else. If you do, I'll sue your ass until hell freezes over."

Doyle's friend got him to his feet and got him breathing again. As he led him back to the car, Doyle yelled, "You haven't heard the last of this!"

"Yes, we have," Marc quietly said.

THIRTY-ONE

Major Paxton O'Rourke finished applying a very light pink lipstick on herself. She smacked her lips together and stared at her reflection in the mirror. Paxton was the progeny of an Irish-American father and a half-Persian, half-Italian mother. Fortunately, she got the best of both of them. Almond shaped dark eyes, silky black hair and her mother's oval face. Coupled with her father's intelligence and Irish gift of gab had made Paxton a pretty good package.

She continued to stare at the mirror again wondering if she should let her hair grow out. Currently, it was cut into a very stylish pixie cut, short even by Army standards.

"Stop stalling," she said out loud to her image. "The sooner you get this over, the better. Get at it, soldier."

Paxton O'Rourke was a thirty-seven-year-old prosecutor with the Army's JAG Corp. A graduate of the University of Illinois College of Law on an Army scholarship, she had been with the JAG Corp for twelve years. Originally, she intended on doing four years to repay the Army then go into private practice. Instead, she found she enjoyed the life and had become one of JAG's top prosecuting trial lawyers. A little more than a year ago the case of the U.S. vs. Samir Kamel dropped in her lap and she had regretted it ever since. This morning was a reminder of why that was so.

At 0850 hours, Paxton took a seat in the anteroom of her boss, Brigadier General Keith Mills. Paxton hid it well, but Mills was a man she despised. Aside from his natural political abilities, Paxton could never understand how this man obtained the star he wore on his shoulder. Along with that were his often less than subtle hints that Paxton's career prospects would be enhanced by a friendlier attitude toward him. Never enough for her to bring a harassment charge but very obvious all the same.

"You may go in, Major," the general's aide, a captain who had hit on her more than his boss, told her after hanging up his desk phone.

While walking the few steps to Mill's office door, Paxton smoothed her skirt and could feel the captain's eyes on her behind. She knocked lightly twice, opened the door and went in. She marched up to the man's desk, came to attention and formally addressed him.

"Sir, Major O'Rourke reporting as ordered, sir."

For the next two seconds, she had to fight off a smile. Sitting alongside Mills' desk was Mills' boss, a man Paxton liked and admired, Major General William Conklin. Mills would have to behave himself.

"At ease, Major. Have a seat," Mills told her.

"Is this thing going to go to trial sometime soon?" Conklin asked.

"We hear he fired his old lawyers and brought in a new one. Another civilian," Mills added.

"Yes, sir, that's true," Paxton replied. She was seated in front of Mills' desk sitting straight up as if at attention in the chair.

"Are they looking for another continuance?" Conklin asked with clear displeasure.

"Yes, sir," Paxton replied looking at him instead of Mills. "I don't believe he will get it. Colonel Dorn, Kamel's military counsel, was told in no uncertain terms there would be no more continuances. Colonel Dwyer, the judge, was adamant. Plus, we are opposing it."

"What happened to his former lawyers?" Mills asked.

"He fired them, sir," Paxton replied.

"Why?"

"May I speak bluntly, sir?"

"Please do, Major," Mills said.

"Because they didn't do dick, sir. All they were after was publicity for themselves. They are so far behind in their preparation they're going to have to bust ass to be ready for trial."

"Do you have a specific trial date?" Conklin asked.

"Yes, sir, Monday, October sixteenth," Paxton replied.

"Are you going to be ready?" Mills asked.

"Yes, sir."

"Do you need anything else?" Conklin asked.

"No, sir. I feel very confident, sir."

"Good, because we're getting heavy political pressure on this. I know that's not your concern, but this building," Conklin told her referring to where they were, the Pentagon, "whether we like it or not, must always be aware of the politics across the river."

Paxton squirmed in her chair and nervously looked around the room and the two generals.

"Something on your mind, Major?" Conklin asked. "Go ahead, say what you need to say. You're among friends."

"Well, sir. We're getting very close to inappropriate conversation, sir."

"That's enough, Major," Mills sharply said.

"No, no, Keith," Conklin said. "She's right. Major O'Rourke, thank you for stopping by."

Seeing a quick way out, Paxton jumped to attention, saluted, turned and got out of the office as fast as she could.

"What do you think, Keith?" Conklin asked after Paxton left.

160

"She's very good, Bill. She's careful and methodical. It's the only case she has and she'll have it all lined up and ready to go. She'll convince the jury members this Muslim leaked that list," Mills replied.

"Okay," Conklin said. "Damn good-looking woman. I bet she looks good to a jury."

"She does and she will," Mills said.

"Are you done?" Marc Kadella asked the technician.

"Yes, sir. Found nothing, again," the man replied. He was the supervisor of the team of technicians brought into Sammy's quarters to check for listening devices, cameras or any other type of surveillance equipment they might find. "I almost wish we had but sorry, nothing."

"Satisfied?" Carvelli asked Marc. "This is the third time they've swept the place now…"

"I know," Marc said.

While Marc was writing a check to the technicians from the expense trust account, Tommy Lee Dorn arrived. With him was a man in a somewhat rumpled, inexpensive, civilian suit.

Dorn waited for the technicians to leave, then introduced the man to everyone.

"This is Warrant Officer Dave Smith," Dorn said.

All of them, Marc, Tony, Sammy and Madeline, were seated around the dining room table. They all stood to greet the man who shook hands with each.

"I could never figure out what to call a warrant officer," Marc said to him.

"Dave will be fine, sir," the man said.

"And you can skip the 'sir' part," Marc replied.

Smith sat down on the sixth and final chair of the dining room set and looked over the group.

"We got a call when Captain Oliver Townsend was found dead in his garage. He was Army, so the D.C. cops notified us. I got the report, verbally, of their investigation. They're finding it to be an accidental suicide. The autopsy revealed a blood alcohol content of point two-three. There was also an empty pint bottle of vodka on the passenger side floor."

"Will you be getting the written reports? The police report and autopsy and lab results?" Dorn asked.

"Yes, sir. I should have those in a few days. I'll get you a copy. They are public record reports."

"Good and thanks," Marc said.

"There's more," Smith said. "There's something bothering me. The night before he was found, remember how hot and humid it was?"

"About like it's been, I guess," Marc said.

"Actually, a little worse. I got a report from the U.S. Weather Service. At ten o'clock that night, in D.C., it was eighty-seven degrees with over ninety percent humidity; a hot, steamy August night. Pretty typical," Smith said.

"Okay?" Marc looked at him.

"What's bothering me is that both the driver's side window and passenger side window on Townsend's Benz were open," Smith said.

"It was hot and humid. His windows were open, so?" Marc asked.

"And his air conditioning was on. Why would he put down the windows on such a muggy, hot night and run his air conditioning inside the car at the same time?"

"He was drunk," Carvelli said. "I'll bet that's what the cops told you when you asked about this didn't they?"

"Exactly," Smith agreed. "That is precisely what they said."

"But he wasn't drunk when he went out and that's when he made sure the A/C was on," Carvelli said.

Smith pointed a finger at Tony, smiled at him and replied, "That's what I said to the cops."

"Did they dust the car for prints?" Carvelli asked.

"Yeah, they did. They found a lot of them," Smith said.

"Any other than his on the driver's side?" Carvelli asked.

"No, just his. I asked," Smith said. "The windows open on that car is a loose end and I don't like it."

"Will the cops keep investigating?" Marc asked.

"No," Tony replied. "They'll clear it as an accident unless you can come up with more."

"Officially," Smith said, "I'm out of it. Sorry."

"Do you know the places he hung out?" Marc asked Sammy. "The bars we might check?"

"Not really," Sammy replied. "I didn't party with him so I didn't pay much attention to it. I was usually in bed when he got home."

"I'll get you those reports and if I think of anything else, I'll let you know," Smith said.

"Why are you doing this?" Marc asked. "Your superiors probably wouldn't like it, you helping Sammy's defense like this."

"Because I think he's innocent," Smith said. "At the very least, he deserves a fair trial."

THIRTY-TWO

"I have the first list you wanted," Sammy told Marc.

They were again seated at the dining room table. Four boxes of documents had been delivered the day before completing the discovery required of the prosecution. A significant amount had been taken from Sammy's workstation at the former Vice President's office. Every piece of paper from there was so heavily redacted as to be virtually useless.

"Look at this one," Carvelli said holding up a single sheet of paper. "The only thing not blacked out is his name."

"At least they're not claiming his name is covered by national security," Tommy Dorn said.

"Let me see your list," Marc said responding to Sammy.

Sammy handed Marc a single sheet of paper with a handwritten list of names on it. There were twelve in all. Each name was an officer, all but one of higher rank than Sammy. Included on the list were two general officers. A one-star and a two-star.

Marc read over the list then asked Sammy, "You think they'll all testify for you?"

As he was saying this he handed the sheet of paper to Dorn.

"I don't know," Sammy replied with a shrug. "Under normal circumstances they would give me an excellent recommendation. Several of them have given me outstanding performance reviews."

Dorn handed the list back to Sammy and said, "Go through your personnel file. Match up your evaluations with the names on the list."

Dorn looked at Marc and continued. "We may have to subpoena them and force them to testify about what they wrote about him."

"Go through all of your evaluations. Especially the bad ones. We don't want to be surprised with them."

"There aren't any bad ones," Sammy said.

"Good. Go through them anyway," Marc said. "How's the other list coming?"

"Good. I'm over one hundred names but I don't have addresses for them," Sammy replied.

"What other list?" Maddy asked.

"A witness list. Character witnesses," Marc said.

"You're going to call a hundred character witnesses?" Maddy asked.

"Of course not. This will be the witness list we turn over. They'll have to check every one of them. Just because we put a name on a list doesn't mean we have to call them. They'll do the same thing to us," Marc said.

"Lawyer games," Maddy said shaking her head.

"Tony," Marc said to Carvelli, "that won't work."

Carvelli was holding up a document and trying to read through the redaction.

"I know," he grumbled. "Going through this stuff is a waste of time."

"Who do you know on the NYPD?" Marc asked.

"I don't know," Tony replied. "No one really. Why?"

"How about you?" Marc asked Maddy.

"Nobody," she said. "I could probably come up with someone through friends in Chicago. Why?"

"There's the unsolved case of a murdered New York Times reporter up there. The one who had the list leaked to him," Marc said. "I'd like to know how that case is coming along."

"That was what, over two years ago?" Carvelli said. "I can tell you right now, that case is colder than a well digger's ass."

"Probably," Marc agreed. "Still, make a few calls and see what you can find out."

"'Colder than a well diggers ass'? Where did you come up with that?" Maddy asked giving Carvelli an odd look.

"Google," Tony replied with a grin. "You can look it up."

"I'm starting to worry about you, Carvelli. Like maybe you're ready for the home," Maddy said. "Have you ever heard that?" she asked Marc.

"Yeah, I have," Marc laughed. "It's a little old but…"

"Me, too," Dorn said.

"And me," Sammy added.

"What is this, like a boys' locker room thing? Stuff you guys come up with when you're not lighting farts?"

The men all laughed but tried to look innocent when they stopped.

"So, all of you guys have done that?" Maddy asked looking them over. Sammy and Dorn looked away to avoid her gaze.

"And you?" Maddy said looking at Marc.

"On advice of counsel I exercise my right under the fifth amendment to remain silent so as not to incriminate myself," Marc replied, trying not to laugh.

"Boys know how to have fun," Carvelli said. "Girls don't know how to have fun. Playing with dolls and other nonsense."

"I played with guns," Maddy said.

"That I believe," Carvelli replied.

"Can we get back to work?" Marc said to settle down the laughter.

"Or, how about colder than a witch's…" Carvelli started to say.

"Don't say it, Carvelli. That one I've heard," Maddy chastised him.

164

"Anyway," Marc said, "the case is probably cold. Check it out anyway. If we could find out who did that, or even suspects, and there's no connection to Sammy, it might help us."

"Could we get it in?" Dorn asked.

"I don't know. Let's see what we can find, first," Marc replied.

"Haven't you ever lit a fart?" Carvelli quietly asked Maddy.

"No!" she yelled and elbowed him in the shoulder.

When the laughter died down, Marc suggested an outdoors break. Fifteen minutes later, they were back at the table.

"Okay," Marc began getting back to business. He looked at Maddy and said, "When Sammy finishes his list, the short one, I'm gonna want you to hunt these people down and find out if they will voluntarily testify on his behalf. Don't push them. Just get a feel for which way they are leaning. Don't mention subpoenas. We can do that later if we have to."

"I don't have addresses for all of them," Sammy said.

"That's okay," Marc replied. "She can start with the ones you have." Marc looked at Maddy and said, "I'll get the list to Jeff, back at the office. He'll find the rest. He's gonna have to find addresses for most of the people on the long list."

"Who's Jeff?" Dorn asked.

"Our office paralegal. Bright guy. Knows his way around the internet. He'll track these names down for us," Marc replied.

"Do you think that CID guy would help me track down where this Oliver Townsend was the night before he died?" Carvelli asked Dorn.

"Probably," Dorn said. "I could ask him. He would have to do it on his own. CID isn't anxious to help us now."

"It's a needle in a haystack," Marc said to Tony.

"If that," Tony replied. "But maybe this Dave Smith knows his way around D.C. clubs where he might have gone. Worth checking out."

Marc's phone went off and he saw from the ID who it was.

"Hi, Mom," he answered the phone.

"Connie?" Maddy asked. When Marc nodded his head she told him to say "hello" for her.

"Hang on, let me write this down," Marc said. He listened for a minute while writing a name, address and phone number.

"Thank you, my love. Tell Jeff I'll be sending him a list of names to locate," Marc said. He hung up the phone and handed the note to Dorn.

"This is our handwriting expert. That was my landlord, Connie Mickelson. She's a lawyer in the Twin Cities and knows everyone. She tracked her down for us. Connie says she's the best," Marc told him.

"Denver," Dorn said. "She's in Denver?"

"She teaches criminology at Denver University. She's a criminalist and handwriting expert. Connie already talked to her so she's expecting us. I'll get a hold of her today."

"When do you go to meet the judge?" Sammy asked.

"Friday morning. He'll want to get out early for Labor Day weekend," Marc said.

"You think he'll give you a continuance?" Carvelli asked.

"I think he'll throw his gavel at my head for even asking," Marc replied. "But I have to ask. Who knows, he might agree to a little bit. A couple of weeks maybe. This meeting is mostly just to meet the guy and the woman prosecuting. She seems reasonable enough on the phone but you can get a better idea of what she's like in person."

"I know her well. She will be prepared," Dorn said, "She will have her case ready and will methodically, thoroughly and professionally present her case. We won't catch her making a mistake or missing anything. Although I am surprised they gave her this. A very high profile case."

"Why?" Maddy asked.

"She's a little junior. She's experienced but there are any number of more senior lawyers they could have given it to.

"On the other hand," Dorn continued, "the case isn't that complicated."

"It will come down to if the jury believes Sammy is a self-radicalized Muslim and did he write that list or he didn't he," Marc said. "That's why we need character witnesses of unquestionable credibility. People who will get on a witness stand and convince a jury Samir Kamel is an outstanding, even excellent, officer of the United States Army and the Samir Kamel they know would never have done anything like it."

"And a handwriting expert who can find flaws in the handwritten list. Enough to cast reasonable doubt that he wrote it," Dorn said.

"That's pretty much the case," Marc said. "That damn list."

"What about the fingerprints they claim are on the list found at that reporter's apartment?" Maddy asked.

"Same thing," Marc replied. "But with fingerprints we need an expert that slings so much bullshit the jury won't know what to believe. We also try to create enough inference in their minds that it's possible someone lifted that sheet of paper from Sammy with his fingerprints already on it. That's what I wanted the roommate for," Marc said looking at Carvelli.

"If we find out it was no accident that killed him, maybe we can still use him," Carvelli said.

"That's a big maybe," Marc responded. "It might take a lot of tap dancing to get it admitted. We'll see."

166

"Here you go," Sammy said handing his short witness list to Marc.

The Army had provided them with a good copy machine and it was set up in the living room.

"I'll make a copy and get at it," Maddy said.

"And I need to call Professor Wendy Carlson, our handwriting expert. I'll see if she knows a good fingerprint person, too," Marc said.

THIRTY-THREE

Marc Kadella exited the house they were renting through the front door. The house was a brick McMansion with four two-story white columns supporting a roof overhanging a front porch that covered the width of the building. Marc descended the three steps and took the concrete sidewalk to his right. Waiting in the driveway with an Army green Ford was Sergeant Larry Esterhazy sporting a disappointed look.

"Good morning, Sergeant," Marc said to his driver.

"Good morning, sir. Ms. Rivers won't be joining us today?"

Marc was halfway into the back when he heard the question. He stepped back, smiled at the young man and said, "Sorry, Ms. Rivers has her own car to use. A rental. Don't look so disappointed."

"Oh, no, sir. Not at all," Esterhazy scrambled to say.

"Morning, Colonel," Marc said to Tommy Dorn as Esterhazy closed the door.

"Morning, Marc," Dorn replied.

Esterhazy drove them onto Ft. Myer and to their destination. It was the Friday before Labor Day and at 9:00 A.M. it was already almost ninety degrees and humid. Esterhazy found a parking space on the street close to Myer-Henderson Hall for Marc's first meeting with the judge assigned to Sammy's case.

Colonel Otis Dwyer was considered a rising star in the JAG corps. Forty-seven-years-old, he had been with the JAG office for over twenty years. A graduate of West Point and Yale Law School, he was on the short list to receive a star; probably within the next two years.

Dwyer had been a JAG judge for five years after being both a prosecutor and defense attorney. Tommy Dorn knew him well and considered Dwyer to be a fair judge. In fact, Dorn believed that because of Dwyer's race, African-American, he leaned a bit toward defendants. The judge had been assigned a temporary office in Myer-Henderson Hall for the duration of the trial.

Marc and Dorn took the stairs up to the second floor where Dwyer's office was. As they walked down the hallway toward their destination, they could see two Army officers, a female major and a male captain, waiting in the hall at Dwyer's door.

"Good morning, Colonel Dorn," the woman said when Marc and Dorn reached them.

"Good morning, Major, Captain," Dorn replied. "Marc, Major Paxton O'Rourke and Captain Greg Bain."

"Marc Kadella," Marc said smiling and shaking their hands. "It's nice to meet you, I think."

Paxton returned Marc's smile and said, "No offense, but I hope Major Kamel finally has a lawyer."

"He does," Dorn replied.

"Judge Dwyer told us to come in as soon as you arrived," Paxton said. She stepped over to the door, knocked and opened it when she heard Judge Dwyer respond.

"Good morning, everyone," the judge affably said as the four of them filed in, Tommy Dorn in the lead. "You must be the new man, Marc Kadella," Dwyer said. He was standing behind his desk, a pleasant smile on his face and his hand extended to Marc.

"Yes, your Honor," Marc replied shaking the man's hand.

"Please, have a seat everyone," Dwyer said indicating the four chairs placed before his desk.

Seated next to the judge was a young woman with an E-4 Specialist insignia on her Class B Uniform. In front of her was a steno machine and on the judge's desk was a recorder.

"I thought we should put this on the record. Any objections?" Dwyer said. "Good," he quickly added before anyone could respond. "Are you ready?" he asked the court reporter.

"Yes, sir."

Dwyer read the case name and court file number into the record. Starting with O'Rourke, each of the lawyers announced their appearance and Marc spelled his name for her.

"The defense has filed a motion requesting yet another continuance, is that correct, Mr. Kadella?"

"Yes, your Honor. I have…"

"Allow me to interrupt," the judge said. "I know your situation and how new you are to the case. And I am not unsympathetic. As Colonel Dorn knows, we were here recently on just such a motion, the tenth or eleventh, I've lost track. At that time, I made it abundantly clear there would be no more continuances. I'm sorry, Mr. Kadella. I know this is not your doing, but I meant it. Motion denied.

"What about discovery? Where are we?" Dwyer said looking at Tommy Dorn. "Colonel Dorn?"

"As far as we know, we have everything except their witness list," Dorn replied.

"As far as you know?" Dwyer asked.

"Well, your Honor," Dorn said with a shrug, "We don't know, what we don't know."

"They have everything," O'Rourke said with an edge in her voice.

"There will be no surprises in this trial. Do I make myself clear?" Dwyer said looking over the lawyers.

"Yes," each answered in turn.

"Go off the record," Dwyer told the court reporter.

"This isn't supposed to matter but we're all grownups here," Dwyer began. "This is not just another case. It has and will receive massive scrutiny. It has political ramifications worldwide. We are going to do this and do it right. Back on the record," he said to the court reporter.

"What about witness lists?" the judge asked.

"We're working on it, your Honor," Marc said.

"What does that mean?" Dwyer asked.

"It means it is incomplete. If they would like, we could provide a partial list say, next Wednesday. Then a more complete one in two or three weeks," Marc said.

"What about that, Major?" Dwyer asked O'Rourke.

"We can wait another two weeks," she answered.

"How about three? We're just now rounding up experts," Marc said.

Dwyer sighed heavily and said to Dorn, "Did that other bunch do anything? You don't need to answer that."

"A lot of press conferences," Dorn said.

"Okay, three weeks," Dwyer said. He opened a pocket calendar and checked for a date. "Friday, September twenty-second. You will exchange witness lists and all discovery. There will be no last minute surprises.

"Now, we have another matter," Dwyer said. He looked at the reporter and said, "Sorry, you can go off the record. Delete what I just said after the part about last minute surprises."

"Yes, sir," she replied.

"Okay, we have received over a thousand requests for press credentials. Obviously, we don't have a courtroom big enough for that. Or, even close to it.

"I've been asked to consider putting in a closed circuit TV for a live feed somewhere to accommodate this. I am not inclined to do this," he continued holding up a hand to stop Marc who was about to object. "What we can do is hold the trial in the post community center. I am told they have space for at least three hundred. Plus, it's on the post and the MP's assure me they can provide security. There are additional personnel resources at Ft. Meade in Maryland if we need them. Any comments, suggestions, objections?"

When none of the four lawyers replied Dwyer said, "Okay, we'll do it."

"How about," Marc began, "giving us a chance to take a look at it?"

"We could do that. Tommy, have you been in there?" Dwyer asked Dorn.

"Yes, judge. I don't think it will be a problem but if Marc wants to take a look first, that seems fair."

"Okay," Dwyer said. He removed a business card from his pocket and handed it to Marc. "Give me a call by next Friday and let me know what you think.

"Anything else?" Dwyer asked. "Okay," he said. He stood and told Marc he was glad to meet him and to be sure to call if anything came up. The other three lawyers all came to attention and Dwyer dismissed them.

Marc and Dorn went out the front door and the heat and humidity hit Marc hard. He took three steps down the sidewalk toward the street and had to stop. He was shaking, sweating, doubled over and having a hard time breathing.

"Are you okay?" Dorn asked.

"No, I have to sit down."

To their right, twenty feet from the sidewalk was a large oak tree with a wooden bench under it. Dorn held Marc's arm and helped him over to it.

Marc took off his suit coat and gave it to Dorn. He placed his briefcase on the ground and for the next two minutes sat bent over with his head between his knees.

Breathing normally again, the shade of the tree offering some respite from the heat, Marc leaned back and looked up.

"Are you okay?" a worried Dorn asked.

"Yeah, yes, I'm all right," Marc whispered. "It's, um, stress. Truth be told, I'm scared shitless about this case."

Marc leaned forward again and placed his elbows on his knees. Dorn placed a gentle hand on his back and silently waited for Marc to speak.

Marc turned his head to Dorn and said, "I'm okay. Haven't been sleeping well but I'm okay. Sometimes the stress gets to me. Funny thing is it never happens during a trial. I guess once we get going I'm doing something and don't have time to let it bother me. Right now, I have too much time on my hands to worry.

"Sammy's in a lot of trouble," he continued. "We need to bring in another lawyer. An appellate lawyer. Someone to work with us, sit through the trial and prepare his appeal."

"You think we're gonna lose?" Dorn asked.

"Tommy, it's going to come down to whether or not the jury believes Sammy wrote that list and leaked it to the reporter. The government has had it with leaking classified information.

"They have three class A FBI experts to testify it was Sammy's handwriting and three more to testify it was his fingerprints on the paper.

171

They have verification that he was studying radical Muslim websites on his personal laptop and his work computer."

"He says he was doing research…"

"That no one told him to do," Marc said. "If you were on the jury, what would you believe?"

"I know," Dorn said. "I have the same thoughts. We're in trouble."

Marc slapped his hands on his thighs, grabbed his briefcase and took his suit coat back from Dorn. He stood up, stretched his back and said, "Damn it's hot out here."

"August in DC," Dorn said.

Marc looked at Dorn, smiled and said, "I guess we better get back to work."

THIRTY-FOUR

Maddy Rivers had been waiting for less than two minutes when the Army private answered the phone on his desk. A couple of quick "Yes sirs" and the young soldier replaced it in its cradle.

"The General will see you now, ma'am," he told her.

Being called ma'am pricked her ego a little bit. She stood up, looked at the private who was barely old enough to shave and decided to let it go. To him she probably was a 'ma'am'.

Maddy went into the third-floor corner office of Brigadier General Russell McKee. The general stood up from behind his desk and extended his hand.

"Madeline Rivers?" he asked as they shook hands. "Please, have a seat. What can I do for you?"

General McKee was a forty-eight-year-old career soldier. He was currently the deputy division commander of the First Infantry Division, the U.S. Army's oldest and most famous combat division, the Big Red One.

"First of all, thank you for taking the time to see me. As I told you on the phone, general, I am an investigator working for the defense team for Samir Kamel. I am interviewing his former commanding officers, those who have given him a performance review, to see if any will be willing to testify on his behalf," Maddy began.

The general noticeably sighed and sat silently for several seconds. He leaned forward, put both forearms on the desk and looked directly at Maddy before continuing.

"Sammy Kamel was an outstanding officer. Intelligent, brave, exceptional leadership qualities and a very likeable, personable young man but..."

"I knew there was a 'but' coming." Maddy smiled. "I've heard that from other superior officers of his before you."

"Yeah, but first off, I haven't seen him for several years. Word through the Army grapevine is he became self-radicalized."

Maddy started to protest but McKee held up his hand to stop her.

"You're going to tell me it's not true. That he's been set up by someone..."

"He has indeed," Maddy said.

"You know something," McKee said. "I believe it, but it doesn't matter what I believe because the second thing is, if you want to stay in the Army and continue to climb the ladder, the word is out to stay away from this. Or, at the very least, don't volunteer anything.

"Let me explain something. The United States Army, Navy, Air Force and Marines, are political institutions whether we like it or not and most of us don't. They always have been and always will be. We are subject to the political winds in Washington and right now they are not blowing in favor of your client. So, no I cannot volunteer to help your client. I'm afraid you've come a long way for nothing."

With a dejected, disappointed look on her face, Maddy slipped the notebook and pen back into her bag. She stood, as did General McKee, extended her hand across his desk and thanked him.

"How did you get here? Did you rent a car?"

"Yes, I did," Maddy said.

"Tell you what, let me walk you to it."

McKee said this with a look on his face that Maddy picked up.

"All right," she said.

Maddy's rental was in the lot behind the headquarters building. When the two of them exited the building the 98 degree Kansas heat hit Maddy pretty hard. General McKee seemed to take it in stride. As they walked the short distance to Maddy's car, they passed two soldiers who saluted the general while eyeing up Maddy. At the door to the car, McKee looked around for a couple of seconds.

"Look," he began, "I can't volunteer because, to be honest, I have to cover my ass for my career. But I'd like to help Sammy. Look me in the eye and tell me you absolutely believe he is innocent."

"I absolutely believe Sammy Kamel is innocent. The Sammy I've gotten to know is no more radicalized than you or me," Maddy said, staring McKee directly in the eyes.

"Yeah, that sounds about right. The Sammy I remember wasn't even all that religious," McKee said.

"I've never seen him pray once let alone five times a day," Maddy said.

McKee smiled and said, "Sounds like him. Okay, get me a subpoena. Force me to get on the witness stand. I'll testify about my evaluation and the soldier I knew. I'll do what I can to help.

"How many others have you interviewed so far?" McKee asked.

"Two," Maddy said. "A Lieutenant Colonel Benton at the Pentagon…"

"I know Howard Benton," McKee said. "He's a closet racist. Did Sammy give you his name?"

"Yes, he did. Why would he…"

"Benton will kiss your ass in public and stab you in the back if he thought it would enhance himself. Don't subpoena him. He'll do you no good. Who else?"

"Colonel Ann Engel. She's at the Defense Intelligence Agency. She worked with Sammy when he was an interpreter in Iraq."

"I know Ann. Subpoena her. She'll be a good witness. Is that it?"

"So far," Maddy said. "Thank you, General. I'll be in touch."

McKee took a business card from his shirt pocket and a pen and wrote on the back of it.

"This is my personal cell phone number. Call me if you have questions about anyone on your list. I'll tell you what I can. And say 'hello' to Sammy for me."

"I will, sir and thank you again," Maddy told him as she took the card.

A short while later, Marc's phone went off. He looked at the caller ID and answered it.

"Where are you?" he asked Maddy Rivers.

"I'm just leaving Ft. Riley, Kansas and heading back to Manhattan," she said. "Manhattan, Kansas, not New York."

"I know the difference," Marc said. "Did you talk to McKee? What did he have to say?"

While Maddy drove, for the next few minutes she gave Marc a report of her meeting with McKee. On Marc's end, he had Sammy leaning across the dining room table eager to hear what Maddy had to say.

"That's interesting about Benton," Marc said. "Wasn't he kind of anxious to testify?"

"A bit, yeah," Maddy replied. "McKee was adamant, don't put him on the stand."

"When are you coming back?" Marc asked.

"I've got a late flight out of Manhattan to Chicago then a red-eye back to Washington. I won't get in until late but I'll see you tomorrow."

After Marc ended the call, he explained to Sammy and Tommy Dorn what she told him.

"Now that I think about it, after what Maddy was told by General McKee, that doesn't surprise me about Benton," Sammy said. "He was a senior at the academy when I was a freshman and he was a bit of a bully. He had the reputation of being a suck up to superiors even then and he was like that in Iraq, too."

"We'll leave him on the list, but not call him," Marc said. "Maddy will find some more. We may have to subpoena four or five of them and just make them go over the evaluations they gave you. There's a risk with that. The prosecution will cross-examine them and get them to admit they don't know what you've been up to recently. We'll just have to take it."

The next day Sgt. Esterhazy delivered Marc and Tommy Dorn at Sammy's quarters promptly at 0800. Sammy had a large coffee maker ready to go and greeted them at the door. Before they were inside, Tony Carvelli's rental pulled up and parked behind Esterhazy. The three of them stood in the doorway waiting for Carvelli. Marc had to suppress laughter when Carvelli grumbled a barely coherent greeting to the MP when he reached the porch.

"What's the matter, Sunshine," Marc said grinning at his PI friend, "a little too early for you?"

"Screw you, lawyer," Tony growled as he stepped past Marc. "Now I remember why I didn't enlist in the Army. Your hours suck," Tony said to both Tommy Dorn and Sammy.

"Welcome back," Dorn said as they went into the small house.

"How you holding up?" Carvelli asked Sammy.

"Okay," he replied. "Part of me is getting nervous about what's coming and part of me is anxious to get it started."

All four men grabbed a cup of coffee from the kitchen then settled into chairs around the dining room table.

"Not much luck in New York, I gather," Dorn said to Carvelli.

"This reporter for the Times, this Bullard guy, he had more enemies than Hitler. Even the people he worked with at the paper hated the guy. The suspect list is the size of a phonebook.

"The cops believe his murder was tied to the list of Muslim names he got but they really don't have a clue. He was shot twice in the back of the head with a small caliber gun. Probably a .22. The bullets fragmented. The forensics are minimal. No way they could tie the bullets to a gun even if they had it. They figure the gun went into the river with the body."

"Sounds professional," Marc said.

"Very," Tony agreed. "That rules out most of the nutcases who sent threatening letters or emails. But…"

"But good luck finding the killer," Marc said. He turned to Dorn and asked, "Any idea about how we get this into testimony?"

"Subpoena a couple of New York cops," Dorn said. "Establish their expertise and see if we can get them to say in their opinion his murder was tied to the list."

"That's a little weak," Marc replied. "The prosecution will be screaming about it."

"Let her scream," Dorn said with a shrug. "She can cross them about it," Dorn replied.

"You know a couple of NYPD cops we could call?" Marc asked Carvelli.

"Yeah. I don't know how cooperative they'll be. Cops don't like to side with defendants. Are we sure about Sammy's alibi for the time of death?"

"Solid," Sammy replied. "I was working late every night that week. There were a dozen others in the office with me and a log that shows it."

"Give me their names for our witness list," Marc told Carvelli. "We have to turn it over this Friday, the twenty-second."

"What about my roommate, Oliver Townsend?" Sammy asked. "Are you sure they won't say it was a homicide?"

"There's no evidence to support anything except an accident," Carvelli said.

"We can put Dave Smith, the CID investigator, on the stand," Dorn said. "He can testify about his suspicions."

"Good idea," Marc said. "We'll do it. Hopefully, the judge will let it in. We'll put the two NYPD cops on first then Smith. Make it look like there's a conspiracy going on to silence people and Sammy has nothing to do with it. Reasonable doubt is all we need."

THIRTY-FIVE

Madeline Rivers stopped her rented, red, Mustang convertible at the end of the line waiting to enter Ft. Myer. The news had broken that Sammy's trial date had been fixed and was coming up. Because of this, the protestors and camera crews were starting to reappear. The day before, there was a minor brawl between the two groups; a microcosm of the feelings once again sweeping the nation.

Maddy's was the fourth car in line. Normally the guards would recognize her and pass her through quickly. The procedure had now slowed considerably. She waited in line for a full five minutes and the MP, a man she recognized and who recognized her, closely examined her pass before allowing her to proceed. Security was getting tight and would likely get a lot tighter before this trial was over.

"How was Ft. Meade?" Marc asked Maddy. She was back at Sammy's quarters after a trip to Ft. Meade, Maryland to interview another Army officer on Sammy's list. This one, a woman, Major Charlene Hughes, was stationed at Ft. Meade and working at the National Security Agency.

"Have you ever been to that place?" Maddy asked Sammy referring to the NSA.

"Yeah, a couple times," he replied.

"It's huge," Maddy said. "What the hell is going on in there?"

"A lot of things no one is allowed to talk about. Did you meet with Charlene?"

"Yes, I did. She had wonderful things to say about you," Maddy said. She leaned forward and looked Sammy squarely in the eyes and said, "You should have told us you had a romantic relationship with her."

"How, I mean, what, um, did she tell you this?" Sammy stammered.

"Is it true?" Marc asked him.

"I can't believe she would tell you that. We were very careful and…"

"She didn't tell me," Maddy said. "I guessed it by the way she talked about you. You just confirmed it."

"Sammy, you can't keep things like that from us. If we had put her on the stand and they found out about it, the prosecution would rip her to shreds. It would look like she's lying," Marc said.

"And her career would be over," Tommy Dorn interjected.

"And it would have saved me a trip," Maddy added.

"We should go," Marc said to Dorn.

"Where are you off to?" Maddy asked.

"We have a pretrial conference with the judge. The prosecutor is blowing her stack over our witness list," Marc said.

"How many names are on it?" Maddy asked.

"A hundred and twenty-four."

"How many are on theirs?"

"Seventy-six," Tommy Dorn said.

"So we're more imaginative than they are," Maddy said. "So what?"

"I think Judge Dwyer wants to have a little chat about all of this. You want to ride along?" Marc asked Maddy. "Maybe you can distract Dwyer a little bit."

"Don't go there," Maddy said giving Marc a dirty look.

"And you," Marc said looking at Sammy, "You go through that witness list again. If there is anyone on there you even had a lustful thought about, I want to know it."

"I don't think there is, but…"

"Check it anyway," Dorn said.

"Yes, sir," Sammy meekly replied.

The prosecutors, Paxton O'Rourke and Greg Bain, were waiting for them when they arrived at Judge Dwyer's office. After introducing Maddy, Marc made a little joke about him not being used to punctual prosecutors. Neither O'Rourke nor Bain cracked a smile about it which made for an awkward moment.

"Okay, that went well," Marc said.

This elicited a slight smile from Major O'Rourke. She rapped on the judge's door and opened it after she heard him respond.

"Come in, everyone," Dwyer said to the group.

Marc introduced Maddy and received permission for her to stay. They all took a chair in front of the desk and waited for the judge. "One hundred and twenty-four names on your witness list," he said looking at Marc, "and seventy-six on yours," he continued turning to Paxton O'Rourke. "This trial is gonna take six months."

When neither lawyer responded Judge Dwyer continued.

"I can tell you we're not trotting a hundred character witnesses up on the stand," he said again looking at Marc, "nor are we putting seventy experts or FBI and CID agents on the stand, major."

"I understand your position, your Honor," Marc said. "But at this point, we're not sure exactly who we're going to call as character witnesses. We're not finished interviewing them."

"Is that right, Ms. Rivers? You're not done interviewing potential witnesses?" Dwyer asked Maddy.

"That's correct, your Honor," Maddy replied.

Dwyer turned back to Marc and said, "I can't tell you who to call or whom to put on your witness list. I know you're not going to call all of the people you have here," he continued holding up Marc's list. "More than a half dozen character witnesses all saying the same glowing things about your client and the jury will stop listening. You know it, I know it and Major O'Rourke knows it."

Dwyer turned to O'Rourke again and sternly pointed a finger at her and said, "You will provide the defense with a summary of what each of these people will testify too…"

"They have already received copies of our experts' reports, your Honor," O'Rourke said.

"I don't care. Do a summary of everyone on the list. You may want to pare it down a bit," Dwyer said.

"Your Honor, if I may make a suggestion," Marc said.

"Go ahead."

"She has several experts with the same basic report for both handwriting comparison and fingerprint analysis of the list of names they claim my client leaked to the media. One should be enough."

"If we can get all of their reports admitted through that witness, your Honor," O'Rourke quickly said.

"Would you agree to that?" Dwyer asked Marc.

"No, your Honor we can't…"

"There you are," O'Rourke said. "If he won't stipulate and at least allow in the reports then we need to call all of the technicians. His fingerprint and handwriting witnesses are going to testify that ours are wrong. We need to put all of them on the stand."

"How about you?" Dwyer said again looking at Marc. "How many experts?"

"Just two, your Honor. A fingerprint analyst and a handwriting expert."

"Well, that's a little progress," Dwyer said. "If you get a written report from either of your experts you will turn it over to the prosecution."

He looked at Paxton O'Rourke again and asked, "Have you made a decision about the death penalty?"

"Yes, your Honor, we have," O'Rourke replied. "We will not be requesting the death penalty at sentencing."

"All right, I'll make an order containing that stipulation. Since that is the case, the convening authority has determined the appropriate number of members of the jury shall be nine. Any questions?"

"Yes, your Honor," Marc said. "Who is this convening authority? Is this a person or…"

"His name is Major General William Conklin. He has been designated the convening authority for this case. Colonel Dorn," Dwyer said looking at Tommy Dorn. "I take it you will educate Mr. Kadella about jury selection process and procedures?"

"Yes, your Honor. It's on my list," Dorn replied.

"Anything else?"

When no one replied, Dwyer dismissed them.

It had been discussed and settled that there would be no conversation about the case in the car. Sgt. Larry Esterhazy seemed like a personable, pleasant, young man but they were taking no chances. Marc and Tommy and now Maddy talked about nothing of consequence on the short ride back to Sammy's quarters.

Once inside Sammy went right at them to find out what happened.

"They took the death penalty off the table," Marc said. "They stipulated that if you are found guilty, they would not request it at sentencing."

Sammy sat back in his chair, thought about it for a moment then said, "God that's a relief. I mean, well at least that isn't hanging over my head."

"There is a reason she did it," Dorn said with little enthusiasm. "In a death penalty case, they have to have a twelve-member jury and the verdict has to be unanimous. Now, there will only be nine members and they only need to get six to vote for a conviction."

Sammy leaned on the table, frowned and said, "That's right. I remember that now."

"Either way, with twelve members, the verdict, guilty or not guilty, must be unanimous. Now, they need to convince six, we need to convince four. So, it both helps and hurts," Dorn said.

Maddy was seated at the table next to Sammy and asked Dorn, "How are jurors selected?"

The door opened and Tony Carvelli walked in leading a small, slightly built man. Marc stood up and quickly went to the door to welcome him.

"Hello, Professor. Thanks for coming," he said to the older man as they shook hands.

"You must be Marc Kadella," the man said with a warm smile.

Professor James Sanderson taught Constitutional Law and Civil Procedure at the University of Virginia School of Law. He was a small man, barely five feet six inches, mostly bald with a fringe of gray hair circling the back of his head. Sanderson resembled everyone's Norman Rockwell version of the cheerful grandfather right down to the wire rim glasses he normally had on his forehead. He also had a sterling reputation as a first-class appellate lawyer. He had argued criminal appeals in every significant appeals court in the country, including more than a dozen appearances before the U.S. Supreme Court. Despite being on a first name basis with several Supremes, he had yet to achieve his ultimate goal; James Sanderson was using every fiber of his being to have the death penalty abolished nationwide.

"It is an honor to meet you, sir," Marc said as he released the man's hand.

"Oh please, call me Jim, or James if you feel you must be more formal. I don't even let my students call me professor."

Marc led him into the dining area and introduced him around the table. When he got to Maddy the little professor held her hand in both of his.

"Now I know where I'll be sitting," he told her. "Watch out, young lady, I'm younger and more dangerous than I look," he smiled and winked at her.

Maddy laughed, then said, "I'm sure you'll be a lot more charming and better company than these rogues."

Sammy found another chair and placed it at the table next to Maddy.

"Thank you, professor," Sammy sincerely said. "If there is an appeal, I understand you'll handle it and from what I've been told, it will be in very capable hands. But I want you to know, I am innocent. I have been framed and made a patsy."

"Well then," Sanderson said, "let's hope my services won't be necessary."

"Back to my question," Maddy said looking at Tommy Dorn. "How is the jury selected?"

THIRTY-SIX

"All rise," the commanding MP, Captain Al Dreyfus, ordered the small crowd. It was Monday, October 18 and the trial of Major Samir Kamel was about to get underway.

The courtroom was the auditorium of the Ft. Myer Community Center. With the furor and worldwide publicity surrounding this case, the Army wanted to hold it in a room large enough to accommodate a good cross-section of both the public and the media. There were three hundred uncomfortable, metal folding chairs set up. A hundred of these were allocated for the media and the rest for the public.

A month ago, it had been announced and widely publicized that a lottery would be held for tickets. More than half a million private citizens had gone online and filled out a request for one of the seats. Two hundred lucky winners had been electronically selected and passes were sent to them. Each ticket was assigned a specific seat number. It was being reported that ticket scalpers were selling them for as much as $25,000.

There was one exception; Clay Dean, through the Carver's political pull, obtained a ticket at Darla's insistence. It was his job to attend the trial, keep an eye on the proceedings and make periodic reports. Usually each day.

The seats allocated for the media were assigned the same way. No cameras or electronic recording devices would be allowed.

Security was tighter than for most presidential events. There were over five hundred Military Police temporarily assigned to Ft. Myer just for the trial. The community center was closed for the duration and guarded twenty-four hours per day. Every inch of it had been swept for explosives, recording or listening devices and anything else that might be out of the ordinary. This would continue daily throughout the trial.

Everyone entering the building, including the lawyers and any support staff, were subject to being searched. Bags, purses and briefcases were searched and everyone was swept with a wand outside while being surveilled by several serious looking MP's. Inside, before going to their seats, everyone had to walk through a metal detector and have their bags pass through a conveyor belt x-ray similar to those at airports.

The room itself was made to look and function as a normal courtroom. In front of the gallery chairs, a courtroom rail, complete with a swinging gate, had been erected. It had been anchored into the floor and was quite sturdy.

The Army had also built a judge's bench approximately three feet higher than the floor. Next to it, to the judge's right, was the witness stand two feet lower than the judge.

Along the wall, also to the judge's right, the left-hand side from the audience facing the front, a jury box had been provided. It contained nine, very comfortable, padded, individual armchairs for the members.

Set in front of the rail were two tables with the same chairs as in the jury box. These were for the prosecution and defense. Facing the judge, on the left, nearest the jury box was the table for the prosecution. The table to the right would be used by Marc and the defense.

There was a podium set up about six feet forward and in between the two tables facing toward the judge and the witness box. The lawyers would conduct their questioning from here.

Finally, you had better get there early. Every day, precisely at 0900, whether or not court had convened, the doors were locked and not even President Timmons would be allowed in. Anyone still in line waiting to enter would not be allowed in. This was also the case when the lunch break occurred. If you were not back inside and seated by the time court resumed, you were out of luck. After the doors were locked, the attendees could leave anytime but would not be allowed back in until the next session.

Outside, during the day when court was in session, there were twenty MPs armed with M-16's and sidearms surrounding the building and patrolling the grounds. Every street intersection within a two block radius was set up with a Humvee armed with a fifty caliber machine gun and another eight to ten soldiers in complete combat gear. Anyone trying to drive through after 0900 would be turned away.

Just to be on the safe side, the Army had six Apache attack helicopters circling the area. The Air Force was also involved providing a pair of fully armed F-16 fighters flying CAP—combat air patrol—over Ft. Myer.

There was one final touch for security purposes; the room was surrounded by floor-to-ceiling windows. Every one of them was covered with a thick, heavy, black-out curtain.

Judge Otis Dwyer entered the hall from a small room. Military courts-martial judges do not wear black robes. Colonel Dwyer was in his Class A dress uniform; gold-bordered epaulets, dark blue blouse and lighter blue slacks with a gold stripe running down each leg. When he took his seat, the six-foot-four-inch African-American man cut an imposing and no-nonsense figure.

"Be seated," he intoned.

For this morning's session and until jury selection was completed, the courtroom would be closed to the public. Dwyer had allowed the media to select six people to sit in. They were seated in the front row behind where the defense table would normally be. The defense and prosecution tables were both moved to sit perpendicular to the front of the room. Also, the podium was turned to face the gallery in case Judge Dwyer allowed the lawyers to question the prospective jury members.

On the left-hand side of the gallery, the jury pool was seated. There were thirty-six Army officers and per regulations, all of them outranked Major Kamel. These had been selected by the trial's convening authority, Major General William Conklin. Judge Dwyer had made it clear to both sides that they were going to quickly select the nine members from this group.

There was one other person besides the six members of the media. In the front row, right-hand side, seated next to the center aisle was an Army Lieutenant Colonel. There was a "reserved" sign on his chair. His name was Brent Collins and he was there at the behest of Army Chief of Staff, General Dirk Carney. He was assigned to attend every part of the trial and report daily to General Carney at the Pentagon. He was also there as a not so subtle reminder that the Army expected everyone to do their duty and deliver an image-clearing, ass-covering guilty verdict. It was no secret within the Army, indeed the entire U.S. Military, that a guilty verdict was expected.

Two weeks ago, every member of the jury pool had delivered an informational form to the court. Copies of these were provided to both the prosecution and defense. The forms contained basic information about each of them. Included were such things as name, rank, marital status, current billets and former military postings. In addition, Marc had their religious affiliations put on the form as well.

Of the thirty-six prospective members, twenty-three were men; eight African-Americans, two Latinos and two of Asian descent. Of the thirteen women, there were four African Americans, one Asian and no Latinos. The other nineteen, both men and women, were white. It was a fairly good cross-section except every one of them was a Christian. There was not a single Muslim or Jew selected.

Judge Dwyer settled himself into his chair on the bench and looked down at the stenographer. It was the same Army specialist who was in the judge's chambers whenever there was a conference there. She silently nodded to the judge that she was ready to go.

"Good morning," Dwyer began. He read the case name and court file number into the record and when he finished he looked at the lawyers.

"Is counsel present?"

Paxton O'Rourke stood up for the prosecution and Tommy Dorn for the defense. All four lawyers—Professor Sanderson was not attending jury selection—gave their name and rank for the record and agreed counsel was present. Dwyer also noted Sammy's presence.

"I'm going to take a minute to explain our jury selection process," Dwyer said. "This is primarily for the benefit of our guests from the media."

Dwyer continued to look at the six reporters and said, "Before I do that, I want you to understand why I closed the courtroom for this. Jury selection can get a little boring if you're just watching it. As you probably noticed, security for this trial is extremely tight. I didn't want a lot of bored people in here because, as you know, we are locked in. After the jury has been selected and we start taking testimony we will allow the gallery to fill up.

"Jury selection for court martial will be conducted like this: I will ask questions of the panel as a whole. I may, but I don't have to, allow counsel to ask questions themselves. Both sides have submitted questions to me to go over and I will.

"When we are finished with the panel as a group, we will then sequester them and have them brought in one at a time for individual questioning. This will continue until we have nine members for the jury. Both the prosecution and defense have one peremptory challenge. This allows each of them a chance to dismiss a panel member without having to give a reason."

Dwyer then began the selection process. For the next forty-five minutes, Dwyer went through his list of general questions. Most of these were designed to give the panel members a chance to try to beg their way off the jury. Being high ranking officers with many years of service and knowing the futility of even trying to bail out, none even attempted it. The judge also used this opportunity to ask about potential biases. The most obvious one being any preconceived beliefs about the guilt or innocence of Major Kamel. Because of the notoriety and media interest of this case, it was ludicrous to try to find nine people, especially Army officers, who had not heard about it. And it was extremely unlikely to find nine who did not have an opinion about his guilt or innocence. What Dwyer was really doing was giving them all, even the three general officers, a stern lecture to set those thoughts and feelings aside.

"All right," Dwyer said when he finished. "We're going to take a fifteen- minute break then begin the individual questioning." He looked down at the court reporter and told her to go off the record.

Dwyer looked at the panel and said, "The MPs will escort you into the rec room. You'll be comfortable there. There are machines for soda, snacks and a coffee machine. There are magazines, newspapers and a TV. It will be boring and I apologize for that. You will not discuss this case with each other and there will be guards in the room to ensure that.

186

There are also restrooms. When we break for lunch it will be brought in for you. Thank you for your patience."

He looked at the counsel tables and said, "I'll see counsel when the room has been cleared."

"We still want the generals excused, Judge," Marc said after everyone had left. "By virtue of their rank, they can exert too much influence."

This was a request Marc and Dorn had made as soon as they received the questionnaire forms. Paxton O'Rourke had argued to keep them on. As a prosecutor, she believed they would be inclined to be biased in favor of preserving the Army's image, although she did not say this. At the time, Dwyer said he would take it under advisement.

"Do you have anything new to argue against the defense request to excuse the three generals?" Dwyer asked Paxton.

"No, your Honor. You know our position. No bias has been shown and…"

"I get it, Major," Dwyer said holding up a hand to stop her. "But," he continued still looking at her, "I am inclined to agree with Mr. Kadella. I'm going to excuse them. Your objections are already noted and on the record.

"Captain," Dwyer said to the MP Officer, "you can tell the generals they are excused and release them."

"Yes, sir."

It took until late Tuesday afternoon to get the nine lucky ones selected. Two majors, both women, one black one white. Both outranking Sammy by date of rank. There were also four lieutenant colonels and three full colonels. The ranking officer on the panel who would act in the same capacity as a civilian foreman known as the President, was a black woman, Colonel Odessa Lewis. The panel consisted of six men, three women. Five whites, three African-Americans and a Japanese-American lieutenant colonel from Oregon.

"What do you think?" Dorn asked the assembled defense team. They were all back at Sammy's quarters hanging out with a beer in the living room.

"I think they'll be fine," Marc said speaking up first. "They are a highly educated, intelligent group. They should have no problem understanding the burden of proof, innocent until proven guilty and all the rest of it."

"It is what it is," Sammy said.

187

"I think they'll be fine," Maddy said. "They all looked like they were taking it seriously and were not looking for a way out."

"Well, we'll get started tomorrow," Marc said raising his bottle in an ironic salute.

THIRTY-SEVEN

Sergeant Esterhazy drove Marc, Tommy Dorn and Maddy Rivers into the parking lot behind the community center. They had made the drive from Sammy's quarters in silence following the MP van transporting Sammy. Security protocol would not allow the prisoner to ride with his defense team. Not only was Sammy locked inside the bulletproof van, but there were three armed MPs inside with him. And just to be sure, his hands were shackled to his waist and his ankles were shackled together.

Esterhazy parked in the closed off parking lot while the van drove up the sidewalk to the back door. Scattered around the grounds were at least a dozen MPs in full combat gear, each armed with a holstered sidearm and an M-16 assault rifle. All of the guards, as did Sammy, wore Kevlar helmets and Kevlar vests. This security procedure had been standard starting on the very first day. There had been hundreds of death threats through various mediums. The Internet and social media were aflame with self-proclaimed patriots expressing outrage that Sammy would not be put to death. Somehow this news had leaked out enraging enough idiots to keep the FBI busy for a decade tracking them all down.

By the time Marc and the others reached the defense table, Sammy was already there freed from the chains, helmet and vest. In his Class A dress uniform, Samir Kamel looked like a recruiter's dream poster boy. Unfortunately, a jury made up of his superior officers were not as likely to be impressed with that as a civilian jury might.

When Marc finished setting up the defense table he walked the few steps over to the prosecution side.

"Morning, Paxton," Marc amiably said. The two of them had established an informal greeting shortly after Marc had taken the case. Initially, he addressed her as Major O'Rourke and she called him Mr. Kadella. This barely lasted beyond two interactions.

"Hi, Marc," O'Rourke replied.

"Tell you what," Marc said, "Let's skip all this trial nonsense. What do you say? Let's arm wrestle for it."

"Deal, I'll kick your ass," Paxton replied. "I'm not a wussified civilian. I'll even go best two out of three."

Marc laughed and said, "You're probably right. I can't remember the last time I had time to go to a gym."

"Marc," she quietly said as she closed the distance between them. "Good luck. I mean that."

"You too." Marc smiled. "After it's over, winner buys dinner."

"Deal," Paxton agreed and they shook hands.

189

While this was taking place, the doors were being opened and the crowd was starting to trickle in. The first ones in were Sammy's family. His father, mother and his two brothers, their wives and his two sisters and their husbands were escorted to the front row. There were ten chairs at the bar directly behind the defense table reserved for them. Security would not allow Sammy to touch them but Marc, Maddy and Tommy Dorn greeted each of them with handshakes or hugs.

Marc took his seat, the chair on the left closest to the podium. Next to him was Sammy, then Tommy Dorn and Maddy Rivers to his right. A fifth chair next to Maddy was currently unoccupied. It was for Professor Sanderson, Sammy's appellate lawyer. Due to his schedule, it was not possible or necessary for him to be present for the entire trial.

Marc had his trial notebook handily placed directly in front of himself at the edge of the table. The notebook was a three-ring, loose-leaf binder with his preparation and sections for each phase of the trial, both his case and the prosecution's. Obviously, with a witness list with over seventy names on it, Marc could not know with certainty exactly whom the prosecution would call. In their own preparation, with everyone's input, they could make a good guess.

At a few minutes past 0900, the MP captain ordered everyone to rise as Judge Dwyer came out and onto the bench. Dwyer spent a few minutes making it clear to the people in the gallery he would tolerate no misbehavior. He also explained it might be necessary to empty the courtroom if testimony would include reading classified information.

When Dwyer finished addressing the spectators, he looked at the Captain Drefus and said, "Captain, please bring in the members."

The courtroom remained silent while the nine members of the jury filed in and took their seats.

"Is the prosecution ready to make its opening statement?" Dwyer asked looking down at Paxton O'Rourke.

"We are, your Honor," she replied.

Major O'Rourke stood and walked to the podium which was turned to face the jury box. After laying her notes on it, she looked at the solemn faces staring back at her and the case of the United States of America vs. Major Samir Kamel got underway.

"Good morning," she began. "My name is Major Paxton O'Rourke and I am lead counsel for the prosecution."

As Tommy Dorn had informed Marc, she was meticulously prepared, methodical and thoroughly complete. For the next two and half hours, with a fifteen-minute break thrown in, she carefully walked the jury through the government's entire case. She rarely needed her notes but even so, turned the pages of them as she moved along.

"It is our job, the government's job, to prove the defendant guilty beyond a reasonable doubt. You have all heard that phrase many times. It is the burden of proof required of criminal prosecutions and is a bedrock principle of civilized law; a burden I wholeheartedly agree with.

"But keep in mind that it is 'beyond a reasonable' doubt. That is not the same as beyond all doubt. And, at the end of the trial, you will see that we have met that burden. We will have presented the evidence to establish beyond a reasonable doubt that the defendant, Samir Kamel is guilty of the worst, most heinous crime there is; treason."

After she said the word "treason", there was absolutely no sound in the entire room. O'Rourke stood at the podium for almost ten seconds and let that word hang in the air like the sword of Damocles hanging over Sammy's head. While she stood there for those ten seconds, which seemed like an hour to those at the defense table, she made unblinking eye contact with every member of the jury.

Marc, without realizing it, was not breathing. He stared straight ahead and was looking at nothing. He did not dare to even look around. Marc knew, despite their promise to keep an open mind, if the members were to vote at that moment, Sammy would be toast.

He snapped out of it at the same moment Major O'Rourke broke eye contact and started to gather up her notes. Marc looked at Sammy who was staring straight ahead trying to maintain his impassive look.

While O'Rourke walked back to her seat, Marc whispered into Sammy's ear. "Relax, there's a long way to go. Breathe."

"Mr. Kadella, is the defense going to give its opening statement now?" Judge Dwyer asked.

Originally, Marc had decided to defer. As in civilian trials, the prosecution puts on what is called its case-in-chief first. The defense is allowed to defer their opening until the prosecution has finished presenting its case and has rested. The quality of O'Rourke's opening and her presentation of the evidence they had and would be submitted was giving him second thoughts.

"Mr. Kadella?" Dwyer asked again when Marc failed to respond.

In an instant, Marc realized this was not the time to change his mind. Stick to the case as planned and prepared.

"Um," Marc started to say as he stood to address the bench, "the defense will defer its opening until it presents its case."

"Very well," Dwyer said. "Major O'Rourke, have your first witness ready to go at 1400. That's 2:00 P.M. to our civilian audience. Recess."

191

For security reasons, Sammy was not allowed to leave the building until court adjourned for the day. Within the community center are numerous smaller activity rooms. One of these was designated for the defense and one each for the prosecution and jury members. The judge had his own office within the building.

There is a sandwich shop nearby with a reputation for good quality food. Potbelly's was less than five minutes from Ft. Myer. In order to facilitate lunch breaks, they had been contracted to deliver lunches for all of the participants and the Kamel family.

When Dwyer called for the lunch break, all parties went to their individual rooms. The lunches were supposed to be waiting for them. Unfortunately, the caterers did not arrive until almost 12:30.

While the girl who seemed to be in charge of the sandwich deliveries was stacking them on the table in the defense team room, Marc and Maddy walked over to her.

"I'm really sorry we're so late," the pretty blonde apologized.

"What happened?" Maddy asked.

"There's a huge crowd at the entrance. There must be five thousand people out there," she answered.

"Maybe not five but at least three thousand," the MP who stood waiting for her said. "And they're getting a little out of hand."

"We waited in line for almost an hour just to be let in," the girl told them. "We're really sorry..."

"Don't worry about it," Marc said and smiled at her. "We have plenty of time to eat."

Marc removed a twenty-dollar bill from his pocket and handed it to her.

"Oh, no," she said holding up a hand to stop him. "Lunch is paid for."

"I know, this is for you and your crew."

"Don't be so cheap," Jahid Kamel said. He was holding a one-hundred-dollar bill for her. "Please, take it," Jahid said.

"Thanks for making me look bad," Marc said.

"You're welcome," Jahid replied, smiling.

At 1:45, there was a knock on the door and an MP lieutenant came in. He looked at Marc and Dorn and said, "The judge wants to see you."

They followed the young officer to Dwyer's office and joined up with Paxton and Captain Bain on the way.

"What's this about?" Marc asked Paxton.

"I don't know," she said with a shrug.

"Come in," Dwyer said answering the knock on his door.

The MP lieutenant opened the door and the four lawyers filed in. Dwyer picked up the refuse from his lunch and dropped it in a wastebasket. Standing next to his desk was all lieutenant colonel in combat fatigues. "There's a riot going on at the gate," Dwyer said. "It seems emotions are running a little high."

"We're not sure how or what started it," the lieutenant colonel said. The man's tag read Henderson. "We have it pretty well contained. About fifty to sixty people have been taken to the post commissary. Mostly minor injuries. Basically, it became a large fist fight. It was all off-post so the civilian police were called in. There were at least a couple hundred arrests made. I thought you should know. You might want to consider adjourning for the day."

"I've spoken to the officer in charge of court security. He believes we should be okay. Probably a number of spectators will be held up and locked out. Are your witnesses here?" Dwyer asked Paxton O'Rourke.

"Yes, sir," she replied. "We're ready to go. We have two for this afternoon, sir. The two FBI agents that located the pilfered list at the home of the New York Times reporter after he was found dead."

"Was the media out there, Jack?" Tommy Dorn asked the lieutenant colonel.

"Oh, yeah," he replied. "A shitload of them. The film's already running all over cable news and the internet."

"Thank you, Colonel Henderson," Dwyer said. "Keep us informed. We'll start taking testimony in about fifteen minutes."

193

THIRTY-EIGHT

"You may call your first witness, Major O'Rourke," Dwyer said to start the afternoon session.

Thanks to the disturbance by the protesters at the entrance to Ft. Myer there were barely fifty people in attendance. Outside the locked community center were over two hundred angry ticket holders, some of whom paid a lot of money.

"The prosecution calls Samuel Arnold, your Honor," Paxton stood up and said.

Less than a minute later the witness was sworn and took the stand. Arnold gave his name and occupation for the record. He was a special agent and a fifteen-year veteran of the FBI. His current assignment was in the Manhattan office.

O'Rourke took fifteen to twenty minutes establishing the witness as an investigator with an excellent record. She went over his career and the numerous commendations he had received. She then had Arnold explain in detail the policy and procedures required for handling evidence in the field.

Being first a police officer for eight years and an FBI agent for fifteen, Arnold had testified in too many trials to remember. Plus, Captain Bain had done a good job preparing him. All O'Rourke had to do was wind him up and let him go and he expertly explained how he came to find the list that had been leaked to the reporter, Melvin Bullard. Or at least the list he had found in Bullard's spare bedroom/office in his apartment.

Marc had anticipated the FBI agent being the first witness. The government would want to get their most incriminating piece of evidence, the list, before the jury as soon as possible. When O'Rourke and her witness reached that point in his testimony, O'Rourke smoothly went through the steps to get it into evidence as Exhibit One. At the same time, she had him identify the envelope the list was found in. It was in a separate evidence bag and marked as the government's Exhibit Number Two.

The list was in a sealed bag with a chain of evidence slip of paper attached with several sets of initials on it. The first one was Arnold's. After it was entered, O'Rourke handed the bag to one of the jurors to give them all a chance to look it over themselves. While it was passed around the jury box, Marc watched as each member checked it out. After passing it to the next person, every one of them looked at Sammy with a very stern expression on their face.

O'Rourke made a feeble attempt to get Agent Arnold to testify about the handwriting and fingerprints found on the document. Judge

Dwyer quickly sustained Marc's objection but the message was clear; there were fingerprints on it that belonged to Sammy and the handwriting matched his.

When O'Rourke finished, Marc took her place at the podium. He introduced himself to the witness and started his cross-examination.

"Special Agent Arnold, did you obtain a search warrant…" Marc began to ask.

"Objection," O'Rourke said almost jumping to her feet. "We thoroughly covered this in a motion hearing. The defendant has no standing to object to the lack of a search warrant nor does he have an expectation of privacy in the apartment of Melvin Bullard."

"I was just wondering if he had a search warrant, your Honor," Marc replied holding up his hands' palms out trying to sound and look as innocent as possible.

"She's right, Mr. Kadella," Dwyer admonished Marc. "The New York police had one. The objection is sustained. Move along."

For the next twenty minutes, Marc went over the FBI's procedures with Agent Arnold looking for even a little crack in how the evidence was handled. Not surprising, Marc was unable to create one. Arnold and his partner, Gayle Lockett, had even personally transported the item in its plastic bag to the FBI crime lab in Quantico, Virginia. He finally realized the futility and gave up.

"Your Honor, may we approach?" Major O'Rourke asked before calling her next witness.

Dwyer waved them forward and the lawyers met at the bench.

"Your Honor, my next witness was going to be Special Agent Arnold's partner, Gayle Lockett. She was going to be a backup if we ran into a problem getting Exhibit One entered into evidence. Since that's been accomplished I think it would be redundant to call her. However, I do not have another witness for today. Given the time…"

"Let's adjourn," Dwyer said interrupting her. "Unless you think you can punch holes in the admission of Exhibit One through Agent Lockett," Dwyer said looking at Marc.

Realizing the judge was basically telling Marc not to waste their time, he quickly agreed.

"No, your Honor. I'm okay with that. But if I find a reason later to call her, I reserve the right to do so."

"Fair enough," Dwyer said.

Thursday morning, promptly at 0900, Dwyer came out and again found every seat taken. When everyone had retaken their seat, Dwyer told O'Rourke to bring in the next witness.

"Sir, the government calls Simon Kohl."

A well-dressed, somewhat serious-looking, middle-aged man in an expensive business suit and tie was led into the courtroom. He walked with an air of arrogant authority through the gate and to the witness stand. Major O'Rourke swore him in and he took the chair next to Judge Dwyer.

"Please state your name, job title and current position, sir," O'Rourke said from her place at the podium.

"Simon Kohl spelled K-O-H-L. I am the Deputy Director of the Department of Homeland Security," the man politely answered.

"How long have you held this position?"

"Six years," Kohl answered.

O'Rourke then took him on a trip through his curriculum vitae, a copy of which had been provided to Marc. It took almost a half-hour but when she finished, O'Rourke had established the witness as one of the most important people involved in the nation's security and with impeccable credentials. This was not a political appointee. Kohl was a real security expert and not a pal or fundraiser of President Timmons.

In a broad and general sense so as to avoid discussing in open court confidential security details, Kohl testified about the war on radical Islam. Especially those efforts that were being undertaken at the time the now infamous list had been leaked to the media and to WikiLeaks.

"Director Kohl, how would you describe the effect the dissemination of the names on that list had on our efforts to combat radical Islam?"

"Devastating," Kohl said. "The damage done was absolutely incalculable."

"Please explain, sir," O'Rourke said.

Kohl turned to face the jury and said, "It destroyed years of intelligence gathering. That list contains the names of the top leaders of one of the most dangerous groups out to destroy Western civilization. Dozens of people risked their lives doing incredibly dangerous undertakings to find out who these people were and where we could find them.

"Keep in mind," he continued, "these fanatics had killed hundreds if not thousands of people including their fellow Muslims, maybe even especially their fellow Muslims. They were responsible for radicalizing hundreds of people and killing and maiming hundreds of Americans. After that list of names was made public, these people scattered and set us back to square one in our search to find them and stop them. You cannot overstate the damage that was done."

"Director Kohl," O'Rourke said when he finished, "in your opinion, would you say that leaking that confidential top secret list of names to the media gave aid and comfort to our enemies?"

"Objection," Marc said as he arose to address the court. "The question calls for a legal conclusion for which there is no foundation that this witness is qualified to answer."

Paxton O'Rourke had anticipated Marc's objection and was certain Dwyer would quickly overrule it. Instead, Dwyer looked at Marc for almost thirty seconds with a solemn thoughtful expression. While he did this, O'Rourke stood rigidly at the podium not breathing as a thin line of sweat broke out on her hairline. If the objection was sustained O'Rourke's case would be finished.

"Overruled," he finally said. "The witness has been sufficiently established as a national security expert to give his opinion. The witness will answer the question."

"Absolutely. We believe, because of the subsequent uproar across the Muslim world, it had been an enormous boost to their recruitment and again, had set us back years. It has also caused significant damage to our relations with allies and made us look bad in the eyes of our enemies. It also made it more difficult to find the people on that list."

"Thank you, Director," O'Rourke said now anxious to end her examination. She had gotten what she wanted and it was time to sit down.

"Your witness," she said to Marc.

Marc almost ran to the podium to show how anxious he was to get at his cross-examination. Before he got there, Dwyer stopped him by calling for a break.

After the break, Marc introduced himself and began his cross by asking, "Who exactly is this enemy that you believe was given aid and comfort?"

"Radical Islam," Kohl replied.

"Have we declared war?"

"There is an authorization for a use of force."

"Is that a 'no' to my question, Director?" Marc politely asked.

"It's the same thing," Kohl replied.

"On December 8, 1941, Congress declared war on Japan. Has Congress declared war on radical Islam?"

"They passed a use of force authorization," Kohl replied clearly annoyed.

"Director Kohl, I noticed when Major O'Rourke was asking you questions you were very cooperative. Are you willing to give me the same level of courtesy and cooperation, sir?" Marc asked with an innocent expression.

Kohl hesitated for a moment, gathered himself then said, "Certainly."

"Isn't it true, sir, Congress has not declared war on anybody called 'Radical Islam', yes or no, sir?" Marc asked.

"No," Kohl quietly admitted.

"Isn't it also true that a significant number of both House members and Senators openly dispute this so-called 'War on Terror' or 'Radical Islam'?"

"Yes, I suppose that's true," he meekly replied.

"During your previous testimony, you said after Exhibit One was leaked to the media it became difficult to locate the people on that list, is that correct?"

"Yes," he said nodding for emphasis.

"To hunt them down and kill them with drone missile strikes, correct?"

Kohl went silent and did not answer.

"Isn't it true you had a lot of difficulty locating these people all along, yes or no, Director Kohl?"

"Yes, that's true but leaking the list made it worse."

"Nonresponsive, your Honor. I ask that the answer be stricken."

"So ordered," Dwyer said. "The jury will ignore the last statement by the witness."

"Director Kohl, in your testimony you claimed the leak of Exhibit One was used as a recruiting tool for 'Radical Islam', is that correct?"

"Yes," Kohl emphatically replied.

"Do you have any empirical evidence, any polling, surveys or any data at all or maybe some recruiting literature from these so-called 'Radical Islamic' terror groups to back up that claim? Yes or no, Director Kohl?"

Kohl hesitated and squirmed in the chair a bit before answering. "No, but we have seen an increase in recruits."

Marc quickly, silently deliberated deciding whether or not to have the answer stricken as nonresponsive. He decided to let it go.

"How do you know that isn't because McDonald's, Burger King and Starbucks haven't provided jobs in the Muslim world? Many people believe this is why young men become radicalized."

Kohl remained silent while the laughter throughout the courtroom died down. Instead of waiting for an answer Marc continued.

"What about climate change or global warming? A significant number of politicians are claiming this is the reason. Could it be this?"

Again, Kohl sat silently glaring at Marc until the laughter died down.

"Director," Marc said, "not enough rain or air conditioning?"

"There is no evidence of that," Kohl replied.

"No, you're right," Marc agreed. "And there's no evidence that the government's Exhibit One is causing it either, is there?"

"It's obvious," Kohl replied.

"Isn't it true that the real effect, the real problem with the leak of Exhibit One was the embarrassment it brought to the U.S. Government for hunting Islamic clerics and summarily executing them and not the aid and comfort you claim was brought to an enemy that is, at best, ill-defined?"

"No! Not at all," Kohl almost yelled.

Before the witness could finish answering, Marc said, "I have nothing further," then packed up and walked away from the podium.

"Redirect?" Dwyer asked O'Rourke.

"Absolutely," she answered glaring at Marc. Before Dwyer even asked the question O'Rourke was out of her chair on her way to the podium.

O'Rourke allowed Kohl thirty seconds to sit back, take a deep breath and calm down. In less than ten minutes, she had undone the damage and made it obvious that this leak was a serious security breach that brought aid and comfort to a very real enemy.

When Clay Dean was a mile away from Ft. Myer and still in his car, he called his real boss, Tom Carver. Having Clay attend the trial may have been Darla's idea but Tom made sure Clay checked in with him first.

"How was the first day?" Tom asked.

"The prosecution's opening statement was very good. I think she'll do great. She seems to have an excellent handle on the case. She came across as very sure of herself and she makes a great impression.

"They got the list into evidence right away. Simon Kohl was next up and the defense lawyer hit him pretty good."

"How? What did he have?"

"He tried to cast doubt on the list being leaked giving aid to the enemy. He had Kohl going pretty good, but the prosecutor fixed it."

"What do you think?" Tom asked.

"On the whole, the first day went fine," Clay replied.

"Okay. Call Darla and make sure you embellish the part about the lawyer kicking Kohl's ass. Give her something to worry about," Tom said then chuckled.

"Will do, boss," Clay said smiling at Tom's deviousness to stick it to his wife a little bit.

Late that afternoon, Lt. Colonel Collins, the Army Chief-of-Staff's personal representative at the trial, met with 2 four-stars at the Pentagon.

They were the Chief-of-Staff himself, General Dirk Carney and the Vice-Chief, General Troy Morin.

"Deputy Director Kohl had a tough time on the stand," Collins began his report to the generals.

"That's a shame," Morin sarcastically said. "The arrogant little shit."

Carney smiled then told Collins to continue.

"The defense lawyer, the civilian, hammered him a bit. I don't think it worked though. He tried to show that what really happened was just an embarrassment to the government. He rattled Kohl a bit but Major O'Rourke straightened it out. She's pretty good, sir, from what I've seen so far."

"Yeah, except for taking the death penalty off the table," Morin bitterly said.

"We've been over this, Troy," Carney reminded him. "It makes getting a conviction easier. They wouldn't vote for death anyway.

"What's up for tomorrow?" Carney continued, asking Collins.

"They knocked off early today, before lunch. I'm guessing she'll start with forensics people tomorrow. Techs from the FBI. Fingerprint and handwriting experts," Collins replied.

"It's going okay?" Carney asked.

"Yes, sir. But it's early."

"Very well. You can go, Colonel, and thank you," Carney told Collins.

THIRTY-NINE

The CNN anchor turned away from the camera to look at the man seated to his left. The anchor, Ken Wallis, had made a brief introduction to their topic of discussion and was now turning it over to his guest. The guest's name was Randy Austad and he was this week's paid expert. He was a defense lawyer and former member of the Army JAG Corp. The topic was the trial of Samir Kamel.

"So, Randy, give us your take on the trial, so far," Wallis said.

Austad had not spent one minute in the courtroom; his opinion and commentary were going to be based entirely on second-hand news reports he had heard and seen. This was, of course, quite normal for TV news. Put someone on the air who looks good and sounds authoritative whether they know anything of substance or not.

"I believe the defense did a fairly good job of creating at least an argument for reasonable doubt," Austad began.

Wallis turned back to the camera and flashed a big shot of the $10,000 of pearly, white capped teeth he had and still looking at the camera, asked, "How so?"

"Well, Ken, Major Kamel as you know is charged with a single count of treason. There are specific elements for the crime of treason. I won't go into all of them right now," Austad continued because he could not remember what those elements of treason are, but, he continued, "The prosecution must prove each one. And they must prove each one beyond a reasonable doubt. In my opinion, the most important one is giving aid and comfort to the enemy. In order to convict Major Samir, it isn't enough to prove that he leaked the list of names to the New York Times. They must also prove, beyond a reasonable doubt, that what he did provided aid and comfort to the enemy."

"That seems obvious," Wallis chimed in again flashing the smile to the camera.

"Sure," Austad replied nodding at the anchorman. "But in a court trial, you still have to provide evidence of this. Someone has to get on a witness stand and testify as to exactly what that is. What aid did it provide the enemy?"

"I see," Wallis solemnly said into the camera again.

"Kamel's lawyer can at least argue there is no enemy in the traditional sense. No, country or army we are at war with. And he'll argue that the prosecution fell short of providing evidence that leaking the list provided aid to radical Islam," Austad said.

He then put his right hand to his right ear because he was hearing from the director's booth. In his ear was the voice of CNN's director reminding him not to use the term radical Islam.

"Do you think the defense lawyer was successful?"

"If I had to guess, probably not," Austad answered the anchorman that Austad was beginning to realize was a lightweight, fluffhead. "The jury is made up of senior Army officers. They're not going to be impressed with doubts about who the enemy is or how much aid they received from the leaking of the list."

After that comment, Darla Carver clicked off the TV. She had been watching CNN to get some information on the trial.

The lawyer's comments at the beginning caused her a momentary twitch of panic. Clay's phone call was unsettling, to say the least. His comments about the lawyer's cross exam of Simon Kohl worried her. But she felt better now. The answer about the jury make up of Army officers made sense to her. In fact, she was delighted the decision had been made to try him by the Army. Army officers were not as likely to be sympathetic as civilians on a jury.

For the first time today Darla was alone. It had been another long day of campaigning, speechmaking and handshaking. She was in a Sheraton Hotel in Stamford, Connecticut. To Darla, this was the equivalent of being sentenced to Devil's Island. Something to be endured and left behind as soon as possible. It was after 10:00 P.M. and she was about to enjoy her favorite part of the day. A nice long soak in a hot bubble bath to wash off the grime of consorting with the masses. The whirlpool in the Executive Suite was ready and a snifter half-full of Remy Martin was waiting for her. Her staff knew that woe be unto anyone foolish enough to bother her at this time of night.

The campaign itself was a mere formality for her Senate seat. Polling had her in the sixties and her opponent barely in the thirties. For all practical purposes, with the election only three weeks away, Darla Carver was no longer campaigning for the Senate. This was a trial run for the big one that would begin in barely a year.

Despite her personal disdain for people who worked for a living, Darla was impressed with the enthusiasm and size of the crowds that greeted her wherever she went. Today was quite typical; four campaign stops with huge crowds waiting hours just to see her. And for the past week, the number of "Darla for President" signs were increasing daily.

For the next ten days, she was leaving her new home state. Her popularity and political appeal were starting to spread. The next two days she was campaigning next door in New York for other party candidates. Then it was on to several others, she could not remember all of them, to help other candidates. Of course, this was also to nail down future support.

With her election to the Senate locked up, the national media was already buzzing about her taking on President Timmons. Every opportunity they had to ask her a question was about the presidency. Thanks to the phalanx that always surrounded her these situations were rare. The less she said to the media, the better. Her relationship with them during Tom's presidency had been barely civil.

The media, even the party friendly ones, had portrayed her as cold, ruthless, and ambitious. Unfortunately for her, she was constantly being compared to her husband. Despite the fact that almost everyone knew he was a philandering pig, at times a borderline sexual predator, no one seemed to care. Pleasant, personable and charming, Tom was a natural politician. Darla had to work at it.

Darla walked into the spacious bathroom holding the cognac. She set the glass down on the small table next to the tub and stood in front of the full-length mirror. She let the silk robe drop to the floor and stared at herself, naked, in the mirror.

Not bad, she thought. *Getting a little broad across the beam in behind and at the hips but on the whole, she still looked good.* How she envied her fat-ass husband. Thirty extra pounds around his waist and women still flocked after him.

Darla slipped into the tub which was a tad too hot. It felt good though and she knew it would cool down. She settled in and turned on the whirlpool jets.

Darla picked up the snifter and held it up in front of herself.

"Life is good," she said out loud. "And nobody deserves it more."

With that, she downed a healthy swallow and settled into the cloud of soap suds and bubbles. A half-hour later she slipped in between the sheets of the king-size bed.

Darla heard a light knock on her door. She looked at her watch which read 7:00 A.M. exactly. *Right on time*, she thought. Darla was fully dressed and ready to go.

"Come in," she answered unnecessarily

Sonja Hayden had already opened the door with her key card and stood aside as the young man wheeled the serving cart into the suite. He quickly set up Darla's breakfast on the dining table. Before leaving, the obviously gay man turned to her with an adoring look.

"Mrs. Carver, I just want you to know what a privilege it is to meet you. I can't wait for Election Day to vote for you. I only regret that I can only vote once. All my friends are voting for you too. It's just wonderful…"

"Thank you very much," Darla warmly told him. She extended her hand and he took it for a light shake.

"I may never wash this hand again," he gushed.

"That's probably not a good idea," Darla said with a laugh. "You'll have to excuse me, I have a busy day ahead."

"Oh, of course! I'm sorry. Thank you again," he said as he backed out pulling the cart.

When the door closed and Darla was sure he was gone, she said, "I hope that disgusting little queen didn't give me Aids."

Darla sat down and started eating. Her breakfast consisted of a half of a grapefruit, a small plate of fruit, two pieces of wheat toast with marmalade and Chai tea. While Darla ate, Sonja performed her morning duty and went over the day's itinerary.

When she finished eating Darla went into the bathroom to brush her teeth again. She straightened her hair and checked herself in the mirror. She came out to find Sonja waiting by the door, her bags packed and ready to be picked up. Darla slipped into her shoes and a jacket that matched her skirt. She looked at Sonja and smiled slightly.

"Well, on to Buffalo," Darla said.

While the two women were walking down the hotel hallway to the elevators, Darla said, "'On to Buffalo'. That sounds like it should be the title of a Country Western song about going to prison. That's how I feel; On to Buffalo. On to prison. It has the same level of appeal."

Even the usually staid and solemn Sonja had to laugh at the thought.

FORTY

Major O'Rourke called her first technical expert first thing the next day. A moment later all eyes turned to the back to watch a five-foot, one hundred pound Latina named Manuela Santana march up the center aisle. O'Rourke swore her in and she took the stand.

"Please state your name, occupation and current employment for the record," O'Rourke told her from the podium.

"Manuela Santana. I am a fingerprint analyst and I am employed at the FBI crime lab in Quantico, Virginia. I have been a fingerprint technician with the FBI for nineteen years. I am one of two supervising technicians in the fingerprint lab."

"Tell the jury, please, where you were educated."

Having been given this witness' curriculum vitae before trial with her long list of impressive credentials, Marc did not want them read into the record.

"Your Honor," Marc said interrupting O'Rourke. "The defense will stipulate as to this witness' qualifications."

"So noted," Dwyer replied. "You may continue, Major."

Great, Marc thought as he sat down. *Now she is going to get Santana to tell the jury her qualifications and I just put it on the record that I agree she is an expert.*

Manuela Santana was not only an expert witness, the tiny woman was a veteran witness. It took little prodding from O'Rourke for Santana to give the jury a detailed rundown of her education and numerous awards for her field of expertise. She was also able to explain the times she spent training others in fingerprint science at police departments across the country and in a dozen other nations. The good news for the defense was it wasn't long before the members were showing signs of boredom. Little did they know that this was to be the highlight and most interesting testimony they would get for the next two days.

Manuela was not only a veteran witness, she loved being a witness. She had worked hard the past twenty years and was proud to display it every time she had a chance. Despite personally preparing her testimony, O'Rourke could not get her to speed it up. It was a few minutes past noon before she finished explaining just one of the three methods of print analysis she used.

Despite their best efforts to appear interested, it was clear that the members needed a break. When Manuela finished explaining Alternate Light Source Analysis, Dwyer jumped in and called for the lunch break.

O'Rourke had a serious discussion with her witness over lunch about moving things along. Unfortunately, it did not have much effect.

With an afternoon break around 3:30 it took until almost 5:00 for Manuela to finish her detailed dissertation on the other two analysis methods. The second one being cyanoacrylate, the use of superglue fumes. The vapors given off by cyanoacrylate found in superglue brings out prints on non-porous surfaces such as glass, metals and varnished woods. Smooth surfaces, primarily.

The third and final one is by applying chemicals such as ninhydrin to reveal fingerprints not readily detected. This is especially effective on paper.

Fortunately for the audience, Manuela included in her testimony how she personally used all three methods on both the list and the manila envelope in which it was found. Because of this, it only took her another hour to go through her slide show. A big screen, HD television was wheeled in. Using a metal pointer Manuela gave the jury a vivid education of the ridges, grooves and patterns on the fingerprints found on the list. Alongside each photo on the TV screen, she displayed its counterpart from the prints of Samir Kamel on file. When she finished, she retook the witness stand.

"Ms. Santana," O'Rourke began when she sat down on the stand, "in your expert opinion that even the defense concedes, what is your opinion about the prospect of a match between the prints found on the list, Exhibit One, and the defendant's fingerprints?"

"They are a match, no doubt about it," she answered with certainty.

"A one hundred percent perfect match?" O'Rourke asked. She wanted to get this out before Marc could.

"Nothing's perfect," Santana replied. "But using a formula I have developed I can explain it to the jury if you'd like."

O'Rourke looked at Marc who, knowing what her mathematical formula found, quickly said, "No, that won't be necessary."

A relieved O'Rourke thought, *Thank you, Marc.*

"Please, go on," O'Rourke said to Manuela.

"As I was saying, using a formula I have developed, I found a ninety-nine point two percent match. The prints on the list and those on file of Samir Kamel are a match, in my opinion."

"I have nothing further," O'Rourke told Dwyer.

Sensing the judge was going to halt for the day, Marc quickly stood up and said, "Your Honor, I only have a few questions. I won't be long."

"Very well, counsel. You may proceed."

"Ms. Santana, can you tell the jury when the prints found on the list, Exhibit One, were put on it?"

"No, I have no idea. We can't…"

"Thank you. Now, you found no prints at all on the envelope, Exhibit Two, isn't that correct?"

"Yes, that's true."

"You testified that there is a ninety-nine point two percent match, in your opinion. That also means there is a point zero eight percent likelihood of there not being a match. Isn't it true that also means that there is a point zero eight percent likelihood it could be someone else's print?"

"Um, I ah, don't, um…"

"You testified it is not a perfect match, that there is this small chance it could be someone else's print. Isn't that true?"

"I suppose so, yes."

"There are roughly three hundred and twenty people in this room. Point zero eight is eight tenths of one percent, is that correct? I'm a lawyer, not a math whiz, help me out here," Marc said smiling at her.

"Yes, that's correct," Manuela said smiling back.

"Therefore isn't it true that, mathematically, there are between two and three people just in this room who could match those prints on the list, yes or no?"

"Well, I uh never thought of it that way…"

"Yes or no," Marc repeated.

"Well, yes, I suppose so," she agreed.

"Exhibits One and Two were found in New York City, were they not?" Marc asked.

"Yes, that is my understanding."

"There are roughly eight million people in New York. Given this point zero eight percentage you have said that the prints could belong to someone else, isn't it true that there could be sixty-four thousand people who could match those prints in New York?"

"No," Manuela answered. "Fingerprints are too unique for that. You are misstating it. I said there is a ninety-nine point two percent match to your client. That does not equate to anyone else."

"I have nothing further, your Honor," Marc said to Dwyer.

He quickly gathered his notes and went back to his table and sat down.

"Redirect?" Dwyer asked O'Rourke.

"Yes, sir," O'Rourke said.

She stepped back up to the podium and asked one question.

"Whose fingerprints are on the list, Exhibit One?"

"Asked and answered," Marc quickly stood and said.

"The defendant's," Manuela blurted out before Dwyer could rule.

"Overruled," Dwyer said.

With that exchange, Dwyer called a halt for the day.

The next two witnesses were two more fingerprint analysts from Quantico. Because of the significance of this case, the FBI had assigned three techs to analyze the prints from the list and compare them to Sammy's. Unfortunately for the jury members and everyone else in the courtroom, Manuela Santana was the interesting one. She was also the quickest.

Irwin Karr was born to be a laboratory technician. Forty-two years old, shy, unassuming with an undiagnosed touch of agoraphobia. It had taken him until he was twenty-six to ask a girl for a date and he was still married to her. Irwin was a poor witness at best. Irwin should be back at Quantico and not on a witness stand.

Paxton O'Rourke's co-prosecutor, Captain Greg Bain, had been assigned to do the examination of Mr. Karr. Because Manuela Santana had done such a thorough job of explaining the techniques for retrieving fingerprints, Irwin only needed to give his findings of his examinations. The entire direct exam should have taken no more than an hour. Instead, it lasted until the noon.

Judge Dwyer asked Marc if he wanted to wait until after lunch to conduct his cross-examination. Anxious to get at poor Irwin while he was still profusely sweating, Marc answered the judge negatively while walking to the podium. Just for the sport of it, Marc silently stared with a grim expression at Irwin. The poor man looked like he was going to melt into the seat. Finally, after about forty-five seconds of this, Dwyer told Marc to get on with it.

With a series of short, sharp yes and no questions fired in rapid succession, it took Marc less than ten minutes to almost make Irwin faint. Fortunately for the prosecution, Irwin held it together well enough to emphatically reiterate that, in his expert opinion, the fingerprints on Exhibit One were a match to those of Samir Kamel.

"One last question, Mr. Karr," Marc said.

"Yes!" Irwin said as he almost jumped forward out of his seat at the thought of a final question.

"Is it possible someone stole a sheet of paper knowing Major Kamel's fingerprints were on it and forged the list on it?"

"Objection," Captain Bain shouted as he stood. "Assumes facts not in evidence and is beyond the scope of this witness' expertise."

"Sustained," Dwyer ruled. "The members will disregard the question in its entirety." Dwyer was staring a hole in Marc while he said this.

Hopefully, they won't ignore it, Marc thought.

"I have nothing further, your Honor," Marc said.

The afternoon session was taken up by the third fingerprint technician. Her name was Zoe Fields. A thirty-nine-year-old with twelve years at the FBI. She was articulate, smooth and except for the frizzy hair, reasonably attractive and should have made a good witness. By this time the entire room knew more about fingerprints than any of them had ever wanted to know.

Her testimony began shortly before 2:30 and was done, including Marc's cross-exam, by 4:00. When she was getting down from the witness stand Dwyer rapped his gavel and quickly fled to his private bathroom.

While the crowd was filing out Marc ambled over to the prosecution's table. Since the courtroom was locked and guarded each night by armed MPs both sets of lawyers left some things on the table after each day.

"That was mean," Paxton said to Marc but was smiling when she said it.

"What?" Marc said with his hands spread and an innocent look on his face.

"What you did to poor Irwin," she replied. "I thought he was going to faint up there."

"Where did you find him?" Marc asked with a chuckle.

"I take what they give me," Paxton shrugged. "He's actually a very smart man and knows his stuff. He just has trouble with crowds."

"Actually he did okay," Marc said. "Have a nice evening. I'll see you tomorrow."

"You too, Marc," Paxton replied.

An hour later Clay Dean made his daily report to Tom Carver. When he finished his account of today's testimony Tom told him to tell Darla that the defense lawyer actually did a good job of casting doubt about the fingerprint evidence. Both men got a good laugh out of that and Darla had something to worry about that evening.

FORTY-ONE

Marc and entourage, sans Sammy of course, waited patiently for the hostess to find a table for them. It was Saturday evening and everyone needed a break. Tommy Dorn knew of a great burger joint off-post. Tommy also claimed it was perfectly named as The Great Burger Joint. Because of its proximity to an Army post, it attracted a clientele of soldiers. Tonight was no exception.

The day before, Friday, the prosecution put another expert on the stand. This was the first of three handwriting experts. Axel Bremer, a sixty-eight-year-old with three books and hundreds of lectures on the subject was up first. Bremer spent the entire day comparing the handwriting on the list that was Exhibit One and eight handwriting samples obtained from Sammy.

Unlike most expert witnesses, Bremer was personable, witty and even entertaining. By the end of the day, Marc and company on the defense team were almost convinced the handwriting on the list was Sammy's. Paxton O'Rourke had cleverly put on her best expert before the weekend. The jury members had two days to remember his testimony with little contrary evidence.

Marc had tried to punch a hole or two in the man's testimony. Bremer was so good and experienced that there was nothing Marc could do that Bremer had not dealt with before. Realizing the futility of his feeble attempt to shake the man, Marc quickly gave up. There was little point and nothing to be gained from arguing with the witness.

His explanation to Sammy was simple. This isn't TV. Sometimes you take your lumps and move on.

The hostess took them to a table along a wall near the entrance. Marc ordered a pitcher of beer and four glasses. Maddy was seated to Marc's left, Carvelli across from him and Tommy Dorn to Marc's right.

"What kind of beer?" the waitress asked.

"Do you have real, American beer and not some trendy goop made out of tofu and sunflower seeds?" Tony Carvelli asked.

The girl smiled and said, "I'll see what I can do. How's Michelob sound?"

"That will do fine," Tony replied.

A couple minutes later she brought the beer and while Marc poured he asked the others if they were in a hurry to order. Maddy ordered a couple of appetizers instead of dinner and the four of them sat back for the first relaxing evening they had in months. Before leaving to go out, it was decided by all there would be no discussion of the trial. They all needed and deserved a break from it.

Being football season, the conversation quickly turned to the NFL. Maddy, being a Chicago girl, was a Bears fan. Marc and Tony from Minnesota were long-suffering Viking fans and Tommy Dorn, they found out, was a Green Bay Packer fan. Twenty minutes into the argument, Maddy, who was facing the entrance to the restaurant, tapped Marc on the arm. She pointed a finger at the entryway and Marc turned to look. Standing there in civilian clothes, waiting to be seated by herself was Paxton O'Rourke.

"I think she's alone," Maddy said. "Go ask her to join us."

Marc was up and moving while Maddy said this. He quickly covered the short distance to the door.

"Hi," he said to her.

She was looking at something else and did not see him approach.

"Oh, hi, Marc," she replied smiling.

"Are you alone?"

"Afraid so," she said.

"Well, then please join us. We just got here."

"I don't want to intrude."

"Don't be silly," Marc said. He gently took her elbow and started to lead her to their table. Maddy and Tony both waved to her and she let Marc take her to their table.

Maddy stood up to greet her and Paxton said, "I don't want to intrude."

"Stop it," Maddy said. She looked at Marc and said, "You go find a chair for her. Actually for yourself. Take his chair," Maddy continued as she slid Marc's chair next to her own.

"If you're sure…" Paxton said.

"Relax. Sit down. We've taken a vow of silence about the trial. No discussing it at all," Maddy assured her.

Maddy introduced Tony Carvelli whom Paxton had not met before. Marc returned with another chair and a glass just as Paxton said hello to Tommy Dorn.

"Good evening, Colonel," Paxton said.

"Tommy," Dorn corrected her. "At least for this evening, Paxton."

"Tommy it is," she said. "And you do look like him," she smiled.

"I just wish he was prettier," Dorn replied.

"You a football fan?" Maddy asked.

"Hell yes, Da Bears," Paxton replied.

"Really? I'm from Chicago," Maddy almost squealed.

"Me too," Paxton said as Marc handed her the now full glass. "Actually, Rockford, but close enough."

"These two," Maddy said pointing at Marc and Tony, "Vikings."

"Oh, that's not so bad. I'm okay with the Vikings," Paxton replied.

"Yeah, well, that's not the worst of it," Maddy said. She pointed at Tommy Dorn and before she could say it, Paxton interrupted.

"Don't tell me. Packers?"

"You got it," Maddy said.

"Should we find a different table?" Paxton asked.

"You are all obviously jealous," Dorn smugly said.

"The word delusional does not begin to describe your average Packer fan," Marc said. "The nice thing about being a Packer fan is that no matter who wins the Super Bowl, by the time the next season rolls around, ninety percent of Packer fans will have convinced themselves that they did."

This good-natured ribbing of Packer fans continued for several more minutes. They finished the appetizers and a second pitcher of beer then placed their orders.

Paxton looked at Maddy and said, "I hated you when I first saw you."

"Why?"

"Your hair. I'd like to let mine grow out like that but Army regs won't allow it."

"Seriously? I've been thinking about getting mine cut like yours. It's adorable and it has to be really easy to take care of," Maddy replied.

"That reminds me," Marc said looking at Tony. "I've been meaning to ask you about your hairstyle. What is it called?"

"Haircut," Tony drolly replied.

"Well, it's adorable. Where did you get it done?" Marc continued mildly mocking the two women.

"Barber," Tony replied trying not to smile. "If you say anything about my cute outfit or ask me about shoes I'm coming over there."

"Ha, ha," Maddy sarcastically laughed. "You two should be a comedy team. Have you ever had your ass kicked by a girl?"

"Yeah, but she was naked at the time," Carvelli quickly said.

Tommy Dorn was taking a swallow of beer when Tony said this and almost choked. Even Maddy and Paxton had to laugh.

"I have a question," Paxton said to Maddy when the laughter stopped. "There's a rumor going around that Layne Doyle got a little arrogant and mouthy with you and you laid him out in the blink of an eye."

"It wasn't quite like that," Maddy modestly replied.

"No, I actually blinked twice while she did it," Tony said.

"So, it really happened?" Paxton asked.

"Well, yeah," Maddy replied.

"You're my hero. I mean it. I had to deal with him. What an arrogant ass. And on top of it he tried hitting on me a couple times."

"Seriously? The guy's pushing seventy," Marc said.

"He thinks he's a stud," Paxton said. "He tried to convince me to quit the Army and come work for him. That whole John Adams Project thing. I've come across them before a couple times. I was second chair in an espionage case a few years ago. A private who had access to classified material leaked it to the WikiLeaks clown. These John Adams lawyers came in and tried to make it sound like what his guy did was heroic. They totally lost sight of representing their client. Instead, they made it about how the government is out to destroy liberty and they were saving us all."

"I remember that case," Marc said. "The private got thirty years as I recall."

"Yeah. We offered him fifteen for a plea and they convinced him to turn it down."

"Not enough publicity. Now they have their martyr," Tommy Dorn said.

"Exactly," Paxton agreed.

"I'll tell you something else," Tommy continued. "These lawyers who have wrapped themselves in the cloak of John Adams' reputation are full of horseshit.

"John Adams represented soldiers of his government. It was unpopular at the time but everyone conveniently forgets that they were all British citizens at the time. John Adams did not represent bomb-throwing radicals, cop murderers and international terrorists."

"They need representation too," Marc said.

"Of course, I have no problem with that. But don't compare yourself to John Adams for doing it. If you want a legitimate comparison, do you remember Kent State? The students who were shot and killed by a scared shitless National Guardsmen during a protest against the Vietnam war?"

When everyone agreed, they remembered it, Dorn continued.

"If any of those guardsmen had been charged, representing them would have been the equivalent of what John Adams did. These British soldiers who caused the Boston Massacre were scared kids. Not self-righteous radicals who think they're above all the rest of us. A lot of lawyers represent unpopular clients. It comes with the job sometimes. These people who claim to be the moral descendants of John Adams have enormous egos and are flattering themselves."

"I never heard it put that way," Marc said. "But you're absolutely right. Those British soldiers were scared kids trying to do their job. And they were all British citizens. These John Adams guys were all like Layne Doyle and that bunch. Nitwits who miss the 60s a little too much."

"What they do is necessary," Dorn said. "And it is a good thing that someone does it. But represent your client and not your cause. Too many times they get a little confused by that. I've worked with them on a couple court martial cases and I wasn't impressed."

With that, the conversation became a little more somber. Marc, sitting to Paxton's right, talked to her about herself and her career. Maddy noticed the look in Marc's eyes and wondered if he heard a word she said. Then she saw the same look in Paxton' eyes and wondered if they were headed to the backseat of someone's car.

"We should go," Maddy said bringing the two of them back to Earth. "It's getting late."

"Thanks for letting me join you," Paxton said. "I had a really nice time." She turned her head to Marc and said, "Now, next week, I'm going to kick your ass and send your client to prison."

FORTY-TWO

All of Monday and a good part of Tuesday's testimony were taken up by two more FBI techs. The first was a woman, Marti Conway. She explained the FBI's process for handwriting analysis. She described it as ACE-V. "A" was for "analyze", "C" for "compare", "E" for "evaluate" and lastly, "V" was for "verify".

Axel Bremer, the first tech to testify regarding the handwriting comparison was also the first to do the analysis. Ms. Conway's job was to do all that again, independently of Mr. Bremer and then compare her results to his.

"Did you know what Mr. Bremer's results were before you did your analysis?" Captain Bain asked her.

"No, sir," she answered. "It was assigned to me by our supervisor. I didn't even know someone else had already done the analysis."

"Did you come to a conclusion?"

"Yes, sir."

"And what was your conclusion?"

"The handwriting found on Exhibit One was an exact match to the exemplars we were given for analysis and comparison," she answered.

Exhibit On being the list of Muslim names, targets for drone assassination. There were eight handwriting samples from Samir Kamel, called "exemplars", which were used for comparison. These had already been admitted individually through the first handwriting witness, Axel Bremer.

Captain Bain received permission to approach the witness. He quickly and smoothly had her identify her written report and submitted it into evidence. When it was accepted, like all of the exhibits, Bain walked it over to the jury to let them pass it around.

Back at the podium, using the television set up for the jury, Bain spent two hours having the witness show photos of Exhibit One and each exemplar alongside of it on the TV. She then went over each one point-by-point explaining the process. When they were done, the witness was turned over.

"You've been with the FBI for nine years, is that correct?" Marc asked.

"Yes, that's correct. I have…"

"Please, Ms. Conway," Marc said. "Just answer the question and thank you. Okay?"

"Sure," she replied.

"You did two years as an apprentice in the FBI lab, is that correct?"

"Yes," she barely audibly replied.

"And isn't it true, that during those two years, you received training for a wide variety of evidence analysis, not just handwriting samples?"

"Yes, that's correct."

"Fingerprint analysis?"

"Some, yes."

"Tire print analysis?"

"Yes."

"Ballistics, things like firearms, bullets, gunshots. Were you also trained for these things?"

"Yes, I was."

"And this is standard training for all lab techs with the FBI, isn't it?"

"Um, well, we all learn a variety of things."

"Is that a 'yes'?" Marc asked with a smile just to remind her not to embellish her answer.

"Yes, it is."

"Isn't it also true that you personally spend the bulk of your time with firearms ballistic testing?"

"Well, I, ah…"

"Yes or no, please."

"Yes, that's true," she admitted.

"Give me your best guess," Marc began. He was taking a bit of a calculated risk asking a question he did not know the answer to but he believed he would be all right. "What percentage of your time do you spend on firearms ballistic testing?"

"Oh, I don't know. I'd say at least sixty-five to seventy percent," she replied.

Perfect, Marc thought.

"Have you ever testified in a trial concerning handwriting analysis before today?"

"Yes, I have," she replied.

This is an area that the prosecution would have normally covered. Because they did not, Marc was reasonably sure of his ground in going after her. They, the prosecution, had in fact thoroughly covered this with their first handwriting witness, Axel Bremer, on Friday. Marc had tried the same line of questions on him and was burned. Axel Bremer was a handwriting expert.

"How many times have you testified about handwriting analysis?"

"Twice," she said.

"Isn't it true you spend less than five percent of your time doing handwriting analysis?"

"Oh, I, ah, I'm not sure I would…" an obviously anxious Marti Conway stammered.

"Yes or no, Ms. Conway, please," Marc said.

"Um, yes," she quietly answered.

"Your Honor," Marc said looking at Judge Dwyer. "I move that this witness' testimony be stricken in its entirety. She may be a firearm's ballistic expert, in fact, I will concede that she is. But she is certainly not a handwriting expert. The government is trying to slip a fastball past this jury."

The last part of Marc's statement drew an objection which was quickly sustained. He knew it would be but said it anyway. His point was made and the jury got it.

"No, I will not strike her testimony," Dwyer said after thinking it over for a few seconds. "You made your point and the members can decide for themselves how much weight to give it."

"I have nothing further, your Honor," Marc said then picked up his notes and returned to his chair.

"Redirect?" Dwyer asked.

Bain and Paxton O'Rourke put their heads together and whispered a brief exchange. Then Bain said, "No, your Honor. We will let the witness' written report speak for itself."

Dwyer looked at the clock and adjourned for the day.

While the courtroom was emptying, Professor Sanderson rolled his chair around the table to Marc and Sammy. Dorn leaned over to hear the discussion. Maddy Rivers and Tony Carvelli were not in attendance today.

"He may have made a mistake in allowing her testimony in," Sanderson said. "You did a nice job of showing that she is not qualified as an expert."

"I screwed up," Marc replied. "I should have stopped them when they were qualifying her on direct. I might have been able to keep it out if I had done a voir dire of her then."

"Maybe, maybe not," Sanderson said. "He's right, the jury can decide for themselves," the professor replied.

"Reversible error?" Dorn asked.

"By itself, no," Sanderson replied. "But it's another point maybe in our favor."

"I thought you did great," Sammy said. "I was watching the jury and when you said they were trying to throw a fastball by them, almost all of them looked at the prosecution and they didn't look happy."

"Good," Marc replied. "That's exactly why I said it."

Sammy's transportation van was waiting for him at the community center's rear entrance. While he was shuttling toward it surrounded by guards, his three lawyers stood watching.

"We'll be over after supper," Marc assured him.

"Okay, see you then," Sammy replied while stepping into the vehicle. Before the door closed he stuck his head out and yelled back, "Be sure to bring Maddy."

Sergeant Esterhazy was waiting by their car as the three men slowly walked toward him.

"Maybe we could get Sammy's girlfriend, Major what's-her-name…"

"Major Charlene Hughes," Dorn said.

"Yeah, maybe we can get her to pay Sammy a visit," Marc said.

"We'd have to sneak her in," Dorn said.

"You were in college once, don't you remember sneaking girls in," Professor Sanderson said.

"I remember doing a lot worse than that," Dorn replied. "Let me see what I can do."

The third and final handwriting expert for the government went on the stand first thing the next day. He was Benjamin Hout. His testimony was a more boring version of what everyone endured the day before. Being the third one up and with nothing new to offer made for a drowsy crowd. Even Dwyer had trouble staying focused.

Marc went after Hout for his lack of real expertise. Apparently Bain had done a better job of preparing him for this. Marc scored a couple of points but the man's report went into evidence. The members now had three reports from FBI fingerprint experts all supporting each other. The fingerprints found on the list of Muslim clerics leaked to the world were a match to Sammy Kamel. They also had three FBI lab geek reports with no doubt the handwriting was also Sammy's.

Once again Sammy's lawyers watched as he was put in the van. This time, Maddy watched with them.

"What do you think?" she asked Marc as the van drove off.

"I think when a jury hears the words, FBI lab technician experts, they tend to believe them," Marc replied.

"You think he's in trouble," Maddy said.

"I've thought so all along. We all knew it would come down to whether or not they believe he wrote that list and leaked it to the New York Times reporter. If we knew exactly when that happened, we could work on an alibi. But…"

218

"Yeah," Maddy glumly added. "When do you think she'll put the computer guy on?"

"Probably tomorrow," Marc said.

He was correct. Sammy's laptop and work PC had been confiscated along with all of his work related documents. Pursuant to a valid search warrant, Sammy's laptop and PC had been thoroughly searched. On both, the techs had found over one hundred incidents of Sammy reviewing Radical Islamic websites. Some for as long as two hours. To make it appear even worse, Sammy had the habit of frequently clearing his browser history. Through their testimony the prosecution, Paxton O'Rourke, skillfully made it look like he was intentionally trying to hide these searches.

Of course, Marc had sent the computers to an expert of their own. His evaluation came back basically corroborating those of the FBI lab. The best Marc could do on cross-exam was to get the lab tech to admit for all he knew these were job-related searches. They may have been perfectly legitimate and required by his job. Especially for someone who spoke and wrote Arabic.

Unfortunately, for the next two days, the government put five witnesses on the stand to refute this. The first four were coworkers including a woman who also spoke and could write Arabic. They all testified that as far as they knew, no one on the National Security staff for Vice President Morton was given that assignment

Finally, Sammy's immediate superior was called. The man's name was Darin Montgomery. He was Vice President Morton's handpicked National Security Advisor. A veteran of U.S. Intelligence having worked at both the CIA and NSA. A more credible witness could not be found.

Montgomery was absolutely adamant that Sammy was never assigned to look up jihadist website; whatever he did, he did on his own.

"Did he have anything to do with interpreting Arabic documents, websites or anything like that at all?"

"No, he didn't. Anything like that would have been translated before it came to us. And the Vice President's staff does not do website surveillance or any other surveillance. We are what is known in the intelligence community as an end product consumer. We do not analyze data or obtain raw intelligence."

"Who does?" Paxton asked.

"I won't get into that, sorry," Montgomery replied.

"Samir Kamel did not?"

"No, he did not. It was not his job."

"Did Major Kamel have access to the Vice President's copy of the list, a copy of which is exhibit one?" Paxton asked.

"Objection," Marc said rising to address the court.

"Overruled," Dwyer quickly told him. "She is asking if it was possible. The witness can give his opinion."

"Unfortunately, yes. I hate to say this in an open forum like this, but the Vice President was a little careless sometimes with classified material. Many times I found classified documents on his desk with the door unlocked, including the list you are referring to. So, yes, Samir Kamel could have found it any number of times especially when he worked late or a weekend."

The admission that Vice President Morton was careless with classified material would be headlines in the media that day and the next.

Marc began his cross examination with the question, "By your testimony, any number of people could have accessed the Vice President's list, isn't that true, Mr. Montgomery?"

"Yes, but..."

"Isn't it also true that those same people could have accessed a sample of Major Kamel's handwriting and forged exhibit one?" Marc asked cutting him off.

"Yes, I suppose that's true," Montgomery was forced to admit.

Marc hesitated for a moment deciding whether or not to pursue this avenue of inquiry then quickly decided he got the admission he wanted, could argue it in his closing and moved on.

"Did you see any indication Major Kamel was a radical jihadist?" Marc asked Montgomery.

"No, I did not," Montgomery answered.

"Did you ever see him praying?"

"No, I did not."

"He never asked for permission or breaks to pray five times a day, did he, Mr. Montgomery?"

"No, he did not," Montgomery conceded.

"He was given an annual polygraph was he not?" Marc asked.

"Objection," O'Rourke said as she stood. "Polygraphs are not admissible as..."

"I am not trying to admit the results, your Honor," Marc said. "I merely want the witness to testify whether or not one was administered as a routine part of their security evaluation."

"Overruled," Dwyer said. "The witness may answer for that limited purpose."

"Yes, he was," Montgomery answered.

"Did he lose his security clearance..."

"Objection, he's trying to backdoor the results into evidence," O'Rourke said.

"Sustained. The jury will disregard defense counsel's last statement," Dwyer ruled although the damage had already been done. O'Rourke's objection had the same effect as admitting the results. The members all knew Sammy had passed each polygraph.

"May I approach the witness?" Marc asked.

"Mr. Montgomery," Marc began when he got up to the witness stand. "I'm showing you a document marked for identification as defense Exhibit A. Do you recognize it?"

"Yes," he answered. "It's a copy of an evaluation I did of Major Kamel about a year ago."

"What was your opinion of Major Kamel as reported in Exhibit A?"

"I gave him excellent grades across the board," Montgomery answered.

"Up until his arrest, did Major Kamel give you any reason to believe you made a mistake?"

"No, he did not."

"So, is it fair to say, he was an excellent officer, an excellent soldier and an asset to your staff?"

"Yes, it is," Montgomery admitted.

Marc entered the evaluation into evidence then informed Dwyer he was finished.

"Redirect, Major O'Rourke?" Dwyer asked.

"One moment, your Honor," she said.

O'Rourke quickly thought about asking any more questions. She had obtained what she wanted from Montgomery, definite testimony that viewing radical Muslim websites was not Kamel's job.

"Yes, your Honor," she replied as she stood.

When she reached the podium she asked, "Mr. Montgomery, is it possible for someone to be a radicalized Muslim and you not be aware of it?"

"Objection! Speculation and lacks foundation," Marc said as he jumped to his feet.

"A question or two, your Honor," Paxton said.

"Go ahead," Dwyer told her.

"Mr. Montgomery, in your service as an intelligence officer, have you had opportunity to interrogate jihadist prisoners?"

"Dozens," he replied.

"Would you say you have expertise in how they are trained?"

"Absolutely," he answered.

"Is part of their training devoted to blending in with the non-radical population?"

"A significant part of their training is devoted to just that."

"I am satisfied the witness has sufficient experience and expertise to answer the original question, Mr. Kadella. Your objection is noted and overruled. You may answer, sir," Dwyer ruled.

"I'm sorry, what was the question?" Montgomery said. He knew what it was. He had enough savvy to have it repeated for the jury.

"Is it possible for someone to be a radicalized Muslim and for others, even someone like you with your experience, to be unaware of it?"

"Absolutely," Montgomery replied. "That's what they are told to do and they do it all the time."

"I have nothing further," O'Rourke said.

Unable to quickly think of a way to get out of this hole, Marc passed on recross.

Montgomery's testimony practically slammed the door on any doubt that Sammy could be a self-radicalized jihadi. Paxton O'Rourke, fighting back a smile rested her case. Judge Dwyer, realizing how bad things had gone for the defense adjourned until Monday morning.

"Be prepared to present your defense," he quietly told Marc.

Clay Dean once again checked in with Tom Carver before calling Darla. The two men discussed the prosecution's overall case and decided it was guilt beyond a reasonable doubt. But just to rattle Darla's cage a bit Tom had Clay call her with a completely different take. He told her that it was fifty-fifty for a conviction. Clay also told her he had overheard other members of the audience who had the same belief.

Darla watched every news report she could that evening after Clay called. All of them reported the same thing. Unless the defense could pull a rabbit out of a hat, Samir Kamel was going down. Darla spent a very sleepless night worrying about who was correct.

222

FORTY-THREE

Sgt. Esterhazy dropped Tommy Dorn at his quarters on Ft. Myer. He then drove Marc and Maddy to the rented Colonial in Arlington. During the entire ride Marc sat still silently staring through the right-hand passenger window in the backseat. Maddy had been around him and in trials with him enough to know this was a very bad sign. The day's testimony had not gone well and Marc was probably mentally replaying it to find the ways he screwed up. Maddy also knew the best thing she could do was to let him brood for a while.

When they arrived at the house Marc dropped his briefcase by the door and tossed his trench coat onto a chair. Without a word, he went up the stairs into his bedroom and quietly closed the door.

Maddy got a bottle of Diet Coke from the refrigerator and took it into the TV room. She turned on the TV to CNN just in time to watch another lawyer being interviewed about the trial. Even though the woman on TV had not been in the courtroom, her analysis of the day based on the media reporting seemed spot on with what Maddy had seen. Not a good day for the defense.

She changed the channel to Fox and saw the exact same analysis she had seen on CNN. For the next hour, she watched the news and every few minutes hit the mute button to listen for any noise upstairs. When the news finished it was after 7:00, Maddy was getting hungry and she was sure Marc must be as well.

Marc was lying on his bed still dressed in his suit and shoes except for the suit coat. His arms were at his side as he stared up at the ceiling. He heard a soft knock on the door and shifted his eyes to it just as Maddy opened it and looked in.

"You okay?" she asked standing in the doorway.

"Nope, but I will be. What's up?"

"Are you hungry? We should get something to eat," she replied.

"You're right," he said. He swung his legs over and onto the floor then stood up. "Get out. I want to change clothes."

"You don't have anything I haven't seen before," she cracked trying to lighten the mood.

Marc looked at her with eyebrows raised and said. "Don't be so sure. I don't want to scare you but some men are more equal than others."

Maddy laughed and said, "I'll be downstairs."

A few minutes later, dressed in jeans, sneakers and a Polo pullover, Marc went into the kitchen. He took a bottle of beer from the refrigerator, twisted off the top and tossed the cap onto the counter. As he did this Maddy came in from the TV room.

Marc leaned against the counter and took a long pull on the beer. He held up the bottle and said, "That tastes really good," then did it again.

"Are you gonna talk to me and tell me what's bothering you?" Maddy asked.

Marc finished off the beer, burped, smiled and said, "Excuse me."

Maddy tilted her head and repeated her question.

"It has occurred to me," Marc began to say while setting the empty bottle on the counter, "that Major Samir Kamel may very well be guilty of treason."

"You don't believe that," Maddy quickly snapped back.

"I'm not sure what I believe," Marc said taking another beer from the refrigerator.

"If you believe that, you should withdraw and we'll go home," Maddy said with her best 'annoyed mother' expression. "Besides, how many times have you said it's ridiculous to believe there wouldn't be any other fingerprints on the list or the envelope it was found in?"

"Do all women practice that look or is it some genetic thing? Besides, all of you should have learned by now that men are put on this planet to annoy you. That's our job. Not procreation; any fourteen-year-old kid can do that. Our job is to give women something to be mad about."

"Stop stalling," Maddy said.

"I'm fine," Marc replied. "Besides, withdrawing at this point is out of the question. I could not do that to Sammy or Tommy Dorn. And," he started to say as he tilted the bottle up for more beer, "after thinking it over, I still believe he's innocent."

"But it doesn't matter what you believe," Maddy said.

"No, it sure as hell doesn't. Do you remember how to get to that burger joint we went to Saturday?"

"Yeah, I do," Maddy said.

"Good, you're driving."

"Since you're drinking and don't have a car, I guess I am."

"Good morning, ladies and gentlemen," Marc said beginning his opening statement to the jury. "Again, my name is Marc Kadella and I represent Major Samir Kamel.

"First, let me thank you for your service, your patience and most of all for your promise to keep an open mind and not make a decision until all of the evidence and testimony are in." A not so subtle reminder.

Marc went on to explain in very general terms—so as not to over promise—what the defense would present. He spent quite a bit of his opening telling them about his fingerprint and handwriting experts with

224

significant emphasis on the word "experts". Marc's opening took less than an hour after which Dwyer called for a break.

"The defense calls Professor Wendy Carlson," Marc announced after the break.

An attractive blonde woman was admitted and all eyes watched her as she confidently strolled up the center aisle. She entered the well of the courtroom and was sworn in by Major O'Rourke.

"State your name, home address and current employment, please," O'Rourke told her.

"Wendy Carlson, Denver, Colorado and I am a professor at the University of Denver."

Carlson had arrived in Washington on Saturday, as did Marc's fingerprint expert. Marc was going to conduct the examination of Carlson and Dorn examine the fingerprint expert. Tommy had been hinting around that he wanted to do a witness exam. Marc was actually grateful to let him do one.

Marc spent the first forty-five minutes going over Carlson's three-page curriculum vitae. By the time they were done even he was impressed with her qualifications. The best part was when Chris Bain, O'Rourke's second chair, objected to Marc's continued use of the title professor when addressing her.

"Are you a professor at the University of Denver?" Dwyer had asked her.

"Fully tenured, your Honor," she said with a smile.

"Sit down, Captain Bain. She has earned the title. Overruled," Dwyer said.

Thanks for emphasizing it, Marc thought. He turned to take a peek at the prosecution in time to see Paxton snarl into Bain's ear. Marc smiled then turned back to his witness.

Next, Marc walked her through her extensive trial experience. The professor had testified dozens of times in both civilian and criminal trials. She had also analyzed handwriting samples in five different languages including Arabic and Chinese. Marc entered a copy of her CV into evidence then gave it to a jury member to pass around.

One-by-one she went over the written reports of the lab techs from the FBI. By the time she was done, she made each report seem as if it was written by a college freshman. She even graded each one giving them no better than a D+. This, of course, drew a strenuous objection which was quickly overruled.

Professor Carlson's testimony took up all of Monday and most of Tuesday. She went over everything including the exemplars on the TV screen used by the FBI to do their analysis. Before she finished Marc was beginning to worry that they might be boring the members. Even though they appeared to be paying attention, there was the occasional yawn and headshake to indicate otherwise.

"Professor," Marc began getting to the heart of the matter, "I have put up the government's Exhibit One on the TV. In your expert, professional opinion, based upon all of the analysis and computerized testing that you did, do you believe this was written by Major Samir Kamel?"

"No, I do not believe it at all. It is a forgery. A very good forgery but a forgery nonetheless."

"Tell the jury why you have reached that conclusion, please."

"Because it is too good. It's almost perfect. There isn't a flaw in it. In fact, this is why I believe it fooled the FBI technicians. But it didn't fool me.

"Look," she continued, "no one's handwriting is the same all of the time. There are always inconsistencies from one sample to another. Exhibit One is, again, almost perfectly flawless. It is one of the best forgeries I have seen but it is still a forgery."

"Thank you, Professor," Marc said, finishing up on that obvious high note. "Your witness," he said to O'Rourke.

Paxton practically jumped up, went to the podium and started right in. The best way to discredit a hired expert witness is to go after their pay. Paxton spent the next hour bringing out every penny that the defense had to spend to get her testimony. It was quite effective even though Carlson handled it with ease. She had been through it many times, knew it was coming and was well prepared for it.

When O'Rourke finished, Dwyer gave Marc a chance to redirect.

"Professor Carlson, Major O'Rourke almost accused you of getting paid for your opinion. Almost accused you of accepting money to tell the members something you think the defense told you to say."

"Objection, is there a question coming or is Mr. Kadella testifying?" O'Rourke stood and said.

"Is there a question coming?" Dwyer asked Marc.

"Right now, your Honor," Marc replied.

"Overruled," he quietly said.

"Professor, you have testified on both sides of many trials. Over a hundred you said. Have you ever been hired to examine documents then told the lawyer who hired you the exact opposite of what that lawyer wanted to hear?"

"Many, many times," she answered.

"What happens when you have that news to give?"

"Usually a settlement. But for sure, I don't get on a witness stand."

"So, you're not really paid to tell them what they want to hear?"

"No," she emphatically answered.

Dwyer called a halt for the day. While the crowd was filing out Paxton O'Rourke came over to the defense table.

"You're really good," she said to Professor Carlson. "I was wondering if I could get a card from you. If I ever need an independent document examiner, I'll keep you in mind."

Carlson handed her business card to Paxton who said, "No hard feelings about the way I went at you?"

"No, of course not. I always enjoy being called a professional whore," Carlson said then laughed. "You did your job, I did mine," she added.

The women smiled and shook hands then Paxton said good night to everyone.

When O'Rourke was out of earshot, Maddy asked. "So what do you think?"

"I thought it went quite well," Professor Sanderson said who was again in attendance. "You were very convincing," he said to Professor Carlson.

"I hate to be a killjoy," Carlson said. "But it's my experience that once a jury hears FBI techs and their findings," she shrugged, "that usually does it. Sorry, Sammy. I have to be honest."

"I think Marc will tie it all together in his closing argument," Sammy replied. "We only need four, they need six."

"Maddy has volunteered to get you to the airport," Marc said. "Send me your final bill."

"I will," Carlson said. She shook hands with everyone and wished them good luck.

FORTY-FOUR

During the early part of the trial, Tommy Dorn had hinted around to Marc to let him examine a witness. Marc had agreed to let him have the next one, the fingerprint expert. Her name was Bonnie McAdoo and she had come to them via Tony Carvelli.

Bonnie was a fingerprint expert formerly with the Minneapolis Police Department. Her original training was with the FBI before Minneapolis lured her away. Ten years into her employment with the MPD, a friend and criminalist had convinced her to go independent. That was eight years ago and Bonnie had never looked back.

Tommy Dorn smoothly moved her through her qualifications which were much better than the FBI techs were. She also did an excellent job of explaining why FBI techs were not as reliable and did not have the expertise she did.

The entire day was taken up with her testimony. Bonnie went through all three types of print analysis techniques. Using the written reports from the FBI lab she came up with minor flaws in all of them. By the end of the day she had done about as good of a job of creating reasonable doubt as anyone could.

"Ms. McAdoo," Tommy said getting toward the conclusion of her testimony, "in your expert opinion, is it true that everyone's fingerprints are absolutely unique?"

"Absolutely unique? It's hard to say," she began. "The probability of that is unknowable. With seven billion people on the planet, we can't possibly know if that's true. The police and government prosecutors certainly want everyone to believe it but no one knows. Their own experts came up with three different conclusions as to the percentages that the prints found on the list of names belonged to Major Kamel. The likelihood that those prints matched his. I came up with a different conclusion than each one of them. Is there proof beyond a reasonable doubt…"

"Objection. That is a legal term, and this witness is not qualified to give that opinion." Paxton O'Rourke jumped up.

"Overruled," Dwyer said.

"Go ahead, finish your thought," Dorn told her.

"I don't believe there is proof beyond a reasonable doubt that the fingerprints on the prosecution's Exhibit One are a match to the defendant. There are many instances of innocent people being convicted because of fingerprint matches."

Tommy Dorn had another area to go into with his witness. He wanted her to tell the jury that the same finger can leave a different print in consecutive attempts. Instead, he decided to let it go and end on the reasonable doubt claim she had just made.

Paxton O'Rourke went after her the same way she had gone after Professor Carlson. She tried to paint Bonnie McAdoo as nothing more than an expert for hire. Standard procedure for attacking, Paxton made one little slip-up that opened the door for McAdoo and she went right through it.

"The defense has to hire their own forensic experts. They do not have an organization the size of the FBI to help them. Because of this, there is no such thing as a fair trial."

O'Rourke, horrified at her mistake asked Dwyer to strike the answer as "non-responsive", especially the last part about fair trials.

"The jury will disregard the witness' statement that there is no such thing as a fair trial," Dwyer said.

Thanks for repeating it for us, Marc thought sarcastically while suppressing a smile.

O'Rourke stood silently at the podium trying to think of a way to undo the damage.

"I'm sorry," she said, "I don't recall your answer. How many times have you testified in trials over the years?"

"At least two hundred," Bonnie said. "Probably more."

"During your years with the FBI and Minneapolis Police Department, isn't it true that not once did you get on a witness stand and testify that fingerprints were not unique?"

"Um, yes, that's probably true," Bonnie had to answer.

"I have nothing further," O'Rourke said.

"Redirect?" Dwyer asked Dorn.

Dorn started to rise and Marc reached over, grabbed his arm and stopped him.

"A moment, your Honor," Dorn said.

Marc put his mouth by Dorn's ear and whispered, "If you get up there and have her testify that she always testified that prints are unique, she'll say that was her job. Paxton will drill her with one word: "exactly". That was your job and now your job is to find that prints are not unique. Probably best to leave it alone. We got what we need to argue reasonable doubt."

"Good point," Dorn whispered back.

Tommy turned around, looked at the judge and said, "I have nothing further, your Honor."

Dwyer adjourned for the day.

"Sir, Lieutenant Colonel Collins is here," the captain, an exemplary female admin assistant said into her phone. She was one of several staff members for Army Chief of Staff Dirk Carney.

"Yes, sir," she said then hung up her phone. "You're to go right in, Colonel", she said to Collins.

Collins was at the Pentagon making his daily report to Carney about the progress. An E-7 Sergeant First Class was seated at a desk by the general's door and he jumped up to open it for Collins. Collins nodded slightly at the sergeant as he passed by and entered the big office. Behind the almost aircraft carrier sized desk were three flags. The American flag, the Army flag and Army Chief of Staff flag. General Carney along with the Vice Chief General Morin, were seated at a conference table relaxing with a scotch on the rocks.

"Have a seat, Collins. Tell us what you have," Carney said while not offering him a drink.

"Well, sir," he began. Collins explained the day's testimony in total candor. When he finished, Carney offered him the drink he would have liked to have before he began.

"So what you're saying is the defense is scoring some points," General Morin commented.

"Yes, sir," Collins said setting his glass down.

"And Major O'Rourke made quite a mistake and let their fingerprint witness tell the jury there's reasonable doubt. And Dwyer let her," Carney said.

"Sir, if I may," Collins said.

"Go ahead, Colonel," Carney replied.

"Major O'Rourke has done an excellent job. I don't think that mistake will matter..."

"She's not paid to do a good job," Morin said. "She's paid to win."

"And I think we will," Collins said, "It will come down to, as we believed all along, whether or not the members believe Kamel wrote the names on that list and leaked it to the reporter. I don't believe reasonable doubt will be enough to acquit him. The defense needs to come up with another suspect. Someone else who could have done it. So far, they haven't even hinted at someone else who that could be."

"I hope you're right, Collins," Carney said. "We need to nail this down and move on."

Darla Carver, with Sonja Hayden on the couch next to her, had her feet on the coffee table watching CNN. They were in the living room of Darla's suite in the Hilton in downtown Scranton, Pennsylvania. It was 7:00 P.M. and they were scheduled to appear at three more fundraisers that evening. Two for the party's senatorial candidate and one for the local house seat. Both races were too close to call.

Darla had spoken to Clay an hour ago and she was now watching the news to see if what they said would conform with what Clay told her. There were times when she believed Clay didn't know what he was talking about or was deliberately misleading her.

"This guy is an idiot," Darla said referring to the reporter. "How does someone that stupid get on national TV?"

"He's gorgeous," Sonja said.

"I must be getting older," Darla replied. "That doesn't interest me too much. He should at least be able to ask an occasional follow-up question."

They were watching what CNN claims is a newscast of the day's events. As part of it, the anchor had a Q & A with a prominent defense lawyer about the trial of Samir Kamel. The lawyer almost gleefully presented the day's testimony in a very positive light for the defense.

"This does not sound good," Darla quietly commented. "And it's what Clay told me also."

"Please try to relax. He's a defense lawyer," Sonja reminded her.

"I can't relax," Darla said. She took her feet off the table, picked up the remote and shut off the TV. "My back hurts, my feet are sore, my shoulders are tight and this goddamn trial needs to be done. I need a massage. What time will we be back?" She turned to look at Sonja.

"We'll be lucky to be back by midnight. You have a 6:00 A.M. wake up then we drive to Philadelphia," Sonja replied.

"Where's my husband?"

"The President," Sonja began referring to Tom Carver as "the President", "will be landing at Kennedy in about an hour."

"Good, more money, more connections, more juice for the Carver team," Darla said. "Things are coming along well. How's my latest book doing?" Darla asked referring to the latest book she was writing. Or, more accurately, others were writing for her. Another twelve-million-dollar advance was in the bank and Darla hoped they were doing a good job. After all, her name as the author would be prominently displayed.

"On schedule for release in January. The day after your swearing-in ceremony."

"Good, good. Are you staying on top of it? Is it well written?"

"Yes, ma'am," Sonja replied. "You should get excellent reviews. In fact, there are almost twenty, five-star reviews ready for release."

"For a book that isn't finished yet and the reviewers haven't read," Darla said.

"The reviewers are very well compensated," Sonja reminded her.

Darla stood and said, "Well, let's go have some more buffet carbohydrates. I'll be glad when the election is over so my ass doesn't get any bigger. They'll be slapping a 'Wide Load' sign on it if this campaign lasts another month."

FORTY-FIVE

The clock on the wall of the community center courtroom was fast approaching 9:30 A.M. The gallery was jam-packed and becoming more and more restless. Unlike civilian trials and civilian judges, Dwyer was running a tight ship. Rarely did the trial get going later than 9:05. Today the jury was not seated, the judge was not on the bench and none of the lawyers were at their tables. The only ones in the courtroom well were the MP Captain Dreyfus and an anxious looking Sammy Kamel. Something was up.

Something was indeed up. All of the layers, including Professor Sanderson, were in the room Dwyer was using for his onsite chambers. For the third time, the defense, this time led by Sanderson, was trying to convince Dwyer to allow a certain witness to testify. That witness was the Army CID investigator, Warrant Officer David Smith.

The Professor had come up with some civilian case law he was using to get Dwyer to change his mind. The cases were a little weak, not right on point and worst of all, not binding on a military court martial.

"One at a time," Dwyer said again, patiently admonishing the lawyers.

They were all seated in front of the table Dwyer used as a desk. His court reporter was in the room making a record and she needed everyone to chill out and speak individually. The argument was turning into a real argument. The prosecution believed they had disposed of this issue twice before. Paxton O'Rourke was not even trying to hide her anger about this third attempt.

The issue was Warrant Officer Smith's contribution to the guilt or innocence of Samir Kamel. He had no direct evidence to provide at all. His was clearly circumstantial at best. What Marc wanted him to do was testify that he did not believe Sammy's roommate, Oliver Townsend's death was an accident.

"Your Honor," an obviously dismayed Paxton O'Rourke said, "We've flogged this dead horse twice already. His testimony would be nothing more than a red herring. Townsend's death was ruled an accident. They want to make it look like a murder and with no evidence at all. The windows on his car being down could just as easily be indicative of a suicide. And even if it was a murder, so what? How does that contribute to the guilt or innocence of Major Kamel?"

"I agree," Dwyer said looking at the defense lawyers. "However, I have thought it over and I will allow your New York police detective to testify, on a very limited basis, that the recipient of the leaked list, Exhibit One, was murdered."

"Your Honor," both Marc and Paxton said simultaneously.

"One at a time," Dwyer said. "Major Paxton your objection is noted. And I'm sure you will do a fine job of cross-examining the NYPD detective. Mr. Kadella?"

"Your Honor, our theory is that someone stole a blank sheet of paper with Samir's prints on it and had it forged. Oliver Townsend is the obvious person to have done this."

"I understand," Dwyer calmly replied. "If you can find some evidence then bring it to me, more than just witnesses who will testify Townsend was a closet bigot. Until then, the members are not going to hear this. Are you ready to go?" Dwyer asked Marc.

"Yes, your Honor," Marc said.

"Good, I'll be out in a minute."

"The defense calls, Detective John Spinks," Marc announced when court resumed.

A few moments later a man in an inexpensive, off-the-rack, gray suit, dull tie and comfortable shoes strolled up the center aisle. If Hollywood could cast a real life looking NYPD homicide detective, John Spinks would fit the bill. Mid to late forties, a mostly full head of graying hair, even in this setting he had a hard-case, cynical appearance. A cop who had seen too much and had developed a protective hard shell against the horror people inflicted on each other.

Paxton O'Rourke swore him in and he took the stand. She then had him state his full name and occupation for the record.

Marc spent about fifteen minutes on his résumé as a New York detective and police officer. He wanted to get right to the point, which was the murder of Melvin Bullard.

"Were you the lead investigator in the death of New York Times reporter Melvin Bullard?"

"Yes, I was. Myself and my partner, Calvin Miller," Spinks replied.

"How did he die?"

"According to the autopsy, he died from two gunshots from a smaller caliber gun in the back of his head. His body was then thrown into the Hudson River."

"As a homicide detective with over twenty years' experience in New York, do you have an opinion about how he was murdered?"

"Yes, I do. It has all the marks of a professional hit. This was not a random street crime or someone with an axe to grind against this guy. This was an assassination."

"Objective, speculation," O'Rourke said.

"Overruled. I'll allow it," Dwyer said.

"Has the case been solved?"

"No, we have not closed it," Spinks replied.

"We're you at the apartment of Melvin Bullard when it was searched?"

"Objection, assumes facts not in evidence," Paxton said. It was a minor point but she decided to object just to annoy Marc.

"Sustained," Dwyer said.

"Detective, during the course of your investigation, did you or your partner obtain a search warrant for Bullard's apartment?"

"Yes, we did."

"Was the apartment searched?"

"Yes, it was."

"Were you present?"

"During the search? Yes, I was."

Marc asked for and was given permission to approach the witness. He stepped up to the witness stand and handed a several page document to the detective.

"Do you recognize this document marked as Defense Exhibit C?"

"Yes, I do."

"Explain to the jury what it is please."

"It's a copy of the inventory of items found in the apartment of Melvin Bullard."

Marc walked over to the table where the exhibits entered into evidence had been placed. He picked up the plastic bags containing the list of Muslim names and the envelope it was in that were entered into evidence by the prosecution.

He went back to the witness, verbally identified both items for the record and handed them to Spinks

"Detective, have you ever seen these items before?"

"No, I have not."

"Are they listed on the inventory list of items found in Bullard's apartment?"

"I don't believe so," Spinks said.

"Look it over, take your time," Marc told him.

Spinks quickly looked over the entire inventory list then told Marc the envelope and list of names were not on the inventory list.

Marc handed Spinks another document and said, "Detective, I'm handing you a document marked for identification as defense Exhibit D. Do you recognize this?"

"Yes, I do."

"And what is it?"

"It's a copy of the official list of everyone who entered the Bullard apartment when the search was conducted."

"Did you make the list yourself?"

"No, I did not," he replied.

"Object to this witness testifying about Exhibit D, your Honor. If he did not make it he cannot attest to its authenticity," Paxton said.

"Your Honor," Marc began to reply, "I am prepared to bring the officer who did make each entry if the court finds it necessary. Or, the court can allow me to continue to make the point I want before ruling."

"Go ahead," Dwyer said.

"Detective, are there any names of FBI agents listed in Exhibit D, the sign-in sheet?"

"No, there are not," Spinks answered.

This revelation caused a minor stir which Dwyer quickly gaveled down. He looked at the still-standing Major O'Rourke and asked, "Will you stipulate to the admission of Defense D or do we have to bring the officer in to testify?"

"I'll withdraw my objection and so stipulate," Paxton said then sat down again.

"Detective, can you tell me if there were any gloves of any kind found in the apartment? Please, check Exhibit C for them."

Again Spinks did a cursory examination of the inventory list. He already knew there were no gloves on it and did not need to read it. This was for show only.

Normally cops were never in a hurry to testify on behalf of a defendant. Like most cops, especially NYPD cops, they had no great love for the feds, especially the FBI. Spinks was actually enjoying himself sticking it to them a bit.

"No, no gloves," Spinks said.

Marc took the inventory, placed it into evidence, gave it to the jury and went back to the podium.

"Detective, were the deceased's fingerprints, Melvin Bullard, found in his apartment?"

"Of course," Spinks replied. "It was his apartment. They were all over the place."

"At my request, your tech people went back and dusted for prints on the underside of every desk drawer of Bullard's desk. Were any of his prints found on any of them?"

"Objection, lacks foundation. This witness did not conduct the tests himself," Paxton said.

"I have their report," Marc said. "A copy was provided to the prosecution and they have had ample time to review it and conduct their own examination of the desk drawers. I can bring the tech here to testify or she can stipulate, I'll enter it through this witness and we can move on."

"Major?" Dwyer said looking at Paxton.

"We'll stipulate, your Honor," she replied. "I'll withdraw my objection."

"Were any fingerprints found?"

"None. None at all of anyone."

Marc went through the formality of having the fingerprint report entered then turned the witness over. He got what he wanted. An argument to make that it was slightly ridiculous that Melvin Bullard's fingerprints were not on the envelope or under the desk drawer where it was found. He could even argue that the FBI did not find it in the apartment at all since it was not on the inventory list.

It took Paxton one question to get Spinks to admit that two FBI agents that he knew were in fact at the apartment. Where she ran into trouble was getting him to admit they told him about the envelope and list of names found taped to the underside of Bullard's desk drawer. She asked him at least five different times to admit it and he would not. He simply kept stating that he did not remember it. Marc finally objected, Dwyer sustained him and a mildly frustrated O'Rourke moved on.

Where she successfully and even brilliantly scored was going over the long list of enemies Melvin Bullard had made. Over the years, he had been a thorn in the side of the Mafia and the NYPD knew it. He was even a thorn in the side of the NYPD.

"Isn't it a fact, Detective, this man was generally loathed?"

Spinks leaned forward, made an awkward looking face as if thinking about it then finally admitted it was true.

"You also interviewed coworkers of his at the New York Times, didn't you, Detective?"

"Yes, we did," he admitted.

"How many?"

"Oh, I think it was fifteen. Mostly those who worked in the same department as he did."

"And none of them were at all upset with his death, were they?"

"No, I guess not."

"You guess not? Isn't it true that they had a celebration party and over a hundred people showed up, people he worked with?"

"I'm not sure how many there were. I didn't go but I heard about it," Spinks replied.

"Isn't it true the list of suspects for his murder is fairly long? More than ten or twenty?"

"Yes, I guess," Spinks agreed.

"Including members of the Mafia?"

"You could say that," he agreed.

"Detective, isn't it true that the murder of Melvin Bullard has nothing to do with this case and the leak of the government's Exhibit One?"

"Don't know," Spinks said.

"It's certainly possible though isn't it?"

"You could say that," he agreed.

"I have nothing further," O'Rourke said.

Marc passed on redirect and Spinks was excused. Much to his delight, Maddy Rivers had the task of driving him back to Reagan National. His numerous attempts to get Maddy to go back to New York with him were politely rebuffed. He finally stopped asking when Maddy asked if she would be able to meet his wife.

Over lunch, a dejected Sammy asked Marc if anything good came out of the morning session. Marc assured him it went exactly the way he thought it would including Paxton O'Rourke's cross-exam.

"It's like building something with Legos," Marc told him. "We get a little piece here, a little piece there and in the end you try to have something that looks like reasonable doubt."

Professor Sanderson, who was sitting to Sammy's left, patted him on the arm and assured him his lawyers were doing fine.

FORTY-SIX

Marc had initially presented a list of a baker's dozen of character witnesses he wanted to call. Every one of them were officers, mostly high-ranking ones; colonels and general officers. It took a four-hour conference before Judge Dwyer convinced Marc to whittle the list down to six. Since six was the actual number he wanted, Marc chalked this up as a minor victory. He had gone into the meeting with the knowledge that O'Rourke was arguing for only two and Dwyer had let it be known he wanted no more than three or four.

Following the lunch break at 1400 hours, the first witness Marc called was Navy Commander Landon Beecher. Beecher was the Deputy National Security Advisor for Vice President Morton. He had worked closely with Sammy during their tenure on the Veep's NSA staff, knew Sammy well, liked him personally and admired him as an officer. He was currently the Executive Officer on the *USS Minnesota*, a fast attack submarine. Fortunately, the *Minnesota* was in its home port of Groton, Connecticut which made Beecher available.

Commander Beecher, looking resplendent in his dress blues, was sworn in and took the stand. He gave his name, rank and current assignment. Not wanting to waste a lot of time, Marc got right down to business.

Beecher explained who he was and how he came to know Major Kamel. During his time on the Vice President's staff he had prepared two performance evaluations of Sammy. Both of them were marked as defense exhibits and Marc went through the formality of placing them into evidence.

The commander had given Sammy excellent ratings for every category which Marc had him explain to the members. Marc then smoothly transitioned into having him testify as to his personal opinion.

"Sammy Kamel was as fine an officer, Navy, Army or whatever, that it has been my pleasure to serve with. He is as conscientious and devoted to his duties and service to this country as anyone."

"Commander, would you read the comment you made on the second evaluation you did of Major Kamel for the jury please?"

It was a typed, three-paragraph opinion of Samir's qualities. Beecher took his time, read slowly and emphasized his opinion about Sammy's leadership, dedication and devotion to duty plus his willingness to help others and teamwork. It was a glowing tribute that anyone would want to have written about themselves.

239

"Commander Beecher, did you know that Major Kamel is a Muslim?"

"Yes, I did. I'm not sure how devoted he was to his religion. He never talked about it. I never saw him pray or read the Koran. I don't remember even seeing one on his desk. If there had been one I would not have cared. But he never displayed his religion or talked about it at all."

"Did you have any reason to believe he was a self-radicalized Islamic extremist?"

"Of course not and I still don't believe it," Beecher answered.

"Objection," O'Rourke said. "Nonresponsive and we request that his last comment be stricken."

"Overruled. He knows the defendant well enough to give his opinion. The members can infer whatever they want. You may continue, Mr. Kadella," Dwyer said.

Marc took a moment to go over his notes. He could not think of anything else he could get from this witness. Obviously, he thought highly of Sammy Kamel and didn't believe he was a traitor. Stop here and end it on a high note.

"I have nothing further," Marc said.

Paxton O'Rourke replaced Marc at the podium and wasted little time. Treating the Commander with the respect due his rank, she led him through a sequence of questions designed to elicit yes and no answers. Most of them had to do with three things. One, to get Beecher to admit if someone wanted to fool him about his radical beliefs he would not do anything to advertise it. Two, outside of work, Beecher had spent virtually no time with Major Kamel and had no idea what he did or who he associated with. And three, Beecher did not have Major Kamel monitor jihadist websites at work or at home and to his knowledge, no one else did either.

"Would you have known if anyone on the Vice President's staff had requested that Major Kamel monitor these websites?"

Beecher hesitated for a moment, cast a quick glance at Sammy then admitted that yes, he would have known such a thing.

Marc declined his opportunity to redirect and Beecher was excused.

In defiance of court protocol, Commander Beecher solemnly marched right to the defense table. Sammy stood and the two men saluted each other. They shook hands and Beecher exited the courtroom.

The next day Marc went through three more character witnesses. Two of them were coworkers on the Veep's NSA staff, both civilians. Neither had done a performance evaluation but both had glowing things to say about Sammy. All of it was along the same lines as what Commander Beecher had testified.

As with Commander Beecher, Paxton O'Rourke made them both admit they had little contact with Sammy outside of work. They confessed that it was certainly possible that Sammy was a radical Muslim and they were simply fooled.

The afternoon session was taken up entirely by Colonel Ann Engel. Engel was a watch commander at the Defense Intelligence Agency. She was a West Point graduate who had been in the Army, including West Point, for twenty-two years. The last ten she had worked in Intelligence.

The Colonel had first met Sammy in Iraq when he had transferred out of an infantry unit and into Intelligence. At the time she was a major and Sammy a captain and she was his immediate superior. Colonel Engel had also done an evaluation that was at least as good as Commander Beecher's.

Marc went through the steps of admitting it and then the two of them spent an hour and a half on Engel's personal involvement with Sammy and her opinion of him.

"Were you ever personally involved with Major Kamel?"

"You mean romantically?"

"Yes, ma'am, that's what I mean."

"No," she smiled, "I was not. I admit I was a bit attracted to him. Why not? He's a good looking, polite, considerate man. Solid as a rock. But I was his superior officer and that was that."

"But you did socialize with him, did you not?"

"Sure. We were in a small unit in a combat zone. What little socializing there was, we did with people we worked with."

"Did he seem to be a serious, religious Muslim?"

"I didn't even know he was a Muslim until he had been with us for four months. So, to answer your question, no."

"I have nothing further," Marc said.

Paxton O'Rourke spent fewer than twenty minutes with her. Colonel Engel had not kept in touch with Sammy even though they both worked in the D.C. area. It didn't take O'Rourke long to get her to admit she had no idea if Sammy could have become radicalized during that time.

When she finished with Colonel Engel, Dwyer called a halt for the day. As Engel was leaving, like Beecher, she marched right to the defense table. She and Sammy saluted each other and Engel wished him good luck.

"We need to go see Dwyer," Marc said. He looked at Sammy still seated and said, "We have to put your girlfriend on the stand."

"No! Absolutely not," Sammy declared. "I'll fire you before I let you put Charlene up there."

"What the hell are you talking about?" Marc asked.

"You put her on that witness stand and have her admit to being involved with me, it will destroy her career. I'm telling you, she is on the fast track to getting a star and if you put her up there she's finished. Even if I'm acquitted, she'll be done. I won't do that."

"You were going to before the trial started, what changed your mind?"

"This," Sammy said, spreading his arms out and using them to circle the courtroom. "I had no idea before, now I do. Ann Engel and Landon Beecher came under subpoena. They will be all right. But Charlene will have to say she was romantically involved with me. There are too many senior officers who will never forgive her. No, she would be finished and I won't do it."

"She's the only one who can testify that you weren't getting self-radicalized off duty and…"

"Forget it, Marc. You're doing fine. We'll go with what we have. I still love her enough not to do that to her and that's final."

The next day the morning session was taken up with the final two character witnesses. First up was former Corporal Kyle Fontana from Pine Bluff, Arkansas. Fontana walked through the courtroom using a cane because of a noticeable limp. Fontana took the stand and for the next hour testified about how he got the limp and how then First Lieutenant Samir Kamel saved his life.

Their platoon had been doing recon in an Iraqi village looking for Al Qaeda when all hell broke loose. Fontana was the first one hit and went down next to a small building. They estimated a dozen Al Qaeda fanatics had opened fire and pinned down the platoon.

For the next half hour, Sammy Kamel had coolly directed the platoon and personally came to Fontana's rescue. While the other platoon members gave them covering fire, Sammy had carried Fontana back to safety. Before it was over, four jihadis were dead and the rest had withdrawn. Samir Kamel was awarded the Silver Star for rescuing Fontana.

A wounded veteran is someone Paxton O'Rourke had enough sense to handle gingerly and respectfully. Again, she had the witness admit he had no idea what Sammy had been up to recently. O'Rourke knew when to quit and quickly ended the cross-examination.

Last but not least, Marc put Brigadier General Russell McKee on the stand. The General had been a lieutenant colonel and Sammy's Battalion Commander in Iraq. It was McKee who had recommended

Sammy for his Silver Star. Then after that, McKee personally transferred Sammy to his battalion headquarters as his G-2 Intelligence Officer.

Through McKee, Marc submitted the written Silver Star commendation and McKee's excellent evaluation of Major Kamel. It was also McKee, by then a Brigadier General who had recommended Sammy for a position on the Vice President's NSA staff. All of this testimony was done with a touch of reluctance on McKee's part. Marc knew that he would do this and understood his reason for it. McKee was still a relatively young man and wanted to stay in the Army and pursue his career.

Paxton O'Rourke's cross-exam took less that ten minutes. She steered clear of McKee recommending Sammy for the Vice President's office. One never knew who might be a commanding officer in your future. He did, of course, admit that he had not been in touch with Sammy recently and had to agree he could be radicalized.

As General McKee left the stand he did not go to Sammy at the table. He did manage an unseen wink at him as a clear signal wishing him well.

"Under normal circumstances," Marc began speaking to Sammy across their lunch table from him, "there is no way I would put you on the witness stand."

"They want to hear me say I didn't do this," Sammy said holding his sandwich three inches from his mouth.

By now, everyone at the table, Professor Sanderson, Tommy Dorn, Maddy and Tony Carvelli, was listening while chewing their lunch.

Marc finished swallowing, placed his sandwich on the wrapping paper it came in and said, "Yes, I know. The problem is you can't just get on the stand and say that then come back to the table. Major O'Rourke is proving herself to be a very capable trial lawyer. All she needs to nail your coffin shut, so to speak, is one slip-up."

"They already know you will deny doing this," Professor Sanderson said. "The risk is not worth the reward of testifying."

"I said before the trial, it will come down to whether or not they believe you wrote that list and leaked it to the reporter. Nothing you say is going to influence that," Marc said. "I can't in good conscience, let you take the stand. I don't see where you can help yourself. You can't make it better you can only make it worse."

"And if I insist?" Sammy asked.

"Then I have to let you," Marc replied.

"You need to listen to your lawyer, Sammy," Sanderson said. He was seated across from Marc next to Sammy and gently laid a hand on Sammy's arm.

Sammy thought it over while everyone silently watched him. After a minute he looked at Marc and nodded.

"Yes, I see your point. I was thinking of my career. If I don't deny it and they vote to acquit, there will be people who don't believe it. But I need to set that aside, don't I?"

"Yes, you do. I don't think you can help yourself by testifying and O'Rourke could make you pay," Marc said.

"Okay."

When court was called back into session, everyone was anticipating Marc's next move. Would Samir Kamel testify or not? Without showing it, Paxton O'Rourke was almost praying that he would.

Marc stood to address the court. "The defense rests, your Honor."

A murmuring wave rolled over the gallery and Judge Dwyer gaveled for silence.

"Very well," he said when the crowd settled down. "We'll have closing arguments tomorrow at 0900."

"You mean the sneaky little coward refused to testify?" Darla asked Clay. They were on the phone after the day's testimony and Clay was giving her a rundown of the defense's case.

What Darla said about Samir Kamel being a coward startled Clay a bit. For several days now he had been getting the impression from her that she believed Kamel was guilty. She was starting to believe her own scam.

"His lawyer probably told him not to. I think he has enough now to argue reasonable doubt. Will he convince the jury?" Clay asked rhetorically. "I guess we'll find out."

"What do you think?" Darla asked him.

Seeing a chance to give Darla a good case of indigestion and sleepless nights, Clay said, "I think the defense has done a good job and the jury will come back not guilty."

"Goddamnit, don't say that!" Darla practically screamed into the phone.

"I thought you wanted my honest opinion," Clay said glad she could not see his grin.

"If they find him not guilty, then what?" Darla asked.

"We'll just have to wait and see," Clay replied. "We'll know in a few days, Mrs. Carver."

"Fine," Darla disgustedly said then hung up.

FORTY-SEVEN

"President and members of the jury," Judge Dwyer said addressing the members, "You have heard the testimony of the witnesses, been given the trial exhibits presented by both sides and heard arguments of counsel."

Closing arguments had been conducted the previous day. Major O'Rourke had gone first, then Marc Kadella had done his. When Marc finished, unlike civilian trials, O'Rourke was given an opportunity to do a rebuttal. Her rebuttal was restricted to anything the defense presented that O'Rourke did not cover in her initial closing argument. It was mid-afternoon when they finished and Dwyer adjourned until this morning.

"I will now take some time to give you your instructions and then you will retire to deliberate.

"I realize you have heard this many times during the course of this trial and in your daily lives. In American law, civilian as well as military, the defendant is presumed innocent. That is not just a fancy phrase, a nice sounding legal theory. It is the bedrock of our judicial system. The defendant is presumed innocent and does not have to prove anything. It is up to the government, through its legal representatives, to present sufficient evidence of guilt to prove the defendant guilty beyond a reasonable doubt.

"In the case before you, the defendant, Major Samir Kamel, has been charged with one count only. But that charge is the most serious criminal act there is. He is charged with a single count of treason."

Dwyer held up a sheet of paper and continued reading from it. "The elements of the charge of treason are: One, that the defendant owes allegiance to the United States; and two, that the defendant levies war against them or adheres to the enemies of the United States giving those enemies aid and comfort within the United States or elsewhere."

Judge Dwyer again held up the sheet of paper to the jury then placed it back on the bench in front of himself before continuing.

"The government has the burden of proving each and every one of the elements of treason beyond a reasonable doubt. Put another way, if you have reasonable doubt that the defendant did not commit any or all of the elements of the charge as I have given them to you, then you must come back with a not guilty verdict.

"The defendant chose to exercise his right under the Constitution of the United States to remain silent and not testify. Let me be very clear about this. You are not to make any inference or allow that to enter into your decision at all. The reason for that is you swore an oath, not only as citizens but as officers of the United States Army, to base your decision on what was presented to you in this court only. Put another way, you are not to decide this case on anything that was not presented during this trial. That includes Major Kamel's decision to remain silent. That is also a bedrock, sacred right in our system of justice. If you were to allow his remaining silence to influence your decision, that would be the exact same thing as allowing something not presented during the trial to enter into your decision. I hope that is clear.

"Allow me to make one last point. As you are all aware, there is no such thing as a 'hung jury' in a military court martial. In order to find guilt, you must, by secret written ballot, have a two-thirds majority. There are nine of you. That means that six of you must vote guilty. If four of you vote not guilty, the defendant shall be acquitted.

"What this means in practice is that you will only conduct one vote to reach a verdict. Because of this, I strongly urge you to take your time. Deliberate carefully and thoroughly. I can't tell you what to do or how to do it. It is my suggestion only that each one of you be allowed to speak freely and that each of you carefully listen to each òther.

"You are all officers of the United States Army. However, in this duty, your individual rank has no bearing. No one need be concerned that a higher ranking member will try to use that rank against you. In other words, take your time and be thorough and careful.

"Captain Dreyfus will now escort you back to your room to begin. I will be here until 1700 hours. If you reach a verdict by then, we will conclude today. If not, you will be escorted back to your quarters and come back tomorrow at 0800. If you want to deliberate today beyond 1700 you may do so but let me know before 1700. If you need me for anything, please inform Captain Dreyfus.

"Do any of you have any questions?"

The members all looked around the jury box at each other and shook their heads to indicate they did not. Colonel Lewis, the jury president answered Dwyer's question verbally.

Dwyer looked at the MP officer standing next to the jury box and said, "All right, Captain. You may escort the members out."

"All rise!" Dreyfus loudly ordered as the members rose to leave. A minute later they were gone and Dwyer adjourned.

"You're replaying it, aren't you?" Maddy asked Marc.

They were back at Sammy's quarters, everyone except Professor Sanderson who had chosen not to attend today. Marc was sitting on the end of the couch next to the front window. His head was tilted back bumping against the wall and his eyes were closed. Maddy was in a chair opposite Marc with the rickety old coffee table between them. Dorn, Sammy and Tony Carvelli were seated in the next room at the dining room table drinking an early beer.

Without moving or opening his eyes, Marc replied, "Yeah, can't help it."

"Well, stop it," Maddy said. "You did your best and I think you did great. Don't start second-guessing yourself."

Sammy came into the living room and sat on the couch next to Marc. He gently bumped his right elbow against Marc's left arm, pointed the long neck bottle of Bud at him and said, "Want a plug?"

Marc opened his eyes, lowered his head and said, "Sure, why not? It's afternoon somewhere."

Marc took the half full bottle, tipped it to his lips and drained it. He smiled, handed the empty bottle to Sammy and said, "Thanks, I needed that."

By now Tommy Dorn and Carvelli were in chairs in the living room with them.

"I don't know what else you, I mean we, could've done, Marc," Sammy said. "But you know what, I've believed all along they're going to convict me." Marc's head snapped to the side to look at Sammy with a puzzled expression.

"Seriously? Why do you…"

"Because the Army wants this closed," Sammy replied.

"Yeah but how…"

"Everybody knows that. It's no secret. It's subtle, unspoken even, but believe me, the members know it. That's why that lieutenant colonel had a front row, reserved seat. I didn't tell you this, but he's there watching for the big brass. The Army Chief of Staff and Joint Chiefs," Sammy said.

Marc looked at Dorn and asked, "Did you know that?"

"I suspected it," Dorn replied. He looked at Sammy and said, "They can come back with a not guilty. It's not a done deal."

"Well that's pretty goddamn gloomy," a dejected Marc said.

"We'll see," Sammy said patting Marc on the knee. "I think you did terrific. Who knows, maybe we convinced them. Now, if you don't mind, I would like some time alone."

"Your parents are coming by around 2:00," Marc reminded him. "Don't let your mother find you hanging in the bathroom."

Sammy had a hearty laugh at that thought. "Don't worry, I'm not going to take that route. I'll deal with what happens and keep fighting."

An hour later, Marc, Tommy Dorn, Maddy and Tony Carvelli were at Paisano's Pizza. When they had passed through the gate leaving Ft. Myer they were all astonished at the size of the crowd. There were ten thousand people at least and fairly evenly divided. There were also almost three hundred MPs and state and local police keeping the two

247

sides separated. Fortunately, there was enough traffic flowing in and out so that no one paid any attention to the defense team driving through the gate.

Paisano's had never seen this amount of business. Within walking distance of Ft. Myer, the trial crowd had filled the place for lunch and dinner every day. When the four of them entered the restaurant the place went completely silent. It was like a scene out of an old western when the bad guys walked into the saloon. Every head in the place turned to look at them. The four of them silently looked back.

"Hello, everyone!" Marc loudly said breaking the silence. "Yes, it's us. We eat too."

This broke the atmosphere and almost everyone laughed or at least smiled. The hostess found a table for them while Dorn ordered a pizza at the counter.

When Dorn left the table to retrieve their lunch, Maddy turned to Marc and whispered, "You know, he might be guilty."

"What?" Carvelli almost yelled.

"We've talked about this before," Marc said. "Besides, don't tell me you haven't wondered."

"I think everybody's guilty," Carvelli replied. "That's my sensitive side."

Maddy and Marc looked at each other and simultaneously said, "Cynical ex-cop."

"I'm surprised you two bleeding hearts could think that," Carvelli said.

"Think what?" Dorn asked as he set the pizza and another pitcher of Diet Coke on the table.

"Think that Sammy could be guilty," Carvelli said.

"Oh, that," Dorn replied. He sat down and said, "Yeah, he could be. It's not our job..."

"Look, everybody," Marc said spreading his hands out. "I'm fine. What happens will happen."

While they ate their lunch, as the crowd started to thin out, at least a dozen people stopped to congratulate Marc. Every one of them believed Sammy would be found guilty but they all thought Marc did a very good job for him.

After finishing lunch they went through the mob at the gate to go back to Sammy's quarters. As Dorn drove through the gate—Esterhazy, having been dismissed—they all looked over the angry faces.

"No matter what the verdict is," Carvelli said, "there's going to be an explosion out here."

The rest of the day was spent with Sammy and the Kamel family. It was a beautiful, late October day and the little house was too crowded.

It was almost summer-like and they all went outside and hung out on the tiny lawn. The unspoken was that Sammy might not have many more days like this.

At ten minutes past five, Marc's phone went off. He looked at the ID, then answered it.

He listened for thirty seconds or so then said, "Okay, that's fine."

He listened some more then thanked the caller and ended the call.

"They're done for the day. No verdict. They will start again at 8:00 tomorrow morning," Marc announced to the small crowd.

"What do you think?" Sammy's dad asked.

"I think we'll get a decision tomorrow. There isn't that much for them to go over and it's not like a civilian jury. They don't have to spend three or four days trying to convince one or two holdouts."

Marc said to Sammy, "I'm really tired. It always happens. Once the trial is done, the stress leaves and the release is exhausting. I'll see you in the morning. Get some sleep."

"I'm fine. Don't worry," Sammy replied.

The next morning everyone was again back at Sammy's. Now they were running out of small talk and were sitting around watching the small TV. It was tuned to a cable news channel and of course, the day's hot topic was the jury deliberations. To help kill time, Marc and Tommy Dorn, with Maddy and Tony listening in, were discussing the next possible part of the trial; sentencing.

In a civilian trial, if a guilty verdict is delivered, the judge will set a date for sentencing several weeks out. This is to allow for a presentence investigation and report to be conducted and prepared. Military courts-martial conduct sentencing as soon as the verdict is reached. And it's the same jury that decides the punishment.

Both sides must be prepared to present a sentencing request and argument when the verdict is announced. The defense, especially, is given broad discretion if the judge so chooses. They can argue basically anything including the defendant's character, the weakness of the evidence, pretty much whatever will help mitigate the sentence. They can also present witnesses such as family members to beg for mercy. During their preparation for this phase, Sammy had been rock-solid adamant that he would not allow this. He said it was too difficult to put his family through the trial. He would not allow them to get on a witness stand, break down and beg. He believed his service to the nation should speak for itself.

Tommy Dorn had been tasked to conduct this part of the trial. As much as anything, he had far more experience at this than Marc and a much better grasp of what to say. Also, the defendant could address the members and make an unsworn statement on his own behalf.

At precisely 10:00 A.M., Marc got the call. Within a half hour, all of the principals were back in court and the members had taken their seats.

Judge Dwyer went through the formality of inquiring of the President, Colonel Odessa Lewis, if the verdict had been reached. Answering in the affirmative, Dwyer turned to the defense table.

"Major Samir Kamel, you will rise and address the members," he ordered. Sammy, in his Class A dress uniform, stood up and alone marched in military-style up to the jury box. He stopped approximately six feet in front of Colonel Lewis and came to attention.

Although it was unnecessary, everyone at both the defense and prosecution table stood and faced the jury. Perhaps out of respect, perhaps to get a better view before the verdict was read, everyone in the capacity-filled crowd silently and reverently stood as well.

Colonel Lewis stood and read from the charging sheet. "In the matter of the United States of America versus Major Samir Kamel on the single count of treason, we the members of this court martial find the defendant guilty."

Sammy saluted Colonel Lewis who returned his salute. He then did a perfect about face. With the only sound in the still courtroom the weeping of his mother in the front row, Sammy stoically marched back to the defense table.

Darla Carver watched a replay of the news at her campaign headquarters in Hartford. She was seated at the desk of her campaign manager with several staff members around her, including Sonja Hayden.

"Twenty-years, a ten-thousand-dollar fine and dishonorable discharge," Darla said out loud while watching film of the protestors having at each other. "I guess neither side is happy."

"How many arrested?" one of the young, male volunteers asked.

"Over three hundred and probably more to come," Sonja replied. "You should make a statement," Sonja said to Darla.

"Good idea. Get one written up. You know, the usual stuff. Put this behind us. Come together and let the country heal. The usual thing politicians say at a time like this. Set up a press briefing and make sure there are national media cameras. Might as well look and sound presidential."

FORTY-EIGHT

"Thank you, Mr. President, I appreciate the call," Darla Carver said into the hotel room phone. She listened for a minute then replied. "Yes, sir. I'm sure we'll be able to work together to get a lot of things accomplished and I'm looking forward to it."

President Timmons ended the call and Darla hung up the phone. She looked at her husband and said, "How can you stand to be in the same room with that man?"

"Better get used to it," Tom replied while swirling the ice cubes around in his highball glass. "It's just politics. He probably hates you as much as you hate him."

"And I'm sure he knows we're coming after him," Dan Stone, Darla's pollster chimed in.

They were in the Executive Suite of the Hilton in downtown Hartford. The polls had closed two hours ago and within minutes, every network was declaring Darla the winner. Her opponent, a man whose name Darla barely remembered, had called and conceded ten minutes later.

Seated around the suite's living room area were Tom Carver, Sonja, Darla and Clay Dean. From her campaign were her campaign manager, Andy Peyton, her pollster Dan Stone and chief fundraiser Lawrence Jacobs. Also in attendance was the Chair of the National Committee, Sarah Bennett-Lerman.

Ever since the race was called and Darla's Senate seat confirmed, she had been deluged with congratulatory phone calls. The phone rang again and Sonja answered it. Darla was seated across the room and shook her head at her aide to indicate she should lie to the caller. She was not in the mood to take any more calls.

"Just a moment, sir. I'll see if she's available," Sonja said. She pressed the phone to her stomach and said to Darla, "You'll want to take this. It's Sherwin Field."

"Yes, I'll take it," Darla quickly said. She picked up the extension on her side of the room and began schmoozing the caller.

Sherwin Field was a multibillionaire hedge fund operator and generous contributor. He also was an excellent fundraiser with contacts all over the country. A month ago Tom had spent several days in the company of Field on his private Caribbean Island. It was a poorly kept secret that Field kept the island's forty-million-dollar mansion/playground well stocked with young females for his special guests. Even very young males for those with different tastes.

During that long weekend, Field let it be known to Tom that he would do everything he could to support Darla's presidential ambitions.

And all he wanted in return was an appointment as ambassador to the Court of St. James. A very reasonable price, Tom admitted.

Darla spent fifteen minutes on the phone with Field and verified that he could count on the appointment. When she finished the call she smiled at her husband and told him Field invited Tom down to the Island in two weeks.

"When do we start fundraising for the presidency, Larry?" Darla asked Lawrence Jacobs.

"Tomorrow," he replied. "I'm flying to California to start right in on it. I've got several Silicon Valley guys to meet with."

"Good," Darla replied. She picked up her watery Vodka tonic, tossed it down and said, "Well, we should get over to the Convention Center and thank the troops.

"Tomorrow, I'll go to Washington and get going on redecorating my office. The taxpayers have decided to generously contribute half a million bucks for it," she continued. "You get started on the campaign," she said to Andy Peyton.

"Already am," the heavyset, bald man replied.

"Where are you off to?" Darla asked Tom

"Dubai. Fundraising for the charity. Plus a few bucks for speaking fees," Tom replied.

"Those are going up," Darla winked at him.

"Oh, yeah," Tom said and nodded with a sly smile.

Darla stood up to leave and said, "Sarah, I want you on stage with me."

"My privilege, Senator," Bennett-Lerman replied. "Party unity and all. Whatever you need, let me know."

"A little early, don't you think, Sally?" Darla asked.

"It's a Bloody Mary, big deal. It's like having breakfast," Senator Sally Newport replied.

It was two days after the election and Darla had flown to D.C. to get started. She was at a table having an expensive brunch at Axel's, a trendy Georgetown restaurant, with her good friend and soon-to-be Senatorial neighbor.

When the two of them were being led to their table, everyone in the crowded restaurant had stood to applaud. To a normal human, even one with some serious celebrity, this response would have been cause for at least mild embarrassment. Darla Carver took it in stride. Of course, she smiled and waved around the room to at least show her appreciation for this spontaneous display of adoration. Even from normally cynical Washingtonians this was unusual but Darla saw it as her rightful due.

252

The previous day, the day after the midterm election that brought her to the Senate and back to D.C., the cable news media was already lit up with speculation about her next step. President Gary Timmons' poll numbers were fairly good, mid-forties, but his party had been hammered on Tuesday. People generally regarded him well personally but his policies were not exciting anyone. On top of that, his detractors were downright contemptuous of his foreign policy ignorance. The general consensus was that Timmons could be beaten and kept from a second term. And Darla Carver was already the leading horse in the race to do so. While the two women ate their meal and chatted, a tall, distinguished-looking gentleman in a three-piece suit walked up to them. While he did this, most of the people in the dining area watched him.

"Hello, Carson," Sally said to the man.

Senate Majority Leader Carson MacCallum took Darla's right hand in both of his and leaned down and gave her an affectionate kiss on the cheek. In his soft southern accent, he said, "Welcome back to Washington, Darla. I'm delighted to have you joining our little club."

"Thank you, Senator," Darla said looking up at the most powerful elected official in her party. "Please, have a seat. Join us."

MacCallum sat down and placed a hand lightly on Darla's shoulder. At the same time, he slyly reached under the table and squeezed Sally's upper thigh for which the married senator gave him a lascivious smile.

Within seconds the waiter was back pouring coffee for MacCallum and placing a shot of his favorite bourbon next to the cup. MacCallum barely acknowledged the young man as he poured the shot into his coffee.

While stirring his drink, MacCallum said, "Sally tells me you're looking for something substantial. She even made a couple of suggestions."

"Oh," Darla smiled and replied. "What would those be?"

"Foreign Relations and Armed Services," MacCallum quietly said then took a swallow from his cup. "A little pick me up after a trying night," he said while winking at Sally who turned a light shade of pink and stifled a knowing smile.

"Since you are not a typical freshman senator," he continued, "I can certainly treat you differently. I have no problem putting you on both committees. But I can't make you a chairman of either."

"I didn't expect that, Carson."

"I can get you an important subcommittee chair. How about you chair the Armed Services Subcommittee on Strategic Forces. The current chair is Senator Whisler and he's retiring. There's gonna be a couple people pissed about it but I'll smooth that out."

"Thank you, Carson," Darla said.

"I'll also get you on the Foreign Relations Subcommittee on Europe and Regional Security. It's kind of a plumb post. Lots of vacation time—I mean fact-finding trips—to Europe if you want them. All on the taxpayer's dime, of course."

"That's the NATO subcommittee isn't it?" Darla asked.

"Yes, it is. We'll have to get you an updated security clearance. That won't be a problem."

"Again, Carson, thank you," Darla said.

"I never forget my friends," MacCallum said. "There is one other thing. I need a favor from you."

"Okay," Darla cautiously replied.

"I need you to fill Whisler's seat on the Agriculture Committee," MacCallum told her.

"No problem," Darla said.

"I know it's not one of the glamour positions but it is important and I'd appreciate it."

"I said no problem, Carson, and I meant it," Darla said patting him on the hand.

The waiter was back with more coffee and another shot of bourbon for MacCallum. He refilled Darla's cup and nodded his head at Senator Newport. Sally was holding up her almost empty Bloody Mary glass indicating she wanted a refill.

"I'm here to make friends," Darla said.

At that moment a woman with an extremely pretty young girl of three or four approached the table. Darla looked at them and smiled.

"I'm sorry to disturb you, Mrs. Carver, I mean Senator Carver. But I'm a huge fan and I was wondering if I could get a picture with you and Marisa?" the mother asked referring to her daughter.

"Of course!" Darla said. "Come here, sweetheart. She's adorable."

The little girl, with an almost panic-stricken look on her face, allowed Darla to pick her up and hold her on her lap. The mother took three or four quick shots with her phone and the kid climbed down.

"Thank you so much," the mother said.

"Oh, let me see," Darla insisted.

The woman held the phone for her to show her the photos.

"She's beautiful. Please send me one to my office," Darla said. Darla took the phone and showed the pictures to her tablemates who both cooed over them. After a minute or so more the interruption was over and the woman and child scurried off.

"Well, I guess I should be grateful she didn't pee on me," Darla said. "Do you ever get used to that?"

"Not really," MacCallum replied. "Anyway, welcome back to Washington. Has your campaign started?"

"What campaign is that?" Darla smiled.

"That's the worst kept secret there is. Will she run or won't she?" MacCallum said. "Let me know if I can do anything for you. We need the White House back in its proper hands."

FORTY-NINE

The Cadillac limousine carrying the very urbane, tailored and well-dressed Russian Ambassador, Grigory Tretiak and the Russian Embassy's crude, top spy, Viktor Ivanov pulled into line. It was Saturday, January 21 and the two top men of the Russian delegation in Washington were in front of the British Embassy.

They had been invited to a cocktail party, along with a couple of hundred others, for an informal diplomatic evening. The new Congress of the United States had been sworn in on the 3rd and forty or fifty high ranking Senators and Congressmen and women would be in attendance. This would be the first opportunity for diplomats to semi-officially meet them.

There were at least a dozen cars ahead of theirs waiting to drop off the VIP's. An impatient Viktor Ivanov opened his door, got out and stood alongside the limo in the street. While he did this he smoked a Marlboro Red, his favorite American cigarette. As he smoked he walked alongside the car as it slowly moved up.

"You really should quit those things, Viktor," Ambassador Tretiak said when Viktor returned to the limo's backseat. "They will be the death of you."

"We all die from something," the spy grumbled.

It took another twenty minutes until the two men were finally delivered to the front of the British Ambassador's residence. Once inside they found a fairly large crowd milling about, introducing themselves and making polite small talk.

While the two Russians worked their way through the crowd, Viktor Ivanov casually checked out the wait staff. Three of them, two men and a young woman, were in fact, agents of his. Of course, Viktor was certain, almost the entire catering staff were agents of some country including the hosts, Britain and the U.S.

The two men casually circulated, greeting people they knew and introducing the ambassador to those they didn't. It took almost a half-hour before Viktor spotted the main reason they were in attendance.

"There she is," Viktor whispered in Russian to his compatriot. "Over there by the fireplace speaking with the Ambassador of India."

"Good. Well, we must go across the room and congratulate her," Tretiak said.

They slowly made their way through the crowd then stepped up to their objective. Tretiak shook hands with the Indian Ambassador and politely apologized for the intrusion and asked if they could have a word with the freshman senator from Connecticut. The ambassador graciously acquiesced and moved away.

256

"Senator Carver," Tretiak said smiling at Darla. "Congratulations on your splendid victory."

"Thank you, Grigory," Darla replied while shaking the man's hand. Tretiak had been the Russian Ambassador for over a decade and he and Darla were well acquainted despite disliking each other intensely.

"Have you met our trade representative, Viktor Ivanov?" Tretiak asked Darla.

"No, I haven't," Darla replied. The two of them smiled at each other, warmly shook hands and Darla asked, "And how are things in the SVR, General Ivanov?"

Viktor and Tretiak both laughed and Viktor replied, "I assume all is well with the SVR, as far as I know."

"Senator," Tretiak continued, "I was wondering if protocol would permit a private word between us. Something informal and off the record."

"Certainly, Ambassador," Darla replied. "I'll simply assume you are wearing a recording device and watch what I say." Darla actually winked at Viktor the Spy when she said this.

"You are very suspicious, Senator," Tretiak said with a grin. "Please, there is a small room over here where we can talk. Viktor will wait here for us."

Tretiak led Darla into what appeared to be a well-furnished conference room off the main dining area where the guests were. They each sat in a comfortable leather armchair facing each other. Darla crossed her legs while sipping her champagne waiting for the Russian to speak.

"I have something for you. A photo, to be precise," he said while reaching into the inside pocket of his suit coat.

"What is it?" Darla asked as she reached for it.

"I think you will recognize it," Tretiak said staring into her eyes, looking for her reaction.

Darla looked at the photo and for the briefest of instants, her face and eyes gave her away. She quickly regained control, held the photo up, shrugged and said, "I have no idea what this is."

Tretiak looked down at her crossed legs and sadly shook his head, two or three times. He looked back into her face and heavily sighed.

"Please, Senator, let's not do this. You're lying, I know you're lying and you know you're lying. We both know what it is. It is a photograph of the list of Imams targeted by your husband for assassination. It is the list you leaked to the murdered New York Times reporter, Melvin Bullard. It is proof of your treason madam. We have verified the handwriting and the fingerprints, both yours and his, on the original that you tore into pieces. Next time burn it or flush it down the toilet. But for now…"

"You fucking bastard," Darla snarled at him. She was leaning forward her facial muscles tight as a drum, her eyes narrowed to slits, her lips tight and barely moving. "I'll have you and your head spy killed."

"And the original will be released the next day."

"What do you want?"

"We want to have a close, personal and mutually beneficial relationship with you," Tretiak said as he sat back, smiled and held up both hands in a friendly gesture.

The two of them sat silently staring at each other for almost two minutes. Finally, Darla inhaled a deep breath through her nose, sat back and looked at the photo again.

"How did you get this?" she quietly asked.

"Senator, we both know that is immaterial at this point," Tretiak replied.

"How do I know this is real?"

"You know it is. But if you wish to see the original, I can arrange a private meeting at our embassy."

They sat silently for another minute or so. Someone knocked on the door and a man opened it, looked inside, saw them sitting there, apologized and quietly closed the door.

The Russian leaned forward, patted a dejected Darla Carver on the knee and stood up to leave.

"It was a pleasure seeing you again, Senator. We will be in touch," he said.

"Yob vas," Darla replied which caused Tretiak to quietly laugh.

Tretiak took two steps toward the door turned around and looking down at the still seated Darla said, "I almost forgot. I hope you and your husband appreciate the speaking fees he has received. And the money contributed to your charity."

"What? Why?" Darla asked, a puzzled look on her face.

"Because many millions of it have come from us, either directly or indirectly. It would take your FBI very little effort to trace this back to us."

He paused for a moment while Darla stared, open-mouthed at him.

"Oh please, Senator. Did you really believe your husband was so eloquent and had such marvelously wise things to impart in his speeches to make them worth a half a million dollars for an hour? And the luxurious accommodations that were provided for him? Not to mention the young, cooperative female companionship he received, two and three at a time? I have not seen the film of these trysts but I am told they are quite entertaining.

"One last thing," he said as he took a step back toward her. "You will run for president as planned. Do not even consider resigning and walking away. We have every confidence that the two of you will regain the White House and establish very beneficial relations with us. Yob vas, Senator."

The bellhop started to use his pass key card to open the suite's door. He inserted it into the electronic lock then was stopped by Darla.

"No, I don't want this one. I'll take the one next door," Darla told him.

"That one isn't as nice as this one," the young man replied.

"I don't care!" Darla snapped at him. "I want a different room, now!"

"Yes, ma'am," the thoroughly cowed young man said.

It was the Sunday evening after her meeting with the Russians. Darla and Sonja Hayden were in New York. Because of her status as a former First Lady, she was still under Secret Service protection. There were two agents with them, a man and a woman, in the hotel's hallway. And it was becoming more and more difficult for the Service to keep agents on her detail. One of them recently took a posting in Bismarck, North Dakota just to get away from her.

The bellhop opened the door of the second room then stood aside. The male agent made a quick but thorough sweep of the one-bedroom suite and pronounced it clear.

"When my husband and Mr. Dean get here, bring them right up," Darla said to the agents.

"Their ETA is ten minutes, Senator," the female agent replied.

"Good. Now get out," Darla dismissed them with a flip of her hand.

"What a mess, what a mess," Darla muttered for at least the one-hundredth time as she sat down in one of the living room chairs.

Sonja had immediately gone to the room's dry bar and made her mistress a drink. As she handed it to her, Sonja said, "The President and Clay will know what to do, ma'am. I'm sure of it."

Sonja sat next to her boss and the two of them waited silently for Tom Carver and Clay Dean to arrive. Because of the secrecy Darla wanted for this meeting, she and Sonja had arrived through the service entrance. Twenty minutes after entering the room, Darla was on her second vodka when her husband with Clay Dean walked in.

After greetings that were less than warm, Tom Carver sat on the room's sofa. Clay mixed a scotch and soda for the former president then sat down next to him.

"All right, Darla," Tom began. "Tell me what Tretiak said to you. Slowly and get all the details."

When Darla finished replaying her meeting with the Russian Ambassador the room went silent for a few minutes. Darla handed her empty glass to Sonja who went for a refill.

"What do you think?" Tom quietly asked Clay.

"We need to get it back," Clay replied referring to the list.

"Well, no shit, genius!" Darla practically yelled.

Clay was used to Darla's inability to deal with stress rationally. He ignored her outburst knowing Tom would say something to her.

"Darla, get a grip. We have a problem to deal with," Tom said.

Sonja handed Darla her third drink as Darla replied, "Yeah, and don't forget about your bimbo problem."

Tom silently stared at her, a stern, "Dad is pissed" look on his face and she shrunk back in her chair.

Clay said, "The Russians are going to come to you requesting something specific. It will be something they already have. It will be a test to see if you will cooperate. Do it. Go ahead and give them something minimal to satisfy them. You're going to have to play along.

"I want you to call Malcolm Brewster for me," Clay continued referring to the former director of the CIA, "Tell him I need to see him. Tell him he is to cooperate with me and ask no questions. Don't tell him anything about what I want. Just tell him to meet me and soon. I'll go to him."

"What do you want from Brewster?" Tom asked.

"I'm gonna need information about personnel in the Russian embassy. Specifically, who works in the spy department," Clay answered his boss.

"What if he doesn't know?" Darla petulantly asked.

"He can find out," Tom quietly replied.

"Maybe I should call him," Tom said to Clay.

"Probably best to keep you out of it. In fact, Sonja, you call him. You calling will let him know where it's coming from but give the Senator deniability if anything leaks," Clay said.

Sonja looked at Darla who nodded back at her. "All right, I'll do that," Sonja said to Clay.

"Then what?" Darla asked.

"Then I'll start looking for someone to steal that list back for us," Clay told her.

FIFTY

Malcolm Brewster was still a good, loyal soldier for the Carvers. Of course his political antenna went off the instant Sonja Hayden called him. Doing a favor for Darla Carver, the likely next president, was never a bad idea. Within forty-eight hours of meeting with Clay Dean, Brewster delivered. Using his CIA contacts, he had been given copies of a dozen dossiers of embassy personnel. Of course, these items were highly classified and several dozen felonies had been committed to deliver them, but those were little people concerns.

Clay had gone over them in his Georgetown townhouse, a fancy name for an expensive apartment. He quickly narrowed down the list of possibilities to four.

Working alone, Clay began his surveillance of the four candidates. He was looking for something he was not even sure of. A vulnerability of some type that he could exploit. Because he wanted to check them out on his own, the weeks turned into months. Gradually he began to eliminate them. Mostly because three of them did little outside of their embassy duties. One of them was even transferred back to Moscow. Or at least somewhere out of Washington.

By early June he was down to one candidate. This was also the one Clay had originally believed would be the best one, if he could turn to him.

A late June Saturday night Clay found himself sitting at the bar of a popular Georgetown piano bar. At his age, now past fifty, Clay had been concerned he would stick out like a beacon of light. The bar was near both Georgetown University and George Washington University. Frequented by yuppie, spoiled kids Clay figured he would have thirty years on most of them. Instead, there was a good mix of all ages even though the majority were under thirty.

At first, Clay was so focused on his subject, he did not notice there was something strange about the crowd. After about ten minutes, he looked around and did not see one woman in the entire place. And all of the men were acting very friendly toward each other.

At the end of the bar, Clay had a clear view of eighty percent of the place. His target, the thirty-two-year-old, unmarried, top aide to Victor Ivanov, Mikhail Sokolov, was clearly enjoying himself. There was an open pool room and it appeared Mr. Sokolov handled a pretty good stick. He had been playing for over an hour and after each game, his opponent peeled off a couple of bills and paid him.

A half-hour ago something very interesting caught Clay's attention. A man in his late twenties had a brief conversation with Mikhail. Mikhail gave him some money and the man discreetly placed something quickly in Mikhail's other hand. The entire exchange lasted less than five seconds. Mikhail slipped into the men's room and a few minutes later he was back, sniffing and wiping his nose with his fingers and palm.

Having seen enough to get the picture of what Mikhail was up to, Clay decided to watch Mikhail's car. He had also brushed off the advances of two men close to his age which made him very uncomfortable.

Around midnight, Clay saw Mikhail leave the bar through the back door. Clay was in his car watching Mikhail's embassy car, both vehicles parked in the lot behind the bar. There was a lot of light and even a security guard stationed in a small booth at the lot's entrance.

Mikhail was by himself which mildly surprised Clay. It was also a relief. Clay was not homophobic, he really did have a 'live and let live' attitude. At the same time, he had no interest in viewing two men together.

Mikhail smoked a cigarette and while doing so standing next to his car, he was obviously discreetly surveilling the parking lot. When he looked toward Clay's car, Clay ducked down.

Mikhail drove off in his embassy Ford Taurus with the diplomatic plates. Clay followed him and due to the light, late night traffic, Mikhail was back at his apartment three blocks from his embassy by 12:30.

Clay parked and stayed long enough to make sure Mikhail was in for the night. When he saw what he believed to be the bedroom light go out he started his car for the drive home.

"A gay druggie," Clay said out loud to himself as he pulled away from the curb. "I don't imagine the boys in the Kremlin would be too crazy about that."

As Clay pulled away from his parking spot, an unseen figure in the darkened apartment stood next to a window. Mikhail watched the American's car until it turned at the corner and was out of his sight.

"Have you been approached yet?" Clay asked Darla.

It was mid-July, over six months since their first meeting about the Russians. Clay was now devoting himself full-time to the life of Mikhail Sokolov. If Mikhail went anywhere besides the embassy, Clay knew about it. Clay had also employed some operatives, specifically some of the men who had been involved with the elimination of the reporter, Melvin Bullard. These men were thorough professionals and absolutely trustworthy. Plus, they all knew who Clay worked for and the kind of clout he had. These men had no doubt the U.S. Government could and would make any of them disappear with a single phone call.

262

Clay was meeting with Darla and her appendage, Sonja, in Darla's Senate office. Even though she was a U.S. Senator and her official offices were sacrosanct, Clay saw to it that Darla's office was electronically swept for bugs at least weekly. There were rumors that certain Senators had been "accidentally" and "unintentionally" recorded while on the phone.

"Yes," Darla replied, annoyance in her voice. "Why do you think I called you to get your ass in here?"

Clay ignored Darla's attitude and calmly asked, "What are they asking for?"

Clay was seated in a very comfortable, cloth armchair in front of Darla's glass-topped table she used as a desk. Sonja was seated next to her boss.

Darla stood up and impatiently began pacing about in front of the French doors leading to her balcony. She looked at Clay and said, "Something about the order of battle of the Czech Republic's Army. Whatever the hell that is."

The corners of Clay's mouth turned up in a tight smile. He replied, "It is the specifics regarding the Czech Army. Do you have it?"

"Yes, I found it in one of the briefing books for NATO," Darla said casually pointing at a bookcase along the far wall.

"Okay, give it to them," Clay said. "I guarantee you they know it better than the Czechs do. It's your test. They want to know if you are going to cooperate."

"And what are you doing to put a stop to this?" Darla asked.

"As I told you before, I have a man selected to…"

"Who?" Darla asked.

"Better that you don't know," Clay said. "I have him under surveillance. I believe he is a gay man with a taste for the good life of a swinging American. Including drugs. I don't think he's a junkie but he does like to get out and party once in a while."

"What are you waiting for? This needs to stop. Can he get his hands on the list?" Darla asked, her anger and impatience rising.

"This is taking longer than I had hoped it would," Clay admitted. "He's fairly high up on the food chain in the Russian Embassy. He's also very careful. We need some evidence, real evidence not just suspicions. I have quite a few photos of him in a gay bar in Georgetown. I also have a few that look like he is buying drugs in this same bar. I need more detailed proof. I haven't even gotten a shot of him leaving the place with another man."

"Are you sure you're with him all the time when he's not in the embassy?" a calmer Darla asked.

"No, I can't be sure. He's a highly trained Russian intelligence officer. Is it possible for him to, say, leave his apartment and slip past us? Hell yes. There's not much we can do about that but stay patient."

"It's just so damn frustrating," Darla said.

"Be a little patient," Clay said. "We'll get him."

"Soon," Darla replied.

"Has Timmons reached a decision about putting a missile defense into Poland, the Baltic States and the Czech Republic?" Clay asked.

Toward the end of Tom Carver's second term, he had negotiated an agreement with Poland, the Czech Republic and all three Baltic states. They had agreed to let America place a protective missile defense system into their countries. In fact, all of these smaller members of NATO situated near the Russian bear were anxious to have it done. When Gary Timmons became president, one of the first things he did was to unilaterally cancel this project. He did this to show the Russians he was starting a new era of relations that would be a more touchy-feely diplomacy and not as confrontational. The Russians saw this as a sign of weakness, which it was, and Timmons was having second thoughts.

"No, he still thinks he can show the Russians how nice he is and how nice they can be to us. I hear he is becoming a little more practical though," Darla replied.

"That will likely be the next thing they try to get from you," Clay said. "The Russians are scared to death of a missile shield that close. They will want to know what's going on with it and what exactly we might put in there."

Darla, who was seated at her desk now, looked at Clay, sighed and said, "We'll cross that bridge when we come to it. In the meantime, nail this guy down and get that damn list back."

Ten days later, on a Friday night toward the end of July, Clay was on duty following Mikhail. He had been inside the bar for an hour observing. Around 10:30 he had left to wait in his car. Forty minutes later Mikhail came out the back door with another man. Clay recognized the man as one of the guys Clay suspected was selling drugs to Mikhail.

The two men were holding hands as they walked through the parking lot. When they got to Mikhail's car they both lit cigarettes. Clay could see them laughing and talking while they smoked. Using his camera with a 300 mm lens, he snapped off a dozen shots of the two of them.

Mikhail was leaning against the passenger side front door while this was going on. They dropped their cigarettes together and crushed them out. Then Mikhail opened his car door for his friend and as he was getting in, he lightly kissed Mikhail on the lips. Clay had his camera going and was able to get two clear photos of this little act of affection.

"Well, that's something," Clay whispered to himself. "But not enough."

FIFTY-ONE

Clay Dean hated D.C. in August. Little wonder everyone who could flee this place during July and August did so. Who and how it was decided to build the nation's capital on swampland was a mystery. Probably someone who sold the place to the government for triple its value. The first real estate scam perpetrated on the taxpayers.

Clay was again on surveillance and again in the parking lot of Mikhail Sokolov's favorite gay bar. Clay was getting impatient and tired of Darla's ball busting. The Russian's were starting to squeeze her, putting more and more pressure on her for information. What they really wanted was for Darla to use her influence to kill the Eastern European Missile Defense bill. This was the bill to fund the missile defense system the Russians were apoplectic about.

Labor Day weekend was a little over two weeks away. Both the House and Senate were in recess until after that weekend. When the members returned, at the top of their agenda was the funding bill for the missile defense systems to be put in the Czech Republic, Poland and the Baltic States. President Timmons had finally awakened to the reality that Vladimir Putin was not his pal. Timmons had not actually decided to put the missiles into Eastern Europe. In fact, political gossip had it that Timmons wanted Congress to deny him the funding so he could avoid making a tough decision and then blame it on Congress. This was getting to be a standard ploy of the indecisive President.

Darla Carver was using Timmons' waffling as a springboard for her campaign. Or so the press was reporting. Darla was leading the opposition for the bill in the Senate. She had even come up with a slogan for her foreign policy; "Firm but friendly". Darla was advocating a new approach to Russia. Less antagonist but with a firmer hand than Timmons. Of course, very few people knew the real reason for Darla's conciliatory attitude. Killing the funding bill had been ordered by her pals in the Russian Embassy.

Clay had been sitting in his car in this familiar parking lot for over an hour. To avoid suspicion he sat with the engine and air-conditioning off. He had two windows open but there was not the slightest hint of a breeze. The temperature that afternoon had hit 92 and the humidity 96. Even now, several hours past sundown, the heat and humidity were stifling.

Clay had a damp hand towel on the passenger seat. He used it to wipe away the sweat from his face and neck. He tossed the towel onto the passenger seat when he saw Mikhail come out the back. This time he was again with someone. Clay took a quick look through his binoculars

266

and with the lights in the lot, recognized the young man with Mikhail as the same one he had seen him with a couple weeks ago.

"Okay, here we go," Clay said into his handheld radio. "He's with that guy with the apartment in Rosslyn." Clay was talking to two men in a car a couple blocks from his location. If Mikhail followed his friend home, they would drive right past his companions.

"Roger that." Clay heard the reply. If Mikhail was going home alone or his friend was going with him, they would turn right out of the parking. If they turned left, they were headed for Rosslyn.

Clay waited as each got in his own car. When they drove past the parking lot attendant's shack, Mikhail was following his friend and both turned left.

"They're heading toward Rosslyn. Do you remember how to get to this guy's apartment?" Clay asked through his radio.

"Affirmative," came the terse, one-word reply.

"Go ahead and get on post. I'll follow these two and keep you informed," Clay told the two men.

"Copy that," the voice answered.

As Clay was pulling out he muttered to himself, "I gotta get some ex-cops and get rid of these military guys. They all have the personality and intelligence of an eggplant."

Clay easily stayed with the two cars across the Key Bridge into Virginia. Knowing where they were headed he stayed back a good distance and kept one or two cars between him and them. Traffic was light and a mile from their destination Clay's accomplices radioed to let him know they were in place. The more he drove, the more the car's A/C relieved his lousy mood.

"How long do you want to wait?" Brent asked him.

Clay was in the backseat of the Chevy the two men were using. Mikhail and friend had gone into a ground level apartment fifteen minutes ago.

"Do you really want pictures of these two having at each other?" Dale, the second man asked.

Clay ignored the comment then said, "We'll give them another ten minutes."

Exactly ten minutes later Dale gave the entryway door a kick and it blew open. Guns drawn, Dale and Brent went into the apartment to find Mikhail and friend seated on the living room couch. Both of them were stripped down to their undershorts, holding hands, sharing a marijuana cigarette watching a bad skit on Saturday Night Live.

Dale held his 9mm semi-auto on them while Brent snapped a half-dozen photos with his phone. In the meantime, Clay had casually walked in and looked over the scene. The two on the couch looked terrified and then the apartment's tenant found a bit of courage.

He stood and said, "Who, who are you? What do you want? Get the hell out of..."

His courage quickly disappeared after a quick backhand across the face from Brent. It broke open the man's lip and bounced him down so he was half laying on the couch. Brent held an index finger to his mouth and shushed him to shut him up.

Clay looked at Mikhail and quietly said, "Get dressed Mikhail. You don't know it yet, but I am your new tovarisch."

Clay looked at the cowering young man with the bloody lip and calmly said, "We were never here. Understand?"

"Yes, yes," he meekly replied.

An hour later Mikhail was led, with a hood over his head, down a set of carpeted stairs and into a basement. They were in a house in Bethesda, Maryland. Clay had driven his car with the hooded and shackled Mikhail in the trunk. Brent had followed in Mikhail's embassy Taurus with Dale bringing up the rear in the Chevy.

Mikhail was placed in a comfortable chair in the home's finished basement. Clay pulled off the hood while Brent unlocked the shackles and handcuffs. Dale handed Mikhail a small glass half-full of a clear liquid.

"Drink it," Clay said. "Relax. It's just vodka. Stoli. Relax, if I wanted to harm you, drug you or poison you, I would have done so already. Go ahead," Clay smiled, "drink it."

Mikhail tossed the liquid down and felt its warmth throughout his abdomen. He took a deep breath and with a worried look, asked, "What do you want?"

Clay sat down in a chair he had pulled up to Mikhail so close their knees almost touched. Brent and Dale went upstairs. They had no idea who Mikhail was or why Clay wanted him. Clay began lightly brushing off some unseen lint from Mikhail's knee. "In your embassy..."

"How do you know...?"

"Do you think we don't know who you are? Now, just listen. In your embassy is a piece of note paper that was torn to pieces and your people put back together. It has a list of names on it. Muslim names..."

"I don't know what you're talking about," Mikhail said.

Clay slapped him across the face hard enough to knock him sideways. Mikhail sat up holding the side of his face, the defiant look in his eyes now replaced with fear.

Clay silently stared at him for over a minute to make sure Mikhail got the message.

"Please don't lie. I find that insulting. Do you understand?"

"Yes," Mikhail meekly replied.

Clay sat back and crossed his right leg over his left.

"We've been following you for months. We have hundreds of pictures of you in a gay bar having a good time and buying drugs. I don't think Viktor would be happy with your behavior. You will get this piece of paper we want and any pictures or photos that were taken of it."

"I, ah, I don't know how I can do that," Mikhail stammered.

"Find a way," Clay said.

"You don't understand. It is kept in a safe behind a man's desk..."

"Viktor Ivanov," Clay said.

"How do you know that?" a bewildered Mikhail asked.

"We're not fools," Clay answered. "But you obviously do know what we want and where it is, don't you?"

"Yes," Mikhail reluctantly admitted.

"Good, that's a start."

"How do I know if I get this for you, you won't come back for other things?"

"You don't, do you?" Clay replied.

"I don't see how I can help you. I think I should just take my chances and say 'no' to you," Mikhail said with more conviction than he felt.

"Okay, but I'll leak it to your people that you helped us anyway and let them have the pictures we have of you. How long before you're on the next flight back to the Motherland and a firing squad? Do they still use a firing squad? Or do they do it the old fashioned way, the Stalin way? A single bullet to the brain stem?"

"Bastard!" Mikhail snarled.

The two of them went silent for another minute and sat looking at each other. Finally, Mikhail quietly said, "I'll need some time. I don't have the combination to the safe. It won't be easy. And afterwards I will have to defect. I'll need money and a new identity."

"We'll cross that bridge when we come to it," Clay replied.

"What? What does that mean? I don't understand. You must help me. They will know who did it."

"We will deal with that when the time comes. I can tell you this, money and a new identity won't be a problem."

Mikhail went silent again, then after a minute or so asked, "May I have more vodka please?"

"Sure," Clay said. Clay went to the bar to pour the drink. He poured a shot for each of them. While he did this, he could hear Mikhail muttering in Russian.

"What? What was that?" Clay asked as he handed Mikhail his drink. Mikhail tossed it down and held the glass out for more. Clay had the bottle and refilled his glass.

"I said, 'I must be crazy to betray my country like this'. If I wasn't such a coward, I would shoot myself and get it over with," Mikhail told him then tossed back the second shot.

Clay laughed, refilled Mikhail's glass then held up his own in a toast and said, "Well, here's to cowardice and a long life."

FIFTY-TWO

The ballroom of the Hilton Hartford in Darla's 'home state' Connecticut, was set up and waiting for her. Every broadcast and cable news network was in attendance with strategically placed cameras. In addition, the print media was also well represented. Since the driving time from New York City to Hartford was less than three hours, the room was crowded with over two hundred journalists awaiting the announcement.

For three months at least, since the Iowa straw poll in August, the big political question of the season was: Will she run? There were already six candidates vying for the opportunity to run against President Timmons next year. All of them had practically taken up residence in the Hawkeye state. The quadrennial political invasion of the small Midwestern state was, once again, well underway. So far, the clear favorite, Darla Carver, had not made a single appearance. The crowd in the Hilton Ballroom believed that was about to change. With the election barely a year from now, it was time for the big decision.

The announcement was scheduled for 11:00 A.M. Eastern time to make the noon news. It was now 10:50 and the attendees, despite the free coffee, juice and pastries provided, were getting a little restless.

Upstairs in the Presidential Suite, a professional makeup artist was applying a couple of last second touches to Darla. She was seated in the living room with Tom, Sonja and three campaign people preparing for the big moment. Darla stared at the mirror with smug satisfaction. Even she had to admit her hair looked perfect, the makeup excellent and for a woman in her mid-fifties, she looked pretty damn good.

"It annoys me what women have to go through and men only need to shave and comb their hair," Darla said while checking the slight crow's feet by her eyes.

"Give it a rest, Darla," Tom said. "Women need to stop whining about all of this double standard crap. It's getting old and it makes you sound whiny."

Darla turned to her husband, squinted her eyes, pursed her lips and holding her left hand near her body, flipped him her middle finger.

Tom yawned, looked at his watch and said, "I have plans. Let's get this over with."

Darla entered the ballroom and with Tom and their two children with her, Natalie now 29 and Jefferson, 26, stepped onto the portable stage. Along with their children, Darla had insisted Natalie bring her husband and two-year-old daughter. With Jefferson was his fiancée with

271

her multiple tattoos covered up and nose and lip studs removed. And the cherry on the sundae to show off Darla's All-American family, Natalie was noticeably pregnant. Unknown to Darla, Natalie was praying that her husband was, in fact, the father. Natalie had grown a little too close to a couple of her Secret Service escorts.

No one in the audience who knew anything about the Carvers was fooled for an instant. This bunch was about as dysfunctional as any family could be. Your typical All-American family.

Darla stepped up to the podium and stood silently for fifteen to twenty seconds. This was to give the cameras time to get a good picture and the still photographers to get their shots.

"Ladies and gentlemen, thank you for coming. For the past three years we have all watched as President Timmons performs, at best, poorly as President and Commander-in-Chief. I am here today to announce my candidacy..."

Grigory Tretiak, the Russian Ambassador, along with Viktor Ivanov and Viktor's top aide, Mikhail Sokolov watched Darla's announcement live on CNN. Tretiak and Viktor were seated together on a plush, leather couch in the Ambassador's office. Mikhail was in an uncomfortable chair behind them.

When Darla finished her statement, Tretiak clicked off the set. He reached forward and placed the remote on a coffee table in front of the two men.

"How are things working out?" Tretiak asked Ivanov.

"She has been reluctantly cooperative," Ivanov replied.

"She did an excellent job of defeating the Polish and Czech missile defense system funding bill," Tretiak said. He stood up and began pacing slowly in front of the darkened TV.

"Yes, she did," Ivanov agreed. "Our source in the White House reported that President Timmons was delighted the bill was defeated. It was a decision he did not want to make."

"And our next plan?" Tretiak stopped pacing, looked at Ivanov and asked.

"Now that she has formally announced her candidacy, we will go forward. It will be a small step to help her win," Ivanov replied.

"Well," Darla began to say, "what do you think?"

They were back in her suite and her small entourage could see Darla was pumped with excitement. She stood before them, a look of genuine curiosity on her face, her arms spread wide waiting for their input.

Tom stepped up to her, kissed her on the cheek and told her, "It went well. You looked and sounded great."

"Yes, Mom," Natalie chimed in. "I agree with Dad. I'm really proud of you. And excited too. You deserve to be the first woman president."

For the next few minutes, there was a lovefest in the room as everyone sang her praises. Even the prodigal son got in the act. Of course, he would soon be asking Tom for an increase in his living expense allowance and a little extra for the girlfriend's next abortion. Apparently, Jefferson was having problems remembering how to avoid this woman's health issue.

At noon, the hotel's room service arrived with their catered lunch. Everyone enjoyed a nice buffet complete with celebratory champagne. When it was over, Natalie informed her parents they were headed back to New York. Jefferson was able to pull Tom into the bedroom for his little chat. A disgusted Tom, after being reminded by Jefferson of his own behavior, caved in and made a note to get him some more money. Soon afterwards, Jefferson and the girlfriend, whose name Tom never remembered, slipped out as well.

"Where the hell is Clay?" Darla asked Sonja.

"He's on the way. I thought he would be here by now," Sonja replied.

"Call him again," Darla impatiently ordered her.

While Sonja made the call, Darla huddled with her campaign manager, Andy Peyton. Also present was her pollster, Dan Stone and chief fundraiser, Larry Jacobs.

Even though it was November and the Iowa caucuses were only two months away, Darla's campaign structure in Iowa was fully in place. Andy Peyton had done an excellent job for her. Of course, it helped that the other candidates were featherweights compared to the Carvers. Each of them together and individually were about to get hammered. Peyton had the TV, radio ads and robocalls and the money all set to flood Iowa. Every four years, the people of Iowa put themselves through this. But they were about to be blitzed like never before.

In the meantime, Tom Carver would be working New Hampshire. The people of New Hampshire considered it a personal insult if the candidates did not shake their hands at least five or six times before the primary. Darla had a significant advantage. Despite Tom's well-known lust for money and women, he was still extremely popular in New Hampshire. The campaign had even rented a house for him in Concord.

While Sonja was on the phone talking to Clay, there was a knock at the door. It was one of the Secret Service agents assigned to Darla who was waiting in the hall who opened it. With his phone to his ear still talking to Sonja, Clay Dean walked in smiling at her for the trick he had played.

"Very funny," Darla said. "Where the hell have you been?"

"On my way," Clay replied while shaking hands with Tom.

"Please give us some time," Darla said to her campaign people.

The door was barely closed behind them when Darla started in on Clay.

"When the hell are we going to get that damn thing back?" she angrily asked referring to the list the Russians were using to blackmail her.

"He thinks he'll be able to get it this weekend. Ivanov is flying back to Moscow for a few days. Most of the staff will be off and he believes he'll be able to get it then. Of course, we have to protect him. When Ivanov gets back, he'll know who is responsible."

Clay and Sonja were on the couch, Darla and Tom in separate, matching club chairs. Darla was lightly tapping her lips with her right index finger, obviously thinking about what Clay had told her.

"Maybe we should simply eliminate the problem altogether. Will we need him for anything else?" she asked.

"He has a lot of valuable intelligence in his head," Clay reminded her. They had been through this before and Clay was tired of it and let it show. "We're going to treat him like a legitimate defector and turn him over to the FBI."

Darla narrowed her eyes while looking at Clay. There were times when his insubordinate attitude toward her was more than a little annoying. Like now. Perhaps she would have to get Tom take care of this.

"I suppose. The important thing is to get that damn list back," Darla said.

"You have no one to blame but yourself for this," Tom reminded her.

Darla's head snapped to the side to glare wickedly at her husband. He had seen this look hundreds of times over the years. It used to have an intimidating effect, but not since leaving the White House.

"Don't bother with that look, Darla. I'm no longer impressed. A divorce wouldn't bother me in the least but it would doom your shot," Tom said.

"Asshole," Darla snarled.

"Let's keep our eyes on the ball, my darling wife," Tom said with a big grin.

FIFTY-THREE

Mikhail Sokolov approached the Iwo Jima Marine Corp Memorial and spotted the lone man seated on a park bench. From this distance, he was still a couple hundred yards away, he could not be sure if it was the man he was meeting but he assumed so. This was the Sunday following the America's Thanksgiving Holiday. In Moscow, this late in November, there would already be a foot of snow on the ground and temperatures below zero Celsius. Here, across the Potomac from Washington, it was a pleasant, sunny, plus twelve Celsius. The Americans, indeed, had a lot to be thankful for.

Mikhail was acting the part of a young American male. He wore black jeans, a leather coat and basketball sneakers. The man whose name he still did not know was clearly in his vision. Clay Dean sat casually on the bench. His trench coat hung open in front, his right leg lazily crossed over his left and his left arm resting casually on the bench's back.

Mikhail silently sat on the opposite end of the bench and waited for the man to speak.

There was a moderately sized crowd milling about the memorial. Even late November this almost holy sight attracted people from all over the nation.

"I love coming here," Clay finally broke the silence and said. "It's a powerful reminder, don't you think?"

"I suppose," Mikhail said.

"Do you know what this is for?" Clay asked referring to the Suribachi flag raising.

"Yes, an insignificant battle by your storm trooper Marines during the great Patriotic War," Mikhail replied. "You Americans always think you were the only ones who fought the fascists. Twenty-five million Russians died…"

"Mostly because of Stalin's incompetence," Clay interrupted him.

Clay removed a small electronic device, about the size of a pack of cigarettes, from a coat pocket. He pushed a button on it then used it to quickly search Mikhail for any wires or listening devices. Satisfied, he shut it off and returned it to his pocket.

"Did you bring it?"

"How do I know I can trust you?" Mikhail asked.

"You can't," Clay replied then laughed. "What choice do you have? It's either us or your pals in Moscow."

"I suppose you are right," Mikhail said with a heavy sigh. "How do we do this?"

"We've been over this a dozen times," an irritated Clay Dean said. "You give me the plastic case with the torn up list in it. Then I take you to meet an FBI agent I know. I tell him you approached me after seeing me with President Carver asking me to help you defect. The FBI squeezes every drop of intelligence they can out of you over the next five or six months. Then they give you a new name, new identity, help you find a job and a new home. If you mention one word about our arrangement, we'll deny it. We'll claim you're not a real defector and the FBI hands you back to your friends at the embassy."

"When do I meet with the FBI agent?"

"Right now if you brought what I want. Did you pack your clothes and personal items like I told you to?" Clay asked.

"Yes, they are in my car. It's parked in the lot," Mikhail told him.

"Okay," Clay said as he stood up. "Let's go."

Clay, using a handkerchief so as not to touch it, removed the plastic case with the list in it from his coat pocket and set it on his kitchen counter. He removed his coat as he walked back toward the front door. When he got there he slipped off his loafers and hung the coat in the small hallway closet.

Clay returned to the kitchen, pulled a bottle of beer from the refrigerator, twisted off the cap and took a large swallow. He opened the freezer compartment door and shuffled several food items around. He pulled out a plastic bag with two sheets of paper and an envelope in it. They were a copy of the list and the original of the note Darla had written to Melvin Bullard. Both were in her handwriting. Clay carried this to the counter where the plastic case lay and set it down.

He put on a pair of surgical gloves from a box of them he kept under his sink. He removed the copy of the list he had removed from his freezer, the one he had made from the original list, and placed it on the counter. Using a six power, handheld magnifying glass, he spent the next hour carefully comparing his list to what Mikhail had given him. Clay checked every letter of every word and was finally satisfied that Mikhail had given him the real deal.

Clay put his copy back in the plastic bag and put it in the freezer where he had kept it for the last few days. He would return it to the safe deposit box in the morning. He opened another beer and speed dialed a number on his cell.

"Yes," Sonja Hayden answered his call.

"I got it," Clay replied. "I'll see you on Tuesday.

"Thank you," Sonja said and hung up.

Sonja slipped her cell phone into her left-hand skirt pocket and looked at Darla.

"He has it," Sonja said.

"Wonderful!" Darla replied clapping her hands together. "What a load off of my mind."

They were in the Hotel Julien in Dubuque, Iowa. They had made three appearances that day and had another scheduled for this evening. Andy Peyton and his staff, almost all of them veterans from her husband's campaigns, were doing an exemplary job. The schedule was brutal, especially for the number of delegates Iowa had to offer. But in politics, perception is reality. And the reality was that Darla not only needed to win the February 1st caucuses, she needed to dominate them. The last thing she needed was a real challenge from her own party. Crushing victories in Iowa and New Hampshire would dry up her competitor's money and force them out. Then she could concentrate on President Timmons.

"Wait a minute," Darla said, a worried look on her face. "How does he know it's the real one?"

"I don't know," Sonja conceded. "I guess he figures you will know. It's your handwriting."

"Yeah, that's fine," Darla said. "Shit I should have kept that photo," she quietly said mostly to herself.

"What photo?" Sonja asked.

Darla looked at Sonja for several seconds before answering. "When that sonofabitch Ambassador Tretiak told me about this, he proved it by giving me a close-up photo of it. That's how I knew they had it. I shredded the damn thing. I could have used that for comparison."

"I'm sure you'll recognize it," Sonja said.

"Yeah, you're right. I'll recognize it. Where to tomorrow?"

"Waukon," Sonja said.

"'Walk On'? Where the hell is 'Walk On'? Who would name…"

"Not 'Walk On' two words," Sonja told her. "Waukon, one word," she said spelling it for her boss.

"Oh, okay," Darla said. "Where is it?"

"Northeast part of the state. About two hours north of here," Sonja replied checking her day planner. "Population, thirty-seven hundred. We'll be spending the week in Northeast Iowa then we'll go to New Hampshire for two weeks. We'll break for Christmas, then back to Iowa in January. You knew what you were getting into," Sonja reminded her.

"I know," Darla agreed. "Some of these small towns are…American. And I must admit, after years in Washington and the East, the people out here…"

"In flyover country," Sonja said.

"Yeah," Darla laughed. "They're almost too nice. I'm not used to dealing with such polite, pleasant, courteous people. Anyway, walk on to Waukon."

Clay Dean leaned against his rental car on Main Street in Waterville, Iowa watching the crowd across the street. There were at least a hundred people in front of the Waterville Diner trying to get a look inside. There were four big, black, SUVs parked in a row across from Clay. The presence of these vehicles was how he had tracked down Darla and her campaign entourage.

Clay had flown into Des Moines that morning and rented a Chevy. The GPS assisted drive took three and a half hours and but for the GPS, he would still be wandering around the state. While he waited for Darla to reappear, he was reminded that the weather in Iowa in December could be quite different than what he left in D.C.

Clay's hands were stuffed in the pocket of his trench coat, his shoulders slightly hunched together while he examined the dark, gray, overcast sky. While he was looking skyward, he did not notice a man in local attire, jeans and a Carhartt coat approach him.

"We're supposed to get wet today," the man said to Clay. "Rain mixed with snow."

"Hey, Rich," Clay said to Rich Mason, an assistant campaign manager. The two men shook hands.

"What brings you out to flyover country?" Mason asked.

"I need to see Her Majesty," Clay replied.

"Business or personal?" Mason asked.

Clay thought about the question then said, "Is there a difference with her?"

Mason chuckled then said, "No, I guess not. She should be done in there pretty soon. It's a little after noon so we'll go back to the motel for a bite to eat. She has a full day scheduled."

"Okay, I'll follow you guys," Clay said.

"This is actually quite nice," Clay said referring to Darla's room at the Stoney Creek Inn.

Clay was sitting on the edge of the queen size bed. Sonja was in a chair at the room's table with Darla. Darla was leaning over the table using Clay's magnifying glass to examine the list Clay had received from Mikhail Sokolov.

The three of them sat in silence for another twenty minutes while Darla used the magnifying glass. When she finished, she pushed the plastic case with the torn up list in it across to Sonja. She handed Sonja the glass and told her to check it. While Sonja examined it, there was a knock on the door.

Clay went to the door, opened it and found the head of Darla's Secret Service detail standing there.

"I'm told it's time to go," the woman, whose name Clay could not remember, informed him.

"I'll let her know," Clay said. "I think we're almost ready."

A few minutes later, Sonja set the glass down, looked at Darla and gave it her approval.

"Me too," Darla said. "It's the genuine original. Thank God."

Having anticipated this moment, Clay walked over to the table and handed Darla a book of matches.

"I thought you might want to have the honor," he said.

"Oh, yeah," Darla said with obvious relief. She picked up the plastic case and pried it open. The individual pieces of the list fell onto the table. Darla scooped them up and took them into the bathroom. Using the wastebasket, she burned each piece then flushed the ashes down the toilet.

Clay was standing in the doorway watching her. She turned, saw him and sincerely said, "Thank you, Clay."

"My pleasure, Madam President," he replied.

FIFTY-FOUR

When February rolled around and the Iowa caucus took place, there were six other candidates competing with Darla. By the time Iowa and New Hampshire were finished, there were only two left. Darla's campaign, with enough money to start her own small country, swamped South Carolina. She took almost sixty percent of the vote and afterward was the last one standing.

Unknown to the public, at least three prominent, potential candidates who had considered running had stayed out. This was brought about primarily by Darla's friends at the National Party Committee. Of course, these people at the National Committee were supposed to be disinterested but were anything but neutral. All three of these potential candidates, a male governor, a black male senator and a female senator, were not so subtly warned to stay out of it. Each could have given Darla a real race but this was Darla's turn.

Following her victory in South Carolina and with the last opponent gone, the race for the nomination was over. Darla and the Carver Money Machine could turn their full attention toward Gary Timmons. Which they did with a vengeance.

President Timmons approval ratings had hovered in the low to mid-forties for almost two years. The man could give a stirring speech when he wanted to and this was what had propelled him to the presidency in the first place. His problem was the perception that he preferred the golf course to the Oval Office. The simple fact was the man was a bit lazy and not too interested in doing the job. Or, at least, that was Darla's campaign theme against him.

By the time the August conventions rolled around, a half a billion dollars in TV and radio ads would be spent by the Carvers making that point. Timmons was portrayed as weak on terror, inept at home on domestic matters and lazily running a power hungry, out of control government bureaucracy. And in case that was not bad enough, there were ads featuring jokes about his golf game and what a poor golfer he was.

By the time Darla's party coronation rolled around in mid-August at the Boston Convention Center, she had a ten-point lead and that was growing. The election was being called hers to lose. All she had to do was not make any major gaffes such and it was a done deal.

"What I wouldn't give for a small terrorist attack in October," Darla said to no one in particular.

She was in the living room of the Presidential Suite of the Boston Harbor Hotel. There were nicer, more expensive places in Boston fit for political royalty. But Darla liked the 16th-floor view of the harbor and it was far enough from the Convention Center for privacy. With her were the usual suspects from her campaign. They were all sitting around the plush room watching Tom Carver's speech to the convention. It was Wednesday evening and the convention had been a Carver lovefest. Much to Darla's annoyance her husband was still the party's darling.

While she watched him fire up her crowd she thought, *Tomorrow night it will be my turn and I'll use the opportunity to take over the party.* Of course, because so many people in this room owed their first allegiance to Tom, she kept her thoughts about him to herself.

There was a sharp knock on the door then one of the Secret Service agents, an older woman, opened it for Clay Dean. Darla watched him come in then go to the bar and open a bottle of water.

"That reminds me," Darla whispered to Sonja. "Make a note. When we win the presidency I want only young, good looking men on my protection detail. If men can be sexist pigs, so can we."

Darla looked at Clay who was standing by the bar. She held up her hands in an inquiring manner and asked, "Are my children here?"

"Yes, they are," Clay replied. Clay had been given the task of making sure Darla's All-American family were on stage with her tomorrow night.

"When is Natalie's baby due?" Darla asked Sonja.

"September twenty-eighth," she replied reminding her for at least the tenth time.

"A new baby and grandmother again for the last month of the campaign. That's good timing," Darla replied.

"I need a word in private, Mrs. Carver," Clay said. "Please."

Darla put her drink on the glass-topped table to her left and stood up. Clay and Sonja followed her into the master bedroom. When Clay closed the door behind them an annoyed Darla looked at him and asked, "What?"

"Mikhail Sokolov," Clay said.

"Who?" Darla asked.

"He's the Russian who defected after returning that paper they had to us," Sonja said reminding her.

"Sure, okay. What about him?" Darla asked.

"He's disappeared," Clay said.

"I don't understand," Darla said. "What do you mean he's disappeared?"

"He has slipped his FBI handlers. They don't know where he is. Poof, gone," Clay said.

"How is this our problem?" Darla asked. "What can he do to us?"

"I don't know," Clay replied.

On the day Clay met Mikhail at the Iwo Jima memorial, Clay had taken Mikhail to an FBI agent he knew. Ever since then, almost nine months ago, Mikhail had been in FBI custody. For the first six months, he had been kept in comfortable isolation while the FBI interrogators squeezed him for information.

At first, Mikhail was very reluctant to talk. He saw himself as a loyal, patriotic Russian citizen. Clay had explained that Mikhail came to him because they had met at a Russian Embassy reception. Mikhail was fearful that his homosexuality was suspected by his boss. If it came out, he would be sent back to Russia in disgrace and face prison.

Gradually his interrogators made him realize there was no going back and if he wanted their help he would have to cooperate. Mikhail's dream was to get a new identity, a job and a home in San Francisco. This was the carrot the FBI dangled before him.

At the end of six months, around the first of June, Mikhail, at least to his handler's satisfaction, had proven himself. He was then allowed to move into an apartment close to the FBI facility in Quantico, Virginia. Gradually he earned more and more freedom of movement as he continued to cooperate.

On the Monday morning of the week of Darla's nominating convention, two agents went to the apartment. There was a briefing and questioning session with the CIA scheduled. What the agents found was Mikhail and his clothing gone.

"I got a call from the guy I know earlier today," Clay said after telling the two women about his disappearance. "The FBI has a high-security BOLO out for him. They've looking for him for three days and so far, not a peep. Nothing."

"Can he hurt us?" Darla asked, meaning, of course, can he hurt *her*.

"I don't know," Clay replied. "I don't know how. What's he going to do? Go to the cops? The media? He can make all of the wild claims he wants but he has nothing to back it up."

"Would he have a copy of…well, you know," Darla said.

"Possibly. I checked him and everything he took with him for that. But even if he has a copy we would just claim it's a forgery. He'd look ridiculous."

Darla, who was sitting in a chair by the bed, sat silently thinking over what Clay had said. After a minute or so she nodded her head as if agreeing with Clay's assessment then looked at Sonja.

"I think he's right," Sonja agreed. "I don't see how he could hurt us. I don't know what he might have but I can't see how he could hurt us now."

"I agree," Darla said. "But," she continued now looking at Clay, "you stay on this. Find him and… well, you know what to do. Make absolutely certain he does not become a problem."

"I'll see what I can do," Clay replied.

Darla stood up and took three steps to move up to Clay, "No, goddamnit. You don't see what you can do. You're paid very well to take care of things like this. If you had done your job when he came to you, this wouldn't be happening. Get it done!"

"Thank you, Mr. President," Darla said into the phone. "That is very gracious of you and I won't forget it."

She listened for a while then said, "Of course, Mr. President. I harbor no ill will toward you and I certainly hope you feel none toward me. It's just big stakes politics."

Darla looked around the hotel suite at the crowd and gave them all a thumbs up. President Timmons was calling to concede. As quietly as possible so as not to be overheard on the phone by Timmons, everyone in the room began hugging and dancing about in celebration.

"Yes, sir," Darla continued. "And the very best to you and Laura and your family. I know you love our country and I wish you nothing but the best."

With that last lie, Darla Carver ended the call and screamed for joy. With the official concession by Timmons, Darla Carver would become the first woman elected President of the United States.

It had been a much closer election than anyone had anticipated. After Labor Day Weekend, every poll had Darla leading by as much as fifteen points. Gary Timmons, despite his weak job performance, proved himself to be a terrific, energetic campaigner. When the final polls came out on Monday, the day before the election, it was too close to call. It took until fifteen minutes ago, 3:00 A.M. Eastern Standard Time, before the Associated Press called it for Darla. All of the major news networks quickly followed suit. Timmons, to his credit, saw the handwriting on the wall and made the phone call to a woman he truly despised. Of course, that feeling was more than reciprocated by Darla toward Timmons.

For her running mate, Darla had chosen wisely. She had selected a popular senator from Texas, Jared Galvin. Her hope was that Galvin could deliver Texas with its 39 precious electoral votes. He was also half Latino and would help with their votes.

The problem had been convincing Senator Galvin, now the Vice President-elect, to run with her. Senator Galvin knew both Carvers quite well and was none too fond of either of them. Plus, giving up his place in the Senate was a difficult decision. Like all U.S. Senators, he dreamed of being president but believed attaching himself to Darla Carver would kill any chance of that happening. It took Tom at his persuasive, political best to convince him.

Darla went around the room receiving congratulatory hugs from everyone. Even the Vice President-elect was enjoying the moment. At least until he overheard Darla whispering to Tom.

"Now we can go to Washington and make the bastards pay."

"We'll make everybody pay," Tom whispered back. "My fees just went to a million bucks per speech, minimum."

"What have I gotten myself into?" the Vice President-elect quietly whispered to himself.

FIFTY-FIVE

Marc Kadella parked his car in the lot behind the Reardon Building. He turned the collar up on his overcoat, picked up his briefcase from the passenger seat and looked out the side window one last time. The rain had turned to snow and it was the slick, wet, sloppy, heavy snow common to Minnesota in late November. A harbinger of things to come.

Wishing he had worn shoe rubbers over his best dress shoes, Marc opened the door, got out and sprinted—or at least for him what was sprinting—across the lot to the rear door. Once inside, he shook himself to knock off the water then went up the back stairs.

"It's a mess out there," Marc said to no one in particular when he went into the office.

"Good morning, sunshine," Carolyn Lucas said back to him.

"Now is when we all start to wonder why we live in this state," Marc's landlord, friend and fellow lawyer, Connie Mickelson, growled. "I saw two accidents on my way in. It's like the idiots in this place can't remember what it's like to drive in snow from one year to the next."

"Those are transplants from Arizona," Marc replied.

"Who the hell would move from Arizona to Minnesota in the winter?" Connie asked.

"The ones who can't drive in snow," Marc replied as he hung up his overcoat.

"Got a lawyer joke for you," Connie said to Marc. "Guy walks out of court after his divorce and goes straight to the nearest bar. He goes in and loudly says, 'All lawyers are assholes.'

"Another guy sitting by himself at the end of the bar says, 'Hey, do you mind? That's not necessary. Have a little more respect, will you?' The first guy says, 'Why, are you a lawyer?' The second guy answers, 'No, I'm an asshole.' "

Marc chuckled and all of the staff laughed along with Connie.

"Judge Stennis told me that one," Connie said.

"Don't tell me," Marc said with a disgusted look on his face. "You weren't in the sack…"

"No, no. Old Harry hasn't had it up for ten years. We're friends is all," Connie said.

"I have a lawyer joke, too" Sandy Compton, one of the secretaries said. Everyone turned to look at her and she said, "What do you get when you cross a blonde with a lawyer? Nothing. There are some things even a blonde won't do."

Once the jocularity died down, Sandy told Marc, "I made an appointment for you this morning at ten o'clock. He called right at 8:00. Said it was urgent he got in to see you."

285

"What for?" Marc asked.

"Don't know. He wouldn't say," Sandy said.

"Probably some kiddie diddler sex crime pervert," Connie said. "They never want to talk over the phone. They don't want people to know what sick little twists they are."

"Connie…" Marc started to say.

"I'm just saying," she shrugged.

"What's his name?" Marc asked Sandy.

"Scott Duncan," she replied. "You know him?"

"No," Marc answered. "You?" he said to Connie.

"Nope."

"Damn it's a mess out there," Chris Grafton said as he came through the door.

"Does the name Scott Duncan sound familiar to you, Chris?" Marc asked.

Grafton stopped and thought for a moment then said, "No, I don't think so, why?"

"Made an appointment but wouldn't say why," Marc said.

"Probably some sex pervert thing," Grafton said. "Tell him to throw himself on the mercy of the court then have him taken out and shot."

"Okay," Marc said. "I guess we have this case resolved."

At 9:50 Marc's office phone buzzed. It was Carolyn informing him that his ten o'clock appointment was here. Marc waited a few minutes to give the man time to finish filling out the intake form. He slipped on his suit coat and went out to get him.

Marc led the man back into his office, offered him a seat then closed the door. He took his seat behind his desk and could see that the man was a little nervous. Marc looked at him and noticed a scar above the man's left eye.

Puzzled, Marc asked him, "Have we met? Somehow, you look familiar."

Scott inhaled a large breath of air then replied, "Yes, we have. Once, many years ago and very briefly. You had a client, a dear friend of mine, Billy Stover…"

Marc instantly, and much to his surprise, recognized the name. "There's a name I haven't heard for a long time," Marc said. The light of recognition came on then and Marc snapped the fingers of his right hand and pointed his index finger at Scott Duncan.

"You're the guy who interrupted my dinner in the hotel restaurant in Colorado. The prison guard who was Billy's friend."

"Yeah," Duncan admitted. "Good memory."

Marc sat back and looked past Duncan at the wall behind him. "Billy Stover," he quietly said as he worked his memory to recall the case.

He sat forward and placed his forearms on the desk. "I always felt bad about that. Especially after what you told me about the Carvers."

"Yeah and now she's gonna be president," Duncan said.

"Why are you here?" Marc suddenly asked, truly mystified.

"I want to show you something," Duncan replied. He pulled a folded up newspaper from his coat pocket and spread it out on the desk so Marc could see it. It was the front page of the Denver Post from the morning after the recent election. In full color there was a four-column photo of Darla Carver, Tom, their kids and a number of their political entourage. They were on the stage celebrating Darla's victory and her speech.

"Okay, so?" Marc asked. "Yes, it makes me sick too."

Duncan was standing and he leaned over Marc's desk and pointed to one of the people behind Darla. It was a serious looking man who did not seem to be enjoying himself as much as the others.

"I know this guy," Duncan said. "When I saw this photo and saw him, I thought he looked familiar. It took almost three days trying to remember who he was and where I saw him. Then, when I wasn't even thinking about it, it came to me."

Duncan sat down again and continued.

"His name is John Estes and he was at the prison the day Billy was murdered. I remember it because everyone, the warden and all his lackeys were tripping over themselves kissing this guy's ass."

"And he's with the Carvers," Marc quietly said.

"Looks like it," Duncan replied.

"So what? I mean, he was at the prison and later Billy was found hanging in his cell. Could just be a coincidence," Marc said.

"I don't think so," Duncan said. "You remember Al Bass?"

"No, I don't," Marc said after a moment.

"He was Warden Carlyle's number one asshole. Nothing happened in that prison without Bass knowing it. I overheard Bass and Carlyle use this guy's name, this John Estes. That's how I got his name."

"Okay," Marc said.

"And Captain Munson, Howard Munson. He was there too. I heard the three of them saying things like whatever this guy Estes wants they gotta do. A while later I asked Bass who he was and Bass got really pissed. Grabbed me and slammed me up against a wall. Told me to mind my own business. You didn't mess with Al Bass. No one did. So, I let it go. That night, Billy died and I was too upset to think about anything else."

"I remember, you and Billy were planning on going away together," Marc said.

"Oh, do you remember when you left the prison?" Duncan continued. "It was Bass who followed you."

"That's right," Marc replied nodding his head in agreement.

"Then Warden Carlyle ran his car over a cliff a few days after you left. Al Bass was shot dead in a robbery attempt in Denver a month later. Two days after that, Captain Howard Munson retired and we heard he moved to New Mexico. Shortly after that I quit and got a job with the Boulder police department. I'm a patrol sergeant. One thing I know is all of this is a little too coincidental."

"So you believe this Estes guy is the cause of all of this? That all of this was done on behalf of the Carvers?" Marc asked.

"It all came back to me after I saw this picture," Duncan said pointing at the newspaper still lying on Marc's desk. "I've been thinking about it for two weeks. I know beyond all doubt, this is the guy I saw at the prison with the warden and Bass and Munson the day Billy was killed. This was a few days after Tom Carver's election. I believe they had Billy killed to shut him up. To make sure the Carvers were covered."

"That's quite a stretch, Scott," Marc said.

"Billy told me the Carvers were responsible for that girl's death. That she was in Tom's room. He was having an affair with a teenage girl, she died as a result and they covered it up. And I believe this guy," he pointed again at the photo, "was in on it up to his ass."

Marc sat back and laced his fingers together behind his head. He sat quietly like this for over two minutes obviously thinking. He finally sat forward again, placed his folded hands on the newspaper and looked at Scott Duncan.

"The stories about these two are such that I'm not sure I would put anything past them. Tom Carver is a sexual predator, that's well known. Darla is power hungry to the point of pathological plus she can't open her mouth without lying. But murder?"

Marc let the last part, the question, hang in the air.

"What do you want from me?" Marc asked Duncan. "What do you think I can do about it?"

"You've become a fairly well-known lawyer," Duncan said. "I don't know. You were Billy's lawyer and I know you wanted to find out the truth about how he died. I didn't know who else to go to. The Carvers in Colorado, well, they're gold. Untouchable. No one would be willing to tangle with them.

"I don't know what to do," Duncan continued. "Maybe, I don't know, you might have some way of looking into this."

"Well, you've certainly piqued my curiosity. Are you going back to Boulder?" Marc asked.

"Yeah, I took a couple days off but I have to go back tomorrow."

"Leave the paper so I can have the photo," Marc said. "Let me look into it and see if I can find out who this Estes guy is."

FIFTY-SIX

As soon as Marc had shown Scott Duncan out he knocked on Connie's office door, went in and sat down. Over the years Marc and Connie had become close friends and he had learned to value her counsel.

Connie Mickelson was an old-school feminist. The daughter of a successful Jewish lawyer and businessman—she had inherited the Reardon Building from him—and because of her upbringing, Connie believed in individualism. Her attitude was that if you wanted something for yourself, get an education, roll-up your sleeves, get off your lazy ass and go get it. Today's brand of self-absorbed entitlement junkie feminists was not who Connie Mickelson was. Plus, in her late sixties, she had come of age during the 60s and 70s when misogyny was real and not an excuse.

"I need to talk to you," Marc said. "I need your opinion, some advice."

"This sounds pretty serious," Connie replied. "What's going on?"

So Marc told her. He went back to the very beginning when he was with Mickey O'Herlihy and told her the entire story. Connie listened politely. At one point she wheeled her chair back to a window, opened it, lit a cigarette and blew the smoke out into the snow. When she finished it, she tossed it out but left the window open. When Marc finished his story, Connie sat quietly for a few seconds.

"That's quite a tale," she said. "And this guy in the picture here on stage with Her Majesty," she continued tapping the newspaper now lying on her desk, "you don't know who that is?"

"Just a name: John Estes," Marc replied.

"What do you want to do?"

"I don't know," Marc said. "This isn't a simple question. These are the most powerful people on the planet."

"If you shoot at the King, you better not miss," Connie said jumbling the famous quote a bit.

"Exactly," Marc agreed.

"But if what this guy, Scott..."

"Duncan," Marc said.

"Yeah, Scott Duncan, says is true then these people need to be exposed," Connie said. "What else have they done? Who is this John Estes guy? This is America not some third world shithole where one gang of crooks kicks the ruling crooks out so a new gang can rob the place. At least it's not supposed to be."

"I was thinking I'd give Tony a call. He has that master hacker in his pocket. Maybe Tony can get this picture to him and find out who he is," Marc said.

"What's this guy's name, this hacker of his and why isn't he in jail?" Connie asked.

"Tony thinks he's being protected by the cops, the MPD and at least a couple of FBI guys. They use him clandestinely to skirt the Constitution to find people and get information on the side."

"Hello, Big Brother," Connie said.

"Look, if I start down this road, it could be all of our asses if I shoot at the King and Queen and miss. To tell you the truth, it scares the hell out of me."

"Bullshit. You're a lawyer, I'm a lawyer. We still have an independent judiciary in this country and we know how to use it. If these two are as corrupt as most of us believe, it's time they paid for it. It's time someone held them accountable and showed the Carvers they need to abide by the same laws as the rest of us."

"You're right and I guess that's what I wanted you to tell me. Besides, there may be no proof of anything. Let me have your phone," Marc said.

Connie handed her office phone to him then Marc dialed a number he knew by heart.

Connie said, "This could be fun. I'll help you any way I can."

"Thanks," Marc told her. "Hey," he said into the phone, "I need to see you."

"What's up?" Tony Carvelli asked.

"Not on the phone," Marc said. "Can you come by the office?"

"Yeah, I can be there in fifteen minutes. See you then."

Marc hung up and handed the phone back to Connie.

"Who's your client? Who's going to pay for this?" Connie asked.

"Good question," Marc answered her.

While they waited for Tony Carvelli, the two of them chatted a bit about cases, business and some personal things.

"How're things with the judge?" Connie asked Marc referring to Marc's girlfriend, Judge Margaret Tennant. Margaret was a Hennepin County District Court judge with her courtroom in downtown Minneapolis. They had been involved for several years, off and on but mostly on.

"She's humming those 'Wedding Bell Blues' again," Marc said. "What is it with women and wanting to be married?"

"They like the commitment," Connie answered him. "Plus, like myself, you can make a pretty good living with marriage and divorce. Just be careful who you marry."

"She has more money than I do," Marc said.

"There you go," Connie said. "Something to think about."

"We both live in Hennepin County. If we ever got divorced, I'd still have to pay no matter how much more money she has."

"Good point," Connie agreed. "Either stay single or move out of the county."

They heard a commotion in the reception area and accurately concluded Carvelli had arrived. Tony could charm about anyone if he chose to and always made a splash when he came to Marc's office.

"I think we need to let everyone know what's going on," Marc said to Connie after they came out to greet Carvelli.

"Yeah, I think you're right," she agreed. "Okay, everyone into the conference room," Connie announced. She looked at Jeff Modell, the office paralegal and asked, "Is there a client in with Chris?"

"No, I'll get him," Jeff replied. He knocked on Chris Grafton's door and told him to come out.

The fourth lawyer, Barry Cline, was already out of his office joining the group going into the conference room.

Everyone found a chair and for the next twenty minutes Marc gave them a shorter version of what he told Connie. He let them know he was going to check out who Estes was and his connection to the Carvers. They were heading down a path toward extremely powerful people and could be opening up a serious problem for everyone.

"Rock and roll," Barry gleefully said when Marc finished. "Whatever I can do to help..."

"Me, too," Chris agreed. "It's not like the Carvers aren't capable of doing something like this, covering up the death of a young girl in the sack with Tom Carver."

"Let's not get ahead of ourselves," Connie said. "We don't know anything at this point." She looked at Marc and said, "Be careful."

"Absolutely," Marc agreed. "We just thought you should know what we're up to." Marc looked at Carolyn and Sandy then asked them, "Any thoughts?"

Carolyn said, "I voted for Timmons. I've never trusted Darla Carver."

"Do what you gotta do," Sandy said.

"We could make history," Jeff said.

"God, don't say that," Marc groaned. "Let's hope it's not true."

292

"Thank you," Connie said. She looked at Carvelli and said, "Let's go into Marc's office."

"What do you want from me?" Carvelli asked after they situated themselves in Marc's office.

Marc handed him the newspaper and Connie, sitting next to Carvelli, pointed a finger at the man in the photo behind Darla Carver.

"His name is John Estes and we need to start with him," Connie said.

"Scott Duncan," Marc started to say to Carvelli then looked at Connie and asked, "Is *he* my client?"

Connie shrugged and said, "I don't know. Why not?"

"Anyway," Marc said to Carvelli, "Scott Duncan, the friend of Billy Stover, says this Estes guy was at the prison and the warden and senior guards were kissing his ass. Then Billy Stover," Marc paused, looked at Connie again and said, "maybe he's my client."

"His estate," Connie said.

"That'll do," Marc replied.

"Anyway," Marc continued, "they were all bowing and scraping to this Estes guy. When Duncan asked about him he got hammered and was told to mind his own business. That night Billy Stover hangs himself in his cell."

"And we think maybe this Estes guy ordered a hit from the Carvers to shut him up?" Carvelli asked.

"Who knows? It does seem a little fishy, if you believe Scott Duncan that he and Billy were gay pals and we're gonna take off together when Stover got out. He was up for parole in a few months and…"

"It stinks," Carvelli said. "And this was a few days after Tom Carver was first elected?"

"Yes," Marc replied. "Can you take that photo to your hacker guy and see if he can find out who this Estes guy is and how he's connected to the Carvers?"

"Sure," Carvelli said. "How am I going to pay him?"

"Don't worry about money," Connie said. "I have plenty. I'll cover it."

"We could bring Vivian in on this," Carvelli said to Marc. "And for sure we're gonna need Madeline if this goes anywhere."

"Let's leave Vivian out of it for now. I'll call Maddy and have her come by and bring her up to speed. You go see your guy and see what he can find out."

"You got it," Carvelli said as he stood to leave.

"You can afford it?" Marc asked Connie as she also stood.

"I've had several successful marriages and more successful divorces. You know that," Connie replied.

FIFTY-SEVEN

Tony Carvelli, the collar on his black leather coat turned up, his head drawn in like a turtle's, slopped quickly up the sidewalk. He had called his genius hacker before leaving Marc's office and was now hurrying through the snow to the man's front door. The snow was coming down harder and mixing with the water from the earlier rain on the sidewalk. Carvelli was quietly cursing up a storm because of what the mess was doing to his Italian leather loafers.

He reached the front door, opened the aluminum screen and pounded several times. A moment later the home's owner opened the door and without a word Carvelli stepped past him.

Paul Baker, christened Pavel Bykowski by his devout Roman Catholic mother, was a world class hacker. Whatever there was to know about someone, Paul could dig it out of the Internet.

Baker's office was the entire second floor of his South Minneapolis mortgage-free home; mortgage-free because Paul had hacked the lender and wiped the debt clean. There were two bedrooms upstairs and the wall separating them was gone creating sufficient space for his setup. Tony knew of two FBI agents and at least four and maybe even five or six MPD cops who also used him. He suspected the man had another dozen or more cash clients as well. It was enough to keep Paul Baker supplied with the latest equipment, at least three or four luxury vacations each year and all the best weed he desired.

"Messy out there today," Baker said while Carvelli took off his coat.

"Yeah," Carvelli grumbled, "and getting worse."

The two of them went into Baker's living room while Carvelli smelled the air.

"Give it a rest, Tony," Baker said when he noticed Carvelli smelling for marijuana.

"Thanks for seeing me on short notice," Carvelli said, then sat on the couch.

"No problem. You're my favorite customer," Baker said.

Carvelli paused and looked at the hacker for several seconds before saying, "You are so full of shit it's coming out of your ears. I have a serious job for you. I need you to find out everything you can about someone."

Carvelli pulled out the copy of the Denver Post and spread it open on the coffee table. He pointed at the picture on the front page and said, "This guy here. We have a name for him: John Estes. First thing is to do facial recognition to find out if that's his real name. Can you do that with this photo?"

"I'll go into the Denver Post and get a print of the original. Then I'll run it with that. Who's the woman in the picture?"

"The next president," Carvelli said with an incredulous look on his face.

"Oh, yeah," Baker said. "I thought she looked familiar."

"How long?" Carvelli asked.

"Normally I'd need at least a couple days, but for you, I'll have it tomorrow probably by noon."

Carvelli laughed, then said, "For me, you'll have it tomorrow. You are so full of...."

"Yeah, yeah, I know," Baker said with a big grin. "Seriously, if you say it's important I'll get right on it. Call me tomorrow. I'll have some things for you by noon."

While Carvelli was meeting with his hacker, Maddy Rivers was arriving at Marc's office. Whenever Maddy came by it was an event. She had not been there for several weeks which made today's visit more of an occasion. She spent a half hour yakking with the women and by the time they were done, all of the men in the office had joined in.

"Okay, what's going on?" she asked Marc when the two of them finally settled into his office.

Before he could answer, without knocking, Connie came in and joined them. She took the client chair next to Maddy and said, "Well, tell her."

Marc started at the beginning and told Maddy the entire story, in detail. When he finished, Maddy sat literally speechless staring at Marc. After at least fifteen seconds of total silence, she turned her head to Connie then back to Marc.

"I don't know what to say. It's, I don't know, horrible actually. He was president and she's going to be and you're telling me they did this? Caused a young girl's death, covered it up, got an innocent young man to take the fall for it then possibly had him killed?"

"After everything we've seen over the years from these two, you don't think they're capable of that? You don't believe they are money hungry and power mad enough to do this?" Connie quietly asked.

Maddy looked at Connie who stared back at her with a neutral expression except for her raised eyebrows.

"You know what, it's sad to say it, but you're right. These two could do something like this," Maddy quietly said. "It's sickening but..."

Maddy turned back to Marc and asked, "Okay, what do you want from me?"

"Tony and I talked about it. He's meeting with his mystery hacker. He thinks you should go to the St. Paul Hotel and see what you can find.

296

Find an excuse to sweet talk whoever the head of their security is. See if they kept security footage from when the Carvers were there the year before he was elected. Find out what you can about this girl's death."

"I'll tell him I'm a free-lance writer doing a puff piece about the Carvers. I haven't used that one for a while."

"Open a couple buttons on your blouse first," Connie said.

"Connie! That wouldn't be ethical," Maddy said. "Besides, one button is usually enough."

Jeff Modell, the office paralegal, had made several good color copies of the newspaper photo. Marc gave one to Maddy for her use.

"Hello, Mr. Sloan," Maddy said using her best smile on the man, "Thank you for taking the time to meet with me."

Maddy extended her hand to the head of security for the St. Paul Hotel, Randy Sloan, and they shook hands.

Sloan was able to say reasonably well, "Um, please, my pleasure. What can I do for you?"

"As I said over the phone, I'm doing a magazine article for People Magazine on the Carvers. I'm researching their stay here back before Tom Carver became president. And…"

"You want to see if we have any film record of their visit," Sloan finished for her. Randy Sloan was a retired St. Paul cop and head of security for twenty years. Pushing sixty-five, pudgy and bald, Maddy Rivers could have asked him to do dog tricks and he would have enthusiastically complied.

With the arrival of DVDs, storing film was not much of a problem. A single normal-sized file cabinet could store several hundred years of film. It took Sloan less than a minute to find the disks Maddy wanted to review.

For the next hour Maddy, with the eager cooperation and assistance of Sloan, reviewed every minute of all the film the hotel had taken during the Carvers stay.

"I don't see any film for the floors the Carvers used," Maddy said.

"No, we weren't permitted to have the cameras on for the floors they used," Sloan said.

"Why?"

"Their request. At least after the first few hours. The Carvers had two rooms, suites actually, on twelve. No cameras there at all."

"Separate rooms?" Maddy asked.

"Yes. They said one was for private meetings but both rooms were slept in."

"How do you remember this?" Maddy asked.

"Well, first, I've always had an excellent memory. And we don't get presidential visits very often. Theirs is the only one since I've been here," Sloan replied.

"What other floors did they use?"

"Well, they had a lot of campaign staff. Some on eight, nine and ten. Secret service on eleven."

Maddy went back to the TV and a minute later stopped the disk. She was looking at a younger version of the man in the newspaper photo leaving room 1010.

"Who is this? Can you check your records to see who was using that room, 1010?"

"Give me a minute," Sloan said. He typed up the information on his computer. The response came up and he read it out loud.

"It just says 'Carver campaign'."

When Maddy finished reviewing the disks, she decided to ask for real information. "I have to ask about the girl," Maddy said. "She was found dead in one of the staff's rooms. Abby Connolly found in the room of a William Stover."

"I knew you would," Sloan said. "A tragic accident. A couple of young people fooling around with sex and drugs. Fortunately, it didn't hurt the Carver's politically."

"So the story that came out in the papers and in court was accurate?"

"As far as I know," Sloan shrugged. "There was no reason to believe otherwise."

"Sad." Maddy lightly placed a hand on his knee and asked, "Are there any staff still around who might have dealt directly with the Carvers? You know, waitstaff, housekeepers, maids…"

Sloan, electricity running through his leg, thought about it for a moment and said, "You should ask our head of housekeeping. I think she was here then. She worked as one of the housekeeping staff and might have some information. I can't think of anyone else."

"Her name?"

"Consuelo Perez. Terrific employee. Just between you and me, she was illegal at the time. We've helped her get a Green Card and she's worked her way up," Sloan whispered.

"Good for her," Maddy said. "Is she here? Do you think I could talk to her?"

"No problem. I'll take you to her myself."

They found Consuelo Perez in her office. After introductions were made Maddy managed to get Sloan out of the room and closed the door behind him.

Consuelo Perez was a pretty Latina woman approximately forty years old with a nice wedding ring. On her desk were several pictures of her husband and three children. Because Consuelo was a woman Maddy decided to take a different, honest approach with her.

"Consuelo, may I call you that?" Maddy politely asked.

"Of course," she replied with just a slight trace of an accent.

"Consuelo, I'll be honest with you. I am not a freelance writer. I am a private investigator. I work for the lawyer who represented the man who went to prison for the death of that girl who died when the Carvers were here many years ago."

The woman's face went pale. Her mouth turned down, her eyes began to water and she began rubbing her hands together.

"I always knew this day would come," Consuelo quietly said. "You must understand. I was young and scared. I was here illegally and they said they would send me back if…"

"Wait, wait, wait," Maddy said and reached out to take Consuelo's hand. "What are you talking about?"

"The man, I don't know his name, he scared me. He made me tell the police that Mr. Carver slept in Mrs. Carver's room but it wasn't true. He slept in his room. And he wasn't alone. There were two people who slept in his bed."

"Was it a young girl? Was it the girl who died?"

"I don't know," Consuelo said using a tissue to wipe her eyes. "I never saw her. But there was something very strange; there was a sheet missing from Mr. Carver's bed. We never found it."

Maddy showed her the newspaper photo and asked, "Is this the man who scared you?"

Consuelo looked at the picture, nodded and said, "He told me he would send me back, get me deported. Then he gave me money to go to Colorado, five thousand dollars. I was so scared. I left right away but then I came back. I knew this would happen. I knew someone would come looking for me."

"Consuelo, I am not looking for you. I promise you won't get in trouble. But I need you to tell me everything that you know about what happened that day."

FIFTY-EIGHT

Maddy parked her Audi on the street in front of the two-story house on Seventh. She was in South St. Paul, a couple blocks off of Interstate 494 at the home of a retired cop. A mutual friend had called and set up the appointment. The friend was John Lucas, a detective with the St. Paul police and the husband of Carolyn Lucas, one of the assistants in Connie Mickelson's office.

Maddy knocked on the front door and a moment later a man in his late-fifties opened it.

"Detective Mills?" Maddy asked.

"Please call me Parker," the man said.

Mills stepped aside and Maddy went into the living room. She sat in an upholstered loveseat facing the retired detective.

"John Lucas said you wanted to see me about the death of Abby Connolly," he said.

"Yes, sir," Maddy replied. "I work for the lawyer who represented William Stover, the young man who pled to manslaughter for her death. You were one of the detectives who caught the case…"

"Me and my partner at the time, Nate Hough. Nate died a couple years ago. Cancer. He died about a year after my wife."

"I'm sorry," Maddy sincerely said.

"Why are you looking into this, after all these years? I remember seeing in the papers a few years back that William Stover committed suicide. Hung himself in his cell."

"We have come across evidence that casts doubt on how Abby Connolly supposedly died," Maddy said. "And we have reason to believe William Stover did not commit suicide."

Mills inhaled heavily then exhaled as well. "You know something," he said with a troubled look on his face. "Nate and me both had doubts about that case. Something was wrong. The whole thing smelled of political cover-up. That case has always stuck in my craw.

"I remember we interviewed a housekeeper, one of the maids. I don't remember her name but I do remember she seemed real nervous. A couple days later we went back to re-interview her and she was gone. Poof! Vanished. The reason we wanted to talk to her was because we found out a bedsheet was missing from Tom Carver's room. By itself it meant nothing. But we were told he slept in his wife's room. Why was there a sheet missing from his? And they cleaned his room and contaminated any possibility of forensically finding anything. There was something not right about this. Word came down and we were told to stand down. There was political heat that came down on us and shut down the investigation. Then that kid, Stover, took a plea. The whole thing had a stink to it."

"I spoke with the missing housekeeper yesterday," Maddy said.

"You did? Where, how…?"

"She's back at the St. Paul Hotel. In fact, she came back a few months after she went missing. She told me that two people slept in the bed in Tom Carver's suite that night. She was certain of it and remembered it well. She was paid five grand and shipped off to Denver. A few months later, she was lonely so she came back. She's got her Green Card and is head of housekeeping now."

"No shit? Ooops, sorry," Mills said.

Maddy smiled at his slight slip up and said, "No shit. Is there anything you can add? Anything from your investigation that we didn't get?"

"If you talked to her…"

"Consuelo Perez," Maddy said.

"If you talked to her, it sounds like she knew more than we did. Did she know what happened to the missing sheet from Tom Carver's room?"

"No, and she remembered that too. All of it," Maddy said. "She was afraid she was in trouble."

Mills thought for a moment then said, "I can't think of anything off the top of my head. But I'll tell you what. I'll go downtown and check the case file, especially my notes and Nate's. If I find anything, I'll call."

Maddy gave him her card and thanked him for seeing her. Mills escorted her back to the front door. They shook hands and Maddy thanked him again.

"Be careful," he told her. "These are powerful people. And I wouldn't be the least bit surprised if they had this William Stover killed to shut him up."

"We will," Maddy said.

"Tom Carver was responsible for that girl's death. He didn't murder her but he caused it. And that wife of his, our esteemed next President covered it up. I believed it then and I'm more convinced than ever now."

Maddy got in her car and before starting the engine turned her phone back on. There was a message from Carvelli for her. The message was a little cryptic only informing her he had some interesting information. He had called Marc, was on his way to Marc's office and Maddy was to join them ASAP.

Maddy did a U-turn in the middle of the street to head south back to the freeway. She made a quick call, spoke to Carolyn and told her to tell Marc she was on her way.

"Hello, everyone," Maddy said when she entered the suite of offices.

Marc was coming out of his office when she came in and said, "Ah, the Grand Dame makes her entrance!"

Maddy gave him a nasty look and scratched her nose with the middle finger of her left hand. This exchange caused a bit of laughter as Maddy hung up her coat.

"Cold out there today," she said. "Are you waiting for me?"

"Yes, come on in," Marc said referring to the conference room where Tony and Connie Mickelson were already seated.

When Marc and Maddy took their seats at the conference room table, Marc said, "Maddy, why don't you go first?"

"Okay," she replied.

She removed her notebook from her purse and gave the others her report. It took her about twenty minutes to fill them in on what she found at the St. Paul Hotel and her questioning of Consuelo Perez and her meeting with Parker Mills.

"So, Consuelo definitely remembers all of this?" Marc asked Maddy.

"Absolutely," Maddy said. "In fact as soon as I told her who I was and what I wanted I thought she was going to start crying. She said, 'I knew this day would come.' She was afraid she was in trouble."

"But she has no physical evidence, just her recollection," Connie said.

"Yes, that's it," Maddy agreed. "But she was rock solid. There was no hesitation at all."

"And Parker Mills believed her?" Carvelli asked.

"Yep," Maddy said. "But he doesn't have anything either."

"I'll bet he had a list of names of where the political heat came from to shut down their investigation," Marc said.

"Maybe," Connie said. "He might not have known except what his immediate superiors told him."

"Tony?" Marc asked. "What did your guy find out about this John Estes?"

"He says he worked most of the night on it. He said once he got into it he couldn't stop. But he came up with a lot," Carvelli said.

"How much money does he need?" Connie asked.

"A grand?" Carvelli said making it sound like a question.

"Is it worth it?" Connie replied.

"Every penny," Carvelli said.

"Okay, no problem," Connie said.

She looked across the table at Marc who mouthed the words 'thank you' at her.

"Hey, if nothing else I'll deduct it from my taxes," Connie said dismissing his concern with a wave of her hand.

"Good point," Carvelli replied. "This Estes guy's real name is Clayton Dean and he is definitely the Carver's guy, especially Tom Carver.

"He's former Army Special Forces and Colorado Highway Patrol. That's probably how he met the Carvers. Dean was on Tom's protection detail when he was governor of Colorado.

"Dean is divorced and has a daughter, Jordan, now age twenty-five. Jordan had leukemia when she was a kid, ten or eleven. Apparently, about the time Dean quit the highway patrol and went to work as a personal aide to Tom, Jordan started getting treated at Mayo and Sloan-Kettering."

"How does he afford that?" Marc wondered.

"He doesn't. The Carver's must've picked up the tab for all of it," Carvelli said.

"Or their rich pals," Connie added.

"It looks like that's how the Carvers got their hooks into him," Carvelli said.

"He's the guy who paid off Consuelo Perez and hustled her off to Denver," Maddy interjected. "I showed her his picture from the paper and she recognized him. He's up to his ass in the cover-up of Abby Connolly's death."

"And the murder of William Stover," Marc said. "And maybe that warden what's-his-name and the corrections officer."

"Maybe," Connie reminded Marc. "At this point, we don't have any solid evidence of anything."

"No, but it's not a weak circumstantial case, either," Marc said. "Who here isn't convinced the Carvers covered up the accidental overdose death of Abby Connolly?"

When no one raised their hands, Maddy asked the obvious question. "What do we do about it?"

"Remember, if you shoot at the King or the Queen, you better not miss," Connie reminded Marc.

Marc stared back at Connie and said, "Don't give me that. You're not the least bit afraid of these people. In fact, I know you, you'd love to take a shot at Darla Carver."

Connie smiled back at him and said, "Yeah, you're right. I would." She then added, "What about the rest of you?"

Carvelli shrugged and replied, "I'm not doing anything better."

"Me neither," Maddy said.

"At the very least, we can keep digging," Marc said. "We need to take a run at this guy, this Clayton Dean. Since we have solid evidence he had been using a false ID, this John Estes guy, we can at least start with that."

"And do what?" Connie asked.

"See if we can peel him away from the Carvers. I have a feeling he knows where the bodies are buried."

"There's more," Carvelli said. "My guy spent some time looking at this Carver Worldwide Charities. Did you know it took in over a billion dollars in just the past two years?"

"While Darla was on the Senate," Connie said.

"He didn't have time to dig too deep but it looks like more than half the money is going toward Tom and his pals for travel expenses, luxury hotels, private jets…"

"Hookers," Maddy said.

"Probably," Carvelli agreed. "And they have a ton of their political pals and staff on the payroll all making a damn good living."

"And the money they expense to the charity for luxury living is not reported as income," Connie said. "And the people who donate to it claim it as a charitable deduction. So, for all practical purposes, the taxpayers are the ones really paying for this scam."

"Can your guy dig deeper?" Marc asked.

"Yeah," Carvelli said. "In fact, he's like a bloodhound after a fox. He'll find out what's going on there."

"Why doesn't the government, the IRS or FBI look at this?" Maddy asked.

"Get an honest investigation of the Carvers? Not likely," Connie answered her.

"All the more reason for us to make a run at Clayton Dean," Marc said. "Do you know where he lives?"

"The charity has an apartment rented in Georgetown," Carvelli said. "My guy tapped into some street camera surveillance near it and found footage of this Dean guy going into the building."

"Who is this hacker of yours? He sounds scarier than the government. The government can't find its ass with both hands but this guy can find out anything about anyone in a few hours," Connie said.

"Scary, isn't it?" Carvelli replied.

FIFTY-NINE

Darla's professional cosmetologist was finishing up with a couple of minor touches to her makeup. Her hair was perfectly styled, the makeup made her look and feel ten years younger and she was ready for the big night.

Darla was in the Presidential Suite of the MGM National Harbor hotel in D.C. A month and a few days had passed since the election. This Saturday night, the first Saturday of December, was the semi-official coming out ball for the President-elect. The ballroom was set up to accommodate a thousand guests, formally attired of course. Donors, politicians and dignitaries were going to pay tribute to the first female President of the United States and Darla would look her best.

Because of the large number of people working for her who had been involved with her husband's elections, with their experience the transition was going smoothly. It was a little exhausting for Darla anyway. Her obsessive need for control made her get involved in even some of the most minor, even trivial decisions. Due to this, at last count, an even dozen second tier transition team members had bailed out. Tom Carver had finally stepped in and had a long talk with his wife. He made her realize that she would burn herself out if this continued. She agreed to cool it, a promise she had no intention of keeping.

There was a knock on the bedroom door and Darla snapped at Sonja to get it. Sonja, who was in a chair waiting for her boss, stood and headed to the door. Before she got there, it opened and Tom Carver walked in resplendent in his tuxedo.

"It's almost time to go," he said.

"We're ready," Darla said as she stood and faced her husband. "How do I look?"

"Fabulous, Madam President," he smiled as he bent down and kissed her hand.

"Ladies and gentlemen, may I have your attention please," the announcer said into the ballroom's P.A. system. The grand room with its one thousand inhabitants went completely silent in anticipation, waiting for the announcement.

"Ladies and gentlemen, it is my very special honor and extreme privilege to announce the President-elect of the United States of America!"

The audience exploded. With her husband acting as escort, Darla Carver walked into a thunderous ovation. All of her dreams, schemes and life-long ambitions were encapsulated in this moment with the total adulation of the elites of America. And Darla Carver, no longer in her husband's long shadow, was the object of their affection. As the orchestra played "Hail to the Chief", at that moment, what was going through Darla's mind was how many of them were going to pay for any slight, insult or failure any had ever done to her or to fail to adequately support her. Getting even was not good enough for Darla Carver. They had better get in line and back her personally and her agenda.

A twenty-piece ensemble orchestra was on hand to provide the evening's music. It was mostly strings to play light music which people could dance to without looking like fools. A huge buffet had been set up with an assortment of finger food to snack on. And, of course, several open bars were scattered around the room for the main entertainment, free booze.

It took almost two hours for the Carvers to make their way around the room. Everyone wanted a personal greeting and a chance to suck up to the First Couple. They were followed by a watchful pair of Secret Service agents and the ever vigilant Clay Dean.

Toward midnight the Russian Ambassador, Grigory Tretiak, approached Tom and Darla. He was alone, greeted them warmly and the First Couple returned the warm greeting. Tretiak amiably chatted with them while Darla, despite the smile she wore, was thinking about how much she would enjoy watching the man bleed to death. After a couple of minutes, the Russian bent down as if to kiss her cheek. Instead, he whispered in her ear.

"I need a moment of your time for a private conversation," he said.

"I'm not sure I have time," Darla curtly replied.

"What?" Tom asked.

"It would be in your interest and my country's for you to make time, Madam President-elect."

"I don't think it would be appropriate," Darla said.

"What?" Tom asked again only more forcefully.

"I have someone waiting in a meeting room and you and Mr. Dean need to meet. Please. And of course," he continued looking at Tom, "please join us, Mr. President."

Darla looked at Clay with a puzzled expression. Clay shrugged his shoulders in response. Then they all went out of the ballroom, including Sonja who had joined them, across the hall and into the Aria Meeting Room while the Secret Service agents stood guard outside.

Seated near the door at one of the small, round tables were three men, two of whom had their backs to the door. The third man stood as they entered and walked over to greet them. He was well known to the Carvers, Clay Dean and Sonja. He was Viktor Ivanov, the head spy at the Russian Embassy.

"What is this, ambassador?" an annoyed Darla asked when she saw Ivanov coming toward them. "I'm busy, I don't have time for games. Your hold over me is…"

"Not finished," Ivanov said to her sporting a sinister grin. "Allow me to introduce someone to you, or, to Mr. Dean, re-introduce."

The two men who had been sitting with Ivanov had stood when he did but remained standing with their backs to the small group. They turned around and the instant he saw them Clay Dean's face became almost beet red.

"What the hell is this?" he yelled.

Taking charge Tom Carver stepped forward protectively in front of his wife.

"What the hell is going on here, Grigory? Who are these men?" Tom asked.

"Ask your Mr. Dean," the ambassador replied. "He is well acquainted with them."

"Allow me," Ivanov said looking at Tom. "The man to your left is an aide of mine. His name is Mikhail Sokolov. The man to your right is Anton Popov, another employee of our embassy.

"And, Mr. Dean," Ivanov continued, turning to Clay, "you, of course, recognize them both as the young men you thought you had compromised. They are not homosexual lovers. I am afraid they were on assignment when you met them."

Ivanov turned back to Darla still standing behind Tom with an uncomprehending look on her face.

"You see, Madam President-elect," Ivanov said, "the list that we gave you, that Mikhail gave to Mr. Dean at your Pacific War Memorial, that was a forgery. An excellent forgery but a forgery nevertheless. We still have the original in your handwriting and with your fingerprints on it. To prove it, Mr. Dean or anyone you choose may come by the embassy and inspect it."

"We look forward to continuing a long and mutually beneficial relationship with the new Carver Administration," Ambassador Tretiak said with an undiplomatic grin.

"Why?" Darla muttered.

"To let you believe a cloud had lifted over you to help you get elected," the ambassador replied. "And now, if you will excuse us, it is getting late. I'm sure you would like to get back to your guests. We will take our leave. Congratulations, again, Madam President-elect, on your splendid victory."

"How the hell did you manage to create this mess?" a fuming Darla asked while staring daggers at Clay.

The four of them were now seated at a table in the otherwise empty meeting room after the Russians had left. Clay stared back at Darla with a silent, impassive, almost bored expression. He had known the instant he saw Mikhail and the other young man that they had been had by Ivanov. He also knew Darla was going to explode and the shit storm would land on him. Clay had been through it many times before. He knew the best way to deal with it was to let Mount Darla explode then ignore it.

"Stop it!" Tom ordered his wife. "This is not his doing, it's yours. You created this mess when you did what you did to sink Julian Morton's campaign and help Timmons get elected. You wanted to run against Timmons. You did and it worked. Clay did not create this, you did."

Being spoken to like this, even by her husband, only served to inflame Darla more. Tom was sitting across the table next to Clay. If he was closer she likely would have slapped him for his insolence. Instead, she took a deep breath and looked at Clay.

"What are you going to do to fix this?" she quietly asked.

"Well, Mrs. Carver," Clay calmly began, "since I've had barely a minute to think about it, I really have no idea what we can do."

"Do not take an attitude with me, Clay…"

"He's right," Tom said. "We don't need to do anything right this minute."

"I want that fat Russian asshole killed," Darla said referring to the pudgy ambassador.

"I'm going to pretend you didn't say that," Tom replied.

"And that goddamn spy, Ivanov," Darla continued glaring at Clay and acting as if Tom had not said anything.

"Take a deep breath, Darla," Tom said. "Get a grip on yourself so we can go back to the party."

Everyone except Clay went back into the ballroom. Darla and Tom each put on their best politician's face acting as if they did not have a care in the world. Around 1:00 A.M. the crowd started to thin out and by 2:00 Darla was back in the Presidential Suite. Tom had slipped out for a rendezvous with a married congresswoman he had been eyeing up all evening.

While Sonja helped Darla remove the makeup from her face Sonja asked, "What are you going to do about Clay?"

They were sitting in the bedroom in front of the vanity, Darla's back to the mirror while Sonja worked on her.

"What do you think?" Darla seriously asked looking for a suggestion.

Sonja stopped what she was doing sat back and looked at her boss. The two women silently stared at each other for several seconds then Sonja replied. "I think you've put up with too much from him for years. He needs...to be dealt with."

"I think you're right. This fiasco is the last straw," Darla replied. "But how?"

"You should call Malcom Brewster. Promise him a cabinet job. He should know someone from his days at CIA."

"He'll want State or Defense," Darla said.

"Give him Defense. You've promised Sally Newport the State Department. The generals will see to it Brewster doesn't make too much of a mess at Defense," Sonja advised her boss.

"You're right, this could work. I want it done right away. Have him come by tomorrow," Darla told her.

"I already talked to him this evening after we saw the Russians. He'll be here shortly after lunch. Around 2:00," Sonja said.

SIXTY

"Hi, Connie," Marc said into his cell phone. "We're here. We got three rooms on the third floor of the Georgetown Inn."

"Good, what's it like?" Connie asked.

"Nice enough. Should be for a couple hundred bucks per room each night," Marc replied.

"I told you, don't worry about the money. Just get receipts. Are Maddy and the gangster with you?" Connie asked referring to the Italian Tony Carvelli as the gangster. The two of them had a harmless, flirtatious relationship. They both enjoyed a bit of good natured ribbing.

"No. They checked in and drove over to set up on Clayton Dean's apartment. We're less than a couple miles from there. Like we decided, they will spend a day or two watching him to find a chance for Maddy to make a run at him."

"Be careful. I get the feeling this guy is nobody's fool and more than a little dangerous."

"I know. They'll be careful. Tony has Maddy's back. They know what they're doing."

"Stay in touch," Connie said.

"Will do."

Marc, Maddy and Carvelli had flown into D.C. on the Monday after Darla's big party. A coincidence. They had set up shop in a Georgetown hotel near Clay Dean's apartment. It had been decided that the best way to get to him was for Maddy to try to pick him up in a bar, if at all possible.

They both had their own rental car and within minutes of leaving the hotel were on station. The apartment they were watching was on P Street between 30th and 31st. Carvelli's hacker's guess that this was Clay's home paid off within an hour. Just before sunset, shortly after 4:30, they saw Clay exit his building. He walked a half a block up the street toward Carvelli then got into a new Buick.

Using their cell phones and frequently switching off, the two veteran private investigators followed Clay to the MGM National Harbor. Carvelli followed him inside and saw him present his ID to the guard at an express elevator. Unable to follow, Carvelli returned to his car to wait.

It was after midnight when Clay Dean finally came out. He drove straight home making no stops at all. Maddy and Carvelli watched the apartment for a half hour after the lights went out, then drove back to their hotel.

This pattern continued for two days. Having discovered Clay's car, Carvelli had planted a small tracking device on it. Unfortunately, Clay gave them no opportunity to talk to him until the third day, Wednesday.

Clay had gone to the MGM again, which by now Marc and company knew was the transition headquarters for Darla. This evening Clay left earlier than usual, around nine o'clock. Instead of driving home Clay stopped at a local restaurant in Georgetown, Martin's Tavern. Amazingly he could not have chosen a better place for Maddy. The restaurant was less than a block from the Georgetown Inn.

"Excuse me, is anyone sitting here?" a female voice softly asked.

Clay Dean turned his head to his left away from his Dewar's on the rocks and looked at where the voice came from. The woman standing next to the chair was enough to rattle even the stoic, fifty-plus-year-old Clay Dean.

"Um, ah, no, no please," he said to the tall, slender beauty. "By all means, have a seat," Clay smiled.

"Thanks," Maddy said flashing a smile.

"Let me buy you a drink," Clay asked.

"Oh, I don't know," Maddy said trying to act coy. "I'm supposed to be meeting someone. Unfortunately, I'm a little late. I have his picture and know what he looks like but I don't see him."

By this time the twenty-something male bartender was standing in front of her. Maddy looked at him, shrugged and said, "Well, I guess a glass of white wine. Whatever you have."

"Another Dewar's also," Clay said as he slid his empty glass at the young man.

Clay made a quarter turn on his barstool to get a better view of Maddy. He held out his right hand and introduced himself. Maddy, showing just the right amount of hesitation, took his hand and told him her real first name and a fake last name.

The bartender brought their drinks and the two of them chatted cordially. In his fifties now, it had been a long time, if ever, that a woman of Maddy's caliber had been social with Clay. Despite his normally stern, all-business attitude even he could not resist at least a little face time with her.

While they talked Clay, as any straight man would, tried his best to impress her. When she asked him what he did for a living, he told her.

"You work for the Carvers? I mean, God, you know them and everything? I voted for her. What's she like? This is amazing."

Instead of telling her the truth, he sugarcoated everything he had to say about Darla. When he finished Maddy was obviously quite impressed.

311

"Does this guy you're looking for have your picture?" Clay asked while the bartender fetched another pair of drinks.

"I don't know," Maddy replied. "It was a setup by a friend. I'm not sure about him at all."

She looked at her watch, frowned and said, "I think I've been stood up."

"That's hard for me to imagine," Clay said. "Somebody standing you up."

"It's men my age," Maddy said. "I don't know what's happening to them but most of them are self-centered, immature kids more interested in video games and the internet."

They made more small talk and Clay finished off another scotch. Maddy was almost done with her glass of wine. Clay ordered one for himself but Maddy declined. The bartender brought Clay's fourth or fifth scotch and Clay stood up.

"Excuse me," he said. "I need to hit the men's room."

Maddy looked at her watch again and said, "I should probably go anyway. It's been nice talking to a grownup for a change," she smiled.

"Stick around," Clay said. "It's early. We could get some dinner."

Maddy acted like she was thinking it over then said, "Well, maybe one more."

"Great, I'll be right back."

As soon as he was out of sight, Maddy took what looked like a plastic bottle of eye drops from her purse. She casually sipped her wine then passed her hand over Clay's scotch and squirted a clear, tasteless liquid into it.

By the time Clay finished his drink he was definitely feeling the effects. He was slightly nauseous and his pulse was elevated. Although he was seated, the room was spinning and he was starting to perspire.

"Are you all right?" Maddy asked. "You look a little woozy."

"Yeah, um, I don't know," Clay said. "I don't know what's wrong. I must be coming down with something."

He started to tip over almost falling off the barstool. Maddy grabbed his arm and held him up.

"Whoa, cowboy," Maddy said. "I think we better get you out of here."

"Yeah," Clay muttered.

The bartender came over to them and said, "He shouldn't drive."

"I know," Maddy told him. "I'll get him in a cab."

Clay had one arm around Maddy's shoulders while she held him up and walked him out. When she got outside she turned to her right and started down the sidewalk. Before they went twenty feet Tony Carvelli was with them.

"What the hell took you so long?"

"Hey, can't a girl enjoy a night out once in a while," she replied.

With Carvelli's assistance and using the back door and service elevator of the hotel, they had Clay in Carvelli's room ten minutes after leaving the restaurant.

"Oh, shit," a stumbling, almost incoherent Clay Dean muttered as they guided him to the bed. Carvelli held him up while Maddy slipped off his coat. They dropped him on the bed and made him as comfortable as they could.

"Is he going to throw up?" Marc asked. He had been waiting in Carvelli's room receiving periodic updates from Tony down on the street.

"Maybe," Carvelli replied. "Get his shoes and socks off. When he comes out of this, he's gonna be pissed and he'll want to leave."

"Was he armed?" Marc asked.

"No," Maddy said.

They removed his shoes and socks then put them in a drawer of the room's dresser.

"How long?" Marc asked.

"How much did you give him?" Tony asked Maddy.

"Not much actually. Less than half what we had," she replied.

"An hour, maybe two," Tony said answering Marc's question. "We should get some water in him. That will help."

Just before midnight, the effects of the GHB Maddy had squirted into his drink were wearing off. Clay was lying on the bed staring at the ceiling, breathing normally and no longer shaking or sweating.

"You people are in a lot of trouble. Do you have any idea who I am?" Clay said while still lying flat on his back.

"Of course we know who you are," Marc answered him. "How are you feeling?"

When Clay did not answer, Marc continued by saying, "My name is Marc Kadella. I'm a lawyer from Minnesota. We need to talk to you and tell you some things you need to hear for your benefit. When we're finished, you can go. No harm will come to you."

Clay sat up, his back to the bed's headboard and looked at his feet.

"Where are my shoes and socks?"

"Relax, you'll get them back," Marc told him.

Clay looked at Marc and said, "What do you want? Who are you? You look familiar. Have we met?"

"No, we've never met," Marc said. "Like I told you, we want to talk to you is all. You need to hear what we have to say."

Marc sat down in one of the armchairs next to Maddy. Tony half sat, half stood against the dresser at the foot of the bed.

When Clay noticed Maddy he said, "I should've known a woman like you was a setup."

"Sorry," she replied.

"Again, what do you want?" he said to Marc.

"Do the names Abby Connolly and Billy Stover sound familiar?" Marc asked.

For just an instant a worried look flashed across Clay's face and through his eyes. Enough to indicate he recognized the names.

"No, who are they?"

"Don't even try lying," Carvelli said. "The look on your face gave you up. You're an ex-cop, so am I. You know what I'm talking about."

Clay thought about it for several seconds, then said. "Okay, yeah, I remember them. So what?"

"We know what happened," Marc said. "Tom Carver was partying with a teenager and fed her cocaine. Enough to kill her. You, Darla Carver and at least one other person...."

"Probably Darla's sidekick, Sonja Hayden," Maddy interjected.

"...moved Abby's body to Billy Stover's room. Darla probably paid him to take the fall for the girl's death. Then right after the election that put the Carver's in the White House, you were sent to Colorado to permanently shut up him up."

"Good luck proving any of that, even if it were true, which it isn't," Clay said.

"How did you come up with the name John Estes?" Tony asked.

The fact that they had his alias caused Clay to pause. He swallowed hard and a thin line of sweat broke out along his hairline.

"Yeah we know all about him," Tony said.

"So?" Clay nervously said.

"A couple months after his so-called suicide, I went to Colorado to try to find out what happened to him. I got stonewalled by the warden and a couple of his goons. Then one of them followed me to my hotel and a couple days later the warden was run off the road and over a cliff to shut him up." Marc continued. The last part about the warden's death was pure bluff but it worked. Clay cringed just enough to indicate Marc had hit a nerve.

"This is laughable," Clay said as he swung his feet over the side of the bed. "I had nothing to do with anything. I want my shoes, I'm leaving."

"Billy Stover was gay," Marc said. "And we have witnesses. A woman you bribed and sent to Denver to impede the investigation. We found her and a cop who was a guard at the prison who is a gay man and had a relationship with Billy."

Clay, with a slightly worried expression, sat quietly looking at Marc. These revelations had obviously hit home.

"Who are you and what do want?" he asked Marc again.

"I told you, my name is Marc Kadella. I'm a lawyer from Minnesota and I represented Billy Stover. Or, at least, I tried to. The guys from New York who were on the Carver's payroll hosed Billy over before I could help him.

"What do you think we want? We want the Carvers. They are guilty of multiple, serious felonies, including the death of a teenage girl, and she should not be allowed to become president."

Before Marc finished saying this, Clay had started to laugh. "You three think you can take down the Carvers? Do you have any idea who these people are?"

"With your help, we can do it. And you can get out from under Darla Carver's control and become a man again," Marc replied.

"No chance," Clay said. He stood up and said, "My shoes and socks. I'm out of here."

Tony opened the dresser drawer, removed Clay's shoes and socks then tossed them on the bed. Clay sat down and started to put them on.

"Now that Darla has what she's always wanted, how long before she realizes you're a liability and she needs to be rid of you?" Tony asked.

Clay was tying his left shoe. He stopped in the middle of it, looked at Tony and nervously licked his lips.

"Won't happen. Tom will take care of me," Clay said.

"Really? That's what you're going to rely on? The greediest, most corrupt president in history? A man who should be a registered sex offender? You're going to rely on him? Get your affairs in order," Carvelli said.

"Won't happened," Clay replied. He finished tying his shoes and Marc handed him his coat.

"Is this what you wanted to become to help Jordan? What would she think of her dad now?" Maddy asked.

Clay, angry now, narrowed his eyes, looked sharply at Maddy, pointed a finger at her and said, "You leave my daughter out of this!"

Maddy stood up and went right back at him. "You dragged her into this when you sold your soul to the Devils. Don't lay that on anyone but the guy in the mirror."

"Here," Marc said holding a business card out to Clay, "take this. If you come to your senses and see we're right, call me. Anytime. My cell number is on it."

Clay snatched it out of Marc's hand and shoved it in his coat pocket. Without another word, he stomped out of the room and slammed the door behind him.

SIXTY-ONE

"Good morning," Marc said to Carvelli. Marc and Maddy sat down at the table Tony was using. They were in the hotel's restaurant the morning after their confrontation with Clay Dean.

"You're up early," Marc continued.

Carvelli set down the newspaper he was reading while Marc poured coffee for himself and Maddy from the stainless steel carafe on the table.

"Yeah," Carvelli agreed. "Woke up around six and couldn't get back to sleep. Morning, sweetheart," he said to Maddy.

"Morning, Tony," she replied.

"So, Counselor, now what?" Carvelli asked Marc.

"I don't know," Marc admitted. "I thought about it last night. It was unrealistic of us to think this guy would flip that easily."

"We could go to the media," Maddy said.

"I thought about that, too," Marc replied. "But I don't see it. First of all, ninety percent of the media was behind her. More importantly, what do we have?" Marc asked.

"We have a cop in Colorado," Marc said answering his own question, "who says he saw Clay Dean or, more accurately, someone he thinks was named John Estes that looked like Dean, twelve years ago at the prison when Billy Stover died.

"We have a woman at the St. Paul Hotel scared to death of losing her Green Card and getting deported. And we have a retired St. Paul cop who harbors suspicions about the death of Abby Connolly. Not exactly a slam dunk case to bring against a former President and the President-elect."

"You put it that way and I'll start having doubts," Carvelli said. "But he didn't really deny anything which is basically confirmation."

The waiter came and the three of them ordered breakfast.

"I talked to Connie just before we came down here," Marc continued. "She's okay with us staying for a while. The money for the hotel and everything. Let's give Mr. Dean a couple of days to think about it."

"We could take another run at him and try to talk to him again," Maddy suggested.

"Yeah, we could and probably will if we have to," Marc agreed.

"We staying here for Christmas?" Maddy asked unseriously.

"That's almost two weeks off," Marc said. "We'll see."

Their meals came and they continued to chat while eating. When they finished, Carvelli checked something in the paper he was reading.

"What are you gonna do today?" Carvelli asked his companions.

"I don't know," Marc said. "What do you want to do?" he asked Maddy.

"We could go sightseeing. There's a lot of stuff in Washington to see," Maddy replied.

"Why, what do you have in mind?" Marc asked Carvelli.

"There's a vintage '68 Camaro a guy is advertising online. He's down near Richmond. I thought I'd run down and take a look at it."

"Boys and their toys," Maddy said with a smirk.

"What's he want for it?" Marc asked.

"Twenty," Carvelli replied. "He has a picture of it online and it looks good. Twenty grand is a good price."

Marc snapped his fingers as if something just occurred to him, which it had.

"I just remembered," he said to Maddy. "You remember Tommy Dorn? The Army Lawyer..."

"Sure," Maddy said.

"He retired after Sammy's trial and took a job in a firm in Arlington. He does a lot of work defending our military guys who get jammed up."

"How do you know?" Maddy asked.

"We've kept in touch," Marc said as he started scrolling through his phone directory. "I've been meaning to call him. Ah, here it is," he said then pushed the call button.

The number Marc had was Dorn's direct line. Tommy answered it himself. The two of them spoke for about a minute after which Marc and Maddy were on their way to Arlington. Carvelli kept his plan to check out the Camaro that had caught his eye.

"I'll be back later this afternoon," Carvelli had told them. "I'll give you a call when I get back."

After Clay Dean left the hotel, still a little woozy and nauseous from being drugged, he found his car and got home all right. Once inside his apartment, he sat on his couch for an hour until he felt good enough to go to bed. While he waited, he thought about what his kidnappers had said. By the time his head hit the pillow he had dismissed their warning.

Clay overslept and it wasn't until noon that he arrived at the MGM National. Sonja had left a message on his phone while he slept. She told him he was to stay downstairs in the lobby to keep an eye on security. Darla had another full day scheduled interviewing potential cabinet members and would not have time for him. The message from Sonja was Darla's way of telling Clay he was still in Darla's doghouse.

Clay spent the entire day sitting on a chair in the hotel lobby watching the commotion swirl around. The media was everywhere and filming everything, terrified that they might miss something but at the same time not really getting anything newsworthy.

Every time one of the cabinet interviewees came down and got off the elevator, he or she was obliged to make a statement. And every one of them made the same statement. "The interview went well. I would be delighted to serve President Carver, blah, blah, blah."

Except for the hour he took for dinner, Clay kept his solo vigil all day. In the back of his mind was the nagging concern that perhaps he had become very expendable to Darla. Whenever he became a little too concerned he convinced himself Tom would surely intervene on his behalf.

Around 9:00 P.M. he decided to call it a day. He had spent the entire day in the lobby and accomplished absolutely nothing. Clay had not heard a word from upstairs or from Tom.

Clay stopped at the same bar he had been hustled in by Maddy the night before. The same bartender asked him how he was and Clay sloughed it off as no big deal.

It was an unusually quiet Thursday evening which suited him just fine. This bar normally attracted a Capitol Hill crowd and once in a while someone, usually a congressional staffer, would recognize him. Invariably, the idiot would approach Clay for some inside information in hopes of impressing his boss. Clay would politely rebuff them, finish his drink and leave. Tonight he was left alone. He sat quietly by himself then a little after eleven o'clock decided to call it a night.

Carvelli got back to the D.C. hotel at 4:00 P.M. Marc, Maddy and Tommy Dorn were at Tommy's office. The three of them had been there all afternoon as Tommy took them around the building introducing them to everyone.

Tommy's firm was located in a three-story office building in Arlington. The firm he was with occupied the two upper floors. There were fourteen lawyers and almost twenty staff, all of whom were anxious to meet Sammy Kamel's lead counsel. Once the male members met Maddy, their interest in Marc took a significant decline.

Tommy also took them downstairs to the other two firms in the building and paraded the pair around. By the time they finished, Marc's hand was getting sore from all of the shaking.

Of course, when five o'clock rolled around and after Carvelli had arrived, almost everyone in the building headed for a nearby bar. Any excuse to throw a little party. On the way to their cars, Marc asked Tony about the Camaro he went to see.

"Vintage my ass," Carvelli growled. "The picture online is the good side of the car. The other side has cancer and the engine's a mess."

Later that night, when the three of them arrived back at the hotel and were walking across the parking lot, Carvelli teased Maddy by asking, "How many business cards did you get from the guys at Tommy's building?"

It was almost ten o'clock and thankfully, it was a work night or the party would still be going.

"At least a dozen. If I wanted to, I could be a very busy girl," Maddy replied.

"You shameless hussy," Carvelli laughed.

"No kidding," Marc joined in.

Maddy tossed her head and hair back as they walked and said, "Hey, a girl has needs."

"Now I know what to get her for Christmas," Marc said.

Maddy stopped, looked at him and said, "What?"

"A gasoline powered vibrator," Marc replied.

Carvelli was laughing so hard he doubled over. Maddy, a look of horror on her face, slapped Marc across the shoulder.

"That's disgusting," she said. But then she too burst into laughter and said, "Can you really get one? A gas motored one?"

This really got all three of them going.

By the time they got to the elevators, they had managed to calm down. Once inside, on the way up to their rooms in the elevator, they traveled up about two floors and then Maddy started laughing again which triggered more salacious comments and laughter from Marc and Tony.

When they got to their rooms, Maddy, feeling the effects of the party, insisted on a hug and a kiss from her two pals. They said goodnight and retreated to their rooms.

Clay Dean found a good parking space on the street in front of his apartment. He parked behind a neighbor's BMW and got out. The air was chilly and he stuffed his hands in the pocket of his wool overcoat as he walked around the front of his car. He turned to go in between the front of his car and the back of the Beemer. Just before he got to the curb he hesitated to avoid stepping on a dead blackbird. When he did this, the right taillight on the Beemer exploded.

Startled, it took Clay between one and two seconds to realize what happened. He ducked down and took off as the car's back window took a hit.

Clay got hunched next to the car as a third silenced bullet blew the passenger side mirror apart. When it did, a small piece of it grazed Clay's face under his left eye. It sliced open a thin, one-and-a-half-inch gash that started pouring blood.

One more bullet struck the newspaper dispenser near the front of the car. This fourth shot had passed close enough over Clay's head so that he heard it whiz by.

Still crouched down below the side of the BMW, he pulled out a handkerchief and pressed it to his wound. All he could think about was his 1911 .45 cal. in his townhouse and wished he had it with him. If his assailant decided to come looking for him and check out his shooting, Clay would be in a lot of trouble.

Clay stayed down for fifteen minutes waiting. He knew sooner or later he would have to chance it. He would have to make a leap and a dash for the door of his building. There was a good size maple tree next to the newspaper dispenser. If he could get the tree in between himself and the shooter, he had a good chance of making it.

Clay crawled along the curb next to the car and made it to the tree. Still bleeding and holding the hanky on it, he counted to three, then took off. He made it to the building and crashed through the locked front door, tripped and went down in the foyer. Instead of jumping up, he laid there for a moment listening. Hearing nothing, he realized the shooter must be gone. He had drawn no fire at all during his sprint to the door.

Once inside his apartment, the first thing he did was find his gun. Then, gun in hand, he went into the bathroom and pulled out the first aid kit from under the sink. A half hour later he had cleaned, closed the wound with butterfly strips and covered it with a gauze pad.

Clay opened a bottle of bourbon, took a healthy pull on it, and then half- filled a water glass. He jammed a chair under the front door handle and shoved a living room chair in front of that. An hour later, he fell asleep sitting up on the couch with the .45 in his right hand.

Clay woke up at 8:00 when he heard a man on the sidewalk yelling. Groggily he went to the front window, peeked through the curtain and saw the Beemer's owner stomping around and screaming. The man was an Iraqi who worked in their embassy and Clay thought he was a total asshole. Watching the jerk screaming into his phone while inspecting his car brought a moment of humorous relief.

Twenty minutes later, while having his second bourbon-laced coffee, Clay picked up the card Marc Kadella had given him. Before he had fallen asleep last night, Clay had reached a decision. He placed the card on the kitchen table so he could read the phone number and started to dial.

SIXTY-TWO

"What did he say exactly?" Maddy urgently asked Marc.

The three of them were hurrying through the hotel parking lot to Carvelli's rental car. They had been in the lobby heading toward one of the restaurants when Marc got the call from Clay Dean. He had stopped dead in his tracks and listened while Maddy and Carvelli stared with inquisitive looks. When the call ended, all he said was they had to get going right now.

"He said he changed his mind and wants to meet with us," Marc said for the third time. "Something happened, he didn't say what, and he needs to talk to us."

They jumped into Carvelli's car with Tony driving, Maddy in the front passenger seat and Marc in the back. They hurried out of the parking lot and started toward Clay's apartment.

"This could be a setup," Carvelli said when they were halfway there. "He could be wearing a wire."

"How do we check him?" Marc asked.

"We take him someplace public to talk. I take him into a men's room stall, make him strip down and check him. I'll go over his clothes too," Carvelli said.

"Where should we take him?" Maddy asked.

"I don't know, a restaurant maybe," Carvelli replied.

"I know," Marc jumped in. "There's a public library about a mile up Wisconsin Avenue. They usually have private rooms for studying. We go there. Unlikely anyone will follow us in there."

"Good," Carvelli agreed. "That should work."

While his three rescuers were on the way to get him, Clay continued to watch through the front window. The D.C. Metro Cops were finishing up their investigation of the Iraqi neighbor's shot up BMW. As he watched, Clay thought about how much he should tell this lawyer and his friends. They knew about the girl in St. Paul and Billy Stover. So far, they had not indicated having any knowledge of anything else.

There were two squad cars and an unmarked vehicle that looked to be for detectives. The cops were having a big problem calming down the car's owner while photographing the bullet holes and damage. Clay looked at his watch then back outside. The cops were getting ready to leave when he saw the car with the lawyer and his two companions drive up. Thirty seconds later, after running from the door to their car, Clay was in the back seat with Marc.

"What's with the cops?" Carvelli asked.

322

"Somebody tried to kill me last night. They shot up the neighbor's car."

"What happened to your face?" Marc asked.

"Took a small piece of something. I don't know what. A piece of a bullet or the car. I got it patched up. I'll be okay. Where are we going?"

"You'll see," Carvelli replied.

Carvelli drove around for twenty minutes through mostly residential streets. Satisfied they were not being followed, he got onto Wisconsin and drove quickly to the library.

When they got inside, Marc signed for a private study room on the second floor. While Tony was in the men's room strip searching Clay, Marc and Maddy waited in the room for them.

"He's clean," Carvelli announced when the two men entered the room.

"You think I'm wired?" Clay indignantly asked. "I'm the one whose ass is on the line!"

"Take it easy," Marc said. "There's an enormous amount at stake here and we're being careful. Have a seat and let's hear it."

The four of them took chairs around the wood, rectangular conference room table. Clay told them the complete, unvarnished story about the death of Abby Connolly and the subsequent cover-up. While he did this, the others all sat quietly listening. When he finished it was Marc who spoke first.

"That was your mistake," he said. "The bedsheet. It was the loose end that never went away."

"There's always something," Clay admitted. "Now what?"

"Now I want to hear it again," Marc told him.

Being an ex-cop, Clay expected and accepted this. When he finished for the second time Marc looked at Tony and Maddy.

"Sounds right," Maddy said.

"Yeah, he got it right again," Tony agreed.

"What do you want to do?" Marc asked Clay.

Clay looked back puzzled, and said, "That's why I came to you. I need help. I need a lawyer."

"You ready to go to the FBI?" Marc asked.

"Yes, but I don't want to walk in alone. With the clout and tentacles the Carvers have, I might never walk out again," Clay said.

"I doubt they have the FBI in their pocket," Marc said. "And they sure as hell don't have the current Attorney General. Did you have a lawyer in mind?"

"Yeah, you," Clay said. "Since I don't trust any in New York or D.C. or anywhere else…"

"I'm still representing Billy Stover," Marc said. "I have an obvious conflict."

"Tommy Dorn," Carvelli said.

"Yeah," Marc agreed. "We know a guy who can do it. You can trust him and his firm. They fight the government all the time." Marc said this while looking up Tommy's phone number on his cell. He then dialed it and put it to his ear.

"Hey, it's Marc. We need to come see you, right now."

He listened for a moment then said, "Clear your calendar. This is the biggest thing you'll ever do."

Tommy said something then they heard Marc say, "Yes, bigger than Sammy's case. Much bigger. We'll be there in thirty minutes."

Marc, Maddy and Carvelli had been cooling their heels in Tommy's reception area for over an hour. Bored, they had passed outdated magazines back and forth to each other, waiting for Tommy to finish up and come and get them. The receptionist had politely asked three times if she could get anything for them. Each time they politely declined.

Eventually, two lawyers from one of the firms downstairs appeared. They were a man in his fifties and a younger woman who the three Minnesotans had met. They overheard the older man tell the receptionist to call Tommy, then the two of them reintroduced themselves. The man's name was Steve Murdock and the woman was Melanie Ortman.

"Sure, I remember meeting you yesterday," Marc said. "What's going on?"

"Don't know," Melanie replied. "Tommy called down and asked us to come up. Sorry, but he specifically told us not to say anything to you, yet. Even though we don't know anything," she smiled.

"I'm sure Tommy will fill you in on what's going on as soon as he can," Murdock added.

At that moment Tommy came through the door leading back to the individual offices. He took a moment to shake hands with Steve and Melanie.

"I'll be back in a minute then I'll fill you in," he said looking at Marc.

"Okay," Marc said with a slight shrug.

Two minutes later, Tommy was back. He took his three guests to his office and when they were all seated around a round table in the corner, Tommy started.

"Okay, I can't tell you much right now. What this Dean guy told me was in confidence and I'm not sure I should say anything. He probably wouldn't care but you'll have to trust me on this, for now.

"Marc, I have a conflict myself. That's why I called Steve and Melanie. They are both excellent criminal lawyers who deal with the feds all the time. I can't represent him either."

"What the hell did he tell you?" Marc asked. "I thought this was about a girl's accidental death and the cover-up from thirteen or fourteen years ago. What else…"

"All I can say is your case, the girl's death, is barely a tip of the iceberg," Tommy said.

"What else could there be?" Carvelli asked.

"I can't, Tony," Tommy said. "For now, we'll just leave it at that. I'm guessing by the end of the day we'll all find out everything. Just be patient."

Another hour of waiting eventually led to a knock on Tommy's door and Steve Murdock came into his office.

"Melanie's in with him," Murdock said. "We have a meeting scheduled as soon as we can get there."

"Where and with whom?" Tommy asked.

"The Washington Field Office of the FBI. We'll start there. I don't want to go to the Hoover Building with this. At least not yet. We need to keep a lid on this and there are too many political types at Hoover. It leaks like a sieve.

"I know people at the WFO," Murdock continued. "How much did you tell them?" he asked referring to Tommy's three guests.

"Nothing," Marc replied. "Just that you're taking over because Tommy has a conflict."

"So do you," Murdock said. "Bigger than the girl in Minnesota. But you can come with us. I'll tell you what I can when I can. I can tell you this," he said looking at Tommy. "He refuses to ask for any immunity deal. He says he'll take what comes."

"What were the cops doing out in front of his house this morning?" Carvelli asked. Even though Clay had told him Tony, the cynical ex-cop, wanted it verified.

"Somebody tried to shoot him," Murdock said. "We called the D.C. cops and they verified there was a shooting incident involving a neighbor's car. The detective I spoke to, a guy I know, was damn curious about why I called but I put him off.

"Anyway, we're leaving. You might want to follow us. He needs to stop at his bank and get something from his safe deposit box on the way."

While the four of them—Tommy was now waiting with them— waited in a reception area, it occurred to Marc what his other conflict could be.

"Sammy Kamel," Marc said quietly to Tommy.

"What?"

"My other conflict, the one your pal Steve Murdock referred to that was bigger than Billy Stover. The only one I can think of is Sammy."

"Just be patient," Tommy said.

Marc let it go but it certainly gave him something to think about. What did the Carvers have to do with Sammy's case? The only thing he could think of was the whole thing started toward the end of Tom Carver's presidency. Did the government frame Sammy to placate a popular president? Stranger things have happened.

The four of them sat impatiently for most of the afternoon. Finally, at 4:00 P.M., Steve Murdock and a serious looking black man came out to get them. Murdock took a moment to introduce the man as Special Agent Lou Owens. They all shook hands and Owens led the small parade back to a secure conference room.

Owens opened the conference room door and waited while the others entered. It was a fairly large room, with a long, expensive-looking, highly polished, oval oak table in the center. Around it was at least twenty, comfortable, leather swivel chairs.

Opposite the door in the middle of the table sat Clay Dean. Next to him, to Clay's left, was Melanie Ortman. Another chair, to Clay's right, was pushed away from the table. Obviously for Steve Murdock who went right to it and sat down on it.

Seated across from Clay were two men. Both stood up and faced the group coming in. One of the men Marc and Tommy instantly recognized having seen him on TV recently as a candidate for the next Attorney General of the U.S.; an older, distinguished looking African-American named Carter Greene. He was the current U.S. Attorney for D.C.

"Welcome," he affably said to the four new attendees. He stepped up to Marc, extended his hand and with a politician's smile introduced himself.

Marc reciprocated and Greene continued down the line. When he got to Maddy he turned on the charm.

"And who is this lovely lady who graces us with her presence?" he said shaking her hand.

Maddy, having realized who this man was and although not normally awed by much, was barely able to say her name. She also wished she had worn something better than jeans.

"Have a seat, everyone, please," Greene said.

When everyone was seated, Greene continued.

"Mr. Murdock here tells me that the four of you know at least part of this sordid tale or," he continued looking at Tommy Dorn, "maybe even most of it. Normally, I'd be reluctant to bring you into this room. But you probably deserve to hear it all. Better you should hear it from this room than to leave here guessing.

"We've been in here most of the afternoon going over Mr. Dean's revelations. I've been reminded that you, Mr. Kadella, represented Samir Kamel in his trial for treason. Is that so?"

"Myself and Tommy Dorn here," Marc replied nodding toward Tommy. "What does this have to do with Sammy?"

It was Clay Dean who answered him. "I knew I recognized you from somewhere," he said looking at Marc. "I had a seat in the audience at that trial. I was there for the Carvers keeping an eye on it." He looked at Maddy and said, "Now I remember you, too. You were there at the defense table with him. I should have recognized you."

At that moment a thirty-something woman knocked and came in. She looked at Greene, held up a document and said, "We have it."

"Good. Go get her. Right now," Greene replied.

"Yes, sir," she said and left.

Greene turned to Marc and said, "Do you know who Sonja Hayden is?"

"Certainly. Darla Carver's top aide."

"That was a Material Witness Warrant," Greene said referring to the interruption. "We're picking her up for questioning.

"Now I have no authority over any of you," Greene continued talking to Marc, Maddy and Tony. "I do you, Colonel Dorn. If need be, I could have you recalled and put on active duty, but I don't think that will be necessary. Your friends here, I can't order them to keep quiet about what I'm about to tell you. I can ask that you do so until we can investigate and get to the bottom of this. And trust me, we are going to find out just what the hell the Carvers have been up to. In fact, I've decided to tell you this because you deserve to know and so you'll hold our feet to the fire. Somebody needs to do so.

"What Mr. Dean has brought to us is going to shake this country to its very foundations. You know how it began. Roughly thirteen years ago, in a hotel room in St. Paul. A young girl met a tragic death..."

For the next hour, Carter Greene laid it all out for them. Every sordid detail that Clay Dean had come forward with, right up to and including the events of this morning. Except, before he could tell them about what Clay had retrieved from his safe deposit box, Marc interrupted.

"Except uncorroborated accomplice testimony is insufficient for a conviction," Marc said.

"You're right," Greene admitted. "Except Mr. Dean brought with him the envelope that he says Darla Carver used to pass the infamous list of names onto the New York Times reporter, He believes we will find the President-elect's fingerprints on it, her aide Sonja Hayden's prints and the reporter, Melvin Bullard's prints as well. And either Darla Carver's DNA or Sonja Hayden's. One of them licked the envelope to seal it. He believes it was Darla Carver. Mr. Dean recovered it from the reporter's apartment along with the original list and handwritten note she put in the envelope. Mr. Dean assures us the writing on the envelope, list and note are in Darla Carver's handwriting.

"Now comes the really bad part," he continued with a heavy sigh.

"There's more and it's worse?" Tony Carvelli asked.

"Yes, I'm afraid so. Darla Carver, according to Mr. Dean tore up the original list but she didn't thoroughly destroy it. Somehow, he's not sure how, it ended up in the hands of the Russians. It is in a plastic case in the Russian Embassy.

"If this is true, Darla Carver, the woman who barely a month ago was elected president, has committed multiple counts of treason."

"Are you telling me that these people set up Sammy Kamel to take the fall for something Darla Carver did?" asked an incredulous Marc.

"It looks like it," Greene quietly admitted.

"I want him out and I want him now!"

"We need to finish our investigation..."

"No, you don't," Marc said. "This isn't going to drag on for months the way things usually do in this town."

"No, it won't. We need to test the things Mr. Dean gave us, question Sonja Hayden and if what Dean has said is verified, we'll move on it right away. I suggest you go back to Minnesota and wait..."

"I'm not going anywhere," Marc said. Maddy and Tony Carvelli quickly agreed. "We're going to stay right here in Washington and see this through. I owe that to Billy Stover, Abby Connolly and certainly, Sammy Kamel."

SIXTY-THREE

Two FBI agents walked purposefully into the lobby of the MGM National, a woman and her male companion. The woman, Special Agent Sherry Dunham, spotted a Secret Service agent she knew and the two of them went to him. The man, along with several others, was standing guard at the Penthouse express elevator.

"Hey, Sherry," the agent said. "What's up?"

Sherry looked around the lobby relieved to see that most of the media were gone. The ones that were left were paying no attention to them.

"Hi, Paul. Do you know if Sonja Hayden is upstairs with the Carvers?" Sherry asked.

"As far as we know. She hasn't come down or we would have logged it."

By this time the supervising Secret Service agent had joined them. A man Sherry also knew.

"What's going on?" Carl Wilkes asked.

"I need you to call Sonja Hayden and have her come down. Don't tell her why. Lie if you have to. I don't want a fuss made about this," Sherry told him. "Trust me on this, Carl. The less you guys know, the better. We need to talk to her."

"Okay, will do."

A few minutes later, Sonja, by herself, stepped off the elevator. She had an inquisitive look on her face and the ever-present iPhone in her left hand.

"We need you to come with us, Ms. Hayden," Sherry quietly said.

"Why? Who are you?"

"I'm FBI," Sherry whispered to her. "I'll take this," she said as she took the phone out of Sonja's hand.

Sherry gently led Sonja a few feet away and whispered in her ear. "We have been talking to Clay Dean all afternoon. We have a Material Witness Warrant for you. Please don't make a fuss and alert the media."

With the news about Clay Dean, all of the color, what little there was, drained from her face.

"I have to call Mrs. Carver," she stammered.

"No, you're not calling anyone," Sherry said.

"I need a coat. I'll get cold…"

"You'll be fine, let's go."

By the time the three of them made it to the exit, the media was starting to stir. Several of them, obviously smelling something wrong, tried chasing after them. Fortunately, they had parked directly in front of

329

the hotel and a third agent was at the car. They hustled Sonja into the back seat and quickly drove off.

Even though neither Clay Dean nor Sonja Hayden was under arrest, Carter Greene was going to be straight and careful. Clay had brought two lawyers with him. While the agents went to collect Sonja, Greene made a call to the Federal Public Defender's office for D.C. to arrange for a lawyer for Sonja. His name was Jamal Harrison and he arrived a few minutes before Sonja. While waiting for her, after swearing Harrison to secrecy, Greene's assistant gave the man a quick, sanitized version of what was going on.

Sonja was taken into an interrogation room and left by herself for two or three minutes. She was then joined by her P.D. lawyer, Special Agent Lou Owens and Carter Greene. Introductions were made and when everyone was seated, Owens started in.

While Carter Greene sat quietly, solemnly and with a stern, intimidating look, Owens laid it all out for her. Of course, Sonja was unaware that Clay had preserved the envelope that was used to leak Darla's handwritten list and note. When Owens told her about this, the look on her face went from passive to scared feral cat then back to passive in two seconds. Enough for the others to understand she knew it was over.

"What do you want?" she quietly asked when Owens finished.

"Your cooperation, obviously," Greene said.

"You don't have to say a word," Jamal Harrison quickly told her. "And I strongly advise you to keep quiet."

"Read her the Miranda warning," Greene said to Owens.

When Owens finished, Harrison asked, "Is my client under arrest?"

Before anyone could answer, Sonja asked, "Would it be okay for me to talk to Clay?"

This was a question Greene had hoped she would ask. He was confident that Clay Dean would verify what Owens had told her and make her see the light.

"Yes, we could arrange that," Greene said.

"Alone?" she asked.

"No," Greene replied. "He's under arrest."

"How about with all of the recording devices shut off in the room?" Harrison asked.

Greene looked at Owens who shrugged and said, "Why not?"

"Okay. We will monitor the conversation and not record it. Fair enough?" Greene asked.

Sonja and Harrison agreed and a few minutes later Clay was led in accompanied by Owens. These two, Clay and Sonja, could not really be called friends but they had always been cordial and at least friendly. Clay almost pitied Sonja her slavish devotion to Darla Carver. He never quite understood it; why Sonja was so starry-eyed smitten by the woman. But he at least respected her and she him.

"Clay, why are you doing this?" a teary-eyed Sonja asked when Clay sat down across from her.

"It's over, Sonja. I've told them everything," he replied ignoring the 'why' question.

"What should I do? I'll go to prison," she said as the tears started to flow.

"Sonja, I feel so much better now," Clay told her. "I can't tell you what to do but I feel like a great weight has been lifted. I'm done with those two."

"Did you make a deal with them to stay out of jail?" Sonja asked wiping her tears with the palms of her hands.

"No, I didn't. You can and you should," he replied. "I decided I did what I did and I'm gonna take what comes."

"How can I do this to Mrs. Carver?" Sonja rhetorically asked.

"Think about what she would do to you," Clay said.

"What happened to your face?" Sonja asked.

"Sonja, she tried to have me killed last night."

"She did? I knew she was thinking about it but I didn't know she went ahead."

"She'll put you in a grave too if she thinks it's necessary," Clay said. "She is bat shit crazy," he added.

"No, she isn't!" Sonja declared. "She's ambitious and driven."

Clay stood up to leave, looked down at her and said, "We need to stop this. She can't become president. You know that's the right thing."

When Carter Greene, along with several others heard this while watching on a closed circuit TV he said to his assistant, "Call Magistrate Mullin, we're going to need her tonight."

"I've already got the warrants and affidavits going for her," the woman, Carol Davis replied. "They will be ready by the time Mullin gets here."

"Don't tell her anything. Just say it's from me and we need her here as soon as possible. Tonight."

Two hours later, between 9:30 and 10:00, Federal Magistrate Helen Mullin finished reading the three supporting affidavits. There was one each from Clay and Sonja and one from an FBI fingerprint technician. The envelope Clay had preserved had been quickly examined for prints and the prints of three people were found on it. Several prints of Darla Carver and Sonja Hayden, whose prints were on file because of their security clearances. The prints of Melvin Bullard, the Times reporter, were in the AFIS database because of two DWI arrests.

Magistrate Mullin took off her reading glasses and placed them on the table. She rubbed her temples then looked across the table at Carter Greene.

"Holy shit, Carter," she said. "Is this really true?"

"In fact, we're holding back details for now," Greene said. "Helen, we need to move on this tonight. We can't wait until tomorrow. If this leaks out..."

"Either way," Mullin said as she put her glasses back on and picked up a pen, "it's going to be the biggest scandal in American history. Can this possibly be true?" Mullin asked rhetorically.

"Unfortunately, I believe every word of it," Greene replied.

Mullin signed her name to the arrest warrants for Thomas and Darla Carver, a once and future President. She also put her signature to several search warrants for their homes, offices and Carver Worldwide Charities.

"Can I get copies of all of this? Someday my grandkids can make a fortune selling copies on e-bay. I figure that's the least you owe me. If you're wrong, I just signed away any chance I have to get a seat on the federal bench."

Greene laughed and replied, "If we're wrong, the eruption from Mount Darla will bury us all."

Almost an hour later, Greene, his deputy Carol Davis and four FBI agents walked quickly through the MGM's lobby. Waiting by the elevator was a distinguished looking man in an expensive suit and overcoat. His name was Simon Blumberg and he was a name partner in a very powerful D.C. law firm. He had also represented the Carvers.

Carter Greene knew Blumberg well and had called him and asked him to meet him here. Greene had not told him why, just that he needed to see the Carvers and wanted Blumberg present.

"What the hell is going on, Carter?" Blumberg asked while the two men shook hands.

While riding up to the Penthouse, Blumberg scanned the arrest warrants and supporting affidavits. Seconds before they reached their destination, a shocked Blumberg looked at Carter Greene.

"Are you out of your goddamn mind?"

"Simon, be honest, you know these two. You're not really as surprised as you're trying to act."

"I'm surprised you're trying to do this. If you're wrong, God help you."

The elevator doors opened and the grin on Tom's face—who had been called and was waiting for them—disappeared when he saw the determined, serious looks. In that instant, he knew why he had not been able to get a hold of Clay all day and where Sonja Hayden had been taken. He also knew his fate was probably sealed.

"Come in," he quietly said.

"Are you out of your goddamn minds?" Darla Carver screamed when Simon Blumberg explained why they were here. "Do you people understand who I am? Get the hell out!" she demanded. "Get back on that elevator right now and we'll pretend this didn't happen."

"Darla," Tom quietly said. He walked to her with his hands out to take her arms and calm her down. Tom had read the affidavits and knew their game was up.

"No, get away from me!" she screamed backing away from her husband.

They were in the suite's large living room. Greene and Simon Blumberg were standing close to Darla with Greene's deputy and the four agents behind them. Darla had her back to the master bedroom, her arms extended, her palms out, a wild look in her eyes as if she could make this all go away.

"Where's Sonja? I need Sonja," she stammered.

"Darla, Clay and Sonja have talked to the FBI. It's over. We need to calm down now. It's over," Tom quietly said.

He got to her and put his arms around her. Probably the most intimate moment she had allowed him in years. He smoothed her hair and quietly soothed her as she silently sobbed into his chest.

After two or three minutes of this, she finally looked up at Tom and said, "I guess we have to go now, huh?"

"Yes, we have to go with them," Tom said.

"Okay, okay," she said. "Can I wash my face first? Brush my hair?" she asked.

Tom looked at Carter Greene who said, "Sure. In fact, we'll go out through the service exit. No reporters."

"Thank you, thank you," Darla said trying to weakly smile. She took a deep breath, smoothed her skirt then turned to go into the bedroom. Once inside she quietly closed and locked the door. Darla hurried to the dresser, went through her underwear drawer and found what she was looking for.

The people in the living room all stood around awkwardly, silently, waiting for her. When Tom realized she had closed the bedroom door, the light in his head went on.

"Oh shit, no!" he yelled as he turned and started running toward the bedroom.

Too late. Before he got there they all heard the loud boom of the .38 Lady Smith Tom had given her for protection many years ago.

Despite his age and how out of shape he was, the former President hit the double doors of the bedroom like a charging bull. He crashed into the bedroom with the others right behind him. Lying on the floor, alongside the bed, with her blood, brain matter and bone particles splattered about, was the obviously dead Darla Carver.

SIXTY-FOUR

THE AFTERMATH

Carter Greene called in a doctor employed by the FBI. He also called the FBI director and cryptically told him there had been an accident. When the Director arrived along with several more agents, Greene left the situation at the MGM in his hands.

Marc, Maddy, Tony and Tommy Dorn were still waiting at the Washington Field Office of the FBI. It was after 1:00 A.M. when Greene arrived back. He took the four of them into a secure conference room for an update. Sort of.

He thanked them for their help and assured them the government would handle the situation. They all looked at each other wondering what kind of snow job they were being fed.

"What the hell is going on?" Tommy Dorn asked.

"Nothing you need to concern yourself with," Greene said smiling reassuringly. "But in the interest of national security, the government is ordering you, through me, to remain silent about these events. In the interest of…"

"National security," Marc sarcastically added.

"Exactly. Again, thank you and…"

"Bullshit," Tony Carvelli said.

"Unless the First Amendment has been repealed, you have no right to order these people to do anything," Tommy Dorn told him. "I'm Army Reserve so you might have me, but not them."

"You're working a cover-up," Marc said. "You're doing the usual Washington ass covering, feed them bullshit line, aren't you?"

Greene remained silent and did not respond.

"What happened?" Marc asked. "You part of the Carver Corruption Machine?"

"I resent that!" Greene said.

"We're not going to keep quiet," Maddy told him. "We'll go right to the media…"

"And tell them what?" Greene asked. "You don't think we can brush off the wild ravings of three nobodies from flyover country? Guess again. National security will trump everything."

"Do you know who Vivian Corwin Donahue is?" Carvelli asked.

"Of course," Greene hesitantly replied. "She's one of the richest women in America. So what?"

Tony pointed a finger at Maddy and said, "Vivian looks at Maddy as the daughter she'd like to have. And Marc and I are close, personal friends. She has more political clout than you do. Half the Senators and members of Congress will drop whatever they're doing if she calls. So, guess again. We only need to go to Vivian and she will believe every word and have your ass before she's done."

Greene visibly sighed then quietly admitted, "Darla Carver is dead. She shot herself after we told her what we had and that she was under arrest."

The four people at the table sat in stunned silence for over a minute looking back and forth at each other.

"And you guys think you can cover this up? What the hell is wrong with you? Something as historically significant as this blows up and your natural reaction is to lie about it and cover it up. What is wrong with you people?" Marc said finally hitting him with this.

"We believe it is in the best interest of..."

"Yourselves," Maddy finished for him.

"...the nation," Greene replied.

"Bullshit," Tommy Dorn said. "It's one hundred percent Washington ass covering and you're not gonna do it. Not this time. You're going to tell the American people the truth."

"You guys really don't get it, do you?" Marc asked. "You sit around here in Washington and New York with your media bootlickers, in your insulated, incestuous circle jerk telling yourselves how much smarter you are and how you know what's best for the nation and everyone in it. Then you wonder why people out there in real America hate politicians and your media pals. I've got news for you. Ninety percent of Americans don't live and die on what goes on here in Washington. You might think you're that important but most people don't give a rat's ass about who you are."

"Tell them the truth. It will be a shock for a while but the country will move on," Carvelli said interrupting Marc.

Knowing he was whipped, Greene finally agreed. By six o'clock that morning a press release had been issued. President Timmons gave a brief statement telling America and the world about Darla's suicide and the reason for it. He also closed the stock markets for the day and closed the banks for two days. His reasoning was to give everyone a moment to pause and calm down.

For the next eighteen months, three committees of the House and two in the Senate investigated the scandal. Every member of Congress and the Senate who could score positive political face time from it gleefully did so. Those who were in any way connected to the Carvers ran for cover and would not admit even knowing them. Sally Newport put out a press release claiming Darla was barely an acquaintance and certainly not a close friend. By the end of the investigations they had spent tens of millions of taxpayers' dollars and uncovered nothing the FBI did not come up with.

They would pass a few more laws regarding ethical conduct. Millions of words would be spoken about the corrupting influence of special interests and money in politics. When the dust finally settled, these people continued doing what they had been doing all along. No one was surprised that politicians would be reluctant to clean up their own act.

The IRS and FBI descended on Carver Global Charites like flying monkeys. They shut it down and seized everything down to and including pens and paper clips. A couple dozen indictments would follow that eventually resulted in a small number of convictions with minimal jail time to very few, certainly not enough, people.

On January 20th, former Senator and Vice President-elect Jared Galvin was inaugurated as President of the United States. Fortunately for the nation and for him, none of the Carvers corruption rubbed off on him at all. In fact, President Galvin would be the best thing to come out of the entire sordid mess. He was a solid, very capable and calming influence on Washington and the country. He would be rewarded with a second term and would serve with distinction, competence and would be extremely effective.

One of President Galvin's first acts, one Timmons should have done but didn't have the balls to do, was to kick a bunch of Russians out of the country. Viktor Ivanov and his crew were the first to go. A U.S. President has no authority to remove an ambassador but he did let the Kremlin know Grigory Tretiak had to go, which he did.

Galvin also publicly demanded that the Russians return the list Darla had leaked. Of course, they categorically denied having it, but a few months later it was slipped to an FBI agent. By this time the criminal cases involving the conspiracy were resolved. The list itself was stamped Top Secret and put away for fifty years.

Former President Thomas Jefferson Carver was indicted for multiple crimes except for the big one: treason. Technically, a president cannot commit treason. If he decides to declassify something and make it public, he (or she) has that right.

A deal was made and he pleaded guilty to one count of unintentional manslaughter for the death of Abby Connolly. He was sentenced to thirty-six months. He would go on to serve twenty-four months in a federal prison camp, what people call a "country club prison". Upon his release, he was shunned for several years then eventually rehabilitated himself and made millions with two self-serving, disingenuous mea culpa books.

Clay Dean and Sonja Hayden both pleaded to a single count of conspiracy. Clay received ten years and Sonja seven to be served in a real prison. While doing his time, Clay received over two hundred marriage proposals and politely turned them all down. Upon his release, he moved to Alaska and would live out his life as anonymously as possible. He would die happy having maintained a close relationship with his daughter, Jordan, her husband and Clay's three grandchildren.

Sonja Hayden would die by her own hand in prison. She tore up a bed sheet and hanged herself six months into her sentence.

Scott Duncan, the Colorado police officer, former prison guard and love of Billy Stover remained happily anonymous. Despite the fact it was his trip to the office of Marc Kadella that triggered the discovery of the Carvers' crimes, he was not given nor wanted any publicity for any of it. Billy's parents had given him a framed photo of Billy's college graduation picture. Scott would keep it on his dresser in his bedroom his entire life.

Marc Kadella, Madeline Rivers, Tony Carvelli and Earl 'Tommy Lee' Dorn, would all testify before Congress, but only once. A few weeks afterward, they would also be allowed to slip back into quiet anonymity.

Major Samir 'Sammy' Kamel's appeal for treason had been turned down by the Military Court of Appeals. This happened before Darla's suicide and the subsequent revelations of her guilt.

Professor Sanderson had removed Sammy's case to the U.S. Second Circuit Court of Appeals. The Second Circuit, in a three-judge unanimous ruling, reversed it. They held that the exclusion of the testimony of the CID Warrant Officer David Smith was erroneous. They could not simply declare Sammy innocent and release him. That is not the role of an appeals court. Their job is to review the rulings of the trial judge to determine if any mistakes of law were made. Their finding that keeping Dave Smith off the stand was an error by Judge Dwyer gave the Second Circuit the excuse to send it back to the trial court. They were probably wrong to do so, Smith's testimony was not really that important, but it was the excuse they needed. The case was sent back to the trial court. Major Paxton O'Rourke, with every party including Sammy's lawyers and family in attendance, moved Judge Dwyer to dismiss the case and his conviction was vacated.

Sammy Kamel was gratefully reinstated into the Army with the rank of major. He would go on to retire after twenty years as a full colonel. He and Charlene Hughes would be married by then. She retired at the same time, also as a full colonel. They would move back to Minnesota, start a family and live a quiet life.

Tony Carvelli parked his Camaro in a street side spot on West River Road. He was on the Minneapolis side of the Mississippi, a half block north of the Lake Street/Marshall Avenue Bridge. Tony shut down the car and looked out the driver's side window. It was almost midnight on a Tuesday night. The weather was perfect; misty rain mixed with wet, sloppy snow. He had a task to perform. Tony needed a night with bad weather and darkness and this night was perfect. Very few people would be out this late in this mess.

He covered his head with the hood of his gray sweatshirt to protect it from the weather and cover his face. He was wearing it under his black leather coat. Tony slipped on a pair of gloves, got out of the car then reached in back for the bag on the seat. It was a large, black, nylon-mesh gym bag and its contents were fairly heavy.

Tony walked quickly to the bridge then onto the walkway to go toward St. Paul. It was early March, a few weeks after the inauguration of President Galvin. Tony had waited until he was sure the ice was off the river.

To walk across the bridge completely and into St. Paul would take barely ten minutes. Tony was going less than half that far. Before he stopped, he took a quick look back and forth and saw no cars or buses coming.

Stepping quickly to the railing, he lifted the bag up and let it drop. Despite the numerous street lamps lighting up the bridge, the dark bag was out of sight within thirty feet. Tony continued to watch until he saw the white water of the splash as it hit the river's surface. Satisfied that the weight and the cuts he had made in the sides of the bag would put it on the muddy bottom, Tony turned and walked back to his car.

On the morning after the confrontation in the hotel room Tony, Marc and Maddy had with Clay Dean, Tony took a trip by himself. He told his friends he was going to Virginia to look at a vintage '68 Camaro. This was a lie to provide them with cover.

That morning while reading a local newspaper, Tony had read about a gun show by Centreville. He went there and using a fake ID he always carried, he made several purchases. He bought a .223 caliber bolt action Remington 700 rifle with a four-power night scope and under the table, a sound suppressor for it. He also bought two boxes of hollow point shells. Tony then spent almost two hours in a range behind the sale facility practicing.

That night, after saying goodnight to Marc and Maddy, Tony slipped out and went to a perch on a roof he had spotted across from Clay Dean's apartment. He lay in wait less than an hour, getting lucky the first night out. He saw his target arrive home shortly after 11:00 P.M.

Darla Carver had thrown a temper tantrum and railed, mostly to herself and Sonja, to have Clay Dean killed. As of this night, the night Tony waited for him on the roof across the street, she had done nothing to bring it about.

That morning Tony Carvelli had decided Clay Dean needed a little push. A little incentive to have him come forward and turn on the Carvers. Obviously Tony knew nothing about Darla's threats. But they had warned Clay the night before that she would probably do it. Tony was not going to wait.

Being a cop, Carvelli had spent countless hours on a firing range with both pistols and rifles. He was certainly not a qualified sniper. But he was pretty good and he was barely eighty yards away.

The four shots, one into the BMWs taillight, one into the back window, the side mirror and the newspaper dispenser were easy shots. Using the hollow point bullets Tony knew they would fragment and be of little value for a ballistics analysis. When he finished, Tony quickly picked up the ejected brass and was in his rental car and gone in less than a minute.

The rifle, scope and silencer were now resting in the mud on the bottom of the Big Muddy. The current would eventually dissolve the gym bag but its contents would never be found. Even if they were, there would be no way to trace the gun to Carvelli, let alone the Georgetown shooting. Tony Carvelli would gladly live with it.

Although I am both a lawyer and a military veteran, I have never been involved in any capacity with a court martial. As you might imagine, this required a good deal of research into court procedures for the court martial and the differences between them and a civilian trial.

What I found was that there are many more similarities than differences between them. For example, the presumption of innocence, guilt beyond a reasonable doubt, the prosecution's burden of proof and the rules of evidence are the same for both. The most significant difference is with the jury, its selection, makeup and role are all very different than a civilian jury.

First is the selection process. The pool of military personnel from which the jury will be selected is determined by a person designated as the Convening Authority. This can be anyone from the president on down or whomever the president designates. My understanding is that, routinely, this would be the base or post commander where the offense took place. Because of the seriousness of Sammy's trial, I chose the commanding officer of the Judge Advocate General's Corp to be my convening authority.

There is also no set number of members—what the military calls "jurors"— for a court martial. The number of members of the jury is also set by the convening authority. Also, they do not have to reach a unanimous decision for a guilty verdict. The requirement for a finding of guilt is normally a two-thirds majority vote. This is so with one significant exception.

If the accused is charged with a crime for which the death penalty could be imposed, such as treason, is that exception. In that case, there must be twelve members and the vote for guilty must be unanimous and if the jury votes to impose the death penalty, it must also be unanimous.

In a civilian trial, it is the prosecuting authority's decision as to whether or not to seek the death penalty. I did some research and was unable to determine if the prosecution could take away the jury's right to impose death in a court martial. Admittedly, I did not look too far. The reason being, I did not want to find out.

For my purposes, I decided to have the prosecution remove the death penalty before the trial. I did this, call it literary license if you want, for two reasons. First, because the odds of it actually being imposed are virtually zero. Second and more importantly, I wanted a nine-member jury for simplicity sake. Even lawyers can figure out that a two-thirds majority of a nine-member jury is somewhere around six.

Finally, there is the selection process of the members itself. Unlike a civilian trial—in state court trials but to a much lesser extent in federal court trials—the lawyers, as well as the judge, are allowed to conduct the jury voir dire. In a court martial this is not necessarily so. The judge may allow the lawyers to question the jury panel but does not have to and from what I understand usually does not. Of this, I may be wrong. The lawyers can submit questions to the judge but the judge may ignore them if he or she chooses. The judge questions the prospective jurors and decides who will be on it and who will be excused. The lawyers are normally allowed one peremptory challenge to use to remove jurors.

Other than this slight of hand with the death penalty and the number of members of the jury, the trial as depicted is a fair representation. If there is anyone out there who reads this book and is offended by having the prosecution remove the death penalty wrongfully, I will tell you two things: one, I hope my explanation for why I did this is sufficient and two, if not, get over it. We as a society have become ridiculously oversensitive and it needs to stop.

THE FATE OF DARLA CARVER

Some readers may be disappointed with the ending regarding Darla Carver and how she escaped justice. I had basically three choices on how to handle this.

Have her resign or impeached as President-elect before she took the oath of office and then tried for murder and treason.

Have her impeached after she took office, removed as President and then tried for murder and treason.

The Constitution is not very helpful under these scenarios and either would have been somewhat impractical and cumbersome. Also either would have added at least another hundred pages to the book. In my opinion (sorry, mine is the only one that counts) unnecessarily.

I decided to do what I did with her after thinking about, of all people, Adolf Hitler. No, Darla was not Hitler but hers was the same type of personality. Hitler committed suicide because he refused to accept any responsibility for his crimes. His narcissism would not allow him to be put on trial and turned into a spectacle. It does not stretch the imagination very far to see a Darla Carver take that same way out and for the same reason. Plus, it had the virtue of being clean, neat and very final.

Thank you and I sincerely hope you found *Political Justice* entertaining, interesting and maybe even a little educational.

Dennis Carstens

ACKNOWLEDGMENTS

A special thanks to my dear friend, Kathy Kranz for her help and assistance. I will also thank Wendy Carlson for taking the time to explain handwriting comparison and analysis. Her kindness and patience in explaining handwriting analysis was extremely helpful.

Finally, a special thanks to Nelson DeMille (I'm a big fan) for his book *Word of Honor*. I coincidentally read it while writing *Political Justice*. In *Word of Honor*, he wrote about a fictional court martial and it was very helpful providing me with visualizing one in my mind.

79723674R00189

Made in the USA
Columbia, SC
30 October 2017